MW01599261

The Sorcerers and the Marids

The Sorcerers and the Marids

THE MID-WORLD OF THE TRUCE

BOOK FOUR

STEVE DOUGLAS

Copyright © 2022 Steve Douglas

All rights reserved. No part of this book may be reproduced in any form or by any electronic or mechanical means, including information storage and retrieval systems, without permission in writing from the publisher, except by reviewers, who may quote brief passages in a review.

ISBN: 978-1-7778868-3-7

The Sorcerers and the Marids is a work of fiction. The names, characters, businesses, places, events, locales, and incidents are either products of my imagination or used in a fictitious manner. Any resemblance to actual persons, living or dead, or actual events are coincidental.

Illustration and cover design by Thea Magerand
Typesetting by C'est Beau Designs

For our East Coast Douglas Family:
Dwight, my best friend and ally, and Ann,
and all their children and grandchildren who shared time with
our children and grandchildren.

Contents

ONE SIDE OF

The Game of

THE MAN AT ARMS

THE MID-WORLD SPY

THE ILLUSION

THE APPRENTICE

THE CHARMED KNIGHT

THE PRINCESS

THE TALISMAN

THE WEB OF FATE

THE GREY COUNCILLOR

THE MAG[...]

THE ARMED HOST

THE GREAT SPELL

THE WIZARD

THE MASTER

the Masters

THE APPRENTICE

THE CHARMED KNIGHT

THE ILLUSION

THE MID-WORLD SPY

THE MAN AT ARMS

...E CIAN

THE CAPTAIN

THE SENDING

THE MID-WORLD WEAPON

THE ARCHERS

THE MID-WORLD POWER

THE ANCIENT SECRET

THE SORCERER

THE FORTRESS

ALANTÉA

The Forerunner

Far Avalon
(Goblin Market)

Nemesis

Bizere

Erivan Forest

Varaj

Piranus

North Haven

River Barrloch

Wizards Leag

Amalrie

Sea's Edge

Khiva

 Cities, towns, villages

Wizards towers

• • • • • Greenway

— — — Boundary of The
Wizards League

Chapter One

The Mistress of Illusions

H E SAT ON THE terrace of the Mistress of Illusions, sipping chilled wine. It was just after noon, but already the insect swarms had begun to gather and swirl in the distance. The Mistress of Illusions sat beside him, willing cool breezes over her terrace, and those breezes always came.

Kalanin watched her out of the corner of his eye. He no longer cared that her beauty was made complete by sorcery and that he would never be able to peer beyond her many layers of magic to see what she truly looked like. She would be beautiful every day of his life, as he grew older, greyer, more gaunt, and finally died. Long before, of course, she would tire of him and take another lover.

He would leave then, go to live by Khiva and the coast, fishing, ambling about. Then he would take the Long Sleep, and if that was just another fairy tale, he would simply be only another partly intelligent human being who had lived and then was gone forever.

He turned back to the clouds of insects. On the whole, the Mistress of Illusions had created the most humane form of pest control. Other Powers of the Mid-World developed poisons, or created wonderfully efficient predators, while the strongest simply willed them out of existence so that they vanished into nothingness.

"You were right," said the Mistress of Illusions, breaking the silence. "Your old Master is at my borders. There may be others with him."

"He will come for both of us, for Dargas and myself," said Kalanin. "There's still hope for Dargas, is there not?"

"Merlin is considered to be among the greatest of the healers, but the old warrior has been five weeks in a dreaming coma that was close to death. The Long Sleep would have been a kinder destiny."

Kalanin nodded. "I did speak those words to him, but he wanted to hold on."

"Géla told me that the old soldier was strong willed. That's why I...." she trailed off. "Merlin is not alone — an Adept or Apprentice travels with him."

"That will be Julian," he said. "Others may be accompanying them."

"You don't need to stay in my domain," she said softly. "Leave, if you wish, and I will come with you, bringing aid to the Wizards and their League."

"I've retired," said Kalanin, "and besides, it simply wouldn't work. I can imagine you, trying to deal with the Wizards, and I can picture your frustration boiling over — you would leave me then, and return to your own kingdom. You see, I understand how you will tire of me, at some point, but we will only have a very short time together if we become trapped in the Wizards' webs." She rose and kissed him lightly on the mouth.

"It's good that you understand these things."

"I've learned some bitter lessons recently." He thought of himself, again, like a tiny insect trapped in the great webs of Merlin. He felt pity for the insects that spun in the distance, swirling in flight with the images created by the Mistress of Illusions. By nightfall, they would fall, exhausted, dying in masses. And so, he would struggle to avoid death in the Wizard's web.

A door slid open, and at the edge of the terrace, Géla walked toward them, tall and erect, long black hair streaming behind her. Her eyes passed over Kalanin for a moment, showing a measure of respect — mixed with a cool pity. She turned to the Mistress of Illusions.

"You have visitors, my Lady, Merlin and a party of six if you count the Familiars of Julian."

"Galad will be there," murmured Kalanin, "likely with Harlond and Rostov."

"Is it your wish to see them?" asked the Mistress of Illusions.

"I will see Merlin, alone," said Kalanin, "after he has tended to Dargas." The Sorceress turned to Géla.

"Seat them in the main hall; I will come down to greet them while Merlin confers with Kalanin." Géla left.

"So, they will actually be leaving without you," the Sorceress said. "My Divinations showed many paths for you."

"It's very simple — I've resigned," said Kalanin. "Now that you've become more certain of me, perhaps you can tell me what else is happening." She looked at him and laughed.

"You read me so well. I wanted you to reach your decision in a relaxed frame of mind, but I can surely tell you now — or better yet, I'll show you. Come." She led him through the terrace doors, turning first left, then right, through hallways and passages he wasn't familiar with. At the hall's end, the Sorceress touched a massive door with her palm, and it sprang open. Lights flashed on.

"No doubt the Wizards have kept you far from their great gaming boards," she said, laughing. "Yet it would do them little good to show *The Game of the Masters* at this point. Behold!" Kalanin stared at the Field:

the images of the many pieces within *The Game of the Masters* had become ghostly, insubstantial, drifting without purpose about the Field of the Masters. The Mistress of Illusions laughed again, watching as cloudy shapes drifted from end to end, bumping into each other and recoiling, none of them showing any awareness or purpose. "How amusing to imagine all the self important Powers seeking wisdom from *The Game of the Masters*! Now it's defused, awaiting new definitions. Ha!"

Still laughing, she led Kalanin back to her terrace.

"So, there's turmoil all throughout the Mid-World, and considerable fear," she continued. "The Powers are astonished to learn that three Demon Princes remain outside the Mid-World of the Truce. And they know that some great event has taken place in the Western Sea. Merlin advises them that the Marids have been created, new offspring of the Demons, of unknown strength. The Powers are uncertain of Merlin, and the lesser ones, a little fearful of him. Within the Mid-World, a group of Sorcerers has banded together; they blame the League for breaking the Truce. A great hammering and smithing, the building of many weapons has begun, with the formations of many tiers as new armies are created, and somehow, the Sorcerers are mightier than before; there's rumor that some of the Powers are grooming them."

"That's not complicated," said Kalanin. "The Demon Princes are moving again, by proxy, to destroy the League. Why they do not come openly, I don't yet understand. But it's a problem for those wielding magic, in which war leaders and captains are only a small matter, good for dying at the right moments, their blood sinking, wasted into dry, ruined soil. Let the Wizards deal with it if they can." The Mistress of Illusions nodded, sitting back in her chair. They watched in silence through the afternoon, as the insects churned over still waters.

It was late in the day when Merlin finished tending Dargas and emerged from inner halls out onto the sunlit terrace of the Mistress of Illusions. They rose and greeted the old Wizard, and the Sorceress left to greet her other guests. Merlin sat beside Kalanin, watching the insects, nodding as he understood the webs of illusions surrounding them.

"The old Warrior will live," said the Wizard. "His shield arm will need some strengthening over the next months, but he will wield a sword again — if he chooses."

Kalanin nodded. "I hoped you would save him. Dargas was a fine captain and a surprise to everyone: he seemed so set in his ways, yet he was able to adjust to enormous changes at the very last moments. It's a good outcome for Dargas. He will wish for the sword, and shield and the endless watchsfires again."

"What of yourself?" asked Merlin. "Will you take up sword and shield again?" Kalanin shook his head.

"I've retired," he said, and the words were hard to speak. "I've served the League for nearly twenty years. I'm worn out, and it's time to rest."

"Yet it's not weariness that I read in your voice and features," said Merlin gently. "Rather, you are a strong man who has tired of his master's manipulation. Is this not so?" Kalanin sighed. It was difficult to be angry with the gentle old Wizard who had always seemed so reasonable.

"It is true that I wearied of being treated like a simple piece in *The Game of the Masters*. Yet I don't blame you. I can even understand some of the things that happened: you watched as new powers stirred in the ocean, and you saw how the League was distracted, first by the corruptions of its Adepts and Apprentices, then by the complex illusions contrived for Thorian. You set all your pieces in motion, and in the end, you triumphed — after a fashion. Now, the second round begins, and it is an affair of those wielders of magic. I'm no longer involved." Merlin sat, watching insects swarm in the distance. Sunset would come soon, and he understood that all the tiny creatures swirling in front of them would perish.

"The Sorcerers plot against us, armed hosts move to our borders, Ancient Secrets lie smoldering within Alantéa, ready to burst forth, the infant Marids come to power, three Demon Princes plot against us while the Gods, the Powers of the Mid-World strengthen their domains." Merlin spoke in a low voice, almost chanting. "No, it is more than an affair of Wizards, Sorcerers and Magicians. I see, however, that you will remain with the Mistress of Illusions. Before I depart, have you any questions? You were one of the most critical leaders in this last struggle, and you deserve to understand everything." Kalanin was silent for a moment.

"You were always a gracious Lord, and you are courteous even now, at the end," he finally said softly. "I did have one question. What about Orlan, who was senior to me? I was forced to play his role, that of captain — why was this? Perhaps if I had remained in my old role of weapons master and knight, then I would not have felt misused. Why wasn't Orlan chosen as war leader?" Merlin looked away before he spoke.

"Orlan is a fine man, once a great master of many weapons — but his intellect was in no way comparable to yours. He could not have accomplished the tasks given to you." Merlin turned back to Kalanin. "Since that admission has been extracted from me, perhaps you would be willing to listen to a closing lecture. Is this a fair exchange?" Kalanin laughed softly then nodded.

"Then let us talk of the Servants of the Maker and their tasks," Merlin continued. "In the beginning, there is the shadowy figure of the Maker, the Creator, and fashioner of Earth. The First Servants spoke of him as a benign figure, gentle, a great teacher, yet mysterious, quiet, filled with so many aspects. The Maker always cautioned his Servants that there were many surprises before them and that their Service would not always be pleasant...." Merlin sighed again and looked out at the swirling masses of insects. The sun was beginning to set, and those tiny, unaware creatures had so little time left.

"Let me tell you of a service that lies before me, an unpleasant time. I have dreamt of it so many times now, that it must be a powerful path to the future — all my sleep is enchanted, so that I only dream of what was or what may be, and I remember everything.

"My service lies far in the future, beyond Alantéa, beyond the Mid-World, at a time when the great Forces of Sorcery are nearly spent, and men must turn to the forces within nature to deal with the world around them. I am called back to that distant time because there are two *Talismans* of Power lingering within mortal reach: there is a cup known as 'The Grail,' and there is a sword called 'Excalibur.' If men master these *Talismans*, they will be lured into seeking the dwindling force of sorcerous knowledge, rather than building their understanding of the physical world. They will choose the wrong path, leading them to a complete dead end, and so I am sent to remove these *Talismans*, and free humanity to pursue its own, complex destiny.

"I encounter difficult, unpleasant tasks, for with the waning of energies I have only a tiny fraction of my old power. I must use other men for my ends, cruelly deceiving them for the greater good. In my dreams, I watch as good men perish to achieve my goals — ends they do not understand, nor would they assist me if they grasped my true purposes. Yet I persist, for the intent of the Maker is clear. In the end, after battle, and the death of many men, in the middle of great confusion, I remove the cup and the sword, and humanity is free...." The Wizard hesitated for a moment before turning back to Kalanin.

"So, you see that you were used, as I am used, and the Maker will only let all his purposes be known after he wakes us from the Long Sleep, at the End of Time." Merlin fell silent.

"That was a gentle lecture," said Kalanin, nodding, "without reproach or bitterness. You have been a fine master, and I would like to part on good terms." Kalanin rose, as Merlin stood also: the Wizard reached only as high as the warrior's shoulder, but Kalanin understood that enormous power was woven into Merlin's frame, and behind the gentle eyes of the Wizard lurked a mind of matchless subtlety. He smiled down at the Wizard.

"When the Mistress of Illusions tires of me, I'd hoped for a small pension from the League," he said. "Is this still possible?"

"Of course," Merlin said with a slight smile. "That, and much more — if the Wizards' League still stands." The Wizard turned to go, then hesitated. "You know that I have dreamt of this event many times — of the two of us standing in the red light of sunset, as you discuss your pension. Many paths emerge from this meeting. Do not close yourself off from all of them. I say this not to change your mind, but to share my own understanding with you."

"Again, I thank you," said Kalanin, "but I have retired. May you prevail in all your endeavors. You have been an excellent lord. Farewell!" The Wizard gave a last half smile, walked to the terrace doors, and was gone. Kalanin sat, drinking from his goblet, as the Mistress of Illusions returned to rest beside him. Sunset was spreading over the horizon, forming a deep red line.

"That was hard for you, was it not?" she asked. Kalanin drew a deep breath.

"Harder than I ever thought possible," he said shaking his head. "I would prefer to fight through a mass of monsters than to go through that encounter again."

"Yet it's over, and you have prevailed." She turned back to watch the swarming insects.

For each of the tiny dwellers in her kingdom, the Mistress of Illusions had fashioned a mass of luminous, fantastic, utterly compelling lovers. Now the insects massed and copulated uncontrollably, again and again, until dusk when sheets of them began to fall, utterly spent, to their deaths.

· X ·

Far away, under a great weight of dark waters, the infant Marid lies half awake, dreaming of his future. In his watery home, day, and night merge, for the sun's rays cannot reach him. Yet there is light surrounding the Dreaming Infant Marid: masses of decaying particles form clouds of ghostly phosphorescence. In these enchanted clouds are images of the Marids' future:

Here are images of their allies, the Sorcerers, puny in stature, but mighty with magic, who have been armed by Demon Princes and set against the Wizards.

Here are the towers of the Wizards' fortresses, which the Marids together will destroy.

Here is a ghostly image of the Lord of Coils, a being that the greatest of Marids will send into an everlasting darkness.

In his watery home, the infant Marid closes his eyes and dreams. Bane of those wielding magic, Master of all Monsters, and Destroyer of Gods, the Dreaming Infant Marid sleeps, and a slight smile curls his mouth, showing the beginning of boar's tusks, which are slowly emerging from his enormous jaws.

Chapter Two

The Council at Stone Mountain

J ULIAN STOOD AT THE topmost peak of Stone Mountain, where the fortress of Thorian seemed so close to the cloud masses that hovered overhead. Below him, beyond the foothills of Stone Mountain, ocean waves, tiny and white in the distance were foaming against the shore. It was late, and the darkness and dreariness of the day were bringing rain into an even darker evening.

The first sweep of mist droplets washed over Julian, and he pulled his hood over his dark hair, watching the old soldier out of the corner of his eye. It was warmer inside, with fires heating the Wizard's stone chambers at every level, but Julian was unwilling to leave Azaric to stand alone, outside — where the long drop down the mountainside might quickly end the turmoil and self recrimination of Thorian's Steward General. Azaric lifted his earthenware jar, and once again filled his goblet with wine.

"What's been done with the men following Nergal?" Azaric asked. "I suppose you'll convert them to the League, will you not?" Droplets were beading on the old soldier's bare head.

"A few," Julian replied, "but most were too corrupted by Nergal: they warred on villages and townships, stealing women, wine and gold. Those men have taken an oath never to trouble the League again, and they've departed."

"An oath!" muttered Azaric. "They swore an oath to serve the accursed Nergal, and now they swear an oath not to serve him — which oath is more binding? And how many of those dark-hearted servants of evil would abide by any oath?" Raindrops began to run over Azaric's greyish beard. "An oath," he murmured, "if only it were that simple." He drank and poured again. Now his jar was empty, and Azaric cast it lightly over the edge; it seemed to float down, slowly, until it shattered against the cliffside.

"Thorian has taken a new oath to serve the League," Julian added quietly. "He's moving slowly away from remorse, hoping that the undoing of wrongs is a greater purpose."

Azaric drank again from a fresh jar. "That's because the Wizard has some hope of revenge. I have none. I'm finished. And what will my children's children say of me? 'After more than thirty years of service, he joined with a Prince of Demons and a deluded a Wizard and tried to destroy the League. But at the end, he was beaten, outgeneraled by some horsy galloper, a messenger, for the Maker's sake!'" His goblet was empty, and Azaric seemed ready to cast it over the edge, but he stopped and signaled instead for more wine. A cloaked cup bearer raced through the rain, bringing a fresh earthenware jar.

"It was more than that," Julian said softly. "It was the opening move in a struggle that may destroy the Truce, and bring the Gods, the Powers of the Mid-World into open conflict once again. Even *The Game of the Masters* has been stilled, waiting for new forces struggling to emerge and redefine its balance. It was more than a Wizard's failure or a Steward General's deception."

Azaric said nothing but stood watching the rain slide down the walls of the fortress. Julian remembered how damp and oppressive the weather had been: in the strange aftermath of battle, a wet stillness had prevailed, with moss and fungus and lichen flourishing in the stone crevices of the fortress. Now, all the sheets of water rippling down the tower's sides were turning green and brown as rainfall washed growths into the foothills of the mountain's base. Thunder rumbled in the distance: it would be a long, dark night.

Azaric took his earthenware jar and goblet and walked over to the west wall of the tower. Julian shivered a little but followed the old soldier. They stood at the tower's edge, staring down. Along the west wall, and down the face of the cliff, rain was dripping over a series of winches and ropes: a network linked by pulleys, stretching to the ground.

"That was a nice piece of work," Azaric murmured. "My work. If we'd left it to the Wizard, he'd have raised all our goods by sorcery alone. Stone Mountain would have been helpless in his absence, and worse, his presence here would have been trumpeted each time he raised a mass of provisions. It was a good piece of work, but all for nothing."

Azaric wiped the rain from his eyes. "Why was I given the one deluded Wizard to serve? And why was I overawed by the proud fool? Even stray dogs had sense enough to keep their distance from Nergal, but this great Wizard, so powerful with the Gift, he let himself be jerked about like some mindless puppet! Yes, I, even I, had my doubts, but I kept silent. Azaric the humble and loyal, Azaric the fool — so no wonder we failed: like two blind drunkards trying to guide one another down a mountain's side, then toppling from a precipice. No wonder!" Julian shook his head. The rain was coming down harder. The Wizards' Council would begin soon, and he would be called away from the old soldier.

"We were all misled," Julian said gently, "even Merlin with all his wisdom. You are too hard on yourself — look into the face of Harmadast, your counterpart under Balardi. He wishes amnesty, reconciliation, and a new alliance." Azaric shook his head, staring out into the gloom. Mist and clouds were moving in from the ocean, and the shoreline was vanishing from view.

"But I shouldn't try to convince you," Julian continued. "You know more of alliances than I do. I would offer you my services as a healer though: there are times when the mind turns against itself, and invisible daggers form, wounding the inner person as deeply as any metal. I can help you."

Azaric turned to face Julian. He was half a head taller than the Apprentice. His face was puffy, and his eyes were bloodshot. "Do you mean, Apprentice," he said slowly, "that you wish to drug me, and use your magic to tamper with my mind?"

Julian shook his head. "No, as a healer, I would never do that. Nor would any true healer wish to tamper with the mind of any man. I offer only a short time of peace, a time when the mind would be free to heal itself."

Azaric studied Julian's face for a moment. "You're afraid for me, Apprentice, afraid that I'll take my own life, are you not?" Julian nodded and Azaric laughed. More rain was washing over them. "It did cross my mind, but it's gone. Use your Gift, Apprentice. Tomorrow I leave by boat, to live far from here, to raise horses, and totter about my lands, drinking wine and dreaming an old man's dreams."

Julian's Gift reached out, peering into the old soldier's mind: Azaric's desire for death had faded. Yet, it was dark and gloomy at Stone Mountain's peak as nightfall approached — and now, out of the corner of his eye, Julian saw a messenger hovering at the tower door, waiting to summon him to the Wizard's Council.

Azaric, too, saw the messenger and nodded to Julian. "You should go now, Apprentice. I'll be as I can be. On many a dark night I've stood out here in the rain; I'll last through one more."

"The Wizards will have work for me," said Julian, "but call me when you're ready. It's not needed to drift so swiftly from an evil time into the Long Sleep. I can help you." Julian turned and followed the messenger down the tower stairs. Behind them, thunder rumbled as storm clouds shifted even closer to Stone Mountain.

Julian moved quickly down the corridor. Torches fluttered as he sped by — he was late, and the Wizards would have much to discuss. He turned, and raced down a series of stairs, taking the steps two at a time. Within the fortress, storm sounds seemed remote, but every now and again the stone walls would tremble a little as vibrations reached into the inner stonework of the fortress. Julian moved quickly, bypassing the corridor that led to the Council Chamber — he was late, but he was also wet, and it would be difficult to concentrate without a change of clothes. His chamber was down one more level, and if no one intercepted him, he could change, and at least be dry.

He reached his room safely, tearing his cloak off as he entered. Rafir was curled on his bed, sleeping comfortably, far from any dampness. Julian pulled off his wet clothes and hurried into dry ones. A slight tremor reached into the heart of Stone Mountain, and the fox opened an eye, watching the Apprentice push his feet into dry boots.

"They were looking for you earlier," said Rafir, yawning. "You're missing one of their great mumbling sessions."

"I'm late," said Julian, looking around for a dry cloak. "I thought I was doing something important, but I was wrong — as for the 'mumblings', those are over. A full Council has been called, where the great decisions will be made. Didn't they ask you?"

"They couldn't find me to ask me," Rafir said, with a slight smile, "but I suppose I should join you." He jumped to the ground. "There's a dry cloak over on the chair if that's what you're looking for." Julian whipped the cloak from the chair, and in three strides was out of the chamber, speeding down the corridor, with Rafir trotting easily beside him. Though when Julian climbed the stairs three at a time, Rafir panted a little as he strained to keep up with the Apprentice.

They slowed for a moment, taking deep breaths as they came to the doors of the Council Chambers. Guards stood before the great doors, their chainmail glittering in the torchlight. As the guards looked on, they saw a young man and a small red fox. The youth was slender and somewhat bedraggled — his cloak was askew, and his dark hair was soaked, with rainwater still dripping onto his shoulders. They bowed to the young Magician and his servant, then unbarred the heavy oaken doors.

Within the Council Chamber, men were seated around a large oval table. The three Wizards sat at one end of the oval, speaking together in low voices. Julian hesitated for a moment, staring at the three powerful wielders of magic who had not sat gathered together for many long months: Thorian sat highest in his chair, hair silverish white; while Merlin was shorter, hunched, his beard completely grey; and Balardi sat to Merlin's right, nearly as tall as Thorian, and the Wizard's once golden beard now sprouted shafts of grey hair, having aged during the League's long struggle.

Julian stored the image in his mind, then moved quickly to his seat. He took a deep breath then glanced around: more captains and fewer wielders of magic attended this council. Harmadast, stern and austere, sat closest to the Wizards. Galad was slouched at the far end of the oval table, and he turned to wink at Julian. Rostov and Harlond sat near Galad, and they seemed wary of the powerful Wizards. Others had passed from the League struggle: Rurak and Envar had died in battle, while Dargas still struggled to heal. Kalanin and Azaric had fallen away from the struggle and sought peace elsewhere. Also gone were Géla, impetuous warrior maiden, and Baroda, captain of the men of the Dragon's Teeth — both had retreated into the depths of the Mid-World.

Sebastian came and clung to the back of Julian's chair. Everything seemed normal and yet the Gift within him shifted in surprise: the Wizards seemed deeply discouraged, and they were struggling to conceal their own fears...Balardi's voice was lifting a little, just enough so that Julian could make out the words.

"So, you are saying that swift riders are of more use than any Farsight. Very well, but my people can share the work." Across from them, Harmadast nodded.

"I have good men at Narsis and Durian," said Thorian in a low voice, "yet the Asaram and the Saugus are long, with many fords. What of...?" Here, his voice faded, and Julian lost the conversation's thread. Merlin shook his head, face grave.

"No, the Eye is too well known, they are seeking him even now, as I call for his return. We should develop other sentinels or small messengers, but for now, we will trust to the swiftest of our riders." Merlin turned away from Thorian and Balardi, looking to the others seated at the table with a faint, weary smile.

"We were speaking of Farsight and all the many means by which we obtain information from a distance. When the League was strong, there were few places within our borders where something might be hidden from Wizards and their devices. But now our foes have thrown a dark haze over all our distant eyes, as though to blind us — even the eagle's vision has been blocked, and he has been recalled, for they will have a special malice for him after Gravengate...." The Wizard paused, listening to the sound of thunder as it rolled in, muffled by the heavy stonework of the fortress.

Merlin nodded as it receded. "Sorcery, powerful sorcery, has been launched against us, and the elements are shaken in its wake. But who is wielding this sorcery, and why is it directed against us? Why has the League been subjected to these attacks, first by deception, and now by proxy? Why do our opponents not come forward, openly? They were shown to be Demon Princes, unmatched in power. And if the Ancient Adversaries come forward in contravention of the Truce, then why are the Powers of the Mid-

World not leaping to our aid, or compelling the Demon Princes to adhere to the ancient pact? What is this Truce, and what are its terms?"

Balardi shook his head. "We have studied the Truce and the behavior of the Powers for many years. We made little progress then, and those questions will not be answered here in this chamber."

"They will not be answered here," Merlin said, "but now we must set a course that will force those answers to emerge." He looked at each of his captains as though measuring their intellects and tailoring his words to their understanding. "All that we know of this matter will be shared, here in this Council. Kalanin called this struggle 'an affair of the wielders of magic' and when he said this, he was wrong. It is an affair, first for the Servants of the Maker to block the Ancient Adversaries from achieving mastery over Alantéa and the Far Lands. Secondly, it is a matter for humans, whether they will survive, even as slaves."

Julian sat back in his chair, masking his surprise. Gloomy words were to be expected, but the heavy, grim features of the Wizards were surprising. The Wizards were powers in their own right, and a struggle against the Ancient Adversaries should have brought forth all their pride and strength to the surface. Yet they seemed downcast, defeated at the very beginning. What had happened?

"Let us begin then, with the Ancient Adversaries," Merlin continued. "Who are these beings and how did they survive their contest with the Ancient Servants? Many perished on both sides. How did they avoid the Truce? All the Ancient Powers — Seraphs and Demons, Dragons and Spirit Lords — were compelled to give up their old forms and enter into the Truce. And as the Ancient Powers became one with the Truce, they were transformed utterly, becoming Powers of the Mid-World: the Gods of Mankind.

"So completely were the Ancient Powers altered, that we can only speculate as to a Power's previous incarnation; Zos and Wotan, perhaps, were mighty among the Seraphs or Spirit Lords, while Quetzalcoatl or dark souled Set may have been Maker-roused Demon Princes or great Lords of Dragons. Yet all such speculation is idle, for we will never discover the incarnations of the Gods until the Awakening.

"How then did these three Demon Princes succeed in standing outside of the Truce? Why have they now emerged to challenge the Powers for mastery of Alantéa and the Far Lands? We have the answers, or a portion of the answers, not through our own powers, but from Julian." All the eyes of Wizards and captains turned to the bedraggled Apprentice.

"It was not something I tried to discover," Julian said, sitting up and looking uncomfortable. "I was thrown senseless, to the Hall of the Dreamers, where the greatest of the Servants dwell beneath the Cup of the Maker, awaiting His return. I was only a catalyst; nothing was done through my own efforts."

"It was not by my design, either," said Merlin. "We may believe, or hope, that the distant Hand of the Maker aided us —" Another crackle of electrical energy interrupted Merlin, and the Wizard halted, his eyes growing distant, filled with Farsight. Thorian and Balardi sat up, as though following some distant event. The Gift brought Julian the image of lightning racing through dark thunderclouds. Others remained silent, watching the Wizards carefully. Another burst of thunder rolled over the fortress of Stone Mountain, then it passed down to the ocean's edge and out to sea. Merlin drew a deep breath and broke the silence.

"It is done. The eagle will survive, but disaster hovered close by — so many traps were set for him — hailstones and whirlwinds, but it was lightning that we feared most."

"Merlin is overly modest," said Balardi. "While he sat explaining matters to us, he was guiding the eagle through a very great maze of death. It's not something that either I or my brother Wizard could manage." Thorian shifted a little in his chair but said nothing. The great oaken doors to the Council Chamber opened, and the captain of the guard entered, with the Eye of Merlin on his shoulder. The eagle was wet and ruffled, but undaunted, and his eyes flashed quickly over the chamber, observing alert captains, one lone, bedraggled Apprentice, and gloomy Wizards.

"I will stand with the Apprentice," said the eagle, "for he and I, alone, are truly weather worthy." The Eye sank his talons into the arm of Julian's chair and turned to Merlin. "It would seem, Lord, that you have not yet shown your Divination forecasts to these soldiers. Is this not so?"

Merlin nodded. "We should begin, first with the Demons, then with the Sorcerers, and lastly, the Marids."

The eagle's farseeing eyes flashed back and forth between Thorian and Balardi. "Do not be so downcast, Lords. You should know that the League is more than your two fancy fortresses. Our last struggle proved that." Thorian shook his head gloomily but said nothing. Galad looked over to Julian, who shrugged his shoulders, showing that he, too, was puzzled.

"We will talk of Gravengate and Stone Mountain later," Merlin said. "First, the Demon Princes — who are they and how have they evaded the Truce? As a first step, we will attempt to show what Julian learned at the Hall of the Dreamers. Neither mortal nor immortal has ever succeeded in viewing the Dreamers in their contemplations, but we shall make the attempt."

Merlin nodded to Thorian and Balardi, and the two Wizards rose together, pulling aside the drapes that hung on the north wall. Beyond the fabric, Julian saw the outlines of a Divination Spell, framed against the stone walls of the fortress. Balardi and Thorian retraced the symbols with their staffs, and the stone and mortar of the castle walls began to fade, first becoming grey, then misty, and finally transparent, as though a window formed, out into the stormy night.

Yet the image now showed stars, not stormy skies, and the stars were strange, larger, forming patterns unknown in Alantéa. Julian recognized the star patterns of the Land of the Dreamers, and a great longing rose within him. Now, the image passed over the highest of mountain tops, where the Cup of the Maker lay like a wide basin set into the highest peak. Even at night the crystal waters rose and sparkled across the plain, dancing in delight in the fullness of starshine. Julian let out a deep breath, as the image shifted down the hillside, searching for the Hall of the Dreamers: this was the path he had walked, just a brief time ago, yet it seemed as though a lifetime had passed.

Now the image showed a clearing, with the Hall of the Dreamers shining in the distance: the Hall was formed from glass panels, and filled with the light of a thousand candles, as the Dreamers sat at their great high table. The image moved across the field, coming closer to the Hall, but here, the Divination began to flicker and fade. Merlin stepped forward, touching the outline of the spell. The image cleared and brightened. They beheld the high table of the Dreamers: Julian was standing before them, listening to Voritar and Llara.

Suddenly, the image froze. Julian's figure vanished from the image, and the Dreamers turned to regard the Wizards, staring calmly into the chamber at Stone Mountain. With a start, Julian realized that the Dreamers had set aside the Wizards' spell, that they no longer viewed past images of the Dreamers, as Julian had seen those Powers months ago — these were the Dreamers as they sat, that very moment, in their great Hall.

Thorian and Balardi stiffened, sitting back. Merlin bowed to the images of the Dreamers. Llara searched the faces of the Wizards, shaking her head as though in disappointment.

"It is not permitted to view the Hall of the Dreamers," she said softly. "Even the greatest Powers of the Mid-World would be denied entry if they even came to know of our existence. Why have you chosen to attempt this thing?" Merlin shuffled forward, coming closer to the image of the Dreamers.

"We are the last of the Servants of the Maker," he said slowly. "We are by far the weakest and may soon be overwhelmed by the Ancient Adversaries. It is heartening to know that the most renowned of the Servants still live. Yet we are not seeking your aid, only a retelling of the instructions given to Julian, for it has a direct bearing on our struggle. Come, see the matter through my eyes." Merlin stepped forward and extended a hand into the Divination image. Llara met it with her own. Thorian and Balardi sat rigid, tight with tension.

After a moment, Merlin stepped back, withdrawing from the Divination image. The Dreamers sat back in contemplation, searching the faces of the Wizards. At last, Voritar, Prince of Demons spoke, sending his low, rumbling voice rolling through the Council Chamber.

"I am eldest here; I will judge on behalf of the Dreamers. Your search at the Hall of the Dreamers flows from the journey of your Apprentice, and this visit was brought about by the Ancient Adversaries, and not by your own actions — and so this Divination may continue, but you should know that we are not permitted to offer further aid or counsel. Farewell! May the distant hand of the Maker give you guidance!" The Dreamers turned away, and the image blurred and shifted, again showing Julian in the Hall, standing before the great high table of the Dreamers as he had done many months ago.

"I will recall for you the story, the old story, the sad story, if you wish," Voritar spoke to the image of Julian, and the Demon's voice rumbled through their great glass Hall. "Though I was not present at the Beginning; only the Maker knows truly what went through His mind when He began the great Fashioning. And I cannot remember these events, I must relive them.

"I imagine the Maker coming to Earth to breathe life over its dead surface, and I see Him hesitate as He perceives the Demons, asleep in the

Earth's crust, some echo or ghost of an earlier creation in a distant star system. The Maker ponders whether to wake the sleeping Demons, whether they will prosper in Earth's gardens. After an age, He wakes them, but first He fashions the Seraphs, to be brothers to them, Lords of the codominion of Earth.

"Now I am awake, and the Maker is teaching us about the Earth, and all the great energies that surround it. He takes shape as He wishes, neither Seraph nor Demon, and I perceive that He is careful not to overwhelm us. We begin to fashion and tame the Earth, great labors in which the Demons and the Seraphs share the labor. But I and the other great ones of the Demons begin to hold ourselves a little apart for we now understand that our power is unequaled, except by a few of the greatest of Seraphs. The Maker does not put forth His power but advises and counsels.

"Now, Earth's Gardens are tilled and ready for seed. The Seraphs begin the fashioning of the Spirit Lords to aid in the creation of Earth's life. The Maker counsels the Demons to obtain His aid before exploring their own creative energies, but my brothers have begun to mock the Maker, referring to him, in his absence, as 'Elder Brother.' They believe that the Maker is not greater than they, only first. In secret, I and my brothers begin the creation of the Dragons. In this, we have the help of Adonai, the great Seraph, who has compassion for us and is deceived.

"Now, the Dragons burst forth in splendor, sparkling and gleaming with power, so that Seraph, Demon, and Spirit Lord are dazzled. But the Maker is filled with sorrow and remains silent, perceiving the flaws within the Dragons. In a little while, the Seraphs and Spirit Lords bring forth humankind, and these seem pale and feeble beside the Dragons. Though now, others begin to understand the corruption of the Dragons. Adonai repents and the Maker forgives him. I see within the Dragons, Creatures of the Darkness waiting to be born, and great sorrow fills my being. My fellow

Demon Princes turn against the Maker, blaming him for the corruption of the Dragon's seed.

"Now, the Maker stands forth and casts aside His guise as advisor and elder, showing himself as Lord of the Universe. In a quiet voice He says only, 'You will need to seek Me,' and He vanishes without even a flash of light or a whisper of thunder. All the Powers hear those words, and in that hour, I put aside my kinship and declare for the Maker. Five of the wisest of the Dragons understand the flaws within themselves and leave Earth to seek the Maker in the starry universe. Here, in the Hall of the Dreamers, I watch my children often, as they leap from star to star in their quest for the Maker, and the dross burns away from them.

"The War of the Servants and the Adversaries of the Maker begins. I stand with a few of the Dragons for the Servants. A handful of Seraphs and Spirit Lords are corrupted by the Demons and stand with the Adversaries. With my Seraph allies and my children, the Dragons, we fashion a wondrous work, and three of the most fell of the Demon Princes are chained forever. Lucifrage is destroyed, but two of the mightiest Spirit Lords perish in the aftermath of that battle."

At this point, Merlin held up his hand, and the Divination froze, then began to fade.

"Here then is part of the answer," said Merlin. "Voritar tells us that three of the greatest of the Demon Princes are sealed away forever. Alas! It seems that it was not forever, and they have reemerged when the Servants are weakest! How were these Demon Princes sealed away? By the complex Sorcery of four Powers — Demon and Seraph, Dragon and Spirit Lord. I will guess that they fashioned the Guardians of the World to imprison the Demon Princes, but now those beings called Guardians are corrupted or overthrown."

"What of the Truce?" asked Thorian. "How can this Truce of the Mid-World continue after the Ancient Adversaries come forward — and bring forth a new race of evil beings? Surely the Powers of the Mid-World will come to our aid or at least the Ancient Servants will be permitted to aid us."

Merlin shook his head, grimly. "We have never learned the terms of the Truce, but it seems almost certain that our foes know them; and so, they will take care to avoid the Mid-World Powers — until they are prepared. This, I believe, is the reason that the Demon Princes have not come more openly against us. They will avoid antagonizing the Gods until we are destroyed."

"Yet, if we learn the terms of the Truce, we might use that knowledge to our advantage, against our opponents," said Balardi. "Is this possible?"

"To learn the terms of the Truce will be one of our principal goals." Harmadast stirred: the Wizards seemed remote and depressed, what had gone wrong? Out of the corner of his eye, he saw the torchlight flicker — then the doors of the Council Chamber slipped open, revealing a damp messenger who was still spattered with mud. Harmadast went quickly to the door, and the messenger passed a slip of paper to him and was gone. Harmadast scanned it briefly then returned to his seat.

"Near Dahlak lies the secret of the Truce," Balardi was saying. "We should seek first in the Vale of Whispers."

"But is there time for this scholarly investigation?" asked Harmadast. "Here's news of a great tier mass moving to our northern border, and the news is a half day old — they may have forded the Saugus this morning. And there's a rumor of a war fleet sheltering near the Isles of the Sorcerers. No Truce will help us if the League is overrun by scores of tiers."

"They will seek to deny us time to investigate the Truce," Merlin said, nodding. "No time will be left to learn of Marids, either, before they are loosed against us." Merlin sighed. "Yes, in a short while, great masses of men and magic will be hurled against the League. Their sponsors will be Demon Princes, yet they will be led by men."

"Why should men ally themselves with the Ancient Adversaries?" Julian asked. "Surely they must know that the Demons will discard them when they are no longer of use."

"Binding oaths exist even for Demon Princes," Merlin replied. "The Sorcerers are not vain or naive enough to proceed without some guarantees. In exchange for service to the Demons, they will become the greatest of the Mortal Magic Wielders, the new masters, perhaps, of the League." Galad leaned back in his chair and stretched. The Council Chamber itself was well lit, with tapestries covering stone walls, but gloom seeped from the slumping postures and defeated voices of the Wizards, and a dark unhappiness seemed to fill the chamber.

"So, my Wizard Masters, matters are grim," said Galad, "yet there's no need to speak of others as masters of the League — at least now the League is fully marshaled, and we are no longer divided. Who are these Sorcerers who seek mastery? Merlin has told us of twenty or thirty of the mightiest Sorcerers who serve in the Mid-World, or who inhabit the Isles of the Sorcerers to the south. How many, and which of them have come against us? What are they like, and why should we fear them?" Merlin opened his mouth to speak, but held back, glancing at Thorian out of the corner of his eye.

"Yes, I know of these Sorcerers," Thorian said, looking up. "May the Maker curse me for an idiot for all my misjudgments. I had contact with many of the Sorcerers when I should have kept far away from them...I will tell you of them — no, I will show you. It should take me only a moment." Thorian rose and went to the Divination pattern that remained diagrammed against the walls of Stone Mountain. He spoke a few words over the pattern: lights flickered and blurred, with dark smoke filling its design. Thorian stood watching for a moment, then he raised his staff to the pattern, intoning a name. The image shifted and blurred with ripples of light scattering across the pattern. Thorian stood back and barked a sharp, bitter laugh.

"Not only am I a fool, but I have become a weak fool — I sought Houma but could not reach him. Perhaps he lies hidden in the Mid-World, for he was always at the court of one of the Powers, spreading lies as he insinuated himself into the councils of the most powerful of the Gods. Here, at least is an image of Houma, as he appeared when he last journeyed to Stone Mountain." The rippling lights of the Divination faded, and a portrait slowly emerged, of subtle hues, as though painted in oils, of a lean dark haired figure. His upper lip was shaved, and his beard was trimmed and curled. Houma's manner was meek, deferential, but his eyes sparkled with deceit and malice.

"Not everyone will perceive this Sorcerer as clearly as we now see him," Thorian continued. "I believe that he has always been a secret adversary of the League: it was he who first brought Nergal to my court — curse him forever!" The image faded. Thorian took a deep breath, striving to clear the anger and gloom from his thoughts. "Let us then seek for Cronar and Eudox — rumors come from the eyes and ears of the Mid-World that those two lead the forces against our Northern border. And so, they are closer, and may find it more difficult to conceal themselves." Again, Thorian placed his staff on the diagram's edge, calling softly in a muffled voice. An image formed, of blue sky with ripple bellied puffy clouds lumbering across distant skies.

"We approach these with more caution," Thorian murmured. The image moved forward, accelerating as it sought the Sorcerers...the image passed over a small village...over a series of small hills...through a deep cloud bank...then the image slowed as it reached the edge of a wide river.

"The Saugus," Thorian murmured. They passed over the river...the image became even slower...armed guards stood watch on the other side, down beside the riverbank just a little distance from their horses: these watchers were slouched but wary as they stared across the water. On each of their shields was a bright colored emblem...the image moved closer to the patterns on the many shields...painted on each shield was an image of three hands clasping — one hand was covered with beast fur, the second was that of a skeleton, fleshless, and the third was human.

Merlin cursed underneath his breath and murmured, "I might well have guessed."

Harmadast peered at the image frowning. "But what does it mean?" Merlin said nothing, but hunched forward, watching as the Divination image shifted higher, looking down over the riverbank, where a long string of men stood, guarding a line of pontoons.

"They knew that the fords were guarded," Harmadast said softly, "and so they've built temporary crossings." The image shifted, turning from the river, moving north, showing a stream of provision wagons moving south to the League's borders; and there were messengers flowing in both directions. Men were beginning to move behind the wagons, with some groups reaching a full tier strength of five-hundred men-at-arms while others remained at scout level.

"We are watching their vanguard moving into place," murmured Harmadast. Galad nodded, leaning forward, but he said nothing. The image slowed, and shifted, then from a height they looked down to a series of fields that were linked by roadways and muddy tracks. Over the fields many thousands of men were in motion: some were pulling apart great tent cities, while others loaded masses of wagons. In smaller fields, horses were being groomed and fed. In others, temporary wooden structures housed smithies and armories. The image lowered, and the sounds of hammering and shouting drifted from the image into the Council Chamber at Stone Mountain.

Thorian's hand moved, and the image shifted to ground level, where a young man was leaning forward, carefully painting a design on a shield: again, the insignia of three clasped hands — skeleton, beast, and human. Rostov looked to Merlin, framing a question, but the Wizard motioned him to silence. Now the image moved along the ground, shifting from place to place, dancing among shadows, as a partially invisible spy might avoid the light. At last, a small hillock came into view, raised above the flat fields that surrounded it. The top was barren of trees but green, except where footpaths had turned the ground dry and dead. Small streams of people moved up and down earthen paths; then the image moved, shifting behind an older, dark haired captain, following closely behind him as though the image took the same route as the captain's squire.

At the top of the hillock stood a high-ceilinged tent, almost as large as a small temple. A few feet from the tent, two figures sat before a long table of carved mahogany. Both chairs and table were ornate. Red sunlight from day's end threw crimson shadows over the scene. Even through the Divination, Julian could sense the strength of the Gift within the two men: one was white-haired, aloof, and stern; the second was of middle years, with a noble face and soft wet, eyes. Both leaned over a table, as though examining a plan or a pattern.

Thorian tensed, raising his left hand for silence, while his right gripped his staff. The image crept slowly toward the two seated men, just as the elder cast a series of shapes over the table. The image drifted closer, and Julian peered at the shapes, expecting images of *The Game of the Masters*: but these were vastly different, and strange to the onlookers at Stone Mountain.

Suddenly, the eyes of the Sorcerers lifted from their pattern as they sensed the Divination Spell of the Wizards. Their grey eyes narrowed as they struggled to recognize the creators of spells that gathered to them. Thorian murmured in a muffled voice, and a grey, obscure mist seeped through the chamber. The younger Sorcerer stood, intoning a seeking spell. The elder cast his shapes once again, and when he looked up into the Divination image, his features were filled with understanding — and contempt. His palms flashed, and a heavy black smoke surged into the Divination image.

Then, abruptly, the onlookers were seated once again at Stone Mountain, staring at a rock wall of grey stone. Thunder rumbled once again; the Gift brought Julian an image of hard rain sending sheets of water down the mountainside, carrying a tide of moss and fungus down to the sea.

"Once, they would not have broken my spells so easily," Thorian said, shaking his head. "There, at least, were the images of two of our adversaries. The younger is Eudox, the elder is named Cronar. Eudox was once considered an Adept, part of the League, before Julian's time, but others will remember him."

"I remember him only too well," Balardi said grimly. "Those sad, fishy eyes, his noble-seeming face, don't be fooled by them, as I was. Eudox was apprenticed to me many years ago: a quick learner with a full measure of the Gift — and treachery seething in his rotten soul. He departed abruptly, stealing what he could. His theft would have been greater, had the Ancient One not warned me to beware of him." Balardi turned to Merlin. "We are matched against an alliance of four Sorcerers, who are backed by Demons and Demon spawn. Why do they show an emblem of three hands? Only one hand in that design was human. What's the meaning?"

"More deceit, more treachery," Merlin sighed. "The beast hand and skeleton hand have long been an emblem of *The Game of the Masters* and of the Mid-World. Now, these are joined by a human hand — meaning that the Sorcerers will presume to speak for the Mid-World, to put us down in the name of the Truce, claiming that we are the violators because we still speak for the Maker.

"Some of the Powers will be deceived, others bewildered. The Dark Lords of the Mid-World will not be deceived, instead, they will be amused. So, we have seen three of our foes. What of Alcman, the fourth? He is, by reputation, the greatest of the Sorcerers. Has he also been here, at Stone Mountain?"

"The other three, yes," said Thorian, "but not Alcman. I was a fool, yet at my worst, I would not treat with Alcman: he was entirely the pupil of the Powers of the Mid-World, finally expelled from Alantéa before he could overthrow one of their own minor Gods." Thorian stood. "I have not hosted Alcman, yet I have watched him from afar as he amassed power in the Isles of the Sorcerers. We should see what his part in this struggle will be." Again, Thorian used his staff to trace the lines of his Divination.

Now the watchers at Stone Mountain viewed an expanse of blue water on a bright day, with heavy winds whipping up foaming rows of cresting waves. Small islands lay strewn in mid water, with waves crashing onto sandy beaches. In the distance loomed a larger land mass, where beaches were backed by great sandy bluffs. The image surged toward the headland above one bluff as though blown by high winds. Around the land mass were a few fishing boats, with men struggling with sails surrounded by heavy, surging seas. The image slowed, then began to drift to the left, following the island's long coastline.

Nearly a league from the island's northern tip, the beaches curled, as the indentation of the coastline formed a huge, natural harbor. Within the harbor, a vast flotilla of ships was sheltering, armed for war, with streams of men-at-arms and porters moving among many docks. Mounted on the decks of the larger warships were huge siege weapons: some armed with catapults, while others held gigantic crossbows. Julian began to take count of the ships, but there were too many, and their Divination image was sinking. Each of the ships bore a pennant from its highest mast, showing skeleton, beast hand and human hand linked together.

"Behold the second portion of the vise prepared for our League," Balardi said softly. "From the north, countless tiers and numberless wagons. From the south, a vast armada, and Stone Mountain stands between them, like a walnut in a crusher. We can see that Alcman has not been idle." As Balardi spoke the name of Alcman, the image shook and staggered.

"Control is slipping from me!" Thorian cried. Merlin rose, clutching his staff in hand. The image sped across the harbor, as seagulls squealed, dropping toward boat decks. On the hillside above the harbor, one man stood, alone, overseeing the movement of men down to the docks. He was tall, and broad, moving easily like a warrior of midyears; and he was clean shaven, with a necklace that dipped down across his broad chest: on the necklace was a string of tiny skulls, each carved from bone, or ivory. His hands were raised as though invoking the image.

When Alcman saw the Wizards, he laughed. "I was told to expect you! Welcome! I have even prepared a small gift!" His right hand flashed, and he was holding an amorphous, black fluttering creature. The Sorcerer laughed again and cast the creature at them — and it passed through their Divination, and into the chamber at Stone Mountain. Rostov threw himself away from it, crashing to the floor. The creature, gibbering senselessly, flapped away from them, rising toward the roof of the chamber. Galad and Harlond drew weapons. Thorian stood, staff in hand, surging with power.

"Whatever else, I am Master here!" The creature reached the chamber's roof, shrieking in fear, and burst through the stone and mortar, fluttering out into the stormy night.

Bits of mortar and rubble scattered over them and Julian felt raindrops swirling in from the darkness. A wry laugh slipped from his open mouth.

"This has been an impressive demonstration," Julian said, "of the Sorcerers' power. But surely our cause is not so hopeless. The League has fielded a force of men and sorcery for many years. Can the Sorcerers come together and duplicate our efforts overnight?"

"They can if they are weaponed and aided by Demon Princes," Balardi said. Thorian was whispering in a muffled voice, and in a moment the roof closed over, and Stone Mountain was again sealed against rain and darkness.

"You miss the point, Apprentice," said the eagle. "Or rather, the matter has not been fully explained to us." The eagle raised his wings and cast himself forward, coming to rest on the great council table. "You see these Masters of Power sitting grim faced and depressed, and you think, 'they fear the Sorcerers with their new Demon-spawned magic and their countless tiers' — and you are wrong, for these great wielders of magic have not yet shown their real fears." The eagle turned to Merlin. "We have had tales of the Demons; we have seen the Sorcerers. Are the Marids next, Lord?" Merlin shook his head.

"Our Divination spells are too well understood by our foes, and we cannot show the Marids for they are not yet fully grown — what you have seen through my eyes is an image of our future, and it is a grim image colored red and grey by rampaging Marids."

"You mean that you have cast futures, and the results are not to your liking," Julian, said. Merlin nodded slowly.

"I have looked into the future and watched as the Marids emerge from the ocean to pull down Stone Mountain," Thorian added. "The Sorcerers may or may not prevail against us, but the image of Marids, victorious, cannot be shaken."

"In Divinations, I have watched as Marids stride unchecked over the Plain of Gravengate," said Balardi, "and then my fortress becomes no more than a heap of broken beams and stone."

"And I have watched all these things in clear dreams," said Merlin. "Yet they may not come to pass — there may still be a way to prevent them."

"Even if Stone Mountain falls and Gravengate falls, is this the end of the League?" asked Galad. "During the last struggle did we not learn that the League is more than a series of fortresses, but instead a band of many peoples, uniting to preserve themselves?"

"In my forecasts of the future, I have seen the League broken utterly," said Merlin, in such a soft voice that it was almost a whisper. "The last Portals flash, the last of the peoples of the League vanish into the Mid-World, to uncertain futures...." He drew a deep breath. "Yet I cannot believe that our cause is hopeless. If Demon Princes and Marids were certain to prevail against us, they would not trouble with arming the Sorcerers, or with deceiving the Mid-World. Our tasks are to check the Sorcerers, to find a way to counter the Marids and to bring the full force of the Truce against the Demon Princes. How shall we begin?"

"You alone perceived the birth of the Marids," said Balardi. "You are also the most powerful of us, and most likely to avert our destruction. You should return to Sea's Edge and seek some counter to the Marids. As for the nature of the Truce, it is said that Demons and Dragons, Seraphs and Spirit Lords met near Dahlak, in a place called the Vale of Whispers. I will go there if you wish."

"While you were gone, the Sorcerers would overwhelm first Stone Mountain, then Gravengate," said Merlin. "To reach the Vale of Whispers, you must take the Straight Road, unaided by Transfer Portal. Yet across the Straight Road lie the domains of many Mid-World Powers. They would contest your passage — you might surprise some of them, but you would never reach Dahlak." Merlin turned to Julian. "This, I believe, is a task for our Apprentice. If he no longer seems as innocent and weak as he was once portrayed, he is the least threatening of those of us with the Gift. If he is willing, Julian will seek the nature of the Truce at the ruins of Dahlak."

"I am willing," said Julian, "but I know little of the Mid-World Powers."

"We will teach you more, over the next few days," said Merlin. "We will also advise you about the Sorcerer Houma, who has been placed in the Mid-World, perhaps to block us, perhaps to deceive the Powers. But your teaching will be brief, for we must leave Stone Mountain shortly before this fortress finds itself under siege." Merlin turned to Thorian and Balardi. "What is your judgment? With your Wizardry and your many tiers, can you hold Stone Mountain against the Sorcerers?" Thorian hesitated, but Balardi drew himself up.

"They have forged a great design for our destruction, and yet...." Balardi tapped the hand of Thorian as it rested on the council table. "This one and I are a couple of tough old birds — we'll slip from their hammers and anvils and crush their tools. Watch us!" At Balardi's touch, Thorian sat up in his chair, and seemed to wake, for here was the first gesture of friendship between the two old adversaries.

"Sorcerers, at least, will not overcome us," Thorian said grimly. "This much I pledge: though I fought powerfully in my madness, I will struggle with far greater strength to preserve the League. Though Nergal may have spied my most secret devices, others will soon be crafted, to the dismay of our foes."

"I will work with you," added Balardi. "We will surprise them together."

"So, the outlines are set," said Merlin. "Balardi and Thorian with all our tiers will attempt to check the Sorcerers. I will return to Sea's Edge to discover a counter to the Marids. Julian will seek the terms of the Truce. It is done."

Galad sat staring at the wielders of magic with clear bright eyes before speaking. "Then is it true, what Kalanin suggested, that the men at arms are useful only as background, as embroidery, required only to fight and die at the right moments?" Harmadast sat up in surprise, staring at Galad. Rostov and Harlond turned to watch the Wizards.

"No," Merlin murmured, "what Kalanin believed is not true. In this struggle, we, the Mortal Magic Wielders may be the ones used for dying, dying at the correct place, at the right moment."

Chapter Three

Journey into Fear

THEY WENT A LITTLE way with Julian, reluctant to say farewell to the Apprentice. Julian rode Bluescent, with the mare seeming slight beside the much larger warhorses of Galad, Rostov, and Harlond. The four rode slowly westward, remaining within sight of Stone Mountain. Screening parties moved in parallel with them along the roadsides, watching for any signs of hidden foes.

The Eye of Merlin watched too, but from a great height above them, floating through cloudless sunlit skies. But ragged weather was building in the north, preparing to slide down toward the ocean, ready to bring more rain to Stone Mountain and the coast.

"I feel like a small child," Galad commented, "whose mother has instructed him to stay within sight of their cottage. It's a shame we can't travel further with you, Julian."

"You'll be needed back at Stone Mountain," Julian said. "If Merlin is right, warships led by Alcman will reach land in a few days, while other armed hosts break through our northern borders, and so you'll be busy in a while."

"Still, we'll miss you," Galad said. "The Wizards seem grimmer and more humorless with every passing day."

"Galad was wrong when he compared the Wizard's advice to a 'mother's instruction'," Harlond added. "It's like having grandmothers run your life — three of them."

Julian laughed. "Soon you'll have only two grandmothers: Merlin will return to Sea's Edge, before the storm breaks."

Galad sighed. "I wish that you and Kalanin could still be with us. You two knew how to handle the Wizards better than the rest of us. Now, what about Kalanin? Is there a chance he'll return?"

"Not from what Merlin's told me," Julian said, shaking his head, "and yet…Merlin mentioned something about a 'Seraph's death-sting' — something I've never heard of or read about. Is it possible that Kalanin took some wound in his struggle with that demented Seraph? If so, his wound might heal. Who can tell?" They were silent for a moment, then Galad nodded to Harlond and Rostov who waved farewell to the Apprentice, turning to begin a much swifter return to Stone Mountain, while Galad lingered, riding beside Julian.

"Rafir tells me that you've had some interesting discussions with Merlin," Julian said.

"Hard to keep secrets when there's an invisible fox around," Galad muttered. "The Wizards have always needed older Charmed Knights to guide them in matters about warcraft, things that were not magical. When I was young, Orlan provided Merlin with a steady stream of unwelcome news that the Wizard listened to only with difficulty. Kalanin spoke truth to power, and Merlin was forced to hear him out. Now that they are both gone, I have had to step forward and tell Merlin that you are being sent out vastly underpowered with weapons and not properly supported.

"I argued that I should be joining you. I reminded the Wizard that the Tarnished Sword provides a force of mongrel magic, drawing not only on both good and evil forces but also the living and the dead — you should have heard the dead moan when they were called on to add their power to the creation of the Tarnished Sword.

"Of course, nothing could change the Wizard's mind in the end. Merlin said only, 'The Apprentice is weaponed. Ask him about his new weapons.'" Galad carefully looked around, east, west, north, and south before continuing. "Since no other allies are in sight, I must guess that the Stone Golems and Troll Mages sent to assist you have chosen to remain invisible. Am I correct?"

Julian shook his head, then spoke words of magic that called down a Cone of Silence around them, making it very difficult for the Mid-World to overhear their words.

"Our Trolls and Golems," Julian said quietly, "are so completely invisible that they do not even exist. I've been supplied with two small, though formidable allies." Still riding slowly to the west and north, Julian pulled out a slender but rugged necklace formed of thin bands of steel. At the base of the steel necklace, two *Talismans* had been attached — one was grey, mottled and looking quite grim while the second was blue and seemed to glitter in the daylight.

"My tiny allies are two very powerful *Talismans*," Julian said, lowering his voice even further. If I'm attacked and invoke this grim, grey device, armed Specters and Wraiths will come to my aid. Magic is always unfair, but this device seemed particularly one-sided — the weapons wielded by these creatures will slash our foes, but no weapon will cut our own lovely Wraiths and Specters. The only way for our foes to avoid destruction is to drop their weapons and run for their lives. Wraiths and Specters will not pursue them, so let us hope that they have sense enough to flee.

"That's why the grey *Talisman* looks so grim," Julian continued. "As for the more charming looking blue *Talisman*, let us say that if Alcman or Houma were to hurl some enormous dark thunderbolt at us, then this blue

Talisman would not only repel that force, but it would blow that magic right back at the Sorcerer who sent it. Boom! Then hopefully, we would have one less Sorcerer to worry about."

"We have never had that kind of luck," Galad said grimly, shaking his head. Then he lowered his voice just as Julian had. "Even though you are much better armed than I thought, I still think I should be at your side."

Apprentice and Charmed Knight rode in silence for a while, then from above them the Eye of Merlin began coasting downward, sweeping in a wide circle, until he came to rest on Galad's shoulder. They brought their horses to a halt.

"Time to return, is it?" asked Galad.

"Merlin is calling for us," the eagle croaked. "I will guess that Alcman has been sighted."

"So, it begins," said Galad, and he smiled down at the Apprentice. "Stone Mountain is going to be a lively, dangerous place, Julian. You are fortunate to escape."

"The Apprentice travels into great danger," said the eagle, "more than he may understand. Julian, my master has counseled you about the dangers of your journey. I will add my own warnings: beware of the Sorcerer, Houma. Beware of the Dark Lords of the Mid-World — and beware of the old troubles concealed within your own mind. I have looked into the mind of Merlin, and he fears for you, not only because your foes are powerful, but because old troubles can still fester within you, Apprentice, ones that may return if your stress becomes too great. Go cautiously! May you bring the Truce down upon the Ancient Adversaries! Farewell!"

"At least do something to bring smiles back to the faces of our grim Wizards," added Galad. "Goodbye, Julian! After we've crushed the Sorcerers and the Marids and destroyed the Demon Princes, we'll send for you. Take care of yourself!" Julian waved farewell and urged Bluescent forward.

Sebastian sat on Julian's shoulder, and he turned, watching Galad ride back to Stone Mountain: he was returning far more quickly than he had come, and in a few minutes their great friend and ally was out of sight. Only Stone Mountain was still clearly visible, and even now distance was making the fortress seem steadily smaller.

Sebastian turned forward once again, frowning at the eagle's parting words. What was "concealed" within Julian? As a Familiar to the Apprentice, he should have been surprised that such a thing existed, but somehow, he was not: there had always been a core of sorrow, an aloneness within the Apprentice. Now, however, was not the time to explore it.

"What was that warning about the Dark Lords of the Mid-World?" asked Sebastian, shifting his thoughts. "I remember that Merlin cautioned us about Houma, but who are these other beings?" Rafir pushed his head up out of his saddle pouch.

"My old mistress, the Sorceress Héna, told me about them," said the fox. "She was careful not to name them because if they overheard her, they might send assassins to destroy her, so I could tell that she was afraid of them."

"The Dark Lords are Powers of the Mid-World," Julian explained, "like other Gods drawn from the Adversaries, they began as Demon or Dragon, yet they've held themselves apart from the other Gods. Most of the Powers portray themselves as Deities; some are benevolent and others are cruel, but most Powers at least seek the appearance of wisdom and fairness.

"The Dark Lords are openly cruel and evil, caring nothing for justice, only pursuing their own dreams of power and malice. In our last struggle, a Dark Lord held Galad in a far land, until he was forced to release him. Other Dark Lords flourish, perhaps a score — but there are three major Powers, whose names I will only whisper to you in the dead of night."

"Thank you so much," Sebastian muttered. Their pace quickened, as they rode west along the Greenway towards Gravengate. The day was clear, although the land all around them was damp from the heavy rainfall of previous weeks. Breezes blew in from the west, from Gravengate, and the air carried all the strong scents of Alantéa: of flowers, mosses, ferns, wet leaves, and — death. Many of those fallen in previous battles lay buried near Gravengate, in shallow graves. Julian watched as Rafir's nose twitched — with his keen sense of smell, the fox noticed the decay of death more strongly.

"How far west will we go?" asked Rafir. "I mean, will we return to Gravengate first, before heading north?"

"Far enough west to bypass Cronar and Eudox," Julian said, "but we won't make it all the way to Gravengate. Maybe tomorrow we will leave the Greenway and travel north or northwest."

"Then what, a week's journey to Dahlak?" asked Rafir, "and then a week back?" Sebastian snorted.

"You make it sound like a little holiday in the countryside," the Familiar said. "That's not what I expect."

"It might be no more than a journey of a few weeks," Julian added, "but we can't expect it to be easy. For one thing, when we cross the borders of the League, the Powers may take notice of us. For another, Merlin believes that the Sorcerers, or at least Houma, will attempt to stop us. And if we reach the Vale of Whispers, we may find the nature of the Truce difficult to discover. Why, Rafir, are you interested in returning to Stone Mountain?"

"I liked the long, dark passageways, and the feel of all that stone," the fox said. "But mostly I wondered what was going to happen. I mean, I watched the Wizards show tremendous power, much stronger than anything my old mistress Héna used, and yet they seemed so discouraged."

"Stone Mountain will stand for another two or three weeks, at least," Julian said quietly. "The Wizards will discover, once again, how dangerous and resourceful they are. But when the Marids come to the fullness of their power, who can guess the outcome? The Wizards are not hopeful, yet Merlin may find some way to counter the Marids and give us more time to discover the nature of the Truce. That, at least, is my hope."

They rode along the Greenway, carefully avoiding all the villages and farms that lay on either side of them: it had been Merlin's plan that the three of them should vanish, leaving the Sorcerers and Mid-World Powers to focus on Stone Mountain, and on Merlin at Sea's Edge, letting Julian to pursue his quest unnoticed. As they rode through the long afternoon, they skirted other travelers, turning off the road whenever farmers or haulers of grain appeared.

Now, as the sun began to sink, hovering red and golden over the Greenway, Julian passed barns and farmhouses with some reluctance. They would need to pitch a small tent under the stars, far from any campfire. Sebastian, growing colder, gathered a fold of Julian's cloak around his slender body. Rafir was drowsing, hunched into the deepest corner of the mare's leather saddle pouch. Along the Greenway, little more than a league away was a stand of woods — shelter for the night. More houses were passed, where smoke and scattered sparks poured from stone chimneys, and Sebastian pulled Julian's cloak tighter around his small body. They reached the stand of woods just as the sun set and Julian pitched their small tent in the gloom of dusk. Rafir woke and leaped lightly to the ground, speeding away to investigate their surroundings. Bluescent was left free to graze.

"No fire?" asked Sebastian.

"Not tonight, or even the next several nights," Julian said softly, looking down at a shivering Sebastian. "No fire, no acts of magic, nothing that will draw attention to ourselves until we're far from Stone Mountain and Gravengate. But be of good cheer — we have warm blankets!" They made a brief meal under the starlight, eating their cold rations quickly. Rafir returned just as they finished.

"If you need fresh food, there's a garden just minutes from here," the fox announced.

"No doubt you helped yourself without invitation," Sebastian said.

"Don't worry, they always blame it on the rabbits," Rafir replied with a touch of malice. Julian crawled into the small tent. "Are we all supposed to fit into that thing?" asked the fox.

"Stay outside if you wish," said Julian, "but it will be warmer inside." Somewhat dubiously, the fox followed and curled up on Julian's left side. Sebastian was on Julian's right, rolled in several heavy blankets.

"If you turn over too quickly, Julian, my flying days will be over," the little Familiar said.

Julian laughed. "I'll try not to, though we'd best get used to this arrangement — we may be forced to camp out most of the time." Sebastian began to drowse; Rafir's eyes were shut, but his body twitched restlessly.

"Rafir," whispered Julian, "if you go out, take care not to be seen." Rafir nodded, and Julian cleared his mind for sleep, letting his thoughts drift back to Stone Mountain. Thorian and Balardi should have enough power to hold Stone Mountain against the Sorcerers — the League might be hard pressed, but it would hold.

He slipped into a strange, troubled dream: a man and a woman were speaking intently, almost arguing in undertones, back and forth, while he, Julian, lay pretending to sleep, but listening carefully, eyes closed. Usually, the Gift was a dream sentinel, screening out visions that were unclear, troubled, or frightening. But tonight, the Gift watched for real danger, leaving his own sleeping mind to deal with unguarded night visions.

Still, within his dream world, Julian forced his eyes open and saw that the man and the woman arguing were really his parents, as he remembered them from so many years ago. The two fell silent and turned to stare at Julian with eyes that ached with love and loss.

Suddenly, Julian jerked wide awake.

Their foes were looking for him; the Gift inside him was stirring in alarm, as though it had heard his name mentioned in the distant chambers of one of the Greater Gods. Concentrating, he cleared his mind, thinking of nothing but ripples sliding over dark pools where even the moonlight was blocked by high clouds. After a few moments, his fears lessened, and he tried to relax. He glanced to his right, finding that Sebastian was also awake.

"What was that?" whispered the little Familiar.

"Seeking Spells," Julian whispered. "Not a good sign. Merlin hoped that we would be overlooked, but they're searching for us. They passed us by this time — we were lucky. Sleep now, sleep is the best mask; with Gift and Sight at rest, they will have trouble locating us. Sleep." Julian tried to clear his mind, but sleep would not come for a long time.

· ✳ ·

They had been travelling along the main roads from Stone Mountain toward Gravengate, but the next day they turned, heading almost directly to the north, with a slight lean to the west. As they traveled more through side roads and rough pathways, their progress slowed. They met few of the peoples of the League, only nodding to them silently. As Julian read their faces, he saw fear, a sense that a storm was brewing for the Wizards and the peoples sheltered within the Wizards' alliance.

As they traveled, gloom settled over Julian, a sense of danger, a feeling of helplessness. The Gift within him was troubled, sometimes nervous, other times somber. Several times at night, a false warning from the Gift would wake him suddenly with a bolt of fear. At first, Sebastian and Rafir tried to amuse and relax him, but after a few halfhearted efforts, they also fell silent, retreating into their own thoughts. The weather too changed to match their mood: it became overcast and gloomy, with huge cloud masses shifting south toward the coast and the ocean beyond.

From time to time, Julian would press both hands against the *Talismans* carried around his chest. For a while, they spread hope through his body, but after a time, he came to feel less reassured by their strength.

On the afternoon of the fourth day of their journey from Stone Mountain, they neared the borders of the League, where the river Saugus sent torrents of water to the southwest of the League. Julian slowed Bluescent, unwilling to make their crossing at the edge of night. When darkness came, they pitched their tent inside of League borders, but Julian was wide awake, and he led Sebastian and Rafir down the to the river's edge, to stare across its surging waters.

Although dusk had come and gone, Rafir's night eyes could see easily across the river — to the fox, the land seemed much like League lands. For Julian, the Gift showed something quite different: on the other side, all the untamed energies of the Mid-World were spread across the land — gateways, and passageways to the Powers, neutral regions where spirits and lesser beings played or hunted or struggled for mastery. Even now, on the soil of Alantéa, kobolds, mismorphs, and tiny dragons the size of wasps were shuffling in the shadows, waiting for the onset of dark night.

And the Gift brought images of defeat and grim death that lay on the other side: he was searching for gateways to new understandings — Sorcerers and the allies of Demon Princes stood before those gates. He hoped to slip by, unnoticed — but they were waiting for him. He took a deep breath.

"Can you feel it, Sebastian?" he whispered, still staring across the swirling waters.

"There's a sense of menace, of danger," said the little Familiar slowly. "Someone or something is waiting for us. How could they have known?"

"Spies, Divinations, visions of the future" Julian said grimly. He turned to look down on his small companions. "Listen carefully to me. I must go forward because there's no time to change plans. But I want the two of you to return to Sea's Edge and tell Merlin that we were anticipated. He may have other instructions for you after that. In the morning, head south until you reach the Greenway — the rest will be easy."

"No, Julian, we won't go," Sebastian said in a quiet voice. "We've already talked about it and if you send us away, we'll just follow as best we can."

"We saw that you were getting worried," added Rafir. "It was obvious that you would try to send us back, but we won't go."

"So, three have to die instead of one?" Julian asked quietly. "Come now, that makes very little sense."

"It's our struggle, too," Sebastian said, in the same gentle tones. "Anyway, we're not like the Mid-World immortals who expect to live forever. We'll die sometime, with little choice in the matter." Julian turned his head, shielding his thoughts from them: *We'll see — maybe we can shake the hunters from our trail and avoid their traps. But by all the Nine Billion Gods Under the Shadow of the Maker! They've sent two children and a youngling out to save their League!*

·)(·

The next morning, they returned to the Saugus: its waters were dark, deep, and swift; no fords could be seen, and swimming seemed all but impossible. The three searched up and down the riverside, seeking signs of raft or ferry.

Some methods of transportation had to exist so that men and goods could flow freely back and forth across the border. Only the immortal beings of the Mid-World were barred from League soil. Julian rode east beside the river for a while, as Sebastian and Rafir combed the tall grasses. Their first find, a small skiff with a flat bottom, would not hold Bluescent. A few hundred paces further on, they discovered a little bay, overgrown with reeds, where the river currents were reduced to almost nothing. Here, carefully disguised by toppled reeds, was a sturdily built raft, chained, and padlocked onto stone moorings. Julian touched the padlock with his staff and metal sprang apart.

Bluescent stood in a makeshift corral in the middle of the raft, watching as Julian maneuvered the craft with a long pole, then took up a paddle. Julian and Bluescent's roles were reversed, but with sweat beginning to surge from his forehead and shoulders, Julian found little amusement in their situation. In the middle of the river, he stopped to gather his breath, then as the current swept them along, he carefully kicked the padlock into the swirling waters. Sebastian smiled sadly at the Apprentice.

"In the old days, Julian would have left a note, and a bit of silver," the Familiar explained to Rafir. "It looks as though we've become hardened criminals."

"No traces, fewer chances of discovery," Julian muttered, and he began to paddle again, moving them slowly across the swift waters. On the other side, they stepped off into the shallows, unwilling to bring the raft into contact with the riverbank. Julian waded out, leading Bluescent, and he gave their raft one last push into the middle of the river.

"With luck, it will carry out into the ocean," he explained. "If we've been followed, or tracked, running water should put them off our scent."

Julian mounted Bluescent, and they rode up the riverbank through a tangle of brush that led into a glade of woods. The Mid-World ruled unchallenged over most of Alantéa. Like a low hum in the background, Julian's Gift could feel the network, the grid of the Powers, as it fed and renewed all the sorcerous energies of the Mid-World. Portals and sorcerous passages beckoned close by, and in the air were slight, musty smells that wakened old memories in Rafir.

"Mismorphs," he said, sniffing, "and kobolds — hunting, I think."

"I could sense them last night," said Sebastian, "but I couldn't name them. You learned all those smells from the Sorceress, didn't you?" The fox was sniffing again.

"There's another smell I can't quite match," Rafir said. He slipped from his saddle pouch and began searching along the woodland's floor. Julian halted, watching the fox closely.

"It's like a weasel or ferret," said Rafir, looking up, "but it's different. It's been here and now it's gone."

"I can't name it, either," Julian said, "but it might belong to the force that's looking for us. It's gone now, but tell me if you smell, or sense it again." The weight on Julian's spirit shifted a little, and his mood brightened: they had been observed, but daylight and the mass of rushing waters might block their enemies' sight. What was the best way to continue unseen?

As they rode north, seams opened in the cloud cover overhead with winds whipping through the upper skies, and finally, the sun emerged. By midday, they had reached the woods' edge, where a series of small farms began. Julian continued along a rough track that ran between sectioned plots of land. Rafir vanished; Sebastian hid within Julian's cloak, making a small incision in the fabric so that he was able to peer out. Beside the roadway, both on the left and right were laborers, men, women, and children scything grain in the fields.

Julian studied the laborers: they seemed strong and healthy yet subdued as they moved methodically about their fields. Each wore a similar garment, a long shift, and on each was woven an identical insignia — he thought he recognized that of Demeter, Mistress of the Long Grains, a relatively benign Mid-World Power. Across the fields, growth was alternately stunted and lush, as though the lands had been both cursed and blessed. Julian shook his head; the Powers of the Mid-World played endlessly at Godhood, tapping enormous energies to suit their whims.

Faces began lifting to glance at Julian. Whispers followed, with work stopping as twenty or more field workers watched Julian with open curiosity. What was wrong? Rafir was invisible. He stared down at his cloak, looking for Sebastian, then he understood: he traveled alone, bearing no insignia; he had claimed no Power as Guardian. To the workers in the fields, he was naked, undefended, and asking for trouble. Carefully, he edged Bluescent on, moving as quickly as possible from the farmlands.

At the next belt of woodlands, Julian turned aside and dismounted.

"What went wrong, Julian?" asked Sebastian. "Why were they so interested in us?" Rafir popped back into view. Julian smiled at their expressions.

"No, they couldn't see either of you. It was me they watched — in their eyes, I had no insignia, no allegiance, no Power to protect me. Let's see...." His mind turned to the many Powers. He would serve none willingly, but if he were to choose a disguise, then Thoth, a God with the face of a bird, a teacher, and healer — Thoth would be his preference. He stood, looking all around the surrounding woodlands. Everything touched by the Mid-World was filled with illusion and subterfuge; one more disguise should not be noticed. Julian unclasped his cloak and held it a little distance, touching his staff to the cloth, and in a moment, the Ankh of Thoth, God of Wisdom appeared.

They returned to their horse track, riding north slowly, warily, under a bright noon sun. Farmers and villagers still watched them closely as they passed, so Julian changed direction, riding west, seeking the main roadway, one that had once led from Tuvan to Rigal, a roadway on which they should be among other travelers, less noticeable. As they rode, Julian wove still more illusions around them: he became older, showing a growth of wispy brown beard, and Sebastian was shown in the form of a cat, sleek and well groomed. Rafir vanished again, but peered out of his saddle pouch, watching the passing countryside with all his senses alert.

Several hours into a long afternoon, their smaller track merged with the main road, as they traveled north toward Rigal. A steady stream of wagons and riders journeyed in each direction. Almost all bore the emblem or symbol of a Mid-World, a Power, and a God with many worshippers. Even the herders who drove cattle to the north wore an emblem. Many of the travelers were wrapped in illusions or were shielded by heavy cloaks. Yet, on the whole, it was not much different from the League — but then there came a movement in front of Julian, as wagons and travelers began pulling off the roadway.

Harsh music, sung by many voices, was coming from the north. Julian pulled off to his right, watching as a stream of sub-tiers moved southward: these bore the emblem of three hands and were marching toward Stone Mountain or Gravengate. Julian counted more than seven hundred as they passed — grizzled men, hard looking mercenaries, who watched other travelers sourly, out of the corners of their eyes. A sudden shout rang out, and Julian started, but the sub-tiers turned right and moved from the road to fields on the opposite side.

From the south, an enormous figure emerged, striding down the center of the roadway, completely ignoring the humans on either side. Standing three times the height of a man, a sleek, being with grey fur was striding effortlessly toward Rigal. A cudgel tipped with steel was sheathed at the creature's side, while a cloak covered its head, so its features were hidden. Julian searched for a shielding of illusions, but there was none: the creature was as it seemed, a powerful giant born completely unplanned into the Mid-World of the Truce.

As it passed, the sub-tiers reformed, marching south again. Wagons and travelers resumed their journey, as though nothing had happened. Julian followed, watching more carefully, letting his Gift seek the inner nature of his fellow travelers. Often, they were as they seemed: human messengers, some disguised, others riding openly — then the Gift sent a warning through him, like a cold shiver. Behind him, advancing swiftly, was a dark rider mounted on an even darker horse. As Julian pulled off to let them pass, the Gift showed him that the rider was not human —and the horse was not truly a steed, it was a being of the Mid-World, wrapped in illusion, and it was master of the rider.

Then the horse's head turned and snarled at the Apprentice as the creature perceived the probing spell of the Apprentice. Julian acknowledged them with a bow as they passed.

They rode on through the long afternoon. For Rafir, the air was rich with new smells, and new combinations of odors. Just now, there was the scent of fresh cow droppings, mixed with a smell that was entirely different, one that he couldn't begin to place. He peered forward and saw a long string of cattle, moving toward Rigal. On the other side, a chariot moved south, and it was drawn by lizard steeds, three of them harnessed together — and the cattle were shying from the chariot.

As Rafir watched, one lizard steed slipped its harness, and in a flash had downed a passing steer and was sinking huge jaws into it. Other cattle scattered, mooing in fear. The other two lizards dragged the chariot to the fallen steer and began to feed. Julian passed the lizard drawn chariot warily, holding his staff under his cloak. The chariot's drivers watched him pass with a combination of malice and amusement; both drivers wore the emblem of Moloch, Lord of the Dark Flames.

As evening approached, the winds picked up again, sending cloud masses streaming to the west and northwest, into a golden red skyline. Julian could feel the old disquiet growing within him — on the edge of darkness, the pursuit was readying, searching for him by smell and by magic. And others were seeking him...some from idle curiosity...there was even one mind that had found Julian and watched the Apprentice with concern. Julian halted, watching masses of clouds surge west and north, leaving clear skies overhead.

Traffic had lessened along the roadway, and soon he would be left in the dark, alone, and exposed. Behind him, to the south, the hunt for Julian was beginning again. On the road before him, one benevolent mind stood waiting. To the right and left of the roadway level, recently harvested fields offered little cover or concealment. Other travelers had pulled away, seeking inns or rough woodland shelters.

Julian leaned over, speaking softly to Sebastian and Rafir, "We've been discovered, by a friend, or so I think, but we have to be careful, saying as little as possible."

He picked up their pace, sending Bluescent cantering down the road. Just a little in the distance, a crossroads came into view, where one main roadway intersected with many smaller branches. At the crossroads, a woman stood, her cloak fluttering in the winds of early evening. Her horse grazed nearby, munching on long grasses. Her hood was thrown back, and Julian saw that strands of grey and silver ran through her dark hair. As the Apprentice approached, she raised her arms in greeting, face shining in the last light of day.

"Hail, servant of Thoth, Moon god and master of all the magic of the darkness! I offer shelter to the last travelers, rest for the weary, and haven for the night. My only price is a request for good fellowship and small gossip. Will you join me?" Julian studied her cautiously: she seemed to be of middle years, still lean and vibrant, and she had the Gift. No emblem was sewn into her cloak, and she showed no insignia. Daylight was fading quickly now, and Julian could feel the seekers stir, like a distant pack of dark, sleek panthers, gathering in the moonlight. Still, the Apprentice hesitated.

"We need lodging," he said carefully, "and your offer is welcome, and yet you bear no device or emblem. Whom do you serve?" She laughed and whistled for her horse.

"I serve all those of good will in Alantéa." She mounted. "Thus, I serve your master, and perhaps you serve mine." A spasm shook her, as though she was listening to some distant, threatening voice. The smile vanished from her face. Her horse clopped closer, and as she leaned over, touching Julian, she spoke into his mind: *Come now, for Sorcerers and Dark Lords have scented you. I can and will shield you for this night.*

Julian turned, staring south, where the pursuit was building. He nodded, and followed the woman silently, feeling again like a tiny piece in an enormous game. She led them for nearly a league, picking her way over a tangle of dark trails. As they rode, the woman was chanting, murmuring in a muffled voice, in a language that was strange to Julian.

He found himself cloaked from sorcery, sealed away from the sight of those wielding magic, both mortal and immortal. He began to relax, turning to a night sky where a full range of stars was emerging as masses of clouds were pushed south. Sebastian and Rafir stirred, talking together in low voices; they were talking about food, so they must have become hungry.

In the darkness, the stone building before them was almost invisible, but as Julian neared, he sensed that his sight was being blocked, guarding against Mid-World spies — a shielding that even seemed interwoven with the building's foundations.

They dismounted, leaving their horses to graze in the meadows, and entered the building. Once inside, candles were lit, and Julian stood in the middle of a tall stone building, one too large for a house, too small for a temple. The woman set a glittering array of candles on a table in the room's center and turned to Julian.

"Welcome, Julian," she said, then her voice tones changed, so that they became those of Llara, the Spirit Lord who sat beside Voritar centermost in the Hall of the Dreamers: "Welcome, Julian! Welcome, Servant of the Maker!" Julian stepped back, eyes alert, wary of treachery.

"Those words have been spoken before," he said, gripping his staff, "under much different circumstances. Who are you? How do you know of me?"

"I am Maeglan, Servant and Priestess of the Maker," she said, eyes shining. "Julian, I watched you as you stood before the Dreamers in their great Hall. I am your friend and your ally. I saw you when you comforted your enemy on the foothills of the Mountains of the Moon. Trust me!"

Julian relaxed his grip, but his face was filled with uncertainty. "I thought that the Dreamers were so completely hidden, that even Merlin was barred from viewing them."

"Julian, the Gift is different within me. I am not one of the powerful wielders of sorcery, but I see far, beyond the borders of the world. I cannot see the Maker who stands at the Heart of the Universe, at the Center of all Understanding, but I watch as five of the Lords of Dragons race toward Him. Adonai, greatest of Seraphs, leads a second flock, and they have passed light's speed, leaping from star system to star system. The Spirit Lord, a longtime ally of Balardi, wishes to travel in Adonai's wake, but still, he lingers within the circles of the sun. Do you wonder that I am aware of you, that I have preserved you from your adversaries?"

Julian drew a deep breath, and sank slowly onto a couch, carefully setting his staff on the floor. "It's true that I feel safe here. Yet tomorrow the pursuit will begin again. I had hoped to slip towards Dahlak, unnoticed, and that seems so unlikely, now."

"You will never reach Dahlak, unnoticed," Maeglan said, and her voice was grave. "The Sorcerers are behind you, and before you lie the Dark Lords of the Mid-World, who have been enlisted in their search: Un-Maurag is openly seeking you, and spies of Mordred and Haeglin are sniffing at your trail."

"Should I turn back then? Travel in a different direction?"

"A change of direction will not help you," she touched Julian's cloak, her face filled with compassion. "Julian, your two *Talismans* may be powerful, but they cast only a shadow of a doubt over your future. For in my night visions, I have watched you struggle in the dungeons of Un-Maurag. Yet in none of these visions have I seen you die."

"Death seems certain if we become prisoners of Un-Maurag," Julian said, shaking his head. "This is a doomed expedition — and I'm not even sure what we're looking for."

"I will tell you a little, as we eat, but after you must relax and take advantage of this night's shelter." Rafir's ears lifted at the mention of food. Maeglan smiled down at him. "I can seldom see Rafir even with my Farsight, but I have watched him, once or twice as he browsed, unwanted, in well tended gardens. Tonight, he will feed with my permission."

Rafir was let out and Maeglan served a simple meal to Sebastian and Julian. The little Familiar ate slowly, listening gravely to Maeglan and Julian, though he said nothing.

"If the Ancient Demon Princes have emerged to seek dominion over Alantéa, that would be a clear violation of the Truce, would it not?" Julian asked. "Yet thus far none of the Powers of the Mid-World have come forward to aid us. There must be some means to enforce the Truce, and so if I reach Dahlak, will the Terms be inscribed or recorded there?" Maeglan shook her head.

"The Truce Terms were kept secret by design. Divinations might recall the terms if performed near Dahlak." Maeglan paused. "I will tell you what to look for. I have watched visions of the Truce many times: the most powerful of the Ancient Servants and the Ancient Adversaries come together in a great circle; there are somewhat more than thirty of them standing with one another, Seraph and Demon, Dragon and Spirit Lord interspersed. The Adversaries bulk larger, but the Servants glow with a powerful inner light. Neither humans nor Creatures of the Darkness are present.

"The Ancient Powers stand, speaking with one another, and there are bitter, harsh words — not only between Servant and Adversary but also between Demons and Dragons, Seraphs and Spirit Lords. At the end, they link together and the greatest among them call out their invocations, while others listen. These spoken words I judge to be the Truce Terms, though I cannot hear what is being said. After speech, the Wonder begins, for from those Terms springs the Mid-World of the Truce, and all is transformed."

Julian pulled back from the table, sighing. "Even should we learn the terms of the Truce, we may not be able to use them against our enemies."

"That may also be true," said Maeglan, "and yet the Terms have been kept secret, as though knowledge of them conveyed great power. Julian, you are tired now, and fearful. You should sleep, and let your hopes be restored by rest." Julian rose and stretched.

"You're right, of course. I'll sleep soundly tonight, shielded from our foes." He turned to Sebastian with a slight smile. "In spite of our fears, we've little to complain about — we've encountered one truthful and helpful ally and not a single foe."

· 𝕏 ·

At night, Julian lay in comfort, but the Sight within him seethed with tension, and sleep would not come for a long time. After midnight, he slipped into a troubled slumber, and he dreamed: he was small again, only five or six years old, standing under cloudy skies. He was playing with a toy, a rough wooden horse, but his eyes were fixed on his grandmother, an old grey haired woman who stooped a little. She was taking clothes down from a line, folding them neatly into a straw basket...and she was singing or chanting...he could barely make out the words....

In the last hours of Earth, all the Adversaries
will stand forth, murmuring in the twilight:
Demons and Dragons and Creatures of the Darkness.
The Nameless will wake, bellowing in the ocean depths.
Earth's waters will foul, spilling poisons over the land.
From the Mid-World, the Dark Lords will emerge,
crying out, loud and harsh in their triumph.
Monsters will stalk through Earth's gardens,
snarling and seeking human flesh.
Grim music, hymns of crows' calls
will shatter ancient harmonies.
All that is mortal-made will crumble into dust.
Giftless, shelterless, mortals will sob and weep,
fleeing in great fear, to no hiding place.

Yet in the end, it is the Evil Ones who will fall silent, amazed.
For at the end of time, the Maker will lift His voice in song.

In his dream, Julian's grandmother turned her face, staring down at her grandchild, Julian, with a look of overwhelming, everlasting love and pity and sorrow.

He pulled himself free from a sleep that had become a nightmare, waking with sweat beading on this face. He sat up, finding himself in the dark stillness of deepest night. Even though sleep was now farthest from his mind, it was much more peaceful to watch moonlight pour through the upper windows of his chamber than to return to his grim night visions. In the grey light of early morning, while Rafir and Sebastian still slept, Maeglan came to his chamber. Her face, like that of Julian's, was strained and troubled.

"We have both been warned, Apprentice," she said in a low voice, not willing to disturb the small servants of Julian. "I too dreamed of danger for both of us. But I have a hiding place that has been long prepared, while you will be traveling unprotected. I want you to have this." She took a slim silver band from her finger and placed it in Julian's palm. "This is a lesser force compared to your own *Talismans*. Still, it has helped me in the past. The Mid-World is filled with beings of so many levels of strength, and so many motives. A few of these, of intermediate strength, will offer aid to the Servants — they are sometimes extravagant, sometimes halfhearted, and yet at times, they have helped me. Call for the Lords of Light, for they fancy themselves as counterweights to the Dark Lords."

Julian opened his mouth to protest; Maeglan shook her head and closed Julian's hand over the ring. "Nor do we have further time for more discussion," she said. "You will leave early this morning, and I will vanish — if I can." She turned, walking quickly back to her own chambers, no longer serene and confident. Julian slipped Maeglan's ring into a side pocket, but as Julian turned to gather their belongings, he saw that Sebastian was awake and was watching the Apprentice closely.

"It's all gone wrong, hasn't it," the little Familiar said softly. "What she's telling us is that your *Talismans* are unlikely to work and that we never really stood a chance." Rafir was awake now, blinking his eyes at them.

"Too late to turn back," Julian murmured, and he knelt beside them. "Listen, our enemies are prepared, and our future looks poor. Our *Talismans will* work — the question is, will they be powerful enough? But whatever happens, we'll do anything needed to slip through their nets, or fight our way through. We can't let them capture us. Can we agree on that?" They both nodded, their small, serious eyes blinking in the dim morning light. Julian rose and packed quickly.

Maeglan met them at the door, and she embraced Julian, holding the Apprentice in her soft arms. "I should never have shown my own fear to you, Julian. I have been left undisturbed for so many years, that real danger caught me by surprise. But we should remember, you and I, that we are Servants of the Maker. They may kill us, but they cannot destroy us, or bind us to their will forever. Farewell!" She turned to Sebastian and Rafir. "Small ones, I cannot speak for the Maker, yet it is in my heart that He will wake you, too, when Earth passes its life stage. For now, be your master's eyes and ears."

They rode out, traveling eastward back to the main road to Rigel, riding into a golden, mist filled dawn. As the morning haze lifted, the day grew clear and bright.

"I'm glad I don't have either the Sight or the Gift," said Rafir, watching Julian's troubled face. "I used to envy you and Sebastian, but now I don't." Julian patted the fox's fur but kept his eyes on the road.

"We'll need to conceal you," he said to Sebastian, "and we'll change our emblem, too." Sebastian hid himself within Julian's cloak, as Julian wove a new illusion over his garments: the cloak now showed the emblem of their foes — beast, skeleton, and human hands linked together. The image of the Apprentice now grew older, and travel stained, as would suit an aging mercenary messenger serving the Three Hands.

They returned to the main roadway. The sun was hovering bright, hanging over the east, and already traffic was moving north and south to and from Rigal. And the watchers were out, sniffing. Just as they entered the highway, a party of tall riders passed, talking together in low voices, casting wary eyes about them. Julian slowed: the tall figures were Elves, not Elf-Lords mighty with the Gift, but they might have power enough to penetrate Julian's disguise. The Elf party moved on warily, with Julian following in their wake, keeping less than a hundred paces behind them.

Probes intensified, searching for them within Rigal and all the roads leading into and away from that city. Julian clenched his teeth and with an effort, the Gift sealed off his mind.

"Julian!" Rafir whispered urgently. The fox was still invisible, but Julian could see from the shape of the pouch that Rafir's head was out, sniffing the morning air.

"Julian!" the fox whispered again. *"There's that smell — the one you wanted me to remember. And it's fresh!"*

Ahead, the Elf-riders were moving more quickly, as though eager to move through Rigal and beyond. Julian scanned the roadsides carefully. Out of the corner of his eye came a flash of movement — or was it just a shadow?

"That's it!" whispered Rafir. The Gift showed Julian an image, something black as soot, a tracking creature, small, snarling with sharp teeth. Was it aware of them?

From within his cloak, Sebastian was tugging at his jacket, trying to signal him. He stared down at his cloak: the emblem of the Three Hands was fading! Some power was stripping the illusion from him, leaving him naked to the trackers. All along the roadway came cries and curses as travelers became aware of spell changes. Quietly, carefully, Julian wove a second illusion under the image of three hands — and as the image of Three Hands faded, the Ankh of Thoth returned.

Julian continued north, wariness increasing with every step. Every now and again, a flicker of black seemed to flash in the corner of his eye, as though tracking creatures were following just outside of his vision. And tempers were rising all along the roadway, as illusions slipped from the travelers. A large party of the men serving the Three Hands passed them, muttering, and sneering at the Elves as they marched south. A short distance in front of them, a group of herders lost their disguises and were revealed to be armed priests of — was it Rudra? And who would worship a God of Plagues? An equal group, bearing insignia of dark lightning, fell upon the armed priests, testing swords and shields with clusters of sharp spears. The Elves gave the melee a wide berth, watching the human warriors with remote disdain.

Julian slowed, hesitating. *A true healer would stop to aid the wounded, but the Vale of Whispers is far, so far.* The noon sun beat down upon him.

From the roadside, a short black creature pushed through the brush and looked directly into Julian's eyes. Then it hissed at the Apprentice, as Julian backed Bluescent away. From the north, one of the searchers cried out in triumph.

"Un-Maurag! The Apprentice is here!"

With a concussion of thunder, a Portal with a huge arch— an arch formed of black smoke — flashed in the middle of the roadway. From it surged a force of two hundred Uraks, heavy, feared inhuman warriors of Un-Maurag. Throughout the roadway four-footed Vorrs began to race, sleek furred, stronger, faster, and twice the weight of wolves. The Elves gave a great cry of fear and hatred, letting shafts fly at the dark hued Uraks: three went down. Vorrs leaped at the Elves, struggling to pull them from their saddles; Elves hacked at them, trying desperately to flee.

Armed priests and warriors broke off their quarrel and turned south, racing away on foot. Julian turned and rode past the racing humans. The voice called out again.

"Let the Elves and warriors be! Seek the Apprentice — you have his scent!" Sebastian peered out and watched as the Elves staggered, bleeding, to the roadside. Vorrs and Uraks pushed past them.

Now, Bluescent opened her stride, racing south, away from their northern destination. As Julian jostled along in his saddle, he carefully restored the image of the Three Hands on his cloak. Others were fleeing beside him. Behind them, the cries of Vorrs grew sharper as they caught their prey's scent. Julian separated himself from the others. One thing was left before calling on his own magic and the *Talismans*. Just in front of him, men serving the Three Hands had halted, nearly a full tier of five hundred turning to watch the disturbance. As Julian neared, he slowed, rising in his saddle, showing his emblem.

"Treachery!" he called out in a loud voice. "Black treachery! They are coming for us! Check them while I warn the others!" As Julian passed, their commander gave Julian a look of pure astonishment, while his men turned, formed up, then raised weapons against the servants of Un-Maurag. The first pack of Vorrs went down to arrow shots, lying squealing and bleeding on the roadway.

But now the massive, mailed Uraks closed with their human opponents, crushing their lines, no longer content merely to pass the humans — now the Uraks were in a killing frenzy. The men of the Three Hands were smashed from the road, with Vorrs tearing at their flanks. Julian pulled left, turning from the road; a forested slope lay just a little distance away. He might have an advantage there over the massive, mailed Uraks — but Bluescent was tiring. Again, the power charged voice rang out.

"Now, break this off! You are allies! See, I too am of the Three Hands. Now break this struggle off, or you will feel *my* wrath!"

Julian leaned over and cast a pinch of crumbled Heart's Ease in front of Bluescent's nostrils. She sneezed, then her stride lengthened — but the forested slope was too far. Behind him, the pursuit had grown: Men, Uraks and Vorrs followed, but perhaps the Sorcerer and his followers would continue on the roadway.

Julian pulled to a halt, turning and, gripping his staff, quickly calling out the spell of darkened mist. Bluescent sped on; behind them came a moment of confusion, then a great wind whipped the haze aside. Houma had joined the hunt. It was just noon, and Julian was nearly run to ground. He reached into his pouch, drew out a powder, touching it awkwardly with his staff. Casting the powder behind him, he called out a single word of command.

Everywhere the powder touched, soil, branch, and sod burst into flame, sweeping wildfire across the meadows. They raced on. Milling sounds came from behind them, followed swiftly by Houma's lightning and a heavy downpour: flames vanished quickly, and the chase began again.

Bluescent began to labor up a steep slope, breathing heavily. Julian clenched his teeth in anger: he had been trapped so easily, and his small allies would be lost with him!

The incline grew steeper. He leaped to the ground and raced up the hillside, leading Bluescent behind him. Down below, Vorrs and mounted Uraks reached the slope's base and began to climb rapidly. Houma could be sensed but not seen. Overhead, the sky was blue, cloudless, and serene, in mockery of his desperation and the failure of his quest. The road to Rigal could no longer be seen, though sounds of distant fighting still reached up to the hill's crest.

He reached the top, gasping for breath. As Julian turned to look back, a Vorr's head with dark brown fur appeared at the hill's top, followed by more of its panting brethren. A mailed Urak face appeared next, panting as it struggled to reach the crest. Swords and spear point flashed at the edge as other Uraks climbed closer.

Vorrs made snarling sounds like the laughter of hyenas but lower in tone and far more grim.

Now! The Gift within Julian called out. He pulled the dark grey *Talisman* from his steel necklace and tugged at it with trembling hands.

A grey mist poured out, a cloud that separated Julian's party from their attackers. Within the mist, grey bones began to come together, forming grey Wraiths and grey Specters that carried rusted swords, jagged scythes, and greyish black spears. As Wraiths and Specters surged toward the servants of Un-Maurag, their strong smell of decay and death made Julian step backward and shield his face with a fold of his cloak.

"Is this really Merlin's work?" Sebastian breathed out. "I can't believe it!"

"Go back!" Julian called out to their adversaries, his voice croaking. "You must flee — or die!"

Vorrs leaped, snarling and biting — and their teeth closed on nothing but grey mist. Uraks hacked with swords, smashed with shields, but spectral forms passed through them, slashing with rusted dark blades. Uraks and Vorrs fell thrashing, spurting the dark fluids of their life's blood onto long, green grasses, howling and moaning as they died. The rusted weapons of Wraiths and Specters were biting, while those of their foes were useless.

"Merlin has become much more dark and grim," Julian muttered, as he watched a tide of grey Wraiths and Specters milling over dead foes then spilling over the crest of the hillside and down the hillside. The grey *Talisman* had unleashed a tide of grey death, but Julian could hear the distant snarls of Houma forming words of sorcery, rising over the cries coming from dying Vorrs and Uraks.

None of the images flashing in front of Julian's mind brought him images of victory, or even escape.

"I must make a stand here," Julian said. "You must reach Merlin and warn him. Death is not the end for us — we will meet again!" He slapped Bluescent's rump calling on her to ride swiftly away.

"Now, go!" he called out. Wraiths and Specters were sweeping down the hillside, though as they reached the hill's base, a strange hesitation seemed to come over them. A red mist had gathered in front of them and began slipping over them, as though investigating their nature and their purpose.

A red mist sent by Houma.

Grey Wraiths and Specters halted, turning to regard each other as though asking each other, *What exactly are we supposed to be doing here?* Then very, very slowly Wraiths and Specters began to collapse into greyish black dust, slowly covering the slope like dark snow. And now, creeping with the same slowness over the dark hill, a red mist was climbing up the slope toward Julian.

He turned back toward Sebastian, Rafir, and Bluescent. They were only a hundred paces away and had stopped. Sebastian had tugged Bluescent's reins and brought her to a halt. His two Familiars stared back at Julian in defiance, while Bluescent nibbled on long grasses.

"Get away!" Julian cried out. "In the Maker's Name, get away, get away!"

Julian turned from his friends and allies, watching as Houma's red mist reached the hill's crest. Both his hands clutched his blue *Talisman*. As he tugged at it, Julian murmured, "Maker, if you are able to, if you are willing, stand with me on this day."

From his *Talisman*, a blue mist poured out, surging toward Houma's red mist. As the two magics fought together, blue mists were gradually forced back, leaving traces of black ash in their defeat.

Then Houma's face appeared at the hill's crest. He stood fully two inches shorter than Julian, hunched over and much older, with a sculpted dark beard and a shaved upper lip, face shining with malice and triumph. On his chest was a pulsing, red amulet, still radiating red mists.

Houma tugged his gleaming red amulet and Julian's amulet with its blue gleam exploded into black dust.

"Did you really think," Houma said, in a completely reasonable voice, "that any device made by a Wizard would equal the Power of the Demon Princes?"

Julian lashed at the hillside with his staff, calling on the earth to rise in service to the Maker, to fall upon the Adversaries. Power surged toward him, and tremors began to race through the hillside.

Houma's face gleamed as red mists reached out and touched Julian. The hillside stilled. Julian groped for a second spell, but no words would come to him, and his staff slipped from his nerveless hands. He felt no pain, only a sense of weakness, of sluggishness. Julian turned slowly, as though moving under water. Words formed in his mouth, to call out for his companions to flee, but he could only mumble. Rafir and Sebastian stood, wrapped in red mists, gazing stupidly, senselessly at Julian. Bluescent had turned away and had forgotten even to graze.

Vorrs and Uraks surged over the slope, surrounding the Apprentice, crying aloud in triumph. The nostrils of Vorrs were sniffing at Julian, but Houma was shoving them away with hands that pulsed with magic.

"Back away, there will be other flesh for you. This one is destined for the Mouth of Un-Maurag!" and the Sorcerer laughed as he watched the slow movements and stupid gaze of the Apprentice. Julian saw sunlight pass over a tapestry of horror: showing the sleek brown fur of the Vorrs, exposing the grainy dark skin of the massive Uraks. Houma was shorter and much older than Julian, yet even with his Gift dulled by sorcery, Julian could sense the Sorcerer's enormous power. Houma strolled around the frozen Apprentice, smiling, and shaking his head.

"Apprentice, I am saddened that you were caught so easily. So many, many other traps were set, each of them subtler and more exquisite. You must be certain to offer better sport for Un-Maurag, or he will be most annoyed with us." Julian opened his mouth to say, *Take me, I am willing to die in the Dungeons of Un-Maurag, but leave the others, they have done nothing,* but he could only make meaningless sounds. Houma shook his head, a gloating smile still fixed on his face.

"It doesn't matter, Apprentice," he said in reasonable tones. "Nothing you say will matter, ever again."

Julian made one last effort to flee, but only toppled, face first to the ground. Houma turned and held both hands out, calling upon Un-Maurag. As Julian peered up from the ground, a huge, Portal with an enormous arch formed on the upper hillside, opening onto a dark, lifeless plain. The fortress of Un-Maurag loomed in the distance, huge, with many turrets, far greater than Stone Mountain or Gravengate, and it was fashioned of dark metals, mixed with slabs of black basalt.

A single, large Urak hand reached down and effortlessly pulled Julian to his feet. He saw that Bluescent was being dragged toward the Portal, with Sebastian and Rafir each stuffed in a saddle pouch. Both of their eyes were vacant, and drool slipped from small, senseless mouths.

In complete despair, the Gift within Julian lashed out at Houma with its final strength, then it collapsed, dragging Julian down to a senseless abyss.

Chapter Four

The Dungeons of Un-Maurag

JULIAN WOKE, SLOWLY, INTO a nightmare. Images shifted in front of his eyes — of many torches flickering, set into long, dark walls and giving off more smoke than light, of many beings, Urak Lords, and unknown others, staring down at him. And in the center stood a huge throne and seated there was...his eyes closed, and he discovered that he stood supported, for as his legs sagged, hands tightened around his arms, holding him upright. Now, his hearing began to return, or at least his mind was starting to make sense of the sounds around him.

"You were sent to bring me a Wizard," said the voice. Its tones were deep, menacing, and harsh, echoing throughout the chamber. "Where is this Wizard that I was promised?"

"Lord, we said that they might fear to leave their own domains, that they might send this Apprentice," said the voice of Houma. "But take this one — the Gift is powerful within him. And he is so young and innocent; how you will feast upon his terror! Look, even now the Apprentice wakes, as I lift my spell from him." All of Julian's senses surged back to his body — then they recoiled in horror.

His eyes reopened and he saw for the first time the face of Un-Maurag. The Dark Lord sat on a throne of black basalt lined with silver, dwarfing those around him, and his face was massive; his two eyes were like those of insects, with huge ruby clusters, each with many facets, with torchlight glittering a deeper red as it passed through each facet. Beneath his enormous eyes and flat nostrils was the mouth of Un-Maurag, small and dark, like the opening to a tunnel. Un-Maurag was the God of All Insects. Julian sagged back, but the arms held him upright.

"See, Lord, taste his fear. The mouth of Un-Maurag will feast tonight!" Houma stood a few paces to the left of Un-Maurag; the figure of the Sorcerer seemed tiny beside that of the Dark Lord.

"Do you speak, Apprentice?" asked Un-Maurag. "Or do you only sweat with fear?" Julian licked his lips, wondering if his tongue would work again. His eyes glanced around the throne room. Uraks held him; Sebastian and Rafir lay at his feet, senseless, barely breathing.

"Lord, I have done you no injury," Julian said. Even to his own ears, his voice seemed tiny and insignificant. "What of the Truce? Why should you not release me, and let us be on our way?"

"Injury, Apprentice?" said Un-Maurag, in mocking tones. "You damaged my Brother in Darkness. Do you not remember freeing the mortal warrior you call 'Galad,' with his rusty, half-aware sword, as you wielded a scroll and words of destruction against a Dark Lord? I remember all, for I watched with these eyes. But I am just, Apprentice." Here, Un-Maurag laughed, as did the others of his court, studying their master's face carefully. "I am just, and I blame your Wizard Masters, though you must serve in their place. As for the Truce, there is no truce for me, there is no law for Un-Maurag except for his own will." The Dark Lord turned to Houma.

"This one will make poor sport, Sorcerer. I expected pleadings, promises, threats. I will take you also, Sorcerer, for the Dungeons of Un-Maurag." Houma stepped back — a half pace only.

"That was not part of our pact," said Houma, and his voice was steady.

"I have no law but my own will," said Un-Maurag. "Did you not listen as I explained this matter to the Apprentice?" Un-Maurag stood from his throne, his eyes beginning to glow. No smile could come from a mouth that seemed as deep as a tunnel, but Julian could feel the amused malice flow from the Dark Lord. "And did you truly believe that a mortal, any mortal, would be permitted to leave my domain?" Houma stood somewhat crouched as though ready to spring, but now he straightened as he studied closely the glowing eyes of Un-Maurag.

"Lord, in your greatness, all threats are wasted upon you," the Sorcerer said in a soft voice. "Yet I did not come here unprepared. It is said that the eyes of Un-Maurag see all things, including events that are yet to come. Lord, look upon the results that flow from your actions against me." The face of Un-Maurag shifted from the Sorcerer; his eyes stared, glowing, into distant space. Julian tested his arms but the grip on them had not relaxed.

"Strange...yes, strange," said Un-Maurag slowly. "None of the outcomes is certain. First, you might escape with your own strength powered by the amulet you bear, or your brother Sorcerers might free you. And should they fail, the Marids will be unleashed against me — I see them tearing apart my fortress, even down to its very foundations. Behind all these images are the Demon Princes, ready to take reprisals against me. Strange, yes." Un-Maurag laughed again, his courtiers following suit, in a lurid, rattling echo. "But, you see, these things have never stopped me before." The Dark Lord turned again to Houma, eyes glowing brighter. The Sorcerer stood his ground.

"Hold for a moment, great Lord. Did I not say that it was vain to threaten Un-Maurag? But if you let me depart in peace, I will bring you your heart's desire — I will bring you a Wizard to test in the Mouth of Un-Maurag. Have you not seen the League crumble beneath the power of the Marids? When the Wizards are defeated, I will bring all those who survive for your pleasure. You have tasted Sorcerer before; would you not prefer a Wizard?"

Un-Maurag pondered Houma's suggestion for a long moment. "Yes, I will let you depart, the first mortal visitor ever to leave — you will take the necessary oaths?"

"I will, Lord," Houma said, bowing, "and I will spread word of your terror and greatness so that mortal and immortal alike will taste fear." Un-Maurag turned back to Julian.

"So, I must content myself with you for the moment, Apprentice. Release him." The grip on Julian relaxed, and his staff was pressed into his hands. "Apprentice, this is the last you will ever see of me, yet I will watch with pleasure as you writhe in the Mouth of Un-Maurag. Before you depart, I will leave you one, last reassuring thought: your Maker — the God Who Once Was — is gone, never to return, but I, even I may find a way to wake you from your Long Sleep."

Un-Maurag laughed, eyes beginning to glow. Julian spoke swiftly and a cocoon of protection wove about his body and those of Rafir and Sebastian. Beams of white radiance warred with the red rays of Un-Maurag's cluster of eyes.

And then Julian fell senseless before the throne of Un-Maurag.

·)(·

He woke slowly, to the sound of low voices, while the Gift was slow to stir: it lay crouched and cowering inside him, cringing, fearful. The voices fell silent, while around him were soft wet sucking sounds in the background, as though a swamp surrounded them. With an effort, he pulled himself together — as his senses returned, he found himself in a storm center of dark power; tides of dark Sorcery were holding back, waiting to swallow him.

"I never expected this," said a voice, softly. Sebastian's voice. "We're supposed to die here, after a long struggle. It was never supposed to end like this."

"It went wrong from the beginning, didn't it?" asked Rafir. "Maybe we should have gone back when Julian asked us to."

"What use would we have been to the Wizards?" Sebastian asked bitterly. "Not that we'll be much good here, either." Julian opened his eyes. Lights around them were pale, tinged with yellow, though he could see Sebastian and Rafir, huddled on a stone floor beside a pile of gear: their belongings. He stood. Sebastian and Rafir turned toward him; Julian motioned them to silence. He stepped quietly over to the pile, where he found his cloak, and saddle pouches with all his charms and potions, food, and water.

On the top of the pile his staff lay, and beside it was the silver ring given him by Maeglan. So, Un-Maurag was aware of all his resources and was completely untroubled by them. He placed the ring on his left hand and held his staff in his right. Strangely, after being so easily entrapped and defeated by Houma and Un-Maurag, a cool anger was rising within him, and all his inner fears and sorrows were receding from the shores of his mind.

If it's death for me and for my small friends, then let it be a fighting death, and not a slow slippage into madness. Maker, if we come to you through a gateway of violence, know that it was not through our own choices, but by those of your bitter adversaries.

He took a deep breath and began to investigate the nature of their prison. Sebastian and Rafir followed, watching in silence. They were held in a large cavern almost a hundred paces in width, with a high roof that could only be vaguely seen in the dim light of their prison. Peering up, it looked as if the stone of the roof was scarred and pockmarked as though the chamber itself had been hewn from stone by hammers made of steel. The floor, too, was rock, littered with dust, and white fragments.

Julian knelt, picking up a yellowish sliver — it was bone, a large bone, the remains of a human weapons' master, perhaps. He touched other fragments, searching with the Gift: Elf Mages, Trolls, Sidhe, Creatures of the Darkness, Tanu, Mortal Magic Wielders, and even Emissaries of the Gods had fought and died in this place. Un-Maurag had tested both good and evil beings here, and now the shards of their broken, dead bodies lay scattered over the dungeon floor.

Julian shook his head and turned to the wall nearest him; it was rock, solid, polished stone. As he touched it, he sensed that the other walls were far, far different. He turned, keeping his back to the one stone wall, studying the other walls with great caution.

Those three walls seemed to shiver and pulse, with black droplets shimmering down their surfaces, and periodically, a yellow vapor slipped out, spreading fumes over the chamber; from that vapor came the stench of rotting meat.

Julian stood and walked cautiously toward the left wall. As he drew closer, the smell of decaying flesh grew stronger, almost overpowering. Black droplets slipped slowly over the wall's surface like black drool — and the wall was — alive. It pulsed slowly like a wall of dark flesh. So, here was the meaning of "The Mouth of Un-Maurag." And beyond the dark, fleshy walls lurked many layers of cunning Sorceries, waiting to test its victims.

Julian retreated to the one rock wall and sat back against it. Sebastian and Rafir sat, one on each side of the Apprentice. Julian stared out into the chamber, searching for a light source. None could be seen, but the air itself seemed to glow with a pale, yellow light.

"We can speak now," Julian said in a low voice, "But remember that everything we say or do will be recorded for the entertainment of Un-Maurag — I will guess that the eyes of Un-Maurag see both into the past and into the future. He will be able to relive the pain and torment of this place with senses that are stronger than memory."

"There's no real chance then," whispered Sebastian. "I mean, if there was a way in, shouldn't there be a way out?" Julian shook his head sadly and touched each of his small allies.

"It's going to be the end and a hard, painful end at that. It's much easier to die on a battlefield cleanly, surrounded by friends and allies, but here we have no choice. Though, at the last, we might be able to cheat Un-Maurag, if you agree."

"Cheat Un-Maurag?" whispered Rafir.

"Un-Maurag takes pleasure in fear and torment, otherwise he would have destroyed us earlier," Julian lowered his voice and shook his head. "It's so hard to speak of dying — the three of us are gentle and soft spoken. We should be out of here, riding in the sunlight, studying cloud patterns, and laughing together. But here is my advice: we will struggle in the dungeons of Un-Maurag until we are mastered. Then we will hurl ourselves against our enemies and force them to destroy us quickly and cleanly. Rafir, you might want to vanish and live for a while longer. What do you think?"

"No," the fox said slowly. "It's hard to think about dying — but with all these bones, I don't want to be alone here, hanging on just for a little while both of you are dead."

"Isn't there any hope, Julian?" asked Sebastian. "You always said that the Powers were wary of Merlin. Can't he help?" Julian stared into the distance for a moment.

"If the League triumphs, I can see Merlin and Thorian and Balardi leading a mass of tiers to Un-Maurag's borders — and how they would fare against the Dark Lord, I can't tell. But they will have to fight through Sorcerers, Marids, and Demons. We may be revenged, but I —" Some force was moving within the fleshy walls. Julian stood quickly, staff in hand.

From the far wall, sheets of tiny black creatures were cascading down, spilling out onto the chamber floor. Like a horde of insects, they massed and scuttled toward them across the chamber's floor. Rafir vanished. Sebastian leaped up to Julian's shoulder. Julian began the spell that called up flames but held back...the insects' minds were radiating images of feasting...they had a small portion of the Gift. Julian sent a thought out to them:

Come no farther! The insect horde stopped and milled, black, shuffling, confused.

We hunger.... The message came into Julian's mind. *It has been long since we feasted.*

You are carrion eaters, Julian thought at them. *We are still alive. Is this not so?*

It is so, came the thought, slow, hesitating. *Always, the red eyes feed on flesh, the great ones break the bones and feast on marrow. The rest is ours.* Then the thought came with a sudden urgency. *Yet now we hunger!* And the horde came surging forward.

Julian spoke the last words of the fire spell and a broad line of flames appeared. The insects halted, milling in hesitation.

Warm death for us, came the thought. *Why do you wish to live? Nothing lives here, not even we are truly alive.*

You must wait, Julian sent to them, *or you will anger Un-Maurag.* The insects began to retreat from the flames.

We will wait, came the thought. *It will not be long.* The dark horde shrank back and vanished into the walls. At a motion of Julian's staff, the flames also died out. Julian stood waiting for a moment, but the three walls were still. He sat back against the one stone wall.

"Was that supposed to happen?" Julian asked as Rafir flashed back into view. "Only someone like Houma could really understand the mind of Un-Maurag. I certainly can't."

They sat for a while, in silence, surrounded by yellow vapor and the smell of death, watching as dark slime shifted down the far walls. As the sense of danger eased, a deep depression came over Julian. Soft, wet sounds would be the last moisture sounds he would ever hear — he would never again listen to rushing brooks, or crashing waterfalls, or pounding waves. Sunlight, moonlight, and starlight had also ended; only pale-yellow lights remained, radiances that came from nowhere like an invisible sickness. Gone, too, were crisp winds and gentle breezes; only the drifting mists of poisoned vapors remained.

Sebastian sat quietly, thinking of death, and it was hard. Others who died left families behind them, creatures, or people like themselves, who would survive and remember the dead. When he died — first and last of the winged monkeys, it was over, forever. His only family was Julian, and more recently, Rafir. They would all die, together, and it would be over. Perhaps the Maker was like Merlin: gentle, solemn, kind, but that seemed too much to hope for.

Rafir lay, watching the flesh walls, with the smell of rotting meat drifting over him, pressing against his senses. He tried to remember all the fragrances of Alantéa, but they were slipping away from him. The old Sorceress had taught him to recognize by smell and stored within his mind were memories of thousands of odors — things he would never discover and recognize again. Decay and rotting death would be his last memories.

As time passed, it grew harder to imagine that there had ever been a time away from this foul, shadowy darkness. Waiting for death in the snuffling quiet of the Dungeons of Un-Maurag, where day and night merged, eventually, they slept.

And woke, diseased.

Raging fevers raced through Julian's body, and he was painfully weak. Sebastian and Rafir were hot to his touch, lying unconscious, surrounded by shattered bone shards. He crawled to his saddle pouch. Inside his own body, his lungs were half filled with fluid. Heart's Ease was first and in a moment he felt stronger. As he pressed other pieces of the herb to the lips of Sebastian and Rafir, their breathing eased. Julian's mind cleared, and he recalled the spell that would rid their bodies of most tiny intruders.

Once that spell was spoken, Julian felt as though a weight had been lifted from his chest. Rafir turned over, coughing. Sebastian's eyes opened. He tried to speak but could not; instead, he gestured, pointing to a place beside the kneeling Apprentice.

Julian turned and saw a tall wraithlike figure staring down at him. The Apprentice stood slowly, gripping his staff.

"Who are you?" Julian asked, his face hard. "Have you been sent to mock us?"

"No, mortal," the Wraith said, in a thin voice, little more than a whisper. "I pity you; I would never mock you. These are your last moments, here in the Mouth of Un-Maurag. Yet you are fortunate, for you will be released into the Long Sleep, free of the Dark Lord."

"Are you not free, even in death?" Julian asked.

"Alas, no, mortal. I am chained here in everlasting torment. There is no escape for me. Once I was an Elf-Lord, mighty with the Gift. Ages ago I fought here with the Sendings of Un-Maurag. I dreamed of triumph then, but with every victory, the Sendings grew always stronger. Pushed to the limits of my strength, I called out in fear and anger for Un-Maurag himself to come, but there was only faint laughter, filled with malice and hatred. I was defeated then, and with my last strength I called to my brethren to avenge me, yet their passage has always been blocked by Un-Maurag. So, in my lingering death, I have watched in horror as thousands struggled vainly in this place.

"Yet you are fortunate, mortal. I watched Sorcerers here, wielding a power that was greater than mine, and yet when they were defeated, Un-Maurag could not hold their spirits from their Long Sleep. This fortress rocked with his blazing anger, and we hid from his wrath. I was yet —"

Something flickered to Julian's left. Black shadows were seeping from the wall. The wraithlike figure shook with fear.

"No! I have told him nothing!" it cried. Black shadows shifted toward the Wraith. The Phantom fled, whimpering in fear as it vanished into the fleshy walls. Black shadow shapes pursued the wraith figure, and then they, too, were gone.

Now, as though activated by the pursuit, forces of dark sorcery surged and shifted through the chamber. Walls heaved and pulsed like great slabs of quivering flesh. Julian clasped his staff with both hands. Slow sounds came *fwup...fwup... fwup.* Then came a staccato burst of noise.

And hundreds of dark creatures surged from the walls: black stoats, like the trackers on the road to Rigal. Eyes red, fur black, they advanced on Julian, chittering like giant rats.

Julian spoke the Sleep Spell and they collapsed senseless. In seconds they began to fade, shadowy shapes drifting like lost, evil dreams back into the walls.

In an hour's time, they sprang from the walls again, angry voices chittering. Now, the Sleep Spell failed, and they advanced further until the Cold Spell struck them, freezing them to the floor of the chamber. Again, the stoat forms faded, drifting back into the walls.

"What are these *things,* Julian?" Rafir whispered, watching as the walls drew the fading shadows back. "Are they really alive?" Julian wiped his forehead with the sleeve of his cloak.

"Partly alive," he murmured. "The chamber itself lives — in a sense, and it calls on these partially alive creatures to serve it."

"Is there anything we can do?" whispered Rafir. "I might be able to come at them from behind — they really aren't that much bigger than I am."

"Too many," Julian said after a pause. "There are too many of them, but let's think —" The walls began to heave and pulse and with a staccato *fwup, fwup, fwup,* black stoats surged forward again. This time the Cold Spell checked them for only a second, and Julian was forced to use the Paralysis Spell. Then black stoats stood, red-eyed, aware, but immobile. Rafir slipped forward, speeding across the dungeon floor.

"No, wait, Rafir!" Julian called out. The fox halted, hesitating, then he turned back, but in turning his tail brushed against the foremost stoat. Instantly, the creature was freed, and it leaped on Rafir, snarling and biting. The fox rolled away; the black stoat plunged toward Julian, all fangs and red rage. Rafir sprang at it, nipping its flanks. As it neared Julian, it half turned to the fox — and Julian's boot came crashing down, smashing the stoat's neck. It lay twitching for a moment, and then it was still.

Julian knelt beside Rafir, running his fingers over the bite marks on the fox, watching them with troubled eyes. He went to his saddle pouch, drawing a vial, then rubbed a few drops of ointment into Rafir's fur.

"Poisoned bite," he murmured, "and the poison will grow in strength each time a wound is inflicted — if I've guessed right. Still..." he trailed off, staring down at the dead stoat. Its flesh and fur had vanished, but small bones lay still on the chamber floor. "We've learned something too: these things can be destroyed." He took a deep breath. "And, no doubt, they have learned much, and will return stronger, whenever they consider the time ripe."

The walls were quiet now, though they still seeped vapor into the cavern's air. Julian sank back, worn, and tired, against the only wall made of stone. Sebastian pulled bits of food for them from their provisions. They ate, forcing food down despite the rotting carcass smell that hovered through the cavern. Disquiet and depression settled over them in the long silence that followed. Pale lights within the chamber seemed to dim, as though Un-Maurag had grown bored with them, and his huge, many-faceted eyes were staring into the farthest reaches of the Mid-World, seeking new victims. After a while, the three prisoners slept.

·))(·

And again, they woke diseased, and this time there were no internal invaders — or at least Julian could find none. He stood, leaning against the stone wall, weakened and alarmed. War raged in his body, but there were no outside invaders! He touched Sebastian and Rafir: they were weakened, still unaware, yet there were no signs of the tiny intruders that marked all illnesses.

Except...he spoke the spell that reordered the body, righting its functions...inside him, the sense of illness began to fade. Sebastian and Rafir were breathing more easily.

So, their own defenses had been turned, guardians transformed into destroyers. He reached for the Heart's Ease once again...but...walls quivered and shook...black stoats burst out again, surging toward Julian.

He slurred the words and the spell failed. In desperation, he cast an illusion over them — from behind the stoats, white rats seemed to spring from the walls, speeding and leaping on dark shapes. With wild cries, stoats turned and sank teeth into — nothing except one another, leaving snarling masses of black shapes rolling and squealing on the cavern floor. Illusion-created shapes of white rats sped in and out of clusters of wild fighting stoats.

Julian forced more Heart's Ease into Sebastian and Rafir. They woke, staring in amazement as black creatures warred with white illusions — and with one another. But in moments, the black figures were again slipping back into the walls. Except that more than a dozen small skeletons now lay still on the dungeon floor.

"So," Sebastian said grimly, "if we succeed in destroying another two hundred or so, Un-Maurag will turn a different, much stronger force against us."

Julian nodded and whispered, "At least one other level of force lies present in these walls...I can feel them...huge and powerful...charmed against sorcery.... And beyond those, Un-Maurag will watch and create other monstrosities if he needs to. That's why I —" The walls seemed to heave and pulse, as though angered by Julian's whisper.

Again, black shapes burst forward, and now rat illusions leaped among them, unnoticed. The Cold Spell would not stop them — and so Julian called down sheets of scalding steam, many layered, with gasses and water vapors. Steam forced the creatures back into pulsing walls, and those vibrations from walls diminished, leaving only streaks of dark slime that slipped down the Mouth of Un-Maurag's dungeon walls.

Julian stood still, watching and sensing. Nothing seemed changed — pale lights, yellow vapors, black slime, rotting meat smell — everything continued, but for some reason, the Gift was rising inside him. Was this part of the contest, some hope cheating deception?

Rafir sniffed the air — somehow the smell of death was different.

Sebastian tugged at Julian's sleeve. "Something's changing," he whispered. "Could Merlin...." As though hateful of whispers, the walls shook and quivered; black stoats, always increasing in frenzy, leaped out. Hissing steam pressed against them. They halted, squealing in pain, puzzled, though still unwilling to retreat...as if the steams' substances were too complex, made of several elements...the first rank of stoats pushed through the barrier of steam faces glittering with triumph...but then their faces grew slack.

Horns were sounding in the distance, tiny ringing sounds as though coming from a distant universe. Julian's mouth slipped open in surprise:

battle calls were sounding, though they were not from League forces, nor were they human. Yet now the stoats' eyes were focusing again on Julian with more of the creatures emerging from the wall of steam. Julian stepped forward, taking on his Voice of Command.

"Your master has no time for you! Return, and do not distract him!" Fleshwalls quivered and then were still. All the stoat-like creatures stiffened, grew vague and then their shadows seeped back to the walls. Outside, the bugle calls became clearer, ringing through dark gloom like beacons of bright light.

Julian stood frozen in astonishment. He was hearing sounds that every magic wielder learns, but never truly expects to hear: the Horns of Elfland were ringing in the distance. The Elf-Lords had come, seeking revenge against their tormenter, Un-Maurag.

Now came sounds from the fortress: the clanking of arms, the movement of thousands of feet, as the Hordes of Un-Maurag readied for battle. Behind and beneath the sounds, Julian could feel the seething rage of Un-Maurag. Fortress gates clanked open, drumbeats and war-chants picked up, overwhelming the horns of Elfland: there would be no siege; Un-Maurag would seek out and destroy all those who dared to invade his domain.

"Those were sounds that I recognized," Rafir said softly, almost whispering. "The Sorceress taught me — those are Elf-horns, aren't they?"

"The Elf-Lords have come," Julian murmured, watching the fleshy walls carefully. "They have come ages after their brethren perished here, and it may be that they had assistance to gain their entry. I must guess that this is Merlin's counter, or rather his revenge. Even if Un-Maurag does not drive the Kindreds away, he will still have more than enough power to destroy us. Yet we will not die alone, outside of the greater struggle. That's good, at least."

From a distance, sounds of battle came, as the hordes of Un-Maurag hurled themselves against the Elf tiers. The Gift stirred in Julian: Un-

Maurag and the Elf-Lords stood opposed upon the battlefield, hurling powerful enchantments against one another. Julian listened but watched the flesh walls warily as they began to pour out a thick oily vapor. It was becoming more difficult to see, but the Gift was shifting in alarm.

"Stand close!" Julian said intently. "This gas is narcotic. We're supposed to sleep." Outside, the sounds of battle grew more distant, as though the struggle was shifting away from the fortress. Inside, vapors grew darker. Julian spoke the Wake Spell; the vapors shifted to orange and green colors. He spoke the Counter-Sleep Spell; the vapors became crimson.

He tried another spell, one that he struggled to speak, but was too hard to remember. And everything was becoming so dim, as vapors with many, varied colors surged over them. Once again, they slumped senseless to the floor of the Dungeons of Un-Maurag.

·)(·

Julian woke first, with cold stone beneath him, and rotten, yellowish air all around him. He lay motionless, letting the Gift explore his body: hundreds of tiny tumors were spreading inside him, expanding, seething with malignant violence against his organs. While he slept, the Mouth of Un-Maurag had dealt him a death wound, for it was beyond the power of any healer to deal with the civil war that raged inside his body. He sat, taking care not to wake Sebastian or Rafir. The dungeon was silent, and he could feel the presence of Un-Maurag within the fortress, a sense of brooding malice and hatred.

So, the Elf-Lords had failed, an outcome that was not surprising. Here, in the Mouth of Un-Maurag, all was as before, yellow vapors drifting, soft sucking sounds, black slime sliding down walls made of dark flesh. He tried to recall the Cup of the Maker and the Hall of the Dreamers, but those images had become vague and distant. Groaning, he struggled to his pouch. Heart's Ease would lend strength but bring no healing.

Again, he sat, watching the walls. The Gift reached out and examined Sebastian and Rafir; for some reason, they were free of tumors, though it really didn't matter. He had only a few spells left and unless the ring gave aid, he was finished.

The walls began to quiver. Julian stood.

Tiny and thin in the distance, the Horns of Elfland rang out once again, this time from a different direction. From within the fortress came a great cry of rage: the anger of Un-Maurag. Sebastian and Rafir woke, cowering.

"Merlin has created a second gateway for the Elf Kindreds," Julian said quietly. "Elf Legions have been joined by ranks of fell Sidhe, the most potent of armored forces in all of Alantéa. And now bands of powerful, dark skinned Tanu warriors have joined them — even the most powerful Urak warrior is no match for a Tanu. Un-Maurag may regret his alliance with the Sorcerers, although his regret will be too late for himself, and too late for us."

Gates creaked; war chants boomed as the legions of Un-Maurag surged out once more onto the dark, only partially lit plain. They stood for a moment, in silence, as Julian felt the presence of Un-Maurag pass from his citadel.

Gusts of vapor began to seethe from the walls. Julian stepped forward, holding his ring hand upright.

"For the Servants of the Maker, I call for aid!" he cried in a loud voice. "Let those who serve this ring preserve us from the Mouth of Un-Maurag!" Vapors were dulling his senses, but the Gift brought him a sense of distant malice, as though Un-Maurag laughed aloud on the battlefield, surrounded by all his legions of warriors.

The ring given him by Maeglan grew warm in Julian's hand — and it slipped from his fingers, rolling on the dungeon floor. Then it grew, expanding to a great circle, forming a Portal. From the opening, a tall, golden haired figure stepped, shining in the dim cavern light.

"The Lords of Light bring aid, even to those in the Mouth of Un-Maurag!" Rays of light flashed from the tall figure's hands, and dungeon vapors drooped and slipped to the ground. Outside, huge Uraks growled as they hurled themselves against the Elf-Kindreds. Sidhe ranks held them back, while Tanu warriors hammered at their flanks, and the dark skies were filled with the arrows of Elven Archers.

Julian watched the tall golden form carefully as the vapor settled: this Lord of Light was masked in layers of illusion, not wearing his true form, and his eyes darted and shifted with uncertainty beneath his golden, noble forehead.

"The Lords of Light have sent me to stop the Mouth of Un-Maurag forever. I —" Cavern walls quivered and shook. Black stoats leaped out, speeding toward the Power who was wreathed in illusions.

"I bring Rays of Dissolution for those that are half alive!" cried the golden figure, and the stoats were flooded with radiances of many colors as though from a prism. Stoats stumbled, slumped, and then their forms were sucked back into the walls. Outside, the Horns of Elfland rang out, as the Elf-Kindreds countered Un-Maurag.

"Not disease, nor fell creature, nor living stone may hinder a Lord of Light!" cried the tall figure in triumph. Flesh walls heaved and pulsed with renewed violence. Bursting sounds came; one single, huge figure slipped from each of the three walls, taller than the gleaming Lord, each of them radiating power and malice.

The tall, noble-seeming figure stepped back, looking sideways at Julian. Ogre-shaped creatures shuffled forward, long arms drooping below their knees. Lights flashed from the tall figure's hands, spilling many hues over the ogre-shapes — without the slightest effect.

"But the Lords of Light do not fight alone!" called the tall figure. The Ring Portal pulsed, and three golden warriors emerged, each armed with a gleaming sword and shield. Julian was chanting now, spell words leaping from his lips. In the background, sounds of battle grew louder, as the Elf-Lords hammered at the legions of Un-Maurag.

Ogre-shapes and golden warriors clashed, and Sebastian watched in horror as a nightmare ballet followed: three swords struck three dark forms, with black puss surging from their wounds; three huge hands swept down, and three golden warriors crumpled, dead, to the ground. Ogre-shaped creatures turned to the Lord of Light.

"No," whispered the tall, golden figure. Julian was chanting, but nothing was responding to his spell words. The Ring Portal flared again, as the Lord of Light backed toward it. Dark rays flashed from fleshy walls; the Ring Portal vanished. Ogre-shapes advanced, hands groping for the gleaming figure. Suddenly, the Lord cast aside his illusion-shape...he shrank...he was inhuman, gnarled, no larger than a gnome — and desperate. A tiny Portal flashed into existence, and the Mid-World lesser wielder of magic dove through it headfirst and vanished.

Sebastian stared around him: nothing had come of Julian's spell; three golden warriors lay dead on the floor — the ring given to Julian by Maeglan had proved a false hope. As the ogre-shapes advanced upon them, Sebastian clutched a sharp piece of bone to use as a dagger. Outside, the war-cries of massive Uraks rose over the Horns of Elfland. Dark shapes advanced. Sebastian clutched his bone sliver. They would die now, but they would die fighting.

"Do we cheat Un-Maurag now?" cried the little Familiar, tensing to spring. Julian shook his head and sank back against the stone wall. Rafir stood trembling, still visible beside Julian. Huge forms loomed with menace over the Apprentice. He sat, back against the wall. They hovered for a moment, then, finding no resistance, backed away, shuffling, slipping back into fleshy walls.

When they vanished, the fleshy walls pulsed again, and black stoats surged out, clustering beside the dead warriors, ripping their mail aside with sharp teeth, feasting on flesh that was still warm. On the plain, the hordes of Un-Maurag wheeled and struck again, crying aloud in hatred and triumph.

Perched on Julian's shoulder, Sebastian began to weep. Rafir was wild, feral, on the edge of madness. Sobbing, the little Familiar let the bone fragment slip from his fingers: there would be no cheating of Un-Maurag, just lingering horror and a slow, hard death.

Julian touched each of them gently, and to their amazement, a calm strength emerged from the hands of the Apprentice.

He stood, slowly, face set, eyes narrow, as he watched the black stoats feed. Sebastian was amazed — what was happening? Forces were changing in the death chamber. And the stoats, too, felt the difference, raising their heads from their feeding, red blood smeared over dark faces.

Julian spoke the last words of the summoning spell, and the head of Kath slipped into the dungeon.

Sebastian's wings flared and Rafir snarled deep in his small throat. Julian had used the distractions to summon Kath, his serpent ally! The snake was massive, powerful, more than thirty feet in length. Julian was prepared for battle!

Now, the stoats slipped toward them, hundreds of black faces chittering and squealing.

"Strike, Kath!" Julian cried, "but do *not* feed!" The huge serpent spilled into the dungeon — bringing ruin. Broken stoat-shapes flew in all directions as Kath battered and crushed. Poison fangs scraped at serpent hide but could not break the scale of his hide. Julian leaped forward, bolts of force blasting stoats that tried to flee. None reached the walls. Out on the battlefield, Un-Maurag cried out in shock and anger. The Horns of Elfland rang louder in their challenge.

"Back to me, Kath!" Julian cried. The serpent coiled back behind Julian, tongue lashing at the dungeon's yellow fumes. On the cavern floor, hundreds of black forms lay twitching or dead. The walls heaved and pulsed. Julian was lifting material from his pouch, his hands flew, wrapping quickly. Three concussions sounded: Ogre-shapes shuffled from the walls. Julian pressed the packet into Sebastian's hands.

"When I call out, hurl this at them — from above," he spoke quickly as the huge forms shuffled forward. "But shield your eyes! Do you understand? After you throw the packet, shield your eyes!" Sebastian nodded, wings fluttering. At Julian's side, the great tail of Kath swept back and forth as his eyes followed the advancing shapes.

Julian's hand lifted Sebastian into the air. The huge, shambling creatures neared, staring at the little Familiar fluttering above Julian.

"Now!" Julian cried. Sebastian hurled the packet. Julian closed his eyes while shielding those of Kath. A blinding flash lit the cavern. Huge hands lifted to huge faces, as the creatures halted, blinded by the light.

"Now strike, Kath!" Julian cried. "Break their spines!" The great serpent sped behind the hulking forms, out of reach of their huge arms. With enormous force, the massive head of Kath struck three times and left the ogre-shapes writhing on the cavern floor.

Out on the battlefield, Un-Maurag cried out in pain and rage.

In the dungeon, the fleshwalls heaved and pulsed. Sheets of black insects raced from the walls, crying, "We Hunger!" Julian's staff shot flame, transforming them all into ash.

Flesh walls pulsed again, but now the tides of power in Un-Maurag's Dungeon were shifting.

Julian raced forward, leaping over the dead, and dying. Kath followed beside him. Julian placed his staff against the heaving flesh wall; power surged through him.

"Be still!" he called out. The walls hesitated, twitching. Julian raced to the cavern's center.

"Un-Maurag!" Julian cried. "Hear me, Un-Maurag! We are Servants of the Maker, not victims of trials of strength that are no more than torture! Un-Maurag! You are far; I am near! Your power is spent; mine is fresh! Un-Maurag, I claim power in this place! Now let the Mouth of Un-Maurag be stilled!" Power flowed through Julian, surging into the flesh walls.

And the Mouth of Un-Maurag...sighed....

A death sigh, as scores and hundreds of dead immortal spirits, surged from their endless torment and were free.

On the battlefield, Un-Maurag lifted his huge head and gave a cry of everlasting pain and torment.

In the dungeon, the walls stiffened hardening, to become dark stone once again. Sounds of battle surged and ebbed as the Elf-Lords pressed the legions of Un-Maurag.

As sorcery slipped from the Mouth of Un-Maurag, all the soft sounds of the dungeon vanished, the air grew clear, and pale lights dimmed, leaving the stone cavern in complete darkness. Light flared from Julian's staff.

"So, we are masters here, for the moment," Julian said, stroking the serpent's head. "Mighty Kath, they will sing of you for ages, how you bested the Servants of Un-Maurag in his deepest, most foul of dungeons." He straightened, turning to Rafir and Sebastian. "That is, they will sing of our struggle if any of us live to tell the tale. Let's see if there's an exit." Julian spoke the Portal Spell three times, each time with less effect.

"As I feared, no exit for me," he sighed. "Yet, I can return Kath, and you two need to join him. That much, at least, can be accomplished."

"But we should stay at your side," Rafir said. Sebastian stood beside the fox, and he put his small right hand out, rubbing the soft fur of the fox.

"This time, I think Julian is right," Sebastian said gently. "We would just be in the way. And there's something else that Julian's not telling us." He turned to the Apprentice. "I can sense that something's wrong — and it's inside of you. Am I right?" Julian nodded.

"A death-wound, dealt by the Mouth of Un-Maurag. Even if I escaped, I would have only a short while to live. It would be well if you two survived to comfort our friends. Tell Merlin how Kath and I mastered this place because it will ease his sorrow." The two small ones bowed their heads in grief, then they wept.

· X ·

Julian sat, alone, in the darkness, listening to the sounds of battle raging on the half-lit plain. War raged also in his body, and yet he knew that the illness would not have time to destroy him: in the last few minutes, he had sensed a Power nearing the dungeons. It was not Un-Maurag himself, but probably his greatest servant sent to destroy those who claimed power in the heart of Un-Maurag's citadel.

He stood. Anyway, a quick death was so much better than a lingering one, his body rotting from within.

The Steward of Un-Maurag drew closer; Julian could feel its pulsing power as it strode down the corridors — it would not need to disguise itself or mask its strength. Now it stood on the other side of the wall nearest Julian. The Apprentice moved slowly away, staff in hand.

No words were spoken, but he could feel the power of its sorcery begin to focus. Rock began to crumble, dust clouds billowing into the cavern. Outside, the sounds of battle continued unbroken. Dust slowly settled. Julian gripped his staff. Part of the cavern wall had disintegrated, forming an entrance.

Out in the corridor, surrounded by flickering torch lights, stood the Steward of Un-Maurag. Tall, broad-shouldered, a cape flowed beyond it. Yet it had no face, only a mass of hazy darkness looming over its shoulders. Within that darkness, lights flared and trailed across its visage, like pale comets.

Julian raised his staff: a bolt of force flashed toward the creature. The Steward of Un-Maurag lifted a hand and waved the bolt away; it passed, crashing down the corridors. The creature extended a hand toward Julian. Jagged lights, like angry lightning, flashed across its visage. A cocoon of white light spun around Julian.

"Steward of Un-Maurag," came a gentle voice, from beyond the corridor, outside of Julian's sight. "Steward of Un-Maurag, why are you not out upon the battlefield, serving your master?" As if prompted, the Horns of Elfland came ringing in the distance. The Steward turned from Julian, releasing its spell toward the voice.

"Yes, yes, you are powerful," said the gentle voice. Comets flared across the Steward's visage as a second, more powerful force of sorcery was launched.

"And you might have become a Dark Lord in your own right, with your own evil dungeons and nightmare torments." A Portal flashed beside the Steward, and a dark Wraith surged toward the soft voice, but then a curl of vapor touched the creature on its forehead, and the Wraith drifted away, mindless.

"But now you must take the everlasting sleep," said the gentle voice. "For I do not think that the Maker will choose to wake you." Power flowed to the Steward of Un-Maurag, lights flashing across the hazy dome it used as a face — then, one by one, those lights flared and died. The Steward of Un-Maurag toppled slowly, drifting to the stone of the cavern like a column of fading smoke.

Soft footsteps padded along the corridor, and then Merlin stepped into the cavern. The Wizard's face was filled with sorrow as he embraced Julian.

"Why should the Sorcerers have done this to you?" asked the Wizard. "Why feed you to the most evil of Dark Lords when there were thousands of other ways to hinder you? If we prevail, there will be a time of reckoning for those Sorcerers, a time that may well surprise them. Come!"

Merlin led Julian down the corridor, and up a long, winding flight of stairs, then through several passageways. Everywhere, Urak guards and tracking Vorrs lay still, or dead. Each barrier within the fortress of Un-Maurag stood unlocked, half ajar.

"Un-Maurag has watched us for many years, with undisguised malice," said the Wizard. "For that reason, I have also studied Un-Maurag, but cautiously, from a distance. When Un-Maurag aided the Sorcerers in your capture, I opened the way for the Elf-Lords and the Kindreds — the Tanu, the Sidhe, and the Elf-legions."

They neared the main gates of Un-Maurag's fortress. Noises of battle grew louder so that Merlin was forced to raise his voice.

"For many ages, Un-Maurag has preyed upon the Elf-Kindreds, yet they could never force a passage to their tormentor. Now, they will test Un-Maurag as he has never before been tested." They passed through the outer gates and stood looking back up at the massive walls of the fortress of Un-Maurag. In the distance, the Elf-Host gleamed white as it surged against the dark hordes of Uraks. Merlin placed his hands on Julian's shoulders.

"First I will lift this illness from you," he murmured, and Julian could feel the healing strength surging through him.

"I thought..." Julian said, haltingly, almost in a whisper. Merlin shook his head, eyes filled with compassion.

"No, you will live, and remain well. We may all be doomed, but we will not die from illnesses. Sorcerers and Marids and Demon Princes will bring ruin to the League unless we find a way to call the Truce down upon them." Merlin watched the distant battle for a moment, then he reached into his cloak, and drew out a handful of small bits, like black seeds. With a flick of his wrist, the Wizard cast them against the fortress walls. They sank into the caked earth and were gone.

"The Sorcerers have truly won this round, for you have been delayed, as I have been forced to turn aside," Merlin said, staring into the distance. "Yet Un-Maurag will take a very long time to recover his power."

Against the fortress walls, many tendrils of string-like vines were racing upwards: ugly, wire-like, some were tarnished, petals like spores of rust, but growing with incredible speed.

"Those seeds feed on evil and their roots will dig deep," Merlin said grimly. "The fortress of Un-Maurag is doomed." Dust began to seep from the walls, as the growths ate into its stone and steel, feeding on the tortured dreams of Un-Maurag. Merlin turned back to Julian.

"You must go forward. Seek the nature of the Truce, for there must be some way that the Powers can be brought to battle against our enemies, otherwise Houma would not have conspired with Un-Maurag." He sighed.

"I was not able to save Bluescent, for with the malice of Un-Maurag focused on you and your small allies, she was able to break free, running wild until she was slaughtered by Uraks. Yet Sebastian and Rafir are well, waiting for you to emerge from this dark, nightmare place of torment.

"I sought to slip you into the Vale of Whispers, as a slender but powerful flyer might glide into a dark tower, and in this, I made a mistake, almost a disastrous one. Here, at this time, I will supply assistance that should have been yours at the beginning of your quest: concealed within your healer's potions is a shielding spell, one that will mask, even transform you and your party beyond any of the prying eyes of Sorcerer or Mid-World Power. Use it for the last lap, choosing a time when the pursuit has faltered. In addition, I have recreated your Blue Amulet. An unnamed, fiercely anonymous Power with strength far greater than mine has enhanced it; and so, I doubt that it will be so easily overcome.

"Of greater and more immediate help will be Galad and his Tarnished Sword; I am sending Galad with you, though he can poorly be spared from the twin sieges of Stone Mountain and Gravengate. You must understand that I cannot always be the hidden force that emerges when all else fails, for the Sorcerers and the Powers of the Mid-World are weaving Portal-Barriers at every possible sorcerous junction, and soon there will be only the Straight Path, should I need to depart Sea's Edge.

"But for you and your quest, Galad will bring powerful assistance. You and he and your small allies will seek the Truce Terms." He turned back to the battlefield, where Un-Maurag struggled so desperately against the armed might of the Kindreds, and the magic of the Elf-Lords.

"And what is this Truce, that such open conflict is permitted? Is it broken? Is it lost? Have its Terms been forgotten? Find these things for me, Julian, and I will bring an utter, everlasting, and complete destruction down upon our enemies."

Chapter Five

The Temples of Tel-Alantir

SNOW WAS HURLED AT their backs, a last parting gift from the embattled Un-Maurag. Yet to Julian, the cold white flakes were clean things of clear beauty, in sharp contrast with the darkness, decay, and death of the Dungeons of Un-Maurag. Sebastian and Rafir rode with their faces exposed to the weather, eyes bright with life. Galad rode in front of them, the great muscles of his charger powering easily through snow drifts — and Galad rode fearlessly, in the fullness of his strength, as though Death had taken a long nap in some distant corner of the universe.

The Gift within Julian was watchful, while slowly relaxing, with the images of Un-Maurag and his nightmare kingdom slowly fading. As Julian shifted in his saddle, he could barely feel the malice of Un-Maurag. Above him, clumps of wet snow were slipping from the upper branches. Galad rode on, heedless, but Julian dodged when he could, and laughed when the snow pelted his long dark hair. They had ridden beyond Rigal now, avoiding places where those serving the Three Hands would gather, as they prepared to invade the Wizards' League.

Though the land seemed desolate and barren where they traveled, Julian was certain that they would soon find more favored places with fields and livestock blest by the Powers. Even in this blighted, snow-stricken area, they would not be without shelter: clusters of abandoned farms appeared every league or so, groups of buildings that might have become villages had the Powers been more favorable.

Galad led them up a ridge and halted on the hill-crest where snow left only a thin carpet. Below them a valley sprawled in the overcast white afternoon; snow had mixed with rain, and mists seeped from the damp combination. Julian looked for signs of human habitation, smoke from wood-fires, or the snowless roof of some heated house, but the valley before them was damp and cheerless. They spilled over the edge, easing their way down the embankment.

Julian's mood shifted a little. Perhaps it was just as well that their path was cheerless and uncomfortable, otherwise, he would be distracted by sun, shade, and woodlands, rather than considering the Sorcerer's plots. Houma's words came easily to mind: *So many other traps set, each of them more subtle and exquisite.* Without a doubt, Houma had exaggerated, and yet the Mid-World lay everywhere around them, like a huge sea, with currents and eddies of magic flowing and shifting. The Sorcerers swam like fish in that sea, while those from the League seemed sluggish like eels sliding through rocky shallows.

"Why didn't we travel like this before?" Rafir called out, laughing. "It may be cold and dreary but there's nothing that smells of Urak, or Vorr, or even human."

"Un-Maurag and his kingdom are also beyond any of my senses," added Sebastian. "It's amazing that there's no pursuit. I can't believe that he would let us go that easily."

"Un-Maurag may be mighty, but he has made many powerful enemies. And yet," Julian cautioned, "keep watch, both of you! The Sorcerers will still be trying to destroy us."

"Yes," Sebastian said thoughtfully, "I remember how Houma boasted about all his traps. I couldn't move, or think clearly, but I could hear. Rafir and I will keep watch for the Sorcerers."

Down in the valley, the cold had lifted somewhat, and small streams of melted snow were seeking ancient runoff channels. Galad led them through the last hours before darkness, seeking to move as far north as possible. As darkness came, they slowed, seeking shelter. At last, they chose an old building of long logs and mortar. Outside, the building had weathered well, but within, many small creatures had nested. As Galad forced the door open, the small ones sped in flight, crying in tiny voices. Galad hesitated.

"Not very charming," he muttered, turning to Julian. "Should we look elsewhere? There should be many other abandoned shelters cleaner than this."

Julian shook his head and stepped past Galad. "After Un-Maurag, all living creatures seem delightful — particularly when there's no dark sorcery. It's clean here, in that sense, so it's good for one night's shelter." They cleared a small area in front of a corner fireplace. Galad tended their horses while Sebastian and Julian fed a small fire. Rafir nosed about, and the smell of the fox sent other creatures scurrying from the log-house into the snowy dampness. Galad returned, bringing more wood for their fire. They ate a brief meal and Galad stretched out.

"Un-Maurag," Galad said slowly, "by reputation most fearsome of the Dark Lords, but no man has stood in front of him and survived — or so it's said. When the time's right, will you tell me more about this Power?"

"When the time is right," Julian said gently. "Tomorrow, perhaps in the daylight. Discussions at twilight might encourage night visions, and the three of us have had enough nightmares."

"Then we'll talk tomorrow," said Galad, "but it may hearten you to know that word of Un-Maurag had the opposite effect on our Wizards —

when word came to us that Houma had conspired with Un-Maurag against you, then Balardi was moved to real rage for the first time in a long while. Thorian, too, put forth his strength, though he was colder, more measured. For a little while, I had dreams that we might crush the Sorcerers, then move to bring down this Dark Lord — ridiculous, of course, but it was better than the rest of the struggle." Galad trailed off.

"If your news is as grim as ours," Julian said softly, "perhaps it should also wait until tomorrow."

"No," said Galad, taking a deep breath. "'Grim' is the wrong word. 'Depressing' says it better: a slow defeat just before the first disaster. It would be easier if the Wizards were more hopeful, less discouraged, but they seem haunted by images of Marids tearing down their fortresses; men watch them and take little hope from the looks on their faces." Galad looked up to see three puzzled faces staring at him. He laughed. "Not much of an explanation, is it? I'll try to do better:

"They came at us first by sea, Alcman leading a huge war fleet. Thorian and Balardi tried to counter him by wind and wave, but Alcman had the greater mastery of weather in that struggle. A host of ships landed to the east of Stone Mountain, at the mouth of the Asaram. We marshaled a great force, planning to sweep them back into the sea, just as news came from the north that our border was breached, with Eudox and Cronar leading many men over the Saugus. Narsis was abandoned. All our people in the north fled towards Gravengate, with long wagon trains clogging the roads.

"Balardi then moved with many tiers to rout Alcman before the twin pincers of the Sorcerers could be joined, and yet they were prepared for us; the Demon Princes must have schooled Alcman well. In spite of all the power and wrath of Balardi, on that day he was second to Alcman. Monsters and magic and wild weather — nothing could check the Sorcerer. They were well prepared for me also; there were masses of pike, and enchanted nets cast all around me. Many men gave their lives to rescue me, and I was fortunate to survive.

"We fell back to Stone Mountain. That evening, Thorian and Balardi locked themselves away, sitting apart in the Council Chamber of Stone Mountain. For all their early grim words, it must have shocked them to have learned how mighty the Sorcerers had become. The next day, they were brooding and quiet, but at least the old enmity between them seemed buried forever. It may have been a part of Merlin's purpose, to leave the two former adversaries together, and let events force their reconciliation.

"There was a lull for the next few days as we waited for the Sorcerers at Stone Mountain. I sat in on the war councils and after a time I came to see that the fortress at Stone Mountain was a trap as well as a refuge: there was room for less than half our forces, so we could not give battle easily from the castle walls, or we would leave a large portion of our forces exposed on the hillside." Galad sighed before continuing.

"I wonder if Kalanin might not have devised a more intelligent plan. In the end, we left the walls of Stone Mountain lightly guarded, massing our forces at the foothills of the Mountain. On the fourth day after the battle at the mouth of the Asaram, the Sorcerers marched on Stone Mountain, and we were defeated."

Galad shook his head as though the memory disturbed him, then he looked back into the eyes of the Apprentice. "We were defeated, but not broken. Thorian and his men took refuge in Stone Mountain. I was with Balardi, and we forced our way through their lines, falling back towards Gravengate: Harlond and Rostov led a great press of horsemen through their lines; many of the emblems of the Three Hands lay in the dust after that charge. And Balardi was moved to a frenzy, fierce and dangerous, stalking about, growling, and snarling like a wounded bear.

"As we sit here, the forces of the League are separated, but not destroyed. Also, a strange balance prevails: if the Sorcerers press too hard at Stone Mountain, we are at their backs, nipping at their heels; if they send too great a force against us, we fall back towards Gravengate to shelter within the fortress walls. Yet, if they come at us too strongly, the siege at Stone Mountain fails, and Harmadast will lead an attack against the besiegers.

"In the end, we will lose, if only because new forces pledged to the Three Hands emerge every day." Galad was silent for a moment, staring into the flames, then he laughed. "We had one positive event I didn't mention: Dargas returned from the Mistress of Illusions, but changed; he's leaner now, where before he was heavy. And he's become angry and dangerous, meaner than a pit-fiend."

"Is there any news about Kalanin?" asked Rafir.

Galad's face sobered. "None, and it's bewildering. If ever there was a need for him, it's now, and yet he remains in the Mid-World, living in splendid luxury like some kept puppy. I find that very, *very* hard to understand."

"I've thought about Merlin's words for some time," Julian said. "I have to guess that the Seraphs were protected in some fashion so that those who injured a Seraph were in turn tormented. Merlin said only that Kalanin had changed, but there was no injury to heal, none on the surface at least."

Galad shrugged. "It's our loss. Aside from wielders of magic, that man is the most dangerous human in the League, perhaps in all of Alantéa."

"We'll be forced to do without him, for a while at least," Julian said softly. "There are others who have not yet entered this contest: Merlin lingers at Sea's Edge, the Marids grow to power in the ocean depths, and the Demon Princes lie hidden, shrouded in mystery."

Galad turned to Sebastian and Rafir. "Time for bed, kiddies. You've just heard the magician's sleepy time summary."

Julian laughed. "It's true that I've listened to Merlin and Balardi for too long. Who else can I use as a model?"

"Why not try Dargas," said Galad, and he changed his voice, mimicking the old soldier. "'You pumpkin-headed cheese fluffs! Do you think this is only a sunny ride in the country? They're likely to bring all of you back lifeless, stinking with your own gore and dung.'"

"I would need to practice," Julian said, smiling. They watched the fire die down, and as the light lessened, the sounds of small beings grew louder as little creatures pattered over the floor of the abandoned log house. Despite the slight shuffling sounds, sleep came easily to Julian.

· X ·

Morning brought clear and freezing weather, and they found that the top layer of melting snow had iced over. They rode north at daybreak, their horses crunching through the snow with clouds of steamy vapor drifting from their nostrils. Rafir ran lightly over the snow crust, speeding past Julian and Galad, but Julian called him back.

"Rafir, something is different — I was relaxed yesterday, but overnight there's been a change. What can you scent?"

"Man scent, horse scent, a trace of wolf, I think," said the fox. "Nothing different from yesterday."

"I can sense something," said Sebastian. "It's ahead of us, a magic wielder, I believe, waiting for us. A human?"

Julian shook his head. "It's not human, it has the Gift, and it takes no measures to conceal itself — also, there's something behind us, in pursuit.

The thing before us does not seem evil, but behind us, I sense the torture-stained hand of Un-Maurag." Galad pulled to a halt.

"What's to be done?" he asked. "Should we change direction to lose the seekers?"

"No, forward," said Julian, "but we will be more alert, and wary. Rafir should be among us, but not with us, in case some discreet exploring is required."

"You mean spying," said Rafir, and he vanished.

"I can also be your eyes and ears," added Sebastian. The sun had emerged, and a little of the night's chill was easing, but it was still cold to Sebastian. He flew, struggling for height, wishing he had the Eye of Merlin's strength. Below him, the ground was white in all directions; Julian and Galad were small figures, passing slowly over a white carpet. Nothing else moved, except — far to the south, tiny in the distance, brown-furred creatures were leaping over the snow's surface. Sebastian shivered, not just from the cold. He began to glide downwards, back to the riders, seeking the warmth of Julian's cloak.

"Four-legged creatures," he said, shivering. "Perhaps as many as a dozen of them. They're closing fast. From this distance, I can't tell what sort of beings they are."

"Should we turn to meet them?" asked Galad.

Julian shook his head. "We'll go forward. In a while, a magic wielder will greet us. We are heading into an interesting junction." They rode on and as the day grew warmer, the snow crust moistened, and their progress became less noisy.

As the snow softened, Rafir's progress grew more difficult as his feet sank into the moist drifts. He halted for a moment, catching his breath; he lay panting, watching Julian and Galad ride on. The wind shifted a little, and he caught the scent of their pursuers. In a flash, he was up, racing toward Julian.

"Vorrs!" he called out to the Apprentice. "Un-Maurag has sent Vorrs after us!" Julian said nothing, only pointing to a hilly crest that lay before them. On the snow-covered hillock, serene and erect, stood a Ram, and its fleece blended with the snow, except that golden fibers were sprinkled among the white, and on this bright day, the gold strands glittered with sunlight. Behind them, the Vorrs sped on, calling out wild hunting cries as their victims came into view.

Julian and Galad rode forward, dismounting as they reached the hill's crest. Galad drew the Tarnished Sword and turned toward the Vorr pack. Vorrs had slowed, now certain of their prey, and were stalking the last few hundred feet with caution. The Tarnished Sword began to come alive in Galad's hand as the servants of Un-Maurag neared. Julian approached the golden flecked Ram on foot.

"Greetings, Lord of the Mid-World," he said, bowing. "You have waited patiently for us. What do you desire of us?"

"You are summoned, Mortal Magic Wielder," said the Ram. Its voice was as clear as a mountain stream. "You must come and be judged before the throne of Tel-Alantir. But first, you are permitted to dispatch these servants of Un-Maurag. They would appear to offer little danger to you."

Julian turned back, watching as the Vorrs approached, stalking with the motions of unchallenged predators. Nine of them circled the hill, and their brown fur was matted and scarred. Some had partially healed wounds, with red blood still seeping down their sides. Their leader, larger than the others, was unmarked and he led the others forward, mouth open, still panting from the chase.

"We have run you to earth, Apprentice," said the Vorr leader in a voice of low menace. "Now, you will feel the vengeance of Un-Maurag!"

"Will I indeed?" Julian asked gently. "Hold for a moment, before the dying begins." The Vorr leader said nothing, but his stalking motions came to a halt. Others stopped, standing four-legged, panting in the snow. "I know the mind of Un-Maurag, how he greatly desires my destruction. But why has he sent so few of you on so great an errand?"

"He is beset by the accursed Elf-Lords and their Kindred followers, while his fortress slowly collapses!" snarled the Vorr. "And there were more of us at the beginning. Had it not been for the accursed wolfpacks, we would have been at your throats sooner. But nine is enough — I, alone, am enough!" The Vorr's jaws snapped shut and it inched forward.

"No," said Julian, again gently. "Even twenty-five would not be enough, for this warrior, alone. Show them the blade, Galad." The Tarnished Sword was held aloft so that sunlight spilled over its mixed metals. A muffled sound slipped from the blade, as though it feared being cheated of victims.

"Here is a blade that has brought down two of the Creatures of the Darkness and destroyed a First Servant of the Maker. Do you think that your pack would prevail against it?" The Vorrs made no answer. "As for me, I am able to defend myself." Julian pointed his staff to a grove of trees. A bolt of force leaped out, shattering treelimbs, spilling masses of soft white snow to the ground. The Vorr leader looked from Galad to Julian, and back, then he raised his massive head and howled in anguish.

"We must make the attempt, mortals, for Un-Maurag holds our spirits. Only grant us a quick death, not a slow, bleeding, cold one." He howled again joined by his brethren, but then the solemn goldflecked Ram stepped forward.

"I am aware of Un-Maurag's Sorcery. I will lift his hold from you if that is your wish." Vorr faces turned to one another, filled with uncertainty.

"But how will it be without the will of Un-Maurag?" asked their leader. "He has always been our master."

"That moment I cannot foretell," said the Ram Servant of Tel-Alantir. "Yet, I can speak of your second choice — you can spring at these mortals, and you will all die, bleeding red blood into white snow," Vorrs whispered and snarled at one another.

"Then free us," said the leader, "if that is our only hope."

The great goldflecked Ram stepped down from the hill crest, and though the snow had softened, he still moved over the snow's crust, feet barely touching the surface. Three times the Ram walked around the Vorr Pack, chanting as the Vorrs sank back in the snow, shivering, as though still dreading the wrath of Un-Maurag. After the third passage, the Ram came and stood beside Julian, speaking the last words of its spell. A chill breeze sprang up, blowing quietly over them. Then the wind was gone.

The Vorr leader rose from the snow, sniffing about, then he gave a loud cry of triumph. "Free!" he cried. Other Vorrs cried out and began leaping in the snow so that the horses of Galad and Julian began to back away from them. "We are free!" cried the Vorr leader again. "And yet we are unchanged. I feared that we would become filled with nice, clean intentions, but I still yearn for blood and the chase. Brothers and sisters, we are free!" The Vorr Pack howled. Julian knelt beside the Vorr leader, his staff still held steady in his right hand.

"Go in peace, and join the other predators of Alantéa," he said in a low voice. "But remember, humans are also great predators. You have not seen much of men, but they will kill other predators, with various reasons. Choose a place apart from men." The Vorr leader's eyes were filled for a moment with both cunning and malice, but then those eyes grew wary.

"I am tempted to test these men, and yet, perhaps they are dangerous. The ruin of Un-Maurag was brought about by your entry to his kingdom — and so I will heed your counsel." He turned to his pack. "We will go now and leave these to their destinies." Vorrs called out and began to move away. Hesitating, the Vorr leader turned back to Julian and to the gold-flecked Ram. "I still feel cruelty and hunger, but there is a sense of obligation for the mercy shown to us. If we are near, and you wish aid, call upon us. Now, farewell!" And the Vorrs were gone, leaping in exultation over snowdrifts, speeding toward white woodlands.

"That was most strange," said the Ram. "The power within me showed an image of shredded brown fur, pouring red blood over white snow. You were merciful, Apprentice."

"They were enslaved by Un-Maurag and now they are free," Julian said, watching the Vorrs speed away. He turned to the servant of Tel-Alantir. "So, we are summoned by Tel-Alantir. What does your master wish with us?"

"Heavy charges have been brought against you, Apprentice. Yet my Master is just and will hear your side before passing judgment."

"These 'charges' — a Sorcerer named Houma will be their author. Am I correct?"

"You are half right, Apprentice. The Sorcerers Houma and Cronar are now lodged with the Priests of Tel-Alantir."

"These are my adversaries, and enemies of the Wizards' League. They have brought savage war to the south of Alantéa. I should do my utmost to avoid them. What if we do not choose to stand amid the Temples of Tel-Alantir? What are your instructions?"

"To bring you, willing or not. You have been open with me, Apprentice, and I also will be candid with you: to master you seemed an easy task, and yet now I perceive that you might prevail against me — a chance, no more than that. But after, the wrath of Tel-Alantir would pursue you to the ends of Alantéa." Julian was silent for a moment, mind racing.

"This decision affects more than me, alone. I must speak with my friends, a little apart."

"Speak," said the Ram. "I will not listen."

Julian nodded. "I would trust you, and yet I must seal us away from the Divinations and Farsight of our foes." He moved down the slope, a little more than twenty paces. With his staff, he traced the shape of a pentagram on the surface of soft snows. Galad, Julian and Sebastian stood within the shape; of Rafir, there was no sign.

"So, here is the second of Houma's traps," said Sebastian, "but there's a chance we might avoid it."

"This creature seems reluctant to move against us," said Galad. "If we simply ride away, perhaps it will let us depart." Julian shook his head.

"Tel-Alantir's Emissary will obey its master," he said slowly. "There are two Sorcerers ranged against us. If we turn and look at this matter through their eyes, what do we see? The first attempt failed; they sought to overwhelm us, and so the second trap will be more devious, many-layered. Here, we are supposed to resist, either to be dragged as prisoners before Tel-Alantir, or, if we prevail, we may destroy this servant, and have an angry Power at our backs. No, Tel-Alantir is by reputation benign, known as 'friend to man.' Let us go before him and refute the Sorcerers." Galad nodded after a moment's thought.

"Done! For one thing, we're young and innocent looking, bound to make a better impression than a pair of crusty, evil Sorcerers."

"I'm not so sure," said Sebastian, "but I don't have anything better to suggest. Next time we'll send Rafir ahead of us to learn what we're facing." They stepped from the Pentagram.

"We will go willingly to Tel-Alantir," Julian said. "Let your Great God and master be as fair as his reputation."

The gold-flecked Ram studied them for a moment. "Again, this is not what the Power within me revealed. In a different future, we fought, and you fell before me after a most difficult struggle. Yet, at the last, the sword came surging towards me, singing for my blood. It is good to be alive! Blessings come from Tel-Alantir! All praise to my Master, Tel-Alantir! Now, follow me to my master's realm."

The Ram turned north, chanting his Portal Spell. Energies shifted and focused. A great-arched Portal loomed before them. Beyond the Portal they could see a broad avenue, with masses of white structures on both sides, shining with sunlight. They stepped through, leaving behind only snowy tracks that were already beginning to melt in the sunlight.

"Behold the Temples of Tel-Alantir!" cried the Ram. "Mighty is Tel-Alantir, friend to man!" As if in response, music burst from buildings on either side, hymns of praise for Tel-Alantir.

"Holy, Holy, Holy, mighty Tel-Alantir, giver of gifts, friend to man! Tel-Alantir the protector! Tel-Alantir the provider! All praise to Tel-Alantir!" Chanting and singing, first scores then hundreds of people emerged from the temples, surging up the broad avenue, calling,

"Holy, Holy, Holy! Mighty is Tel-Alantir, friend to man." Clouds of incense lifted into sunlit skies. Trees lined the boulevard, and they were covered with blossoms. Petals fell over the procession, with flecks of pink and white, red, and azure drifting over the multitude. Tel-Alantir's Ram Servant led them behind the procession, and as they moved up the broad avenue, more humans spilled from other temples, swelling the procession to many thousands of men, women, and children, faces gleaming with happiness, marching joyfully to the throne of Tel-Alantir. Many bowed to the gold-flecked Ram before turning to march up the avenue.

Julian and Galad walked behind the procession, halting as more worshippers emerged from temples on either side. Galad's face was a studied mask, but open disquiet showed on the face of Julian, the Apprentice. The Ram's eyes remained filled with joy as it marched toward the throne of its Master.

Before them in the distance, no more than a thousand paces away, the throng bowed before the throne of Tel-Alantir, and departed, half passing to his left and half to his right. Tel-Alantir sat upon his massive marble throne, wreathed in incense. The huge arms of Tel-Alantir extended from a white cloak. His arms were like those of a giant man, but his head was ram-shaped, enormous, with ram-horns curling down either side of his massive head. And Tel-Alantir, seated, was more than three times the height of a man. He looked out over the multitude, eyes distant, beatific. Yet his eyes narrowed, focusing on Julian and Galad as they followed his servant to the throne.

The last column of worshippers reached the throne and passed to the right and left of Tel-Alantir. Julian and Galad halted. They could see now that the Priests of Tel-Alantir knelt on either side of their Lord. With a shock, Julian recognized Houma and Cronar — in Priest's garb, kneeling beside the others. Chanting sounds faded, and silence slipped back over the broad avenue, and the temples, and the throne, where Tel-Alantir sat in the sunlight, splendid and powerful.

The gold-flecked Ram approached the throne, kneeling before the feet of Tel-Alantir.

"Welcome, most beautiful of my servants." The voice of the God-being was clear, powerful, and remote. "Well done. As always, well done." The hand of Tel-Alantir touched the Ram, but his eyes focused on Julian and Galad. "I seldom interfere in matters outside of my domain. Yet I have learned of your journey, that you travel openly over Alantéa, seeking to bring the Truce down upon your enemies — you who violate the spirit of the Truce, serving the Departed. What have you to say for yourselves?"

"Lord, the Truce has come to an end," Julian said in a soft voice. "Three of the greatest of the Ancient Adversaries have emerged and claimed dominion over Earth."

Tel-Alantir turned to Houma and Cronar. "This is not as you described. What of this claim of 'dominion'?"

"He lies, Benevolent One," Houma said. "This League, these Servants of the Maker broke the Truce long ago, pushing the Mid-World from their borders. Their acts woke the sleeping Demons. But behold! The Demons hold back from Alantéa, wishing peace with the Powers. When the Servants of the Maker put down their standard, the Demons will set aside their ancient allegiance and be one with the Truce of the Mid-World. We of the Three Hands seek to restore the Truce, putting down the League, thus bringing the last of the Ancient Powers into the Truce."

Julian looked at Houma with revulsion — and defiance. "No cunning lies will change the Demon's own words. When Zikar, Prince of Demons, stood unmasked at the very topmost tower of Gravengate, here were his words: `In the greater game, we are masters of the Guardians of the World. And we have birthed the Marids! The Mid-World lies before us, rich and decaying like a rotted garden. The Maker is gone, and we shall rule!' Houma, had you heard those words, then perhaps you would put aside your treachery."

"Those words were never spoken," said Houma. "You lie."

"What of the other, standing with the Apprentice," said Tel-Alantir. "Is he mute, or does he also speak?"

"Not well, Lord," said Galad. "But think back. We of the League have had peace with the Mid-World for an age. Only as the Demon Princes rose has there been strife in the south."

"This service to the Maker is a magnet for trouble," said Tel-Alantir. "If the Truce is not overtly broken, still this service to an ancient, long departed Deity violates the spirit of the Truce. If the Maker wished mastery, why did He depart? I will not hold it against you, but I am not fond of the Maker Servants."

Tel-Alantir paused for a moment, watching as sunlight poured over the white marble of his temples. "There is another, not now in view, who might serve as a witness." Julian struggled not to react. Had Rafir been discovered? Tel-Alantir stretched out his hand — the Tarnished Sword flew from Galad's side and dropped into the huge palm of the Mid-World Power.

"So, weapon of the Mid-World, have you wisdom or knowledge? Who violates the Truce, Sorcerer or Apprentice?" There was a pause, then the blade answered with a keening ring:

"What is this Truce? Master strikes, I smite. I have tasted both good and evil; they are one to me."

Tel-Alantir nodded, and the blade flew back into Galad's sheath. "The blade is sentient, but not wise. Now, Apprentice and Warrior, I must declare against you. Your accusers are tested and trusted, while you are not —"

"Lord," came a clear voice. "Lord, hold your judgment for a day, at least." Tel-Alantir looked astonished — his Ram Servant had spoken out of turn. "Lord, the Apprentice is a truthteller. I make no statement against the guests of your Priests. Yet, it is not impossible that you have been deceived."

The face of Tel-Alantir became stern. "It is not seemly to raise questions after judgment has been given."

The Chief Priest rose, bowing before his God. "Lord, it is wise to rid ourselves of these Maker Servants. For behold! They have begun to corrupt your own Emissary."

"Lord, great master of my being," murmured the Ram, "hold your judgment for a day, and perhaps more will become known to you." Tel-Alantir was silent, frowning in his majesty.

"Take them from me," he said at last. "I will listen to you this once, fairest of counselors. But heed me! Stay far from these Maker Worshippers, lest you be further corrupted!"

Priests rose from either side of Tel-Alantir. Their faces were stern and hard, and they led the visitors away from their master's throne, showing no signs of friendship or hospitality.

They passed down the avenue of temples, turning right, walking between two massive sets of marble pillars. A zone of open grassy space separated the temples from the city of Tel-Alantir. Fountains and broad benches lay across their routes, but they were not permitted to rest or refresh themselves.

They passed into the city of Tel-Alantir, and it was no less fair than the temples: pleasant houses, built of stone, were surrounded by well-tended gardens. Children stood about, watching the travelers with curiosity, and yet not one of them smiled. The Priest led them to a building larger than most; it was surrounded by high walls, with men at arms on guard both within and without.

"This is my own residence," said the High Priest. "Here you will stay, taking care that you disturb nothing." Iron gates creaked open. Julian, Galad, and Sebastian were taken inside and led to a large chamber on the second floor.

"If this is 'justice,' then I'm a Prince of Demons!" Sebastian muttered. Julian motioned for silence and again traced a Pentagram on the floor, insulating them from hearing.

"First is Rafir with us?" No answer came, and Julian continued, "He brushed against me several times, telling me of his presence, so he's with us, somewhere, perhaps near the throne of Tel-Alantir — he has to be so very careful."

"Tel-Alantir calls himself 'friend to man,'" Galad said. "With friends like that, it's better to have an open enemy."

"He did prejudge us," said Julian. "For some reason, he's hostile to the Maker Servants."

"He called it 'justice,'" Sebastian said bitterly. "Tel-Alantir is a Power. With even a minor effort, he could easily have discovered the truth." Julian stood, watching the outer walls from the second-floor windows: the guards' numbers had been doubled, and in the late afternoon sun, they were casting long shadows over green grasses. Priests of Tel-Alantir walked among the guards, faces down, as though lost in contemplation.

"Tel-Alantir is a Power, though not a very secure one," Julian spoke softly. "Look at the guards! Why should he fear us?"

"Those Priests have the Gift," said Sebastian. "Or at least a portion of it."

"Tel-Alantir has shaped the Gift within them, restricting it somehow," Julian said slowly. "I think that they will be forced to act in concert to accomplish anything of significance. In this way, Tel-Alantir maintains his control over them."

"So, we might succeed in breaking away from this prison if we needed to," Galad said, marking the passes of the guard.

"Where would we go?" asked Julian. He took a deep breath. "At least imprisonment in the Temples of Tel-Alantir is preferable to the Dungeons of Un-Maurag. Let's wait for Rafir. What do you say?" Galad, Julian and Sebastian nodded and stepped from the pentagram.

The three of them wandered about the chambers of the Chief Priest, taking care not to disturb the many ornaments and things of beauty that had been accumulated. Every room was immaculate.

"Has Tel-Alantir banished dust from his kingdom?" asked Galad. "That's a spell the Wizards should learn for their dingy fortresses."

Julian smiled. "You will find that many servants with cleaning cloths are responsible."

In the pantry, Galad called out to Sebastian, "What a splendid host! Shelled nuts for you, wine and other delicacies for me! The Priests of Tel-Alantir live well!" Galad had found a cabinet filled with carefully selected foods. He filled a plate, then poured a glass of wine, winking at Julian. "I'd leave coins for payment, but they have a League stamp on them: it would make these fussy Priests most unhappy." Julian joined Galad, somewhat doubtfully, and his plate was smaller.

At nightfall, the guard was changed; if anything, it became heavier, with masses of armed men interspersed with torchbearers. In the evening, temple bells rang out and the streets filled as men, women, and children streamed toward the temples. Hymns and chants echoed in the distance. The Gift brought Julian an image of Houma and Cronar groveling before Tel-Alantir.

Rafir seemed to have disappeared, and so late in the evening, they pulled window curtains to shield them from the many torchlights of the guards, then slept on the Priest's embroidered couches.

· 𝄪 ·

"Julian!" A voice was whispering, loudly, in his ear. *"Julian, wake up!"* Julian covered his ears and struggled to sit up.

"Shh, Rafir," Julian whispered. "I wasn't dead, just asleep." He yawned, opening his eyes. Torchlight from the guards outside gave the curtains an eerie, shifting glow. "If you've got news, we should wake the others." He stretched, as Rafir went first to Sebastian, then to Galad. The Charmed Knight sat up instantly, rising like some great beast of prey. Again, Julian inscribed a pentagram to seal them from Divinations.

"Rafir, it's best if you stay invisible," Julian murmured, "they won't be able to hear us, but they might view us, from afar. What's happened?" The little fox laughed.

"You won't believe what I've learned," the small voice of the fox seemed to come from nowhere. "If you paid me for the value of my information, I'd be able to retire."

"Come on now, Rafir," said Sebastian. "Think of all the times Julian saved your furry hide. What's happening?"

"First, Tel-Alantir is very, very, unhappy with all of you — *and* he's unhappy with his Priests, *and* his Ram Servant, *and* the Sorcerers. When those sour-faced Priests led you away, I stayed with Tel-Alantir and the Sorcerers. The Ram Servant was given a terrible tongue lashing, and he seemed to droop, but in the end, he did speak, bowing his head before Tel-Alantir: 'Lord, great giver, the Power within me is your gift. Let me use it now to seek the truth regarding this matter.' Or something like that. Tel-Alantir agreed, without grace, and the Ram Servant cast his spell — we watched as the image showed Houma pursuing, with the creatures of Un-Maurag, then delivering you to the Dark Lord. At this, the image faded, and the Ram Servant was unable to see further. Houma and Cronar stepped forward, crying that Tel-Alantir was being deceived. They prepared their own Divinations — this I couldn't believe — but they showed you conspiring with the Elf-Lords, leading an attack on the kingdom of Un-Maurag."

"This, the Demon Princes have taught them, the corruption of Divinations," Julian said thoughtfully. "What then?"

"The Ram Servant stood, head bowed before Tel-Alantir. The Priests argued among themselves, most siding with Houma and Cronar. At last, Tel-Alantir spoke in a terrible voice: 'Enough!' If he'd said it any louder, some of his temples would have collapsed. Anyway, here's the heart of it: Tel-Alantir wants no part of you or the Sorcerers. Tomorrow, you are all banished."

"So, perhaps we might avoid the Sorcerers, this one time," Julian said. "Well done, Rafir."

"But that's not all," continued the small, invisible voice. "I learned all that hours ago. Since then, I've found out more about this city: there are really two cities, one clean and sparkling, with all of Tel-Alantir's worshippers. The other one is dark, grim, and underground, where all the people who displease Tel-Alantir are being kept as slaves. I was following your scent — actually, Sebastian's — his monkey smell is the easiest to follow, when I heard voices, coming from underneath the street. They came up from an air passage, a duct, not big enough for a human, but enough for me. Anyway, I went down, and deep underground there are factories and guards, and teams of men, women, children slaving away — some are even linked by chains. And beneath them, there's even a third level — with a river. I could smell sewage and rats, and other strange things I couldn't identify."

"So," Galad spoke after a pause. "Perhaps this is the reason that Tel-Alantir dislikes the Maker Servants — they remain rivals to his own religion, forcing him into the role of tyrant and prisonerkeeper, rather than 'friend to man.' What do you think?"

"That makes sense," Julian said. "We're caught in the middle of a very ugly situation, but we are powerless to change it. We'll be fortunate to escape, unharmed." They moved closer to the curtains, watching the guards pacing through the torchlit grounds. In the distance, moonlight poured over white spires, and the Temples of Tel-Alantir gave no hint of their dark foundations.

"Only Rafir might leave here, unnoticed. I —" He broke off as the Gift sent a bolt of alarm through his system. A force of power was surging throughout the Temples of Tel-Alantir: dark sorcery. Lights began to flash as rumbles of sound reached them.

"The Sorcerers must be insane!" Julian cried. "They are challenging a Mid-World Power in his own domain!" Galad was up, lashing his light chainmail in place. Sebastian stared, his eyes huge.

"How can they...?" he trailed off as a strange inhuman cry rang through the Avenue of Temples.

"No!" Julian turned to Galad. "That was the death cry of his Ram Servant! Where is Tel-Alantir?" He closed his eyes, letting his Gift search for him, seeking as he murmured, "Tel-Alantir, friend to man...Tel-Alantir... just Lord...." He found nothing but a sense of rage — and impotence.

Tel-Alantir was imprisoned, held by Cronar! Houma warred with the servants of Tel-Alantir. Another rumble of sound rolled over Tel-Alantir's kingdom.

Julian and Galad raced down the steps and out into the Priest's gardens. Sebastian and Rafir followed. Guards drew weapons, barring their way.

"Listen to me!" Julian cried. "The Sorcerers bring warfare against Tel-Alantir and his servants! Let us aid them while there is still time!" Guards said nothing, but the Priests stood stiff faced, frozen in horror — Julian saw that they were linked with their brethren, but unable to help.

Suddenly, they cried out, five of them together, a loud cry of pain and loss.

"Now, it *is* too late," Julian said bitterly. "Houma is free to seek us. Will you at least let us depart?" The Priests of Tel-Alantir stood sobbing in the torchlight. Guards prodded Julian and Galad from the gates with the butt-ends of spears. Galad stood back, face grim, his moaning sword only partially drawn.

"Not yet," Julian murmured. "We may yet need the goodwill of Tel-Alantir." They drew back from the gates.

Galad touched the top of the garden wall — there were no spikes on it. "I can be over this in a flash."

Julian measured the wall with his eye. "I can too, though not in a flash — if you will boost Rafir when the time comes." Shouts echoed in the distance. Sebastian flew to the building's roof.

"They're showing the insignia of the Three Hands!" Sebastian called down. "Houma's leading them!" Guards around the outer wall moved toward the intruders. Priests called out invocations to Tel-Alantir. Steel rasped from metal sheaths as weapons were drawn.

Then the men of the Three Hands attacked the guards, hacking and stabbing them, cutting the unwary guards down in seconds.

"Through the gates and find the Apprentice!" came the voice of Houma. "This time I will destroy him myself!" The Priests cried out in rage, frustration, then pain, as their half-magic lashed at Houma and failed.

"Now!" shouted Julian. He leaped for the wall...after a moment of sweaty scrabbling he was up and over. Galad stood beside him.

"Rafir!" called Julian. The fox winked into view.

"Which way?" asked Galad. Shouts came from within, death cries as the last of the Priests went down.

"We must find and free Tel-Alantir!" Julian whispered hoarsely. They ran toward the temples, Sebastian flying before them. In the garden, sorcery shifted; Houma's voice rang out.

"Seek the Apprentice!" Rafir turned: black ravens were fluttering around the city, a few now hovering over Julian — and Sebastian. Three were dropping toward the Familiar.

"Sebastian, watch out!" cried Rafir. Without breaking stride, Julian sent a bolt of force skyward; two ravens fell in smoking ruin. The third clutched Sebastian and the two flying creatures sank, fighting, near the avenue of temples. Julian sped through the avenue, as more ravens gathered overhead, shrieking to summon others. Behind them, men serving the Three Hands raced toward the raven's calls.

Julian reached Sebastian and pulled the little Familiar up. His raven adversary hopped away, but more were gathering. Houma was calling out again. Portals flashed; huge feline creatures emerged, and a pack of enormous jackals sped after them. As Julian and Galad raced toward the throne of Tel-Alantir; the area was obscured by a hazy mist.

"Where is Tel-Alantir?" Galad cried. The Apprentice pushed toward the throne, but his way was blocked by a force-field of magic.

"He is sealed away from me!" Julian cried. "There's no time!" The first of the huge jackal creatures raced into the avenue, snarling. Galad hewed at it, and the Tarnished Sword swept through its bulging skull. Ravens swirled around them. Julian and Galad pulled away from the force-field and turned into the closest temple.

Inside, the congregation stood, faces filled with fear. Only a few hundred remained; others had fled as their God failed them.

"Escape while you can!" Julian cried, racing down the aisles. Huge jackals leaped through the temple doors, snarling.

"Trap them inside!" Houma cried out. Rafir ran beside Julian, panting.

"These temple crypts lead to the other city. Down!" he gasped. The congregation stood frozen in fear as huge beasts stalked down the aisles beside them. Galad leaped from behind a pillar and the Tarnished Sword swept the life from a second predator.

"Here!" Julian cried. "To me!" Julian stood behind the altar, where a broad reinforced door stood padlocked. He placed his staff to the lock, but his opening spell was barred by counter-magic.

Then, the Tarnished Sword swept down, blasting metal fragments to the ground. They closed the door behind them, blocking all light. Julian's staff flashed — a broad tunnel lay before them with hundreds of steps made from poured stone leading down from the doors. They raced below.

At the next level, its door was open. Julian turned, calling out the Blast Spell, and the roof of the tunnel collapsed behind them. Houma called out the Stun Spell, but this time Julian was able to counter it. They raced down, several stairs at a time.

"There are other ways down." panted Rafir. They reached the bottom. The door in front of them was unbarred. They opened it, spilling out into a vast underground arcade, a mirror image of the broad avenue that lay above, but these streets were layered with grey cobblestones. Along the stony streets were many barred steel doorways in the place of white temples. The air was filled with mechanical sounds, as though vast factories lay on either side.

Galad and Julian halted. Within a few hundred paces, more than thirty guards stood frozen, staring in astonishment at the intruders.

"Listen!" Julian called out. "The Sorcerers have turned on Tel-Alantir! If you wish to aid your Master, seek him above!" Pale lamplight flickered over uncertain faces. Three of the nearest guards drew swords. Galad struck their weapons from them; bits of molten metal sprayed across the underground avenue. One drew a dagger, but Galad smashed it from his hand.

"These stupid lackeys are looking to die!" Galad cried. Other guards began to back away. "Good. If you want to live, find a place to hide — the ones coming after us are not so gentle!"

Suddenly, Julian realized that the mechanical sounds had ceased. He turned to the wall where grey stone alternated with steel bars, for now, there were faces, human faces pressed against the steel. "What are these, slaves of Tel-Alantir?" he asked. The guards were silent. Julian moved closer to the cells. "Why are you here?" A torrent of voices called out, but an old woman finally calmed them then spoke.

"All here have angered the Priests of Tel-Alantir. A few are thieves or spies, but most deny Tel-Alantir, and serve the Maker, the First Fashioner."

"Stand away," called Galad, raising the Tarnished Sword.

"Is it wise to anger Tel-Alantir?" Julian asked.

"To the dung heaps with these feeble, confused, would-be Gods!" cried Galad. "We are Servants of the Maker!" The Tarnished Sword swept down, leaving the bars of the prison factory in ruins.

From down the broad arcade came the cries of men — mingled with the snarls of huge jackals.

"They're through," Julian said, pulling back from the prison. They sped away, all the time moving from the north end, where Tel-Alantir sat on his throne, imprisoned by Sorcerers. As they ran, Galad slashed down more of the prison doors. Men began to emerge, cautiously, into the underground boulevard.

"No time for that!" Julian pulled Galad away. Behind, the jackal pack growled.

Houma's voice bellowed, "Forget the guards! Seek the Apprentice!" They raced on. Julian looked back: the jackal pack had cleared the freed prisoners and was now closing the gap.

"Rafir!" The fox winked into view. "There must be a slaughterhouse nearby, a place where meat is carved — find it!"

"We passed one," panted the fox. "But there's a rotten smell up in front of us — dead meat!" They raced on until Rafir halted in front of a set of iron bars.

"Just a small opening," Julian said. Galad swung a partial stroke; metal flashed. It was still hot to the touch as they squeezed through.

"Are you hungry?" asked Galad. "Is that why we're here?" Julian turned to a group of men who stood dazed, butcher knives in hand. He seized the closest.

"Where do you dispose of the carcasses, the spoiled or wasted parts?" Dazed, the man led them to a round hole: blood trailed down its sides. Flies buzzed in and out of the darkness. Julian's staff flashed. Beneath them, thirty feet down, a river ran, foul smelling and vile looking.

"I'll go first," Julian muttered.

"What?!?" Galad muttered, staring at the trail of blood and filth.

"Down to the third level!" Julian cried, and he slipped into the hole, vanishing. Sounds came from the prison doors: their pursuers had reached them. Galad, Rafir, and Sebastian slid down the blood-slick waste-hole and were gone.

· Ж ·

Below, the river's water was cold, and vile with sewage. Yet its current was powerful, surging south. Julian's staff flashed: the underground river was fifty paces wide, but on its west side, a catwalk had been built. Julian swam a few hard strokes, then pulled himself up onto the walkway, while Sebastian flew to his side. Rafir clambered up a little further downstream, gasping from the stench. Galad emerged and stood on the walkway, looking down in disgust at the tide of urine, feces, dead animal parts and other waste that swirled and foamed through the river's dark waters. In the background, there were squealing sounds as rats fled into the ducts that lay on either side of the tunnel.

"Do you have any idea what you're doing?" asked Galad.

Julian had to laugh. "It's clumsy and dirty, but for the first time, I think I know what to do: we'll go north and try to come up *under* Cronar's blocking spell."

"And if that doesn't work?" asked Galad. Julian shrugged and began to jog north. On either side of the underground river, masses of ducts were dripping waste into the underground river. The stench seemed incredible to Rafir, but there were other smells, ones he couldn't identify. And there were slithering sounds, as larger sewer dwellers began to stir. From behind them came a series of splashes.

"The hunting packs!" Julian hissed, and broke into a run, his staff lighting the way. They raced, speeding toward the throne of Tel-Alantir. But from behind them came a wailing noise of such incredible agony, that they stopped and turned. Light from Julian's staff reached toward the sound — just in time to see a pair of enormous jaws close over a large jackal. Others in the pack whined and cringed. Behind the cowering beasts, another light flashed: Houma had come.

They turned to flee, but Galad could not move: a large and slimy tentacle had lifted from the water, wrapping itself around his ankle. His sword flashed, severing it. They raced away as tentacles swirled and thrashed in the waters behind them.

As they sped through the river turned into a sewer by Tel-Alantir, all its dwellers stirred — and attacked the pursuing Sorcerer and his pack of jackals. Behind them curses alternated with blasts of power. Despite the stench and danger, Galad was forced to laugh.

But up ahead, their way was barred: huge webs hung from the water's edge up to the cavern ceiling; dark shapes lurked in the web's corners. Galad pushed ahead of Julian, slashing webs that were as thick as ropes. Bolts of force leaped from Julian's staff, and creatures from the webs dropped heavily into dark waters. Masses of finned shark-like creatures surged toward their dark bodies as the web spinners thrashed and died. Behind them came more blasts and curses, as Houma struggled with the sewer dwellers.

Julian slowed. "Tel-Alantir is above us," he said in a low voice. They edged further down the walkway. Distant, pale light gleamed from an opening in the cavern's roof. Julian whispered his spell, shielding it from Houma. His hands flashed, then he held a slender, dark cord.

"Tie this above," he whispered to Sebastian. "Steel bars are good." The little Familiar was up quickly, gasping with the effort. Sounds were coming closer — the Sorcerer was enraged, but all the sewer dwellers were surging toward him.

Suddenly, Julian's dark cord swung down. Galad hesitated.

"Now!" hissed Julian, and Galad was up, Rafir clutching his shoulders. Houma was only a few hundred paces away. Yet the waters were seething, with tentacles slithering over the walkway. Houma cried out in frustration. The black cord dangled; Julian seized it and Galad pulled him up.

They stood once again on the second level. Guards were backing away in surprise — and from the stench of the intruders.

"Stairs? Where are they?" Galad advanced on the guards, with the Tarnished Sword moaning. Guards backed away but said nothing — although their eyes flickered to the walls where a door stood outlined. Below, the voice of Houma could be heard, summoning more aid. Again, they ran, through the doors and up a long stairway.

Out on the broad avenue, the Temples of Tel-Alantir still glistened in the moonlight, but dawn was showing in the east. On his throne, Tel-Alantir sat slumped, head sagging, eyes closed, wrapped in the Sorcerer's enchantments. The dead bodies of his servants and acolytes lay all around him, twisted, blasted, dead. Cronar stood before the throne of Tel-Alantir, chanting, face twisted with his effort to control Tel-Alantir. Even in the moonlight, Julian could see that beads of sweat were dripping down the Sorcerer's forehead.

"Tel-Alantir!" cried Julian. "Awake, Master of this land!" He sent a bolt of force speeding toward Cronar, then leaped away. Tel-Alantir shifted on his throne. Cronar called out a new spell.

"Awake, Tel-Alantir!" Julian called, dodging, edging closer to the throne. Houma emerged from the stairway, eyes searching for the Apprentice. Tel-Alantir stirred.

Over their heads, far in the sky, a projection of Tel-Alantir appeared, raging like an angry God of Gods. "In my own lands!" cried the image. "Deceived in my own lands! Held while my servants perished, calling upon me. No torment is great enough for these evildoers!" Bolts of lightning crashed down, leaping toward the Sorcerers. On his throne, Tel-Alantir began to shift, to waken.

"I can no longer hold him!" Cronar cried, his twisted face dampened with sweat. Columns of flame whirled, pouring from the sky, seeking the Sorcerers. Houma was chanting, but now he broke off his spell.

"Curse the Apprentice forever!" he cried. "Let's be gone."

Portals flared; the Sorcerers sped through, just as Tel-Alantir woke — to rage. He stood, Godlike, lightning surging all around him. Julian pulled the others from the temple area.

"It's best to be far from him in the hour of his wrath," he whispered, backing away. They passed into the city and walked quietly, filled with fatigue, back to the mansion of the Chief Priest, seeking their horses and goods. The sun was coming up, clear and bright.

By the plaza in front of the temple, Tel-Alantir raged and stormed. Portals flashed and faded as he sought the Sorcerers. Humans scurried into deep shelters as powerful energies surged toward their God. After a time, the area around the temples grew silent.

They bathed and changed clothes, leaving their sewer-stained garments in the courtyard. As he dressed, Julian suddenly straightened, as though hearing a distant voice.

"Tel-Alantir wishes to speak with us," Julian said softly, "prior to our departure. We are not the objects of his anger — though we will not be permitted to leave without speaking to him." Galad shook his head in disapproval but said nothing. Outside, men were gathering up the slain, hauling them in carts to the Temples of Tel-Alantir. They ate a brief meal, gathered up their possessions, and left. All of the dead Priest's ornaments were left undisturbed, though he was dead and would never again take pleasure in them.

Outside, the sun was shining over the marble Temples of Tel-Alantir, but a sense of gloom and depression lay over the land. As Julian and Galad rode to the Avenue of Temples, their faces became carefully neutral and unemotional masks. Sebastian and Rafir were subdued, quiet. As they neared the temples, they found that all the pink and red and blue blossoms on the trees had blackened, turned to ash by the wrath of Tel-Alantir.

Tel-Alantir, Mid-World Power and God by his own devices, sat on his marble throne, alone. A great funeral pyre lay before him, with all his dead servants interspersed between many cords of dried wood. At the very top, his Ram Servant and Adept lay glistening white and gold in the sunlight.

They bowed to Tel-Alantir in his moment of sorrow.

"These Sorcerers have brought me much sorrow." Tel-Alantir spoke in even, measured tones. "I have sought them, yet they are beyond my reach. Much grief has your visit occasioned, yet you are not at fault, for the Sorcerers have used me as a weapon against you. I cannot strike at this alliance of Adversaries for you, but if I can aid you, I will do so. Speak."

"Lord, what of the Mid-World of the Truce?" asked Julian. "I have been instructed to seek the Truce Terms that govern the Mid-World. If you can tell me of these, I will return to the League and aid the struggle against the Sorcerers and their masters the Demon Princes."

"It is one of the Truce Terms that only the Great Gods may know all of them, and those mighty beings would never tell mortals of those Terms. Yet I will counsel you to go on as before. Take the Straight Path to the Vale of Whispers. If you arrive by Portal or magic steed, the City of the Truce will be barred to you. Go on as you have before."

The Power's great blue and white eyes peered down, focusing on Julian as though peering into the innermost soul of the Apprentice. "There is a brightness within you, Apprentice with an Adept's Gift, almost as though the Maker had touched you, as if He still cast webstrands of power over the Gardens of Alantéa. Thus, when I bid you go forward, I must also share with you my newfound knowledge of your fate: defeat lies before you, a defeat as complete and ruinous as any the Greatest Gods with all their combined powers might ever have devised.

"Defeat, but not death, Apprentice and sentient blade wielder. And beyond defeat, in the aftermath of failure, does your story then continue? I cannot say, for the Gods do not weave such tales. Instead, they devise stories of the invincible might of their chosen servants, and the grievous destruction of any opposing Their will. But your tale has been crafted by none of the Greater Gods, and you two must go forward alone against the Sorcerers and the Marids. Little power have I against these New Adversaries, yet is there further aid I might offer? I have provided you with replacements for your steeds, and provisions for your journey forward. Do you need more tools or weapons?"

Julian shook his head, murmuring thanks, but Galad raised his voice, speaking softly, "Lord, it might ease our hearts if our brethren among you were treated less harshly; and truly, these prison factories lessen your glory."

"I will free the Servants of the Maker," said Tel-Alantir. "They will live apart from my people, but not enslaved. I would weapon them and send them south to aid your peoples in their struggle if your League was not doomed. For, as I sought the Sorcerers, I found images of Marids ravaging your League. Indeed, when your alliance fails, I will shelter many of your people here, protecting them as best I can." Julian and Galad bowed and were silent.

Tel-Alantir put out his hand and flames engulfed the funeral pyre. Sorrow surged across the face of Tel-Alantir. Julian stepped forward, touching the Power's white cloak before speaking.

"Lord, we too now mourn the passing of your Adept and Ram Servant. He was a powerful wielder of magic, filled with a calm justice. We join you in your grief."

Unbidden tears, tiny as dewdrops, surged down the great ram face of Tel-Alantir.

Chapter Six

The Seraph's Death Sting

SEBASTIAN CRIED OUT IN fear as the lancers rode down upon Galad. With the last of the swordsmen on his left cut down, Galad turned to face the charge. The Tarnished Sword moaned in anticipation, but there were too many, and it was too late to flee. From behind Galad came a snarl of frustration, then Julian blasted the lancers, sending horses and riders spilling downward to the earth with shrieking and groaning sounds filling the valley.

"Houma will know where we are now," Galad said quickly. "Where next?"

"West again, then south," Julian said grimly. He mounted again, staring into the distance. "Toward Erivan Forest and always farther from our goal: Houma and all his wretched servants are herding us away from the Vale of Whispers. Let the Maker deal with these evildoers at the End of Time. Merlin, Merlin, where are you now?"

· X ·

Pale moonlight rippled slowly over the pond's shiny surface and the water seemed to grow even more still as shadowy forms stalked one another around its edges. Gradually, the pond's croaking voices became still as the pond dwellers fell into a deathwatch.

"See, there are Vorrs," whispered Rafir, "but they're not following us, they're following Houma's scouts." From the pond's edge, there came swift thrashing sounds then a gurgling murmur followed by silence.

"They have become allies," Julian said, also whispering. "The Vorr pack that we freed is silencing Houma's outermost rangers. We might have one night's rest. Still, so many are looking for us, from so many directions and the use of even weak magic is a beacon for Houma. We should —"

From behind them, many voices burst into cries of triumph. Torches flared as the trackers had once more found Julian and Galad. Furtive shadows fled from the pond's edge.

"Again!" Julian muttered. Galad shook himself awake, throwing packs over horses that struggled to stand. Julian called out the spell words and the torchlights of their foes were blown dead. Beacons of werelight illuminated their paths as they rode south on weary, stumbling horses, moving always farther from their goal.

· X ·

Merlin stared down at his great gaming board, watching as unformed hazy pieces drifted aimlessly back and forth. So many new forces had recently come into being that the Mid-World intelligences that powered The Game of the Masters *were no longer able to define or structure them.* The Game *had collapsed and his own role as Master had evaporated. At this point, he could no longer move himself as even as a minor Power.*

Merlin turned from the long, now useless board, and made his way up a makeshift plank and stoneshard staircase. Most of Sea's Edge had been destroyed by forces serving the Demon Princes, but The Game of the Masters had protected itself by shielding a portion of its chamber. Now, Merlin could stand on a hillock of rubble and stare into the overcast haze and the endless distances that obscured the four corners of the earth.

He stared south: he could sense but not see the warships and provision galleons supporting the Sorcerers' land forces.

And west: where within the underwater Isle of the Demons, the Marids were being nurtured, beings that he might never be able to master.

As he turned east, he could feel the power of their foes as it lashed at the Wizards and their League: Alcman and Cronar and Eudox were struggling mightily to destroy his fellow Wizards and overrun their fortresses.

Then north, north where his greatest anguish lay — toward Julian, his servant, his almost foster son, Julian the brave and steadfast, who was being beaten back, forced always farther from his goal. Though powerfully supported by Galad and the Tarnished Sword, Julian faced both the mighty Houma and more than two thousand of the Sorcerers' mercenaries, supported by Vorrs and Uraks, evil beings created by Dark Lords. Julian and Galad were no match for them.

Now was the time he had planned for his own power to be put into play, whereby he, Merlin, would emerge by Portal Passage and hurl Houma from Julian's path. But the Gods had woven Portal bars, traps, and snares around both Wizards and Sorcerers so that all but a few of the Portal Passages were closed to mortal magic wielders. At least Houma's reach was also lessened, and Julian would not be struck down suddenly by the mighty Sorcerer.

Merlin closed his eyes, shifting his Farsight from the geography of Alantéa and into the Mid-World. There, the Gods ruled amidst their own miracle work, surrounded by thousands upon thousands of servants and slaves. And yet there were other forces in the Mid-World, of both minor and intermediate strength, and these might have an impact, if only they could somehow be activated.

Merlin opened his eyes, staring into the haze that drifted over Sea's Edge. He no longer had the power to shift distant pieces into play. Other forces would have to move them: the distant hand of the Maker, or the Powers of the Mid-World, or the Fates, or Destiny, or even the malice of their foes.

· ☩ ·

The Mistress of Illusions sat in her place of power, watching as images flowed from her outstretched palms: sky-blue, earth-brown, and fire-red mixing with wine-dark water, all forming into patterns of great beauty, combining, then separating, shifting slowly, then moving with sudden flurries of motion. A dreamlike half-smile was fixed on her face, as though the images formed part of some narcotic enchantment. Hour after hour the images flowed, without once repeating a single pattern.

In the early afternoon, sounds of stringed instruments came drifting into her chamber and interrupted her reverie, forcing her to focus. Then, images slowed and began to reform; the half-smile faded from the face of the Mistress of Illusions as she transformed amorphous images into true patterns.

Images settled, and she regarded the siege at Stone Mountain, where Alcman and many thousands brought war and ruin to the fortress of Thorian. Masses of ships swarmed along the shoreline, with catapults hurling rocks against fortress walls. On the western side of the fortress, Alcman had caused gigantic earthworks to be built, and from these, the Sorcerer's tiers assailed Stone Mountain with a hailstorm of arrows and poison darts.

From the air, masses of winged reptiles circled; men were mounted on them, hurling blasting powder down on the fortress. The Mistress of Illusions shook her head: although Thorian fought powerfully, he seemed doomed. Always, Alcman was ready with yet another sorcerous attack, and more men pledged to the Three Hands marched or sailed each day to the twin sieges of Stone Mountain and Gravengate.

Her hands clenched and reopened. Again, her images shifted and reformed anew, showing the siege of Gravengate, where Cronar and Eudox assailed the fortress of Balardi. As at Stone Mountain, there were earthworks formed against the walls, with steady pressure exerted both from the south and the east...the image shifted lower, sinking beneath the walls of the fortress...masses of burrowing creatures scuttled forward, many-legged like gigantic insects, and men were mounted on them, wearing the emblem of the Three Hands. A maze of tunnels had been built, around and beneath the walls of Gravengate. Men of the League were moving with fire and steel against the burrowers and their riders: a harrowing, subterranean warfare was spreading beneath the fortress, and many men would never again see the light of day.

The image shifted again, showing Balardi leaning on his staff, sagging in weariness. The Wizard's eyes were wild, bloodshot, and his beard was matted, disheveled, greyer than gold. Then the Wizard perceived the intrusion and broke the Divination image, waving his staff in a flash of irritation.

Again, her images shifted, reformed, and the Mistress of Illusions followed the quest of the Apprentice, how he was drawn deeper into the Mid-World, struggling first in the Dungeons of Un-Maurag, then fleeing through the Temples of Tel-Alantir. Now, Houma was blocking his way with a mass of nearly three thousand men, forcing Julian away from the north, herding him west toward Erivan Forest.

Always, Apprentice and Weapon's Master fought against Houma's sub-tiers, then withdrew and fought again. The Mistress of Illusions shook her head: the Apprentice would never reach his goal. Though the Wizards and their League were doomed, anyway.

Her hands clenched, and once more images shifted and changed, now showing her own domain. Kalanin and Géla were racing through the lake, sunlight sparkling on their backs. It seemed childish — all her men had been like half grown younglings, never really prepared for adulthood. Yet this one was much more intelligent, more powerful. Also, he was haunted: some very strange, otherworldly being or creature still pursued him.

It was good that she was able to block most of that creature's sorcerous pursuit. She leaned back, letting the shifting images of many colors surge once again from her open palms. Slowly, the dreaming, partial smile slipped once more over her enchanted features, as the Mistress of Illusion slipped more deeply into her own empire of dreams.

· ⋊ ·

Fish leaped up into falling water, flopping in the air, splashing back, leaping repeatedly until they cleared the waterfall and reached the swiftly moving upper streams. Sunlight shone through the haze, glistening as it reflected from flopping fish scales. Kalanin lay back, letting a soft, drowsy warmth settle over him. If his body was still tired, it was a good fatigue, the hardening of muscle, the stretching of sinew. Tomorrow, he would step up the pace, pushing Géla to a greater effort: to the far side of the lake and back, she winning easily at first, sliding through the waters effortlessly while he swarmed and splashed. But lately Géla had gasped too, at the end of the race, and every now and again, she looked at him sideways, as though measuring his strength.

It was good to heal in the sunlight, white scars turning brown, his lungs strengthening, while his body slowly rebuilt itself. And some of his bitterness had faded: Merlin, Balardi and the League seemed distant, remote. He had played his part; now the new life was better — much better, except for sleep.

In daylight, he felt the shielding enchantments of the Mistress of Illusions, but nighttime and sleep — sleep was clouded by dreams, disturbed and troubling night visions.

Kalanin forced his eyes open and sat up. At a discreet distance, a company of guards stood, lightly mailed, armed with spear and dagger. Géla sat, speaking with their captain; both women had long, dark hair, though Géla's was wet, drying in the sunlight. Other guards stifled yawns, bored, or wilted by the sun's heat. He sat back watching the lake's surface.

Torrents of water dropped from waterfalls into the lake's depths, but the water of the lake remained clear and still, sliding slowly to outflow streams. Down on the lake's bottom, the tendrils of long plants waved in cool waters, leaning upward to the vague, diffuse light that drifted slowly down from the lake's surface.

At the water's edge, all was untroubled; a dozing nap was his for the choosing. Kalanin pulled a fold of cloth over his face, and lay in broad sunlight, listening as falling streams poured into deep waters. Bird sounds piped in the distance — nectar drinkers and seed eaters, but none that fed on grubs and flies: the Mistress of Illusions had banished many insects from her domain, leading to a strange, brooding quiet, and in that silence, he turned and slept.

Kalanin's dream visions were clearer now, as though sleep during daytime brought greater illumination, images that were much crisper. He lay, as before, face turned up into the darkness, and over his chest was a vast stifling weight, like a slab of cool marble. His face was exposed to the air, but breathing was a gasping, hard struggle. Yet now, for the first time, he had full awareness of his dream, the same dream that had haunted and pursued him since his last battle.

He shifted his hands. With an enormous effort, he brought his arms around so that his palms lay on either side of his chest, facing upwards. He pushed up against the slab; it eased only a little, but he was able to breathe more easily. He stared up into the gloomy darkness; there was a sense of height, but nothing could actually be seen.

The slab sank back, crushing the air from his chest. Again, he pushed the slab from his body...this time he slid out from under it, only a fraction of an inch with each effort, snakelike, expanding out, drawing the rest of his body behind him. Again, and again, with enormous effort, he slipped inch by bitter inch out from the slab.

Now, his chest was free, and he lay in the cool darkness, breathing stale air. From habit, he wiped his forehead, but not even a trace of dampness could be found. Of course not! He was locked in some grim night vision, the most real and vivid of dreams, but still, nothing that was real. He tried to forget the slab's weight, closing his eyes, and willing himself back to the lakefront.

The sun was beating down on his body, while a few feet from him, cool waters lipped over beds of lake weed.... He was not released; it was still cool and dark, with a crushing weight remaining on his legs. He resumed his struggles, inching slowly from the weight and pain.

At last, he stood upright, staring into the darkness, trying to penetrate the gloom. The air was stale, as though it had moved little in thousands of years.

Was he dead? This seemed more real than any dream! Had he slipped into the Long Sleep, brought down by some hidden injury? If so, it was not the peaceful interval he had imagined — but still, it was better to be free from the slab.

From a distance came the faintest sound, as though a whisper echoed from the deepest caverns of the world. He stepped toward the sound, one hand extended, the other reaching for his sword hilt, but he had neither sword nor scabbard, and he was dressed only in a coarse, ragged smock, as though his body had been waiting for bored gravediggers to discover his corpse and bury him. Again, whispering sounds reached out to him, faint, distant, and he shuffled slowly toward those distant whispers, both hands extended.

He stumbled at the base of a stone staircase. Perhaps it was his imagination, but above, the darkness seemed to lessen, yielding to a gloomy, partial light. He climbed, step by careful step, then more quickly as the light grew stronger. At the top of the stairs, he turned through one passageway then another, walking carefully toward the whispering sounds.

He entered an immense building, larger than any structure seen or imagined — in width, it was only a few thousand paces across, but in length, half a league, or more. Distant, diffuse lights gave only a dim hint of its height; massive pillars suggested the great weight of a marble roof at the building's peak.

Whispers were growing louder now, and there were flurries of motion as shadows passed through the halflight. Though nothing seemed able to shift the stagnant air masses. In the Maker's Name, what was he doing in such a place? Was death stranger than life, or was he still alive? Best to go back downstairs and think matters through. He turned....

A force reached out then, pulling him away from the staircase. He gasped and set his teeth, leaning from the compulsion, but there was nothing to grip, and he was drawn, slowly, into the center of the vast building.

Shadows were slipping toward him, watching his struggle with a vague, distant curiosity. Within each shadow was a form he had been taught to recognize: Demon or Seraph, Dragon or Spirit Lord.

Kalanin understood, then, that he stood in a vast Cathedral of Sorrows, where the drifting shades of the dead Ancient Powers slipped through dim half-light.

"I have no place here!" he cried out, but his voice came as a whisper, hardly breaking the stillness. And no echo came. "If I must, I will yield to the Long Sleep, but take me from this place!" Again, his voice was a whisper, and the pull on his body was greater now. "If you served the Maker once, then help me now!" Only the word "Maker" echoed, and all the drifting shadows halted, expectantly, as though awaiting a call to judgment.

The pull came, harder. Shadows resumed their endless journeys. "In the Maker's Name, I call for aid!" This time the shadowy forms drifted on, paying no attention to Kalanin.

He clenched his teeth grimly and staggered toward the forces that were controlling his body, eyes searching for weapons, things to hurl or smash with. The floor and massive pillars were clear of stones and battle standards — they were even free of dust. Snarling and struggling, he was dragged forward into a great shadowy shape...the shade of a Lord of Dragons, but its eyes were distant, completely without menace...he put out his hands, but they met no substance, only a deep chill, as he passed through the ghost of the dead immortal.

Kalanin reached the far side of the building. A tall doorway gaped wide open for him, like a mouth. He clutched at the stone on either side, spreading his legs so that each foot rested on the side of the Portal. He turned back to the Cathedral of Sorrows, ready to hurl prayers, curses at the dead, shuffling, whispering immortals. Yet they were powerless — and something at this door had power over him.

He lost his hold and was drawn through the doorway. The force pulled him, staggering, down a short flight of stairs. Whispering noises grew faint and were replaced by the sounds of running water. To his left, a ghostly, glowing white light loomed. He was drawn toward it through another passageway. Sounds of running water became louder, and all the whispers were silenced.

One more doorway loomed in front of him, and he was pulled into a wide chamber. On the chamber's floor stood a wide cistern with a broad rim, one that spilled water over its sides, and light, a ghostly phosphorescent light, flowed from the water's surface. Behind the cistern, a Seraph sat in a chair hewn from stone, with white lights from glowing waters rippling over the face of the dead immortal.

Words, never spoken, formed in Kalinin's mouth: **What is that dead thing and what am I doing here?**

As if in answer to Kalanin's unspoken question, blood, with golden hues, thick as sap, still seeped from the Seraph's wound: in front of him sat the being he had slain in front of Gravengate. Yet it was unlike the other Shades, for power and purpose and malice flowed from its glowing form.

The force dragging him finally released his body, and he stood, weaponless and fearful in front of the Ruined Seraph. Ghostly lights bathed both mortal and immortal shades in pale, glowing rays.

"I summoned your sentient sword also," said the Seraph. Its voice was soft, muted, though stronger than a whisper. "It would not heed me, yet you were compelled to come, mortal. Do you understand why?" Kalanin shook his head numbly. Golden blood seeped down the Seraph's white garments, but its face smiled with triumph. "I am a Seraph, mortal, one of the Firsts. Seraph slayers were not free from us, until they themselves passed into the shadows, or were transformed. Though you followed the Servants, and I the Adversaries, there was power in me to haunt you all your days, rising with you in the morning, settling about you in your evening, and haunting you at night.

"And yet, you were slipping from me; all the weights and chains and hidden miseries were lifting. Can you tell me why, mortal, why I should be denied?" Kalanin shook his head, clearing his throat. When he spoke, his own voice was soft, muted, like that of the Seraph, barely heard above the sounds of water spilling from the cistern.

"Why would you seek to torment me? At the last, you called upon the Maker to forgive you. How will He judge what you now do?"

"It was too late for me then; it is even later now," said the Seraph dreamily, half mocking. Then its face turned thoughtful. "I wonder why the Tarnished Sword would not come; it was called, and so it should have come."

"Hear me," said Kalanin, struggling with his own fear and anger. "You are telling me that the Maker gave the Firsts strength to bring remorse to their foes, whenever a First was slain. It might be justice for Demon or Dragon or

Creature of the Darkness to be so pursued, yet I am only a mortal. Is this not a misuse of your powers?"

The Ruined Seraph laughed. "All of the other devices of the Maker have been corrupted, so why should I not pervert this last gift?" The Seraph laughed again, and water quivered in the cistern in front of him. "And see how wonderfully corrupt the Seraph Sting has become: as my hold over you slipped away, I did not surrender and join the Immortals in the Temple of Waiting. No! I brought your soul here, the first mortal spirit to gather at our resting place.

"And then also, I sought the child of my Brothers in Darkness, to prevent you from slipping into your Long Sleep." The Seraph's eyes glinted with malice. "Lastly, I have fashioned a hiding place for myself, far beneath the Temple of Waiting. The Maker may search; but He will never find me."

Kalanin stared at the Seraph in horror: here was a being that had once been holy — and was now no more than an insane ghost. He pulled his eyes from the Seraph to stare into the glistening water. Light came from within the water, or from images within the water — those images showed mounds of decaying matter, shining on the seabed. Beside the glowing mounds was some being — huge, with boar's tusks, and its half-dreaming eyes were locked on Kalanin's. His mind called out: Flee this Demon Spawned Monster.

"Yes, he is unnamed, not fully grown, but behold my foster child in Darkness, the greatest of the Marids." The Seraph laughed its soft, insane laugh. Kalanin's eyes remained fixed in horror on the Marid's face.

"Enough," said the Seraph. "Let me consider other matters. Take the mortal."

Tendrils of vegetation lifted from the waters beside the Marid, up through the cistern, reaching into the chamber to clutch at Kalanin. He recoiled in terror as tendrils of dead matter closed about him. The Seraph laughed. Kalanin cried aloud.

And then he woke.

He stood on his feet, beside the lake, bright sunlight shining down on him. His heart pounded as though it would burst from his chest. He looked for reassurance from the faces of the guards; they stared back at him with expressions of stunned horror. Had he been changed, transformed into some monstrosity?

He glanced down at his body: hundreds of green tendrils had wrapped around his legs and upper body. With a cry of fear and rage, he tore one arm through the leafy bindings. But hundreds more green and brown tendrils reached for him.

Half turning, he saw a vision of horror beyond any nightmare: the lake bottom was reaching for him. Tens of thousands of green leafy tendrils were gathering around his human form. Again, he cried aloud, lurching, falling, writhing. He slid into shallow waters.

Now Géla was at his side, slashing. Other guards were leaping into the lake to fight the green horror. But it was too late. Water slipped over his face. He fought, bursting a few strands, but it was too late. Desperate arms pulled him to the surface. He gulped one breath, then was pulled back under. It was too late. There came a great roaring sound, both within and beyond his hearing. Somehow, it had always been too late.

· 𝕏 ·

Hands were pumping his arms, again and again, as though he had become a set of feeble, floppy bellows. Liquid ran from his mouth, slipping downhill, away from his face. He opened his eyes, and they twitched in horror: it was nighttime, but in the moonlight, he saw that he lay flopped like a dead thing on a green bed of damp vegetation. He was lying on the lake's bottom, with all the lake's water drained away from it. The waterfall feeding the lake had also been stopped, with only a thin stream still spattering down over dying water weeds.

His arms were raised again, and more water flowed from his lips. He coughed, head sagging back onto green lake weed.

"Enough now, Nesse, Fione, we have him, he won't slip away." It was Géla's voice, just a few feet away. "What now, Grandmother?"

"Hush, child," said the Mistress of Illusions. "Send for a litter, then we'll talk a little apart from here. He's under my protection now, and so the danger's over." Footsteps squished away from him, and he was left lying on a bed of lake kelp.

His eyes peered out again: he lay on the lakebed, facing downward to what was left of the lake: green, slimy dead plants. All the leaping, stabbing guards had kept him alive for only a few minutes, but in those moments, the Mistress of Illusions had destroyed the outflow side of the lake. Then, of course, there had been more hacking and slashing at green nightmare vegetation, more sorcery, fire magic, and terror, as he lay bound, lungs filling with fluid. He coughed again. Sounds of conversation could be heard, just at the edge of his hearing.

"A treaty! Accompanied by apologies!" The Mistress of Illusions was angry, but her voice was restrained, and the low voice responding to her was muted, incomprehensible. "That is a rash course, Granddaughter. It galls me, but we have little choice in this matter." Her voice grew more calm, softer, then faded from hearing.

Kalanin rolled, lurching to his feet. It was time to rise, time to leave. At least with the Wizards, he could die a warrior's death. He coughed again, staggering. The conversation on the upper shore broke off. He pushed himself up the hill, staring from side to side. Under the drifting moonlight, the lakebed lay exposed, ugly in its ruin. Beneath all the green and brown masses of dying water weeds, fish, and tadpoles still writhed and squirmed, still struggling to live.

"You have a powerful constitution, my beloved," the Mistress of Illusions called down to him. "Come, and stand at my side, once again." Kalanin felt the lure, the attraction in her voice, and he stood, hesitating — yet there was no exit from this land, except through the Mistress of Illusions. He climbed the bank, slowly, guardedly.

The Mistress of Illusions measured his mood with a glance.

"So," she murmured. "Now, it's 'where is my shield, where is my sword?' My beloved, the Truce is shaken, the Ancient Wars may well be renewed. We are small creatures in a great *Web of Fate*. If we do not move too vigorously, the Lurker in the Shadows may ignore us, and move to consume larger prey."

Kalanin nodded. With all the stress of battle magic, her beauty had not diminished or wavered. "You have the Gift, my Lady — test the matter by Divination if you wish. I cannot remain here. I will go to Stone Mountain, or Gravengate, wherever I am needed."

Her eyes narrowed. "Each of those is closed off, besieged."

"Gravengate was closed off before. There will be a task for me, even in my old role as a messenger." She embraced him with her soft arms, though the weeds from the lake had left a green film over his body.

"Have I offered you so little, that you would turn so quickly from me? I —" The Mistress of Illusions broke off, staring into the distance. "Héna is at my doorstep — she comes, as ever, at the worst moment, like a bad dream at the edge of sleep." She turned away from Kalanin. "This is a very treacherous *Web of Fate*; we may all be ensnared." Abruptly, muttering to herself, she strode from the lakeside, walking purposefully back toward her terraced halls.

Kalanin sagged back onto the grassy bank. Géla looked down at him, uncertainly: with moonlight flowing over his green stained body, Kalanin looked like some defeated, froggy God.

"Not the worst time to tell me the truth, now that your Mistress is preoccupied," he said softly, staring up at Géla. "What's happened, what's going on?"

"It was a close thing, we almost lost you," she said, after a pause. "But our Lady is a Power here in her own lands. When the lakebed would not obey her commands, her sorcery tore the drainage side away, so that the lake emptied. Fire blasts cured the weed of its wayward magic. Some water spirit came against you — called a Marid, I believe."

"Much more than a water spirit, a new Power is rising. What is this pact you spoke of?"

Géla let more hesitation hang in the air, an even longer pause, before she spoke:

"A message from the Sorcerers — they are close allies of these Marids, and will prevent a second strike into our domain, but you must remain here, and the Mistress of Illusions is barred from revenge or giving aid to the League."

Kalanin shook his head slowly. "She would truly consider this?"

Géla sighed. "Fear and rumor now plague the Mid-World, and the Truce seems far less of a shield than it once did. The Mistress of Illusions is cautious, always protecting herself, though she did send aid to your League before the League's struggle became so much greater."

"And who is this Héna?" Kalanin prompted. "Some sort of ally of the Sorceress?" Géla shook her head, and reached down, pulling Kalanin to his feet. He coughed once again.

"You have been asleep, my old commander," she said gently. "You knew Héna from the last conflict." She led him slowly from the lakeside, taking the curved path that led back to the halls with their terraces. "Héna is a Sorceress, patroness of your small fox friend, Rafir; as I recall, the fox referred to her as 'Granny'." Kalanin's legs were weak, wobbly, as he stumbled along the path. "Héna changed after she lost her pet, Rafir," Géla continued. "It is strange how Mid-World beings require their pets."

"One pet stands beside you, and now that will change."

Géla laughed, and put a strong, supporting arm about his waist. "I never believed that you would continue to be a lap dog all your days, but you seemed stricken, cursed."

"It's over. I may be flea-bitten, long in the tooth, yet I will never return to the kennels." He coughed once again. They turned a corner, to behold the Halls of the Mistress of Illusions: splendid stone terraces were still shining in the moonlight. But dark cloud masses were shifting towards those gleaming halls, while cool, strong winds pressed against the upper branches of the massive firs and yews that lay on either side of their path. Géla drew a deep breath and quickened their pace.

"A clear warning is being shown to us," she said in a low voice. "Control is slipping from the Mistress of Illusions. The Sorcerers are displaying the full range of their own power." Tension was beginning to build, as though every particle of matter grew alert. As they entered the halls, dark-haired guards stared at Géla and Kalanin with troubled faces. Storm clouds were lurching closer toward them.

The Council Chamber was empty, nor was the Mistress of Illusions seated at her high table where she sometimes sat, alone, lost in dreams of her own creation. Géla turned quickly and sped up one set of stairs, then another. Kalanin followed, more slowly.

Standing on her highest rooftop, the Mistress of Illusions stood, facing the Sorceress Héna. About them lay the celestial measurement tools of the star charters: fixed machineries of metal and mortar, with elaborate grids set into the roof stones. Above them, storm clouds surged across the moon's face.

"Child, this is a matter that Héna and I must settle, alone." The Mistress of Illusions spoke gently, but her face was hard. Géla said nothing, only staring up into the oncoming storm clouds. Kalanin reached the rooftop. His strength was returning, but he moved slowly, cautiously.

"My Lady," he said in a voice still choked by water from the lake, "you were right before: 'where is my shield, where is my sword?' If I depart, and you resume your affairs, then the Sorcerers will leave you to your own devices." Héna shook her head, strands of white hair shifting over her wrinkled forehead.

"That's no longer true. The Mistress must either serve the Sorcerers by detaining you or suffer the loss of her kingdom. The Sorcerers will now force this issue, and our selective neutrality is over: in a short time, we will be either Servants or Adversaries."

"Are you wishing this fate on me because you lost your own domain?" snarled the Mistress of Illusions. "I have more guile than you, if not more power. Be gone and let me make my own arrangements."

"Some enchanted sleep for this captain, no doubt, while their quest for the Truce fails, and the League falls." Héna sighed, found a stone bench, and sat, then stared up into the enchanted features of the Mistress of Illusions. "Here are my words, not spoken lightly: I cannot permit you to hold this warrior who has become a captain."

"You *permit!* You, an ally?" The Mistress of Illusions stormed over the rooftop, trailing light garments behind her. "Now, hear my words! I will summon Houma and Cronar to my aid — then we shall see what becomes of your permitting!"

"The weasel summons the Dragon and the Manticore; the weasel does not survive," Héna said gently. "And they would not arrive soon enough.

Test this matter — your Divinations will not lie to you." The Mistress of Illusions stared into each of the three faces that stood around her, while each face looked back, impassively.

"With allies and servants such as you three, there's little wonder that I'm endangered. We shall see if there's no exit from this trap!" She turned and strode swiftly away, sweeping quickly down the stairs and passing from their sight.

"She is trapped, there's no doubt to the matter." The old Sorceress spoke softly, almost to herself, then she looked up into the faces of Kalanin and Géla. "Much has happened in a brief time. I'll try to be brief. Julian and Galad seek the Truce Terms, to see why the Powers of the Mid-World have not attempted to check the Demon Princes. To learn these Terms, they journey to the City of the Truce that lies in the Vale of Whispers.

"Of course, the Sorcerers have barred their way. First, they struck at Julian through the greatest of the Dark Lords, Un-Maurag. Then, more deviously, through Tel-Alantir, a Power of the Mid-World. Both attempts failed, but now Houma grows bolder, blocking Julian and Galad with a force of several thousand, armed men. For gold and spoils, many flock to the banner of the Three Hands.

"And Houma has revealed his own sorcerous strength so that the Powers are wary. Julian and Galad have been pursued first south, then to the west, so they stand always farther from their goal." The old Sorceress sighed. "My own little one, Rafir, is with them. I despaired of his life, as he stood trapped in the Dungeons of Un-Maurag. Then, I called upon Houma to free Rafir, or face my wrath — Houma only laughed, and came against me with his Demon tools — and so my little kingdom is no more. Yet even Houma was surprised, for as my sorcerous kingdom collapsed, there came a sudden release of energies: a crater stands far to the north, near Gravesend, far from all my Portal Paths. Who could have known and what might possibly have triggered such an event?"

"Then, this domain will also be threatened. Is that right?" asked Géla.

"Not just threatened, it is doomed, I fear," the old Sorceress said, watching the mass of energies building above them. "Yet, with its doom, much can be done. We can escape with many archers to support Julian and Galad. Perhaps we can steer the wreckage of this land so that it collapses over foe rather than an ally. And yet these choices lie with the Mistress of Illusions." Géla stared down at the old Sorceress.

"The end of this land, if it comes, will it be swift or slow?"

"Sudden — there will be time to flee, but little more."

"I need to warn our people. We need to be prepared." Géla turned and sped down the staircase. Kalanin sat beside the old Sorceress.

"I'm glad that your fox companion still lives," he said softly. "Heroes can be bold and boring, while Rafir was quiet, gentle, and entertaining. But you said nothing about Sebastian, Julian's winged Familiar. Has he survived?"

"Against all odds, you five are alive and whole," she said, touching his arm. "You, Julian, Galad, Rafir, Sebastian — by rights most of you should have passed long ago into the Long Sleep, waiting for the Maker's Return. That you have all survived is not just Merlin's doing. But I will wait and speak to all of you together."

She broke off, watching the Mistress of Illusions as she emerged again into the open air. Her face was strained and haggard. Géla followed a few steps behind, watching her grandmother and patroness with concern.

"Doomed...me and mine all ruined...." The Mistress of Illusions trailed off, then stared down at the old Sorceress. "Why have you helped to bring this about? What have I done to you to have earned such malice?"

"We were both doomed when we aided the League," the old Sorceress replied gently. "It was never my intention to become tangled in a struggle between powerful Adversaries and feeble Servants. But 'doom' is one thing, then it may become something else. My own death in this matter is a clear, unchallenged future, and cannot be averted. But your doom is different: you will lose your land, but you need not die with it. Many future chances lie before you."

"Yes, fleeing over Alantéa, battling monsters, powerful wielders of magic, and Marids who have been spawned by Demon Princes. A fine future!"

Géla touched the Mistress of Illusions gently on her arm. "Grandmother, do you remember when I was small, and I sat at your side watching as illusions flowed from your hands? Recall your own words: 'At the end of time, you will stand before the Maker. Live your life in a fashion that might please Him.' Is it not time to heed your own words?" The Mistress of Illusions stared into the surrounding storm clouds; they stood fixed, curled over her domain, forming an enormous vortex of destructive power. She stood motionless, in silence, struggling with her inner conflict. At last, she murmured in a soft voice, through clenched teeth:

"I will not preserve myself by betraying those whom I love. Therefore, I will become a vagabond, and a small player in an enormous conflict." She turned to Héna. "What is to be done?"

"Counter spells to earn a brief respite, then the strongest Portals you can make. I will aid you in your place of power. We will emerge near Julian if we can. Géla and Kalanin will ready your people." As she spoke, the first tremors of destruction rattled over the land. Black clouds above them began to seethe with red radiances, as though lava boiled inside them. The two women turned and scurried quickly toward the stairs, as howling noises swept in from faraway hills.

The Mistress of Illusions halted at the landing top, waving Géla and Kalanin to leave first.

"Food and weapons only — other cargo is to be left behind. Héna and I will do what we can, though little time remains." Kalanin followed Géla through the lower halls, then through the outer doors. Spear carriers and archers were marshaling everywhere, trampling roughshod over grounds and gardens.

"There will be no battle here!" Géla cried to her captains. "Our Mistress bids us depart. Come!" Seven dark haired women drew to Géla's side. Hundreds of others gathered in fields outside the halls. Kalanin watched on, feeling useless, staring at the reddish sky of sunset. And now, as though giving birth, red clouds surged and collapsed — billows of black insects were released, spiraling downward. Géla broke off her discussions.

"We'll be ready, but there are others I fear for!" Her sub-tier leaders sped away. Géla sprinted toward the stables. Kalanin ran behind, keeping to half speed. Géla mounted, holding the reins of a second horse. Kalanin mounted a third. Géla said nothing but tossed a sheathed dagger to him and rode away. Kalanin followed, waving his sheath's flat at the insects that swirled about them. They sped beyond the first insect mass, but other swarms followed. Their pace quickened, as though in a race, they sped north to a place where Kalanin had never before traveled. The ground began trembling beneath their feet.

Now, insects pursued and bit — their horses began to break stride — but from the halls of the Mistress of Illusions sped hordes of luminescent dragonflies, sweeping devourers that darted through the skies with long wingspans. As though they were linked together, the insect invaders fell back from their huge adversaries. Géla and Kalanin raced through the woodlands over a narrow horse track. Above them, the moon stood encircled by dark, pulsing, red clouds. Again, the ground trembled.

Géla turned left, and before them lay a small, woodframed cottage. As they dismounted, a candle was flickering, uncertainly, from a window. Géla sped to the door, murmuring, "Grandfather," in a low intense voice. Kalanin lowered his dagger as the door opened, and an old man emerged, blinking.

"It's the end then, is it, Granddaughter? I've no Gift, but I can sense it."

"Not the end for us, Grandfather; in only a few moments we can be gone — free from destruction. Come!" The old man stared at her for a moment, sparing only the briefest of glances for Kalanin.

"And the Dryads, my only friends except for you?"

"The tree spirits are doomed! But come, there's hope for us!" His hand was slight, withered, as he touched Géla on her arm.

"Go and save the others, I know how hard you will fight for them. The Dryads may be locked into this sorcerous kingdom, but there are others who can escape." Black clouds above them billowed again and creatures slipped earthwards: Air Elementals, sucking moisture from the land.

"Grandfather...." Sorrow swept over Géla as the old man blew his candle out and turned back to his cottage. Low moaning sounds were coming from sentient trees as moisture was drawn from them. "Grandfather, I will save the others, but leave a horse for you!" She mounted, riding down the trail, calling out in a strange tongue, a light, dancing language; then in a low melody, filled with hissing tones. Creatures cloaked by shadows peered out beside the trail, slowly, hesitantly. Dryads cried out, shrieking as Elementals of Air sucked all life from them.

"In the name of the Mistress of Illusions, we must depart!" Géla cried. Rumbles deepened over the land. Leaves withered and fell around them, as a sudden drought struck the woodlands. From the Mistress of Illusions, counterspells rose against the dryness, with misty droplets swirling over the land.

"Come now, I beg of you!" Géla cried again, and now from the woodlands, a small people emerged, eyes gleaming with gold, halfling height, but tufts of white feathers ran across their arms and shoulders. They bowed, then followed Géla, keeping a few paces behind the horses.

Now the ground began to burst in the distance — a great fissure, as though reaching for them, spread across their path; but as it reached them, it was no more than a foot wide. Géla crossed, crying out, "The Mistress of Illusions departs! Alints follow. Sophors, do not stay and perish here!"

Fissures cracked wider, but now the small golden eyed people were joined by sleek, soft-faced lizards. Géla rode on, calling out, "Portals to Alantéa, there to live or die. But certain death awaits us here!" Some of the small people hesitated, listening to the death cries of the Dryads; others sped behind Géla as her pace quickened, as they tried to escape to Alantéa the Forerunner.

Arid winds began to whip about them, and the suddenly dry forest creaked and groaned. Leaves were strewn all around them: a sudden, deadly autumn. They rode forward, golden eyed, feathered Alints, and soft faced lizard Sophors scurrying behind them. The ground rumbled and cracked wider. Then from the far hills, explosions sounded, with lava bursting out, spilling fire down dry slopes.

They emerged from the forest, followed by hordes of small people. Pausing for a moment, they stared open mouthed at the devastated land: a country once green, now brown — and red, as flaming lava ignited suddenly dry forests. In the distance, only a small island of green survived, where the Mistress of Illusions still held power over her halls.

The air was drying, and breathing was becoming much more difficult. Kalanin felt the tension build and urged Géla forward. She hesitated, looking back to the forest where Alints still emerged from the woods, trembling, but carrying their young. Small Sophors rode on the backs of larger lizards. In the forest, the death cries of the Dryads continued, as though their nightmares would never end. Kalanin reached over, tugging at the reins held in Géla's hand, and again they picked up their pace.

Now, above them, the cloud patterns changed once more as sorcerous energies shifted. Lightning flickered but was sucked back, as power built. A massed weight of lightning gathered, pulsing with destructive power. From the Mistress of Illusions, counter spells surged: waves of rainbow light sprang into dark clouds. Géla and Kalanin raced on. Above them the lightning mass shifted — a heavy weighted bolt surged down, exploding in the forest, blasting Dryads and their lone human companion, Gela's Grandfather.

Géla paused for a moment, then sped on, weeping. Again, waves of radiance surged from the Mistress of Illusions, checking the lightning mass. But now, lava flows were surging closer. The air had grown so warm that lines of sweat were pouring from Kalanin's body. Behind them, golden eyed Alints gasped and stumbled forward. All around them was fire and devastation: they were racing toward a small, shrinking island of life.

Near the Halls of the Mistress of Illusions, mailed women milled, pulling weapons, beasts, and goods to assembly points. Some women wore masks of cloth to ward off the smells of burning death. The old Sorceress, Héna, stood farthest from the Halls. Her arms were held aloft, as she chanted; but her eyes watched the sky fearfully. Before the Sorceress, a Portal with huge arches had formed. Lightning surged again toward the Sorceress, but counterspells from the Mistress of Illusions sent the weighted bolt hurtling over the horizon.

"Now for Erivan Forest and far from destruction!" cried the old Sorceress, stepping back. Géla rode to her side, masses of small, fearful creatures gasping behind her.

"Is it safe now? Can these go forward?" Géla murmured. The Sorceress lowered her arms, standing back. A few thousand paces away, billows of rolling flames were surging toward them.

"It's open to Erivan Forest," said the Sorceress, staring through the Portal, "a safe passage, but we know little of what's beyond." Géla knelt in the middle of the Alints, speaking to them in their own gentle language. Uncertainly, they walked toward the Portal, staring up at the great arch. Géla cried out one word, and they began to pass swiftly through, shuffling, seven or eight abreast. Little could be seen of the other side of the Portal: only woodlands, cool and dark. As the last of the Halflings passed through, Sophors began to follow, hissing with fear as their red tongues flicked at dead air.

Heat began to build; tier leaders moved slowly toward Géla, long, dark hair plastered to their foreheads. Cloud patterns shifted once again — columns of water surged down — explosions burst over the land as water struck boiling, melted stone. Above them, terrace windows shattered with the concussion, making tiny, soft tinkling noises overwhelmed by the sounds of destruction.

"I can no longer even check them." The Mistress of Illusions stood beside them, face shining with tears in the red light of her land's ruin. "All things of beauty must pass, but they should fade, gently." She raised her voice. "Now, allies and friends, we must depart! There will be bitter vengeance for us — keep an everlasting hatred for the destroyers of our lands! Now, away!"

The Mistress of Illusions stood at one side of their Portal, Héna at the other. Women warriors marched beside creaking wagons. Ruin and death rattled through the air, but the tier groups picked up a marching song, singing in clear voices of bright spears and deadly arrows.

Again, massed lightning hovered in the sky, surrounded by pillars of water. The ground shook one last time, and the Halls of the Mistress of Illusions began to slide and topple, like a child's castle made of wood bark. Tier-groups pushed forward, moving from a nightmare of destruction into a cool, dark forest. Kalanin and Géla stood beside the Mistress of Illusions, and all three wept at the end of their homes and lands.

"Maker!" cried the Mistress of Illusions, raising her arms. "Maker, I might have averted this destruction! Maker, I may be corrupt, but I am not utterly ruined!" The last of her tier-groups passed through the arched Portal. Fire and grey death lay only a hundred paces away, surging toward the last island of life. Arms raised, face shining with tears, the Mistress of Illusions cried out in a great voice:

"Maker, I have done both good and evil! Judge me by this act as well as others!" Héna, the old Sorceress, stepped through the arched passageway and was gone. Géla and Kalanin pulled the Mistress of Illusions through the mouth of the Portal, just as the last wave of utter destruction swept over her sorcerous empire.

Chapter Seven

The Great Forest

EVEN IN BROAD DAYLIGHT, the Great Forest was cool and gloomy. Hundreds of feet above them, sunlight was pouring over leafy branches, but on the forest's floor, saplings were stretching for light and dying. Only clumps of fungus were thriving, feeding like carrion eaters on fallen tree limbs and dead saplings.

They moved over the forest floor silently, Kalanin with his sword sheathed, but Géla and her three archers moved with bows notched. Clouds of spoors settled in the wake of their passage, slipping to the ground like dry dust.

They came to a halt at the base a huge tree: here at eye level a double slash had been carved, showing that their cautious patrols had reached this point on their second day in the forest. It was now day four, and there were still no signs of Julian or Galad. They rested for a moment in the dark stillness, one keeping watch, while the other four sat with their backs against a huge tree's base.

"Has our leader, the Mistress of Illusions, ever closed herself away in this fashion before?" Kalanin asked, keeping his voice low. "To my knowledge, none of the Wizards has ever slipped into such a deep narcotic slumber."

"It's not something I've seen in my time," Géla replied in the same low tones. "There was a hint of it from my mother when I was a youngling. But the old Sorceress Héna hopes that she will heal and be well once more. Let's be gone. If you count the next five hundred paces, I'll take the final five hundred."

They moved swiftly but cautiously through the gloomy forest floor, passing through a slight hollow where moisture gathered. Trees were spaced widely, huge trunks more than fifty paces apart. It was dark, still, and damp where they passed, but high above them thousands of birds were calling out, swooping through sunbeams onto leafy green branches.

The first thousand paces were counted, and another tree notched with four lines. A few hundred paces farther, they came to a sudden halt, as though in unspoken agreement: before them, just to the left, shafts of sunlight could be seen, beaming down over a small clearing.

"There's little chance that Julian and Galad would be nearby," Kalanin whispered. "Still —"

"It would be nice to stand in the sunlight again," Géla replied. "And I suppose there's a chance for fresh meat too, though we're too distant from our base to carry anything large." They walked slowly, warily, to the clearing, watching for any signs of movement.

This clearing was still, serene, motionless except for butterflies and finches that fluttered and swooped over the decaying carcasses of huge tree trunks. Some disaster had struck just a few years ago, leveling a small portion of the forest. Even now, saplings had grown to a man's height and were beginning their struggle for domination. Their search party halted, still hidden in the shadows. It was quiet for a moment — for some reason even the bird flocks were silent.

A doe came into view, grazing warily then moving on. As she grazed, something low and menacing crept a little closer; and from their vantage point they saw that it was a Vorr, a sleek brownfurred servant of Un-Maurag, larger than a wolf, and far more deadly; the archers pulled back their strings, seeking a clear shot.

"Still foolhardy," came a voice from above them, "and the females not less than the males." Arrows shifted toward the voice. Both doe and Vorr vanished from the clearing. In the branches overhead perched the eagle, the Eye of Merlin.

"Put your weapons aside," Géla said. "Your arrows were aimed at an ally, though you will soon learn that he is no soft-spoken friend."

"Soft or harsh-spoken, it's good to see you," Kalanin called up. "Have you found Julian?"

"That Vorr you thought to kill was my one link to the Apprentice. For some reason, a pack of Vorrs now serve as his sentinels."

"Can you sense even a direction for us to look?" Kalanin stepped forward and sat in the sunlight. "We've begun a complete search, but that may take weeks, and not be successful if Julian is well hidden." The eagle was silent for a moment, turning awkwardly on his perch until he had faced each direction. Then, with a brief drop and a flutter of wings, the eagle came down beside Kalanin.

"He is blocked from me, as before, shielded from Houma. But the Sorcerer moves openly through the Great Forest, with masses of men surrounding him: more than two thousand and growing daily as men of Alantéa flock to the banner of the Three Hands. How many serve the Mistress of Illusions?"

"Two tiers and a sub-unit of archers," said Géla. "In all, only twelve hundred."

The eagle looked away, then muttered, "In numbers and in force of sorcery, we are outmastered — yet Merlin sees a turning point here, as though the innermost strands of the *Web of Fate* have begun to part. And the Powers watch us as never before, with many scores of greater and lesser Gods concentrating on their Divination Portals. We must find the Apprentice and his ally, the Charmed Knight."

"Will you come back with us?" asked Kalanin. "If your sight is blocked, we may have better luck seeking Julian. During the last few days, we've extended screens to all compass points. One may have discovered Julian even at this moment."

"I will come," said the eagle, "and though my opening words were unkind, I am glad to have you with us again. In this struggle, you and a few others have been catalysts for powerful forces — even now, the great mind of Merlin watches through me, and he cannot foresee the outcome of this intersection of forces."

Kalanin rose, staring at the sky, shading his eyes from the sun. "We'll find Julian somehow: Vorrs, women warriors, Rafir, Sebastian, Houma, men serving the Three Hands — one of these forces will lead us to the Apprentice." They walked back toward the darkened forest, but the eagle lifted from the clearing, circling high above them.

"I will take the passage of the upper airs," he called down to them. "Only call to me before we near your people — your archers are overly eager!" Kalanin strode along the gloomy forest floor, but his mind held an image of the eagle soaring through blue skies above an immense green forest.

After they reached the first of the patrol marks, they moved more swiftly, less cautiously. Géla slowed them, murmuring, "We have found only the eagle, another seeker, so it's too early to relax or rejoice." But their pace was swift as they returned, and they met no one as they sped through the gloomy shadows of the Great Forest.

As the first screen of sentries showed themselves, long spears in hand, Kalanin whistled, waited, then whistled again. Rustling sounds came from the upper branches, with blackbirds calling loud cries against the intrusion.

The Eye of Merlin dropped from above, breaking into a long, sweeping glide, then coming to rest on Kalanin's shoulder: memories stirred in the captain's mind as he moved past the first screen of sentries.

Now within their camp's perimeter, Géla and her archers slung bows over their shoulders and opened their strides. The camp's center was just a few thousand paces away, but only the Eye of Merlin could penetrate the filtered, diffused light. The eagle's mouth opened, letting out a soft, rasping sound.

"Tents are being packed throughout your campsite. People are moving with some swiftness, but they have not yet drawn weapons — and there are other soft sounds coming from creatures that are not human."

"Small beings, Sophors, and Alints," said Kalanin. "They are gentle creatures; predators within the Great Forest will consume them unless we find a sanctuary for them. As for the camp's movements, either we have found Julian, or the men of the Three Hands have found us." They continued quickly; as they passed a second screen of guards, their commander called out to Géla:

"News from the north — and it's not good news, the way the camp is stirring!" Géla waved and moved on.

Their camp had become a jumble of creaking carts and collapsing tents. Subtiers were beginning to assemble, moving to formations at the camp's outer ring. From a little distance, away came the hoots and cries of slender, feathered Alints, who watched on helplessly as their protectors readied to move once again. A single large tent still stood in the camp's center, with the rainbow colored banner of the Mistress of Illusions hanging dull and lifeless from its peak — neither light nor wind moved through the somber, dim forest.

Not far from their tent they found the old Sorceress, Héna, kneeling in front of a wounded ranger, bandaging a leg wound. Next to them lay a second scout, blood seeping from a chest wound, black hair lying limp on the green moss of the great forest. Her face was still and grey; Kalanin could see that she was dead.

"Hail, Sorceress and ally," said the eagle. "Merlin's good wishes are with you." Héna stumbled to her feet, watching the eagle warily.

"I only wish that Merlin had chosen someone other than me." She dusted bits of dead forest matter from her cloak and drew a deep breath. "I wish, too, for this one's sake, that I was more of a healer." She looked down in sorrow at the woman who lay dead upon the moss.

"At least it was a good death, a warrior's death, by the look of it," said Géla. "How did it come about?"

"Men serving the Three Hands lie to the north of us, it seems," said the Sorceress. "How many I know not, but now I sense Houma in the distance, greatly desiring our destruction. Just a few hours ago, your people met Houma's in a clash of arms on the forest floor. At bowshot, your archers are deadly, but some of the Three Hands were horsed, heavily mailed, armed with long lances. This one was speared — a death wound, while others escaped...." Héna paused, seeming puzzled. "They escaped because fierce beasts tore spearmen from their saddles. It's hard to credit, but word is that they were servants of Un-Maurag, fierce Vorr creatures. Why should these beings come against those allied with the Three Hands? Perhaps the tale is garbled, and some other creatures are responsible."

"The tale was not garbled, a twist of fate lies hidden in this struggle," the eagle said. "It is vital that all our allies have knowledge of this matter. Who leads here, who will explain it to the others?"

"The Mistress of Illusions leads if any," said Kalanin.

"There is a sleeping Sorceress near me who cannot lead even her own magically drugged mind at the moment," the eagle croaked. "Now, who leads?"

"I will advise," Kalanin said, "but these tier-groups are not mine to lead."

"And I know nothing of these matters," added Héna. "My little magic is at your disposal, yet another should command."

"Then I will lead," said Géla, smiling at Kalanin with a touch of malice. "My old captain will become a Grey Councilor and advise me. Now, what of these Vorr creatures?"

"You must tell your people to let them be," the eagle croaked, "even if they seem to stalk at the heels of your sentries. For some reason, these former servants of Un-Maurag now aid Julian and Galad. If the Vorrs are slain, then our link with the Apprentice will be broken."

"So, we will share the information that Vorrs are allies, for the moment," said Géla. "What of Houma and those serving the Three Hands? Is there a way to strike at them?"

Kalanin cleared his throat. "Vorrs may be allies and yet not have learned great discrimination. Remember the small ones," he said quietly.

"Yes, there's not much small ground flesh in Erivan," Géla said thoughtfully, "and Vorrs are more likely to seek venison, but we will double the guard protecting Sophors and Alints."

"As for Houma and those of the Three Hands, you are outnumbered," said the Eye, "both in power of sorcery and tier strength: Houma has become a Power, leading more than twice your own force of arms."

"Then, is there no choice except to flee?" Géla asked.

"You may call it an 'armed withdrawal' if you wish," said Kalanin with a slight smile. "But this would be my counsel: move south, seeking Julian while you rouse the Mistress of Illusions."

"That last task is not an easy one," muttered the old Sorceress, shaking her head somberly. "If she were left untended, she would die; I have no great power as a healer, I can only hold her alive."

"But it makes no difference to my Mistress whether we move south or north, does it?" asked Géla. The Sorceress shook her head. "Then, we're gone. South first, southwest, then southeast, a jagged movement as though we flee uncertainly." Géla moved away swiftly, calling sub-tier leaders and sergeants to her side. Kalanin drifted away, with the Eye of Merlin still on his shoulder. They spoke at length of the twin sieges of Stone Mountain and Gravengate, and of the lurking threat of the Marids. What Kalanin learned filled him with a deep disquiet that was more unsettling than fear.

·)(·

In the afternoon they broke camp, leaving with as much quiet as they could manage. Yet their stealth seemed unlikely to conceal their movements from their foes, as deep ruts made by the wheels of their carts left a clear trail for any pursuer.

Kalanin rode beside Géla, but he turned every now and again to the wagon that bore the Mistress of Illusions south through the Great Forest. He watched her face intently, but no noise or jarring motion seemed able to break through her deep, enchanted sleep. As he rode away from the wagon, Héna, the old Sorceress, came riding toward him. She said nothing, but signalled him to join her. The two rode back to Géla; in the same wordless fashion, the old Sorceress encouraged her to ride with them. Still silent, Héna led them a little distance in front of the vanguard.

"If a conference is needed, we should summon the Eye," said Géla. Kalanin stared up: beyond the distant forest tops, the eagle soared through clear skies, keeping watch for both friend and foe.

The old Sorceress shook her head. "The eagle, for all his wisdom, knows little of many matters, including the emotions of humans. I have looked into the enchanted visions of the Mistress of Illusions, watching the torments and fears that she struggles to control. The loss of her realm is a great grief to her, and she fears the outcome of our conflict with the Sorcerers. Yet one other fear adds to her burden: she perceives a future in which she loses lover to granddaughter, captain to warrior maiden."

Héna sighed. "And to the Mistress of Illusions, with her troubled past, and lost land, to be left by a Giftless mortal is very painful." Kalanin opened his mouth to speak but kept silent with an effort. Géla looked away and seemed to slump in her saddle. Behind them they could hear the muffled sounds of many feet shuffling over the soft forest floor, interspersed with the sound of horses' hoofs, and creaking wagon wheels.

Géla drew a deep breath. "These thoughts have not yet stirred in this Captain's mind: weariness and Seraph's Sting and concern for the Mistress of Illusions have blocked all such feelings. If they have stirred within me, I will deal with them. Let us speak, alone, for a moment." The old Sorceress smiled gently at them and turned back. Kalanin held his peace.

"So?" Géla asked quietly, after a pause.

"My own destiny seems better known to others than to myself," Kalanin murmured. "There's nothing new in this."

"Thus, I am a 'destiny' to be confronted by the grim Captain, along with Marids and Sorcerers. Well, you need not fear me. I will free you to deal with Sorcerers and Marids."

Kalanin caught at the reins of her horse before she could pull away. "Just hold on for a moment. See how complicated this matter has become: we march beside an aging Sorceress, served by women warriors, while the Mistress of Illusions lies bewitched by her own enchantments. We have fallen into a contest between Houma on one hand, and Julian and Galad on the other. And we travel through the center of the Great Forest of Erivan — surely there are inhabitants here who will soon take an interest in us. Should we not hold matters like love and revenge in abeyance? Otherwise, our own complications will ensnare us before Sorcerers or Marids or Demon Princes even reach for us."

Géla looked at him coolly. "Spoken like a seasoned diplomat, with evasions and truth all blended together. But I will listen to the Grey Councilor both carefully and cautiously." She pulled away, leaving Kalanin to travel by himself.

·)(·

They moved at a steady pace through the long afternoon, pausing every few leagues for a brief rest. Water was plentiful on the forest floor with brooks and streams running south and southwest, eventually draining into the Bariloch. With care, their provisions would stretch for half a cycle of the moon, and gold would purchase more if they ever emerged safely from the Great Forest. Kalanin measured all these things, but carefully refrained from offering advice. No advice was sought, either; Géla moved among her sub-tier leaders with authority, leaving the "Grey Councilor" to his own devices.

Their passage slowed as it grew darker, and they became more wary as an unseen sunset merged with a gloomy dusk. At last, they were forced to call a halt, making a camp that was almost identical to the one they had left: as before, huge trees towered over them, with birds calling and swooping through the upper branches. Only a few tents were strung, and cold rations were served, as sub-tiers stood quietly in the cheerless gloom. No fires were lit, as they hoped to pass unnoticed amid Erivan's dark quiet.

Kalanin sat, puffing gently on his pipe, hidden in a small tent so the glow of burning tobacco would be shielded from the night watch. He was not surprised when, an hour after nightfall, talons pulled back the tent's flap, and the Eye of Merlin entered.

"A simple task becomes even more simple," said the eagle. "You have the lone male scent in this camp, and to this, you have added the stench of burning weed." Kalanin said nothing, only drawing more deeply on his pipe so that the features of both man and eagle were lit by the glow. The eagle coughed and continued.

"Houma pursues, moving south behind you. Julian remains hidden. Yet, we found the remains of a fallen deer, one killed by Vorrs, just three leagues to the west. I —" Kalanin held his palm up, halting the tide of news.

"Géla leads, as it should be," he said quietly. "She is entitled to hear your tidings first; and if she is wise, she will have new tasks for you tonight. Tomorrow, if there's a lull, I would like to hear more, but it is only a courtesy." The Eye of Merlin said nothing, only studying Kalanin's face closely for a moment, then backing out into the night. Kalanin finished his glowing pipe, then opened the flap of his tent, letting the heavy smoke dissipate into the night air. He imagined the creatures of the upper branches sniffing in curiosity at the strange smells rising through their leafy empire. With his mind free of haunting and weariness, he turned on his side and slipped into a dreamless sleep.

· X ·

Géla sat beside a slight, smoldering campfire, nodding as the eagle advised her carefully, adding more details than he would have if speaking to Kalanin. Still, the Eye hesitated before leaving, sensing an uncertainty on Géla's face.

"So," croaked the eagle, "what else do you need to know?"

Géla nodded. "Every word you have spoken is clear. What I lack is understanding about the Elf-Kindreds whom we are bound to encounter. We have sighted or sensed, Wood Elves, but none of the Sidhe — taller and more likely armored, and the Tanu, larger and most dangerous of the three. What can you tell me of their presence?"

"Even the Mind of Merlin," the eagle murmured, lowering his croaking voice, "does not *know*, but *suspects* that the most militant of the Kindreds are involved in struggles elsewhere — with Mordred, or Haeglin, on Un-Maurag. But! Be cautious approaching the Elves of Erivan, because these are also very determined, and dangerous." The eagle backed from the small, smoldering fire, glanced into the starlit sky, then flapping heavy wings, the Eye disappeared into the night.

· X ·

It was late at night when Kalanin woke again. Voices could be heard outside his tent, the light, steady voice of the guard — and a deeper male voice. He reached for his sword, prepared to slash through the canvas and spring out into the night.

"So, we'll be discreet — neither light nor fire, but for the Maker's sake fetch me a corkscrew, will you?" said the deep voice. "And tell old Captain Hangnail in there that he's got company." It was Galad's voice: they had been found. Kalanin sheathed his sword, and lay back for a moment, smiling. Outside, there were sounds of a popping wine cork. Kalanin slipped out into the gloomy darkness of the nighttime forest.

"I knew that a popping cork would fetch you," murmured Galad.

"Captain Hangnail at your service," Kalanin said, giving a mock bow. Even in the darkness, Galad's figure bulked large beside those of the lean women warriors. Galad passed a battered goblet to Kalanin, then drank himself from the bottle.

"By the Maker, it's good to have a lull in the chase, and it's good to see you again, even after your untimely holiday." Galad stood back, as though measuring Kalanin. "You look none the worse — I expected you to be bulkier than a fattened goose." He glanced at the lean guards who stood to one side. "Though, with all of these social obligations...." he trailed off. Kalanin embraced him, laughing.

"Now is a good time to let your brain catch up with your tongue. Hear me! It's more than I deserve to see you once again, and to aid you in your struggle, even in a small fashion. But where's Julian? Where are Sebastian and Rafir?"

"Julian and Sebastian are with your Sorceress, the Mistress of Illusions. Rafir, no doubt, is with his old patroness, though none can truly follow his comings and goings. I, alone, sought out Captain Hangnail. Come, drink up, then we'll find a more private place, and I'll tell you our tale of woe." They stepped away from the guard, moving warily from the camp's center, taking care not to disturb the sleeping forms that lay sprawled all about them. On the outskirts of their camp, they found the base of a huge tree and sank back against it. Galad poured another half goblet for Kalanin, then drank deeply himself.

"Have a care with that," murmured Kalanin. "By its sound, it's half empty." Galad sighed — a deep relaxed sound.

"There's more wine. The old Sorceress was so glad to see us, she'd have given away her whole treasury. Whatever her level of power, she seems to have little ability as a healer. That's why Julian toils while I sit here, hobnobbing with Captain Hangnail." He slipped the cork back into the wine bottle and set it against the base of the tree trunk.

"Best to save even a bit of the first bottle: talking's thirsty work. I'll begin while you sip." Sitting relaxed in the darkness, Galad spoke of the twin sieges of Stone Mountain and Gravengate, how Julian sought the Vale of Whispers, and of the first moves made by Houma, as he sought to destroy the Apprentice through Un-Maurag and Tel-Alantir.

"It seems that Tel-Alantir has caused the other Powers to become more wary. For the time being, Houma appears to have set aside his subtle 'traps' and comes at us with his main force. It's effective enough though, and we're farther from our goal than ever before, with many hundreds of men seeking us under Houma's direction. Slowly, Julian has become disheartened as we've fallen back from the north. He feels, I fear, that the League will fall unless he's able to bring the Truce Terms back to Merlin."

Galad pulled his wine bottle up and drank once again. "As for me, I've become weary of cutting down all those unsuspecting warriors: for a long time, masses of them would come speeding toward me on horseback or on foot — they seemed overjoyed to find a lone victim — but then the Sword would make short work of them. Lately, they've learned to avoid me, sending volleys of arrows arcing toward me from a distance."

"I take a somewhat more hardheaded approach," Kalanin said with a grim smile. "If you've cut down fifty, then there's fifty men less to deal with. Now, you say three thousand. Is that a guess or a count?"

"A count, courtesy of the Vorrs helping Julian. The count is now several days old with more drifting to the banner of the Three Hands each day."

"That needs to be stopped if we can," Kalanin said.

"Worry tomorrow," Galad said, yawning. "One thing still puzzles me, though. Your Sorceress keeps only women for weapons work — I know they're effective, but what's the reason?"

"It's never been explained to me directly, but I've picked up the story in bits and pieces. For a long time, the Mistress of Illusions barred all males from her domains. It seems that she was once enslaved by a Sorcerer and used cruelly. When she broke free, her hatred of men endured for many years, then her feelings slowly eased, allowing her to entertain male companions. I fear for her now, because her kingdom was brought down by Sorcerers, by other cruel men. I only hope that Julian is able to —"
He broke off; shuffling movements were passing through the forest, just a hundred paces away.

"They're over here, Granny." Rafir's voice carried easily through the gloomy darkness. Kalanin and Galad rose to greet the old Sorceress as she came forward slowly, leaning on her walking stick. The two warriors rose, towering over the old Sorceress.

"Greetings, Sorceress," said Galad. "I was just passing the time with my old commander. Are we needed elsewhere?"

"Not this night," said Héna, and she sat on the forest floor, one hand reaching over to rub Rafir's soft fur.

"What of the Mistress of Illusions?" asked Kalanin. "Has Julian succeeded in waking her?"

"She may heal, I think, but it has not been easy for the Apprentice: he is weary and discouraged, with his own hidden troubles still concealed. And he has been dealing with a mind that is very disturbed. For the Mistress of Illusions to lose her sorcerous domain with such an explosion of destruction was most difficult for her." Héna shook her head and sighed. "I must believe that our enemies intended to drive her into madness, and so they have become as grim and evil as any Dark Lord."

"I would cheerfully slice Houma's throat, given half a chance," Galad said. "Yet Julian, for all his gentleness, would strike first — Rafir, your night eyes are better than mine. Does someone else approach us, or has wine blotted my vision?"

"It's Julian, and Sebastian, with the Eye of Merlin," Rafir said. "There's so little light in this forest that I can't see much better than you, but there's nothing wrong with my nose." Kalanin watched as Julian approached; the Apprentice seemed slumped, weary, depressed.

"Julian, friend — and ally, well met! That we have all survived is amazing!" He clasped the Apprentice in long, strong arms.

"It is not surprising that you survived," said the eagle, coming behind Julian.

"No, it is not surprising, it is destiny," said the Sorceress, in a soft voice, face staring up at the Apprentice.

"Destiny or not, it's good to see you, Kalanin." Julian sank to the ground beside Galad. "If I were not so weary, I would rejoice. Tonight, I think, I'll join Galad in a cup of wine — if there's enough."

"More than enough," said Galad. He reached over and passed Kalanin's goblet to Julian. "Captain Hangnail is slowing down in his declining years."

Kalanin knelt beside Sebastian and Rafir. "I *am* slowing down, but I hope to become somewhat wiser with age. It comes to my mind that in the struggle for Gravengate, I gave little credit or attention to Sebastian and Rafir, Familiars and friends. Without you two, we might easily have failed."

"It's nice of you to say that," Sebastian said, his serious, wise face showing a slight smile. "But we understand that we are small creatures, of little consequence."

"It bothered me once," added Rafir, "but it doesn't really matter."

"It does matter," said the Sorceress, "for the small ones have indeed become important."

"Each one of the five Far Travelers shares a destiny," added the eagle.

Galad laughed. "This conversation is too much like those dramas once enacted at Gravengate for Balardi's amusement: the eagle is Chorus One, the Sorceress is Chorus Two, and each mumbles dire predictions offstage, while the players stumble around the stage in complete confusion."

"Yes, but unlike your Chorus One and Two, the wielders of magic and their servants always explain themselves — in the end," said Kalanin. His eyes were drawn to a device on Julian's chest that gleamed blue, off and on, like a beacon. Ignoring it for the moment, Kalanin sprawled back against the tree trunk. "It's no accident that we have met here, far beyond midnight, in the Great Forest. There's wisdom to be had for us, somewhere."

"There is wisdom," said the Sorceress, after a pause. "I have come to see and understand many things — the Gift within me understands that it will pass soon, with my death, and it is flaring, like a star bursting with light in its final moments. It shows me that there has been a destiny laid upon you five: Julian, Kalanin, Galad, Sebastian and Rafir; you were marked, I think, when you rested in that old, abandoned tower before the onset of the Great Spell. That explosion of sorcerous energy cast four of you to the farthest edges of earth's magic, while Kalanin was saved to begin the resurrection of your League.

"In a strange convergence of power, the Great Spell of your enemies was met by Merlin's counterspells, Julian's hidden strength, and perhaps the powers within the three Great Spells you carried to Balardi were also tapped, as you were hurled to the farthest boundaries of the Mid-World."

"Merlin perceives this convergence," said the eagle. "He also feels that the distant hand of the Maker may be at work."

"That, too, is possible," continued the Sorceress. "Consider for a moment where your destinies have taken you: Galad beyond the borders of the Mid-World; Sebastian and Rafir to the end of all magic, where the sorcerous energies of Earth have run dry; Julian to the Hall of the Dreamers, where the greatest of the Servants await the Maker's return. And now Kalanin has been drawn to the Temple of Waiting, where the dead Immortals wait, in a strange, partial life, like fertile seeds under a mass of glacial ice.

"It comes to my mind that there is only one place of power beyond the Mid-World where you have not yet journeyed: to the Isle of the Demons, a place that lies far from the ocean's surface, beneath a mountain of dark waters. It may well be that your destinies will take you there."

"What, as prisoners when the League fails?" asked Julian, shaking his head. "Drawn to the underwater Isle — the most suffocating, grimmest of fates, and not anything resembling a destiny touched by the Maker."

"Not necessarily as prisoners," said the Sorceress slowly, staring into the gloomy darkness. "I cannot see that far. Yet the substance of my message is this: you five are marked by fate, and neither foe, nor ally, nor your own strong wills can free you. There is only strife, with either victory or defeat at battle's end."

"Fate and Destiny are large words, too large for me," said Kalanin. "I will serve as warrior or captain, however, until this struggle comes to an end."

"Nor will I make any effort to withdraw," Julian added. "But there is an everlasting weariness upon me now. We've been fighting and hiding and fleeing for so many days. Destiny can wait for the rest of this short night. Now I will sleep." Julian stood in the gloomy stillness of the Great Forest, staring upward. Dawn was just a few hours away, but no hints of light were visible, either from Moon or Star; the only light shining was the blue glow of the amulet gleaming from his chest. The others followed the Apprentice back to camp, stumbling occasionally over a sleeping form.

As Kalanin and Galad finished the last of their wine, Kalanin spoke quietly with Galad: "I let them speak of 'destinies' and 'fates,' and so I never did ask Julian about that blue device gleaming on his chest. What is it, and what tasks is it supposed to perform?"

Galad barked out a short, bitter laugh. "His original amulet was supposed to counter Houma and his magic, although, in its first test, it simply collapsed into grey dust. The current amulet was fashioned by one of the Powers, and we hope that this replacement amulet will do better in any future contests. For the moment, when it gleams its blue light in the darkness, it is simply saying, 'Houma is coming. Houma is coming.' And Houma *is* coming."

· ✕ ·

An hour after daybreak, Kalanin walked slowly to the tent where the Mistress of Illusions had lain throughout her enchanted sleep. Géla stood outside, as though waiting for him, and they entered together without exchanging a word. Within, the Mistress of Illusions lay, eyes fixed on the ceiling, face set and drawn.

"Am I still in the Great Forest, hiding from my enemies?" The Mistress of Illusions kept her face turned to the tent's peak, keeping her voice low, as though she spoke with unseen entities.

"We are here in the south of Erivan," Géla said gently. "Julian and Galad have been found, or rather, they have found us. But Houma advances from the north with three or four thousand men who serve the Three Hands."

"Yes, I can sense him," said the Mistress of Illusions. She sat up, her face still grim and worn. "There are others I sense — Sophors and Alints are nearby, and there are others somewhat farther away: Vorrs serving Un-Maurag are at our fringe unless I have lost all my powers."

"Those Vorrs are now allies of Julian and Galad," said Kalanin. "With Vorrs, Sophors, and Alints, our tasks are now confused, cluttered, and the inhabitants of Erivan have yet to make themselves known."

The Mistress of Illusion struggled to her feet. "You must take all these creatures, together with our people, and move south. I, alone, will stay and deal with Houma: on this day Houma dies or I die." Géla and Kalanin glanced at one another, seeking words of restraint. None came.

"I will ready the wagons then," Géla said after a pause. Géla and Kalanin stepped from the tent.

"It's a good time to find the Apprentice and the Old Sorceress," Kalanin said under his breath.

"Our tier-groups will be ready," added Géla.

Julian was not within eyesight, but the Eye of Merlin stood nearby, as though waiting for Kalanin.

"A smell of burning hangs in the air," the eagle croaked in a low voice. "The Sorceress may seem healed on the surface, but peace is farthest from her mind."

"It's a desire to die, I fear," Kalanin murmured. "She wants to destroy Houma, and if I understand the level of Houma's power, there would be no contest."

"I will seek Héna, the old Sorceress," the eagle said, wings flaring. "Julian still sleeps, just to the west at the outermost circle of your camp. Bring him." The eagle launched himself and was gone.

Everywhere the camp was stirring as sub-tiers readied for a shift to the south: wagons were being loaded, tents struck, horses harnessed. Kalanin walked quickly away from the bustling groups of woman warriors, striding through the dim halflit forest. Flocks of emerald jays and starlings jeered down at him, calling from the sunlit heights. Just a little distance to his left, his eyes caught the figure of Sebastian keeping watch over his master's sleeping form. Kalanin covered the distance in a run, treading easily over the damp forest floor. He knelt beside the Apprentice.

"Sorry," he murmured to Sebastian. "Julian, we have a problem, and we'll need your help." The Apprentice stirred, bleary unfocussed eyes blinking out toward the shrouded upper branches.

"Houma?"

"In a sense. The Mistress of Illusions is awake, but she speaks of confronting Houma, and it will not be easy to turn her aside."

"It's a wish for death." Julian rose, rubbing his eyes. "And yet I don't blame her. Houma is evil and needs to be destroyed. I never thought I would feel this level of anger, but Houma has earned it."

"If I could kill Houma with my mind, I'd do it, too," said Sebastian. "But it will take a Wizard to deal with Houma's power." Julian and Sebastian walked slowly back to the camp. Fatigue seemed to weigh the Apprentice down, and Kalanin slowed himself to match his pace.

"You're weary, and I'm fresh. It's a pity I can't help more...." Kalanin trailed off.

"Yes, I know, 'Wielders of Magic are the true powers,'" Julian quoted, then smiled a weary smile. "But recall how the old Sorceress lectured us on our destinies. Your time will come." They picked their way through a camp that had become better organized: with the marshaling nearly complete, their sub-tiers were moving toward food stations.

· X ·

The Mistress of Illusions stood outside her tent, tapping her right foot with unconcealed impatience. Géla was on one side, Héna on the other, speaking in soft voices to the angry Sorceress. The Eye of Merlin watched on in silence as Kalanin and Julian approached.

"Here they come, onetime lover, and dreary, sober tongued Apprentice," the Mistress of Illusions snarled, "bringing more cautious counsel. It will not work. Just let me be and I will deal with Houma."

"You still wish to die," Julian said softly. "The Sorcerer would destroy you in a matter of moments."

"My land was also brought down by Houma," added Héna. "I greatly desire his destruction, but I will not cast my life away so easily."

"Will you let me be!" the Mistress of Illusions cried out. "You cannot turn me from this conflict — you can only delay and confuse me. At least leave me to concentrate on Houma." Silence prevailed for a moment, then the old Sorceress turned to Julian.

"She will perish, if she challenges Houma, alone."

"Yes," murmured the Apprentice, "but if she were aided, what then?"

"Here we have Magic Wielders' folly at its greatest!" the Eye of Merlin croaked. "All three of you dragged into conflict and near-certain defeat."

Héna stared into the distance then shook her head. "It is not certain."

"Houma has lived too long," added Julian. Kalanin and Galad looked on in astonishment: three cautious wielders of magic — Julian, the Mistress of Illusions, and the old Sorceress, Héna — had turned suddenly rash, with all their carefully measured reasoning swept suddenly aside.

"My Lady, will you not reconsider now?" Kalanin asked softly. "Your actions will threaten the lives of many others."

"Houma must die," said the Mistress of Illusions.

"Merlin should know of these matters. I must interrupt his labors at Sea's Edge," croaked the eagle in a strained voice. "Be silent for a moment while I seek the mind of Merlin." Kalanin watched on with the old tension slowly mounting inside him: again, those born with the Gift were settling matters among themselves and there was little he could do to divert or aid them.

Galad studied the weary, grim face of the Apprentice: Julian had been attacked and pursued, again and again, but now he intended to turn and confront his tormentor. Silence hung in the gloomy air of the Great Forest for a time, then the eagle spoke:

"Merlin strongly advises against this confrontation, but he perceives that you three will not be deterred. At the right moment, therefore, he will signal to Thorian and Balardi to put forth their own strength. And so, the Sorcerers will not be free to send Cronar or Eudox against you, and you will face Houma alone. Speaking for myself, I will guard your backs to warn you of any treachery coming from the Mid-World of the Truce. All others should move south, even beyond the borders of Erivan, if need be."

"What of our quest, Julian?" Galad asked uncertainly. "Is this truly a pathway toward the Vale of Whispers?" Julian met his eyes — briefly.

"Houma has barred our way. Now, he will be removed. If we fail, surely the Eye will have new instructions for you."

The Mistress of Illusions looked away from the others and stared to the north. "It is noon, and Houma still breathes. Let us begin."

"Give our fighting forces an hour's distance to get free," said the eagle. "You will need an hour's preparation time at least."

"We will move south," said Géla. "A league from here, we'll halt and await news of your confrontation. We too will hope for Houma's destruction. Farewell, my Mistress! Héna, it was good fortune that brought you to our lands. Well met, Julian. Strike swiftly and hard!"

The three mortals born with the Gift spoke together in hushed tones, as sub-tiers formed and marched away. The Eye of Merlin watched in silence as women warriors strode through the forest, followed by Alints, golden eyed halfling folk. Behind them, Sophors straggled, lagging, for the coolness of the Great Forest had chilled their small frames, slowing their progress. The eagle sensed, but could not see, that the Vorrs serving Julian were still guarding the flanks of the Apprentice.

Time passed, and the marchers faded into the overshadowed, dark gloom. The eagle turned from the fading marchers and watched as the three Magicians traced designs on the forest floor. Their enemies were drawing closer, and Houma had become aware of his opponents. The Eye could envision the smile of hatred forming on Houma's face.

Julian finished first, then stood back, examining his handiwork. Héna, too, halted and walked over to Julian. The Mistress of Illusions labored on, face still set with anger and inner strife. In the upper branches, birds grew silent, as they felt the drift of Houma's sorcerous energies shifting to the floor of the Great Forest. Finally, the Mistress of Illusions halted and stepped back, walking toward Julian and Héna. Light and power slipped slowly over their enchanted framework. Eyes shining with awareness, the Eye of Merlin approached the three Magicians.

"A moment's speech before the struggle begins," said the eagle. "I perceive much of the mind of Merlin, and he understands the levels of power among the Mortal Magic Wielders. Years ago, the Wizards were accounted the most powerful of mortals, but now the Sorcerers have been armed with Demon tools and much has changed. Merlin is untested as yet; we will not rank him. Alcman stands before Stone Mountain and must be considered the greatest of the Mortal Magic Wielders. Thorian stands a little behind him, struggling to survive. Just below these in power are Cronar and Balardi and Houma. Of only slightly less power is Eudox, but his learning increases each day, and he understands many of Balardi's designs from the time he was apprenticed to that Wizard.

"Now," the eagle continued, "so you understand clearly your own places in this hierarchy, I will tell you of your own rankings: you three are middle level Magic Wielders of roughly equal strength." Héna nodded, but the Mistress of Illusions raised her eyebrows, looking askance at Julian.

"Make no mistake in this matter," the eagle said, glancing at each of the Magic Wielders. "The Sorcerers now clearly understand how Julian's real power has been masked; and so, Houma was sent to block him. If our opponents see these matters clearly, then we should not deceive ourselves."

"I feel weak, not powerful," Julian said, "but if Houma makes mistakes or grows confused, on this day he will sleep the Long Sleep."

"Already, he has lived far too long," said the Mistress of Illusions. "Now, he must die."

Héna nodded, adding, "It begins."

Lights were flickering all about their sorcerous designs. Energies hummed, shifting into whining sounds as power mounted. The eagle stood back from the runic shapes, and he felt a strange spasm of pleasure shiver through his clever, enchanted mind once again: Merlin was watching the confrontation through his eyes.

Now, Elementals were drawn into their vortex of power: half aware beings brought whimpering, muttering into their design. On the forest floor, grey mists slipped through the gloomy partial light. Leagues away, the eagle could sense the mind of Houma become alert, as the powerful Sorcerer readied for confrontation. And there was another being, some grim, evil power, waiting for the Sorcerer's call — a terrible convergence of forces was hovering over the Great Forest.

·)(·

"I don't remember that it was this quiet before," said Sebastian. He was perched on Kalanin's shoulder while Rafir rode beside Galad, leaning out of knight's saddle pouch, mouth open, tongue tasting the dampness of the Great Forest. They traveled at the rear of the column, just behind the straggling lizard people who were carrying their younglings on their backs.

"It *is* quiet," said Galad. "Old Captain Hangnail has been demoted. We're not sure whether he's a piece of baggage or some rude warrior, useful only as an easily sacrificed, surly rearguard."

"I always liked the humor, the bits of mockery," said Rafir, "but what's really happening? I see messengers speeding all around us — why aren't they talking to you?"

"Géla commands," said Kalanin, smiling. "There will be a role for me somewhere, sometime."

"If Houma triumphs," murmured Sebastian, "it will be a brief, very sad role."

Rafir looked up at Galad and Kalanin: massive and mailed, the two weapons masters were powerful, quick, with strong intellects — but Julian, gentle and wise, Julian had the Gift. The fox turned to Galad. "Was it madness to challenge Houma? Is there a chance for them?"

Galad shrugged. "Kalanin understood the Magicians better than I did — for myself, I agree that Houma's death had been too long postponed. But I also fear for them. Kalanin?" A brief pause followed, and during the silence, Rafir watched the progress of Sophors and Alints — small fearful creatures who struggled to keep up with the tier-groups in front of them.

"I'm not altogether wise in these matters, either," Kalanin said. "Yet if the attempt on Houma were doomed, then the eagle would have contested the matter with a much harder, more determined, even bitter effort, and Merlin would have become grim with anger."

"Yes, I was surprised when the Eye gave in so quickly," said Rafir, nodding, "and I was also surprised that Sebastian didn't speak up — usually, he's the most cautious."

"This time I agreed with the Magicians," said Sebastian. "Houma has lived too long. I used to think of Un-Maurag as the most evil, most hateful being, but Houma was born like a normal human and has no excuse."

"Maybe Julian will get him this time," added Rafir. "I've never seen him this angry before...."

As the fox trailed off, they could hear the Eye of Merlin croak loudly in the upper skies, a cry that was something between a sound of triumph, mixed with a sense of danger. Something in the Great Forest was changing significantly, perhaps even dramatically.

Chapter Eight

The Elf-Kindreds

THEY CAME TO A halt as the echoes of the eagle's cry died down. In front of them, Sophors and Alints were halting, while in the distant gloom of the Great Forest, it seemed that all their tier groups had also paused. A messenger on horseback was picking her way through the masses of small creatures, apparently seeking Kalanin. They rode to meet her.

"Géla wishes the four of you to join her," said the messenger. Her eyes lingered on the small, winged body of Julian's Familiar. "The inhabitants of Erivan Forest are making themselves known at last — Wood Elves are speaking to Géla, at this very moment and they seem not at all pleased with us. Come!" As they rode forward, the small creatures widened a path for them and watched with blinking, nervous eyes as the massive, mailed knights rode past.

Sebastian now sat on Galad's shoulder staring down at them, his small face filled with pity: here were small, defenseless peoples, uprooted from their sheltered lives, easy prey now to so many different carnivores. The little Familiar raised his eyes as they reached sub-tier ranks; these too, parted to let them pass.

"Captain Hangnail rides again," Galad murmured in his lowest voice. "But why is he suddenly back in favor?" Ahead of them, Géla stood on the forest floor, speaking there with tall, silver-haired Elves; each of the Elf sentries kept a bow at his side, and each bow was strung. Géla stepped away from the sentries and turned to Kalanin.

"These sentries block our way. Have you any words that will move them?" The Elf sentries watched Kalanin, somberly measuring him with farsighted eyes.

"Here, in the south of Erivan, the Kindreds live in peace," said one Elf sentry "We have no wish to quarrel with you mortals, but you must take your strife and warfare elsewhere." Kalanin studied the three for a moment: they seemed wary, but not tense, as though assistance could be summoned at a moment's notice. He stared back into the forest, to the north, where the Magicians fought with Houma and his Demon tools. He turned back to the sentries.

"We have an intersection, a convergence of forces here in the Great Forest," he said slowly. "We should wait here at your border's edge, while other events unfold. A conflict builds behind us: three lesser Magic Wielders face a great and powerful one. Can you sense anything of this clash?"

"I am not an Elf Mage," said one sentry, "but waves of power radiate from the north, so that only those completely lacking any Gift might ignore them. I feel the Sorcerer, as I felt his Waking Spell: a monster now attends him, obedient to his will."

"A Creature of the Darkness?" asked Géla, growing intent.

"We fear that one of our longbound, longsleeping foes has been aroused: The One/The Many, a being that once stalked us day and night. Your presence here has served to raise a nightmare for us. We need you to depart, drawing all your foes with you."

Kalanin shook his head. "We, too, are victims in this struggle. We also sought peace but have been denied it. We will not cross your borders; we will wait here. But I urge you to summon your masters to speak with us — to see whether there may not be some common purpose between our peoples."

"We cannot summon," the Elf sentry said, "though we will send word of your presence. Farewell for the moment. Be wary at night lest the Many seek you out. And do not come any further, for matters will then become far more difficult." The sentries turned, as one, and moved swiftly into the depths of Erivan. Kalanin mounted and turned back, but Géla grasped the reins of his horse.

"No, I'll need you here — but next time discuss matters with me before deciding or instructing. What's next?"

"Some sort of delay, short or long," said Kalanin. "A light meal if your supplies are adequate. With your permission, Galad and I will return north, to wait for our Magicians."

"You don't need my permission," said Géla, releasing the reins. "We will need to work more on the matter of which of us leads and which follows — but later."

They rode north again in the gloomy, overcast forest, leading three horses for their Gift Born allies. Rafir rode beside Galad, while Sebastian sat on Kalanin's shoulder, peering ahead, growing steadily more tense as he sensed powerful magic in the distance. The Great Forest was still; only the murmurs of the little Familiar could be heard in the damp quiet.

"There, not far...I can almost sense him, but...." Suddenly Sebastian cried out loud. "No, it's not the Sorcerer, it's one of the Dark Ones! Watch out!" Then, the little Familiar pulled himself from his trance. "Hurry!" he muttered to Kalanin and Galad. "They've lost, but Houma hasn't won completely either — hurry!" Kalanin and Galad urged their chargers to a gallop, and they sped forward over damp mosses. Above them, the forest seemed to waken, as the force of magic slipped from the forest floor.

"They're just up there," Sebastian said, "or what's left of them. They —" From behind a massive tree trunk, four Vorrs leaped out, snarling. Horses reared, but Galad and Kalanin slipped from their saddles and stood with drawn swords.

"Let them pass, you fools!" The eagle's voice came just a little distance from them. Vorrs backed away snarling, teeth still bared. Swords sheathed, Kalanin and Galad sprinted forward, with Rafir and Sebastian following just behind them.

On the forest floor, the three Magicians lay senseless, ashes from ruined branches and spell shock still drifting from them. The eagle was pecking and scratching at Julian's saddle pouch.

"Here!" cried Sebastian. His small fingers unlashed the pouch, drew Heart's Ease from it, then began to rub the herb first on Julian's lips, then on Héna's. Rafir stood between his old Mistress and his new Master, with sorrow surging over him. Héna's garments were strewn about, and she lay with legs exposed: white, stiff, with blue veins bulging from her calves. The fox knelt and began to lick her fingers.

"They should survive this encounter," said the eagle quickly, "that's not the problem." Vorr cries and snarls echoed beneath the leaves. "There is the problem!" cried the eagle, surging into the air. Kalanin turned back to their horses. Galad raced forward, drawing the Tarnished Sword.

Men serving the Three Hands were moving toward them, horses rearing as the Vorr flock struck at their flanks and the legs of riders. Galad leaped at their leader — and the Tarnished Sword swept the head from the lead rider's horse, with a fountain of blood gushing from its neck. As the carcass of the horse toppled, a second slash felled its rider. Galad turned to face another, but the men serving the Three Hands ripped at their reins, pulling away.

"It's that accursed sword — again," one of them called out. They moved farther back, numbering more than a score, with only three fallen. Their swords and spears were set aside, and they drew bows. Vorrs stalked the outriders, snarling — but the bows were aimed at the fallen Magicians.

The first arrow was loosed, striking the ground beside Julian. The second archer aimed, but the Eye of Merlin came sweeping through the gloom, talons raking the archer's hand and face. And from the left, Kalanin surged through the forest on horseback, spear extended — the foremost bowman went down, and a second was cast from his saddle. Vorrs took the fallen. Galad leaped forward, striking again. The rest fled in panic.

"Well timed, and well struck," said the eagle, wings still flared in killing lust, "but other hunting parties seek us even now. We must be gone, swiftly. How best to move the Magicians?"

"So, they live," said Kalanin. "Must they be kept quiet? Is it safe to move them?"

"They've been stricken by spells for the moment," said the eagle, after a pause, "but not for long, or so Merlin judges." Kalanin looked down at the three fallen shapes — even when cast down by sorcery, the enchantments of the Mistress of Illusions still held, and her beauty remained undiminished.

"Old age might well bring brittle bones for the two Sorceresses," said Kalanin, turning to the eagle, "unless there is some protection?"

"Each of them has guardian spells woven about them, some level of protection," said the eagle, "but of the nature of those spells, I know nothing." Kalanin was silent, listening. Almost at the edge of hearing, there seemed to be shuffling movements; the ears of Vorrs also lifted as though they, too, listened. Then the Vorrs faded once again into the silence of the Great Forest.

"No time left to fashion a litter," Kalanin said, voice low. "Galad, if you'll hold the old Sorceress in front of you on your saddle, then I'll take the Mistress of Illusions. Julian will have the roughest ride."

"And I will draw our foes from your trail," said the eagle, wings flared. "Rafir, go to Géla swiftly. Tell her that our party returns slowly with outriders at our backs." Eagle and fox sped away in different directions. Sebastian helped to lash Julian to the saddle, then the little Familiar watched over the Apprentice as their horses paced slowly southward.

Kalanin held the Mistress of Illusions propped in front of him in his saddle: she seemed like a dead thing, floppy, lifeless, but every few hundred paces she would gasp a deep breath, murmuring in a low hard voice, as though she had just one more incantation to complete.

Their journey back to their armed forces seemed to take forever, but halfway back, a force of twenty passed: dark haired women with hair bound tight, faces darkened, clad in somber forest grey clothes, loping silently past them, bows on their backs, preparing to defend the stricken Magic Wielders. Kalanin breathed more easily and moved to check the Apprentice: Julian jostled along, groaning a little with every sway of his slow striding horse.

Sebastian glanced at Kalanin reproachfully, but then a wagon came creaking forward, led by a mixed force carrying bows and spears. The three Magic Wielders were carefully placed, faces upward, on a bed of straw. Only Héna's eyes opened — but briefly before they rolled up and closed.

Kalanin found Géla at the southernmost edge, at the border where Elf sentries had halted their passage. She shook her head in dismay, as she heard Kalanin's tale.

"We were lucky, this once," she murmured, "but our luck can't last. We're overmatched both in sorcery and in tier strength — curse them! Now the inhabitants of Erivan are turning their backs on us: these sentries are hostile, calling on us to depart. Tomorrow, their leader, named Haldor, will come forward, no doubt to add authority to the Elf-Kindreds' dismissal. Where shall we go? Men serving the Three Hands move toward us from north, east, and west. Elvenfolk bar us from the south."

Kalanin looked out into the gloomy forest: evening neared, and even gloomy light was fading. "I have no answer — except an early sleep, so as to bring our best thoughts for tomorrow's events." He turned to go, but Géla caught him by the wrist.

"Listen to me," she said. "We're a strange mixture: fifteen hundred women warriors, old and young Magic Wielders. But someone must lead, someone must force decisions. I do not have the experience, nor have the others. It galls me more than you can imagine, but you must do it, you must lead."

"It's not that simple," Kalanin replied quietly. "I'm only a guest who has brought ruin and misfortune down upon his hosts. So how can it be my place to instruct them after the disaster?"

"This disaster is not your fault," Géla murmured. "The Sorcerers have brought ruin upon us all; now we must find some way to strike back." Kalanin stared into the distance but said nothing.

·)(·

It was late in the morning of the next day when Elf sentries again sought them out, bidding captains and Mortal Magic Wielders follow a little distance to the south, to meet with their leader. Héna rode propped up in a little cart, while Julian and the Mistress of Illusions each rode on horseback, though neither seemed steady. Kalanin, Géla, and Galad followed, with the Eye of Merlin on Kalanin's shoulder. Rafir and Sebastian trailed a little behind — uninvited, but not unexpected. All were silent, moving through the gloom of the Great Forest as though fulfilling some long promised, but meaningless task.

They entered a wide clearing where the trunks of great trees still appeared at regular intervals, but the upper growths had been trimmed or trained so that sunbeams poured through the highest branches, and patches of blue sky could be seen far above the forest's upper reaches.

A tall figure stood in the clearing's center, arms folded, watching their progress with only remote interest. A roughhewn long table was placed before him, with simple wooden chairs set about at intervals: from this, they judged that the Elf-Lord intended nothing like a lavish welcome.

Dismounting, they left their horses with the sentries and approached the Elf-Lord in silence. As though held by magic, even the upper branches were motionless and quiet. They bowed to the Elf-Lord, watching as the ageless face measured each of them in turn, and found them wanting. Kalanin's teeth set tighter as he perceived the remote hostility confronting them.

"I will not offer 'greetings,' or say, 'well met in the Great Forest.'" The Elf-Lord spoke softly, clearly, and there were hints of distant melody, chords of music woven within the tones of his voice. "You are here in the South of Erivan, clearly intruders, bringing war and conflict where peace has prevailed for ages. Why should we welcome you?" No answer came, but the Eye of Merlin cleared his throat: a harsh warning sound.

The Elf-Lord searched the faces of Julian, Héna, and the Mistress of Illusions. He motioned them to chairs, then sat also, a little back from the table, to be able to view each of them.

"I do not welcome you," continued the Elf-Lord, "but there is no need for hostility. I am Haldor, Lord of the Kindreds here in Erivan. You and your foes threaten to bring war and destruction down upon us. You must pass from the Great Forest. Your enemies have pursued you intently, yet now they will let you move west, unhindered, until you pass from the Erivan. After, you may resume your struggle."

"You mean that they have agreed to set a trap to the west and will permit us to walk into it at their convenience," snarled the eagle, wings beginning to flare.

"I cannot control events beyond the borders of the Erivan," said the Elf-Lord. "The dwellers of the Great Forest are not part of this contest."

"Are they not?" asked the eagle. "Behold our Magicians, how they stand so mournful, almost beaten. What do you believe transpired just yesterday?"

"A matter of mortal struggling against mortal, and not our affair."

"They tested Houma as he has not been tested before," said the eagle, peering intently at the Elf-Lord. "They might well have mastered him had he not called upon one other: a creature of power, some strangely configured monstrosity."

A shadow seemed to pass over the Elf-Lord's face and he bowed his head, saying in a low voice, "You do not realize what you have helped to bring about: after an age of peace The One/The Many has arisen once again, one of our greatest nightmares. Each sunrise The One will choose some shape of power, to assail our strongholds, consuming all ground flesh in the surrounding forest. Then at nightfall, it becomes The Many, a host of specters seeking to draw the life force from both Elves and mortals."

"This is the work of Houma and his dark masters," said the eagle. "They have raised a Creature of the Darkness from the hidden crypts of the Great Forest."

"Be warned: this is no blundering simple Creature," murmured the Elf-Lord, "but a shapeshifter that chooses each form with cunning and malice. In ancient times, The One/The Many was accounted the most powerful of the Creatures of the Darkness after the Nameless."

Haldor was silent for a moment then straightened and turned to Julian. "Still, they are not the only beings with evil servants. Vorr servants of Un-Maurag seem prepared to do your bidding, kill for you, protect you." The Apprentice took a deep breath as though struggling to rouse himself.

"Lord, I understand that you do not wish to become ensnared in our quarrel, and the words I speak now will seem like heavy chains upon you and your peoples: Houma conspired with Un-Maurag, bane of the Elf-Kindreds. I was brought before him and cast into the Mouth of Un-Maurag. The spirit of your brother was chained there, nearly broken by ages of torment. My master, Merlin, forged a Portal Passage for the Elf-Kindreds, allowing your brethren to test Un-Maurag to the utmost limits of his strength. When the Dark Lord's power was stretched thin, I broke the power of his dungeons, so that the dead immortals imprisoned there now are settling peacefully into the Temple of Waiting.

"To gain revenge, Un-Maurag sent a Vorr pack in pursuit of us. Instead of destroying them, I helped them become free of the Dark Lord, and now they aid me, repaying their debts to us."

The Elf-Lord looked at Julian with undisguised astonishment.

"And here are more words, more chains," Julian continued. "In the Hall of the Dreamers, your brother Voll sits, great among the Servants of the Maker, watching over the Elf-Kindreds. Perhaps he watches us now, from afar, and sees that the ancient struggle of Servant and Adversary has begun once again, and he wonders on which side the Kindreds will stand."

A long, slow look of sorrow passed over Haldor's face, and he shook his head slowly. "It is not so simple — yet I am not Giftless, nor filled with self deception. Now that I have spoken both with you and with Houma, it is no great matter to judge between you. Truth has a simple, direct tone, while the deceit of Houma is a complex melody, woven with intricate, perverse harmonies mixed with deep undertones of malice. Still, I cannot aid you directly, I cannot mass an Elven Host and cast down your enemies. Do you understand why?" Julian shook his head slowly; neither Héna nor the Mistress of Illusions made any sign.

"Is it a matter of strength or will?" asked Kalanin. "If I have understood Julian correctly, the Elf-Kindreds have hurled their main strength against their tormentor, Un-Maurag," Haldor spoke for a moment under his breath, and his fingers traced spell words over the table's rough wood grain. Julian felt the distant echoes of shattering sounds as though the links of faraway Divinations were broken.

"That should have been done sooner," Haldor said quietly. "Many forces, both benevolent and evil, have been interested in our words; now they must speculate. For you are correct: there is no Elven Host at my back to be hurled at your adversaries. With our main strength set before the fortress of Un-Maurag, we are weaker than many realize. Yet, if I wished, those of the Three Hands would be assailed by a hailstorm of arrows and slingcasts. This I will not do, for I am wary of the Truce." Julian sat upright, while the dreaming, distant eyes of the Mistress of Illusions focused for the first time on the Elf-Lord.

Haldor took a deep breath. "No, I cannot recite the Truce Terms for you; the Kindreds were not present when the Great Gods reached their pact. We were born later, into the Mid-World of the Truce. Yet there are benevolent Powers, ones who have dealt kindly with us, and the Kindreds are well represented at their courts, as envoys or servants: even now, I am linked with my brethren as they attend the Gods.

"For many ages, Un-Maurag was our tormentor, and we would ask of the most benevolent Powers, 'Cannot you great ones put down or control this monster? Surely nothing could stand against your combined might.' But we were told that the Truce would not permit such alliances, even of two God-beings against a third. Think for a moment on this matter. Why should an alliance of Gods be forbidden?"

"Perhaps they feared that the ancient struggles between Servant and Adversary would be renewed," Julian said, hesitating.

"Beyond that," added Kalanin, "an alliance of Gods would bring about a terrible tyranny, an iron hand clamped down over the chaos of the Mid-World."

Haldor nodded. "You should understand that we, the Elf-Kindreds, would be a third party to this struggle, and violate the spirit of the Truce, should we enter this conflict."

Héna struggled to sit upright. "Those of us who watched the Powers in conflict noted that only one single Power was arrayed on each side: Zòs felling the empire of Typhon; or Marduk wasting his power against the bastion of Amon-Ra. Yet we did not know that these outcomes were determined by the Truce Terms."

"Again, these Terms seem a barrier for us, and a Portal Passage for our foes," Julian said, shaking his head. "What happens next? Both in weapon bearers and weight of sorcery, we are overmastered and must flee. Will you permit us to pass south?"

"You may pass," answered Haldor, "but do not let the Vorrs serving you into the South of Erivan, for my people will pierce them with whatever weapons that are at hand, and, without hesitation. Also, we will replenish your food and weapon-stocks. If there are other needs, state them."

"Food and weapons," said Géla, after a pause. "There's no time for wagon-work or the mending of canvas."

"No — no," croaked the eagle. "Hold for a moment. You three possessing the Gift are still stunned by your conflict with Houma and do not perceive that we are at a crux, an intersection in this struggle, for this was the time foreseen by Merlin, whereby his own power would be put into play. Jealous dark Gods have blocked him with Portal bars, but he perceives dimly that there are other forces, other shifting streams of power. At this moment all our hidden pathways are passing from us as though obscured by banks of enchanted fog."

Kalanin nodded. "I have no feel for these 'intersections' or 'hidden passages,' but there's more to say — you will let us pass through the South of Erivan, and our foes behind us will follow, unchecked, will they not?"

"We are a third party to this struggle," Haldor replied evenly, "and may not intervene."

"But what of this Creature of the Darkness?" asked Kalanin. "Is it not also a third party? Will this monstrosity also be allowed to pass?"

Haldor's face grew troubled. "The One is an ancient enemy, but we have not the strength to stop him, even were he not shielded by so many men and the evil Sorcerer. He would have to pass — curse Houma for waking him! Long ago, Nablus, the Great Binder, sought the Creatures one by one and put them down. But now Houma has resurrected the Nightmare of Erivan."

"So," continued Kalanin, "let us say that we stand our ground, and turn to face the Sorcerer, with his many tiers, and his Creature? What then? Can you bring force, at least against this Creature, your ancient foe, and also a third party in this conflict?"

Haldor turned away, staring into the distance. "Not weapons; I fear that with the tide of battle sweeping back and forth, we would be thrown against the men serving the Three Hands —The One must choose a shape that will make it master of the battlefield, one of power and terror. We will seek some way to counter its raw strength, and its cunning as a spellcaster. If you can fend it off until nightfall, it will be transformed into The Many, beings you might withstand with bright fire and bitter magic. But even should we manage to check this being, you are heavily overmatched. Have you grown tired of your brief lives? Or have you become desperate?"

"Defeat is coming for us," Kalanin said. "We are seeking some way to avoid destruction. While we struggle, we are burdened and cannot flee far: we shield two small peoples, Sophors and Alints, who move slowly and fearfully. Without us, they would become easy prey for the flesh eaters of Erivan. You advise us that the Kindreds are well represented at the courts of the Powers. Can one or more of these God-beings be persuaded to shelter our small charges? Surely that aid will not violate the Truce Terms."

Haldor was silent for a moment, as though listening to distant voices. "It may be done, and easily at that — my people have always advised that the Gods are prone to benevolent gestures, ones that require little effort, and involve few consequences. Is there more you require of me?" Kalanin nodded.

"Yes, there is more, of increasing complexity: a steady tide of men and weapons swells the power of those serving the Three Hands. Can the Powers discourage or halt this flow? It should now be clear that the emblem of the Three Hands is but a device of the Demon Princes, and their agents, the Sorcerers."

"It is not yet clear to the Powers," said Haldor, "though they have become most wary of the Sorcerers."

"Tel-Alantir understands these matters," Julian added. "Perhaps now is the time to ask his aid. Let Tel-Alantir reveal to the other Powers how destructively the Sorcerers behaved in his domain."

"We will approach Tel-Alantir," said Haldor. "What more?"

"Lord, if I may suggest a course for us all," Kalanin said, eyes fixed on Haldor. "First, a rapid departure of the Vorrs from Erivan and Elven bows. Let them spy out a safe passage for Julian's journey to the east. Our tiers will fall back to the South of Erivan, while the Kindreds fashion safe passages for Alints and Sophors. To check our pursuers, the Kindreds need only make a minor show of force, a feint, some pretense of marshaling, then stand back, unless we confront The One." Haldor nodded. Kalanin looked to the faces about him; the eagle was staring back with unblinking eyes.

"Thus far," Kalanin continued, "we have accomplished only a little, a clearing of complexities and a purchase of more time."

"There is another thought," said the eagle, eyes focused on Kalanin, "just at the edge of your consciousness. We stand at a most complex intersection."

"Yes," said Kalanin, taking a deep breath. "I must summon the men of the Dragon's Teeth. Let Baroda, the Grey Captain, pass from the Mid-World to the South of Erivan."

"Yet when I called him from his enchanted sleep," Julian said softly, intently, "he was held only for a time until the struggle between Thorian and Balardi was resolved."

"But *I* never dismissed him," said Kalanin. "And let the Kindreds pass to Baroda this message: let him look to the twin fates of Héna and the Mistress of Illusions. All those who have aided the League have been brought down. Baroda may aid the League while it still stands, or he may face Sorcerers and Marids and Demon Princes alone when the Wizards' League is destroyed."

He turned to Julian, Héna, and the Mistress of Illusions, murmuring "We have more to do, but you will have what you looked for, an intersection, a major struggle of weapons and sorceries, here upon the gloomy floor of the Great Forest."

Chapter Nine

War Plans

THEY MOVED WEST FIRST, then south, then east again, staying at least a day's march from Houma and his tier-groups; but they found themselves always forced farther from Julian's goal, the Vale of Whispers. On the seventh day after their meeting with Haldor, Julian was riding beside Héna, both speaking in hushed tones of ways to counter Houma and his strength of sorcery.

"As powerful as Balardi, the eagle believes," Héna said, shaking her head slowly, "and yet he may not be as resourceful, because Houma has not wielded great power for as long —" She broke off, and they halted, staring into the distance. The Elf-tiers moved silently and were nearly invisible in their grey cloaks, but the Gifts within Sorceress and Apprentice stirred with their passage.

Julian felt some of his grim depression lift: he had allies now, leaders and warriors and Magic Wielders, so he no longer faced Houma alone. Baroda, the Grey Captain was coming, leading a force of more than six thousand men of the Dragon's Teeth, in twelve tiers. And Haldor was providing aid, keeping Houma's forces unbalanced by shifting tiers of Wood Elves to their foe's flanks, while hurling harsh weather at those flocking to the banner of the Three Hands.

Houma's anger hung like a heavy vapor in the air, leaving a weight of tension and the threat of ruin hovering over the darkened forest. Yet Haldor had kept his distance from the Sorcerer, staying outside of Houma's reach for the moment.

"It's so strange being with the two of you, a little like being deaf," Rafir said, breaking the silence. "I know when you're hearing or feeling something, because you both stare in the same direction, while I hear, see, and smell nothing." Héna reached over and ruffled Rafir's soft red fur.

"The Elf-Lord is a far better ally than I ever thought possible," Julian murmured. "I wonder if he understands his peril."

"Or his doom," said Héna. "Houma is one thing and the Marids another — I no longer permit myself to dream, for each nightly vision ends with huge Marids created by Demon Princes rising from the ocean waters." Julian said nothing, but the Gift brought him an image of ocean waters, drawing back from the shore, opening a vast, sandy carpet as though preparing a greeting for monsters. He took a deep breath, telling himself that The One and The Many were monsters enough for now. Clearing both images and thoughts from his mind, he rode silently through the dark forests, shifting to the left to avoid the base of one ancient, moss-covered tree.

· ✕ ·

A few hundred paces away, the Mistress of Illusions rode beside Kalanin, studying him out of the corner of her eyes, reading a portion of his moods and inner thoughts.

"So, that old busybody, Héna, has once again interfered, counseling you and my granddaughter of your fate and future. Ha! No Gift was needed to perceive Géla's interest, but you are dense, as thick as some of these huge treetrunks. And worse, somehow you expect me to —" she broke off, turning suddenly to the east, gazing into the dreary overcast forest.

"Your words seemed likely to be only the beginning of a long speech," Kalanin noted dryly. "What made you stop?"

"Elf Mage Portal Spells," she said quietly. "Very different from our own work. But the effect is the same: Baroda is coming, with many tiers behind him."

"The pieces are nearly in place, and we may yet match our foes in tiers and strength of sorcery. What of this Creature, though? Haldor seemed greatly concerned about this being, The One/The Many."

"It follows, unchecked, and fear surges from those around it, except that Houma fears nothing, neither foe nor ally."

Kalanin smiled. "We might change that, especially if we quarrel with Houma alone, and not among ourselves."

"I'll behave," the Mistress of Illusions said grimly, then she softened. "Of course, there's always a chance that this Baroda will prove far more interesting than my jaded, erstwhile lover, whose eyes have now begun to wander. Come, your ally now waits, and he brings a strange mixture of men and not-men. It would be good if the two of us greeted him first."

Sentries were racing toward them, warning of tier movements to the south, but Kalanin waved them off, riding quickly south beside the Mistress of Illusions, his mind turning over the phrase, "men and not-men." Those born from the Dragon's Teeth had seemed to drift toward one of two groups: mortals, or a second destiny, a Mid-World, perhaps immortal fate — "not-men."

Grey men were becoming visible in the distance, and as they sighted Kalanin, a shout lifted from them, calling out as one, so that the gloom hovering over the Great Forest seemed to shift with the echoes of their voices.

A surge of joy raced through Kalanin's mind as he rode forward: that was the same cry called out when the Ruined Angel had fallen to his death on the battlefield before Gravengate. He passed the first rank of Grey Men, his hand raised in salute. Now, perhaps anything was possible — his thought broke, and he heard a sharp gasp from the Mistress of Illusions: the first of the "not-men" had come into view. Some were gaunt and spectral, transforming into the forms of wraiths, but others were hunched with the first growth of beast fur spreading over their hands and faces. Humans, mortal brothers, stood among these "not-men," completely unafraid.

In the center of these milling tier-groups, they found Baroda, the Grey Captain, standing with arms folded, smiling at them gravely. Kalanin leaped from his horse, embracing the Grey Captain with both arms.

"Well met, Baroda! The tides are shifting against the Sorcerers and their masters, the Demon Princes! Beside me now is the Mistress of Illusions, a Sorceress in her own right, with more than two tiers of archers attending her." Baroda bowed; the Mistress of Illusions regarded him closely, staring down from horseback.

"Here also is one endowed with the Gift or the Sight," she murmured. "Is this not so, Grey Captain, lord of men and not-men?"

"A small thing of little significance," Baroda said easily. "At times I am able to perceive the intent of sorcerous creatures, or of those born with the Gift — all around us I feel pressure from Houma, a heavy menace, not far, but not yet within striking distance, and there are others." He paused, staring into the face of the Mistress of Illusions as two pairs of cool grey eyes measured and tested one another.

"Madam, ally and future friend," continued the Grey Captain, "will you excuse us for a few moments? Out of old practice, I would like to walk my former commander through our tier strength and let him describe the balance of forces building in Erivan." The Mistress of Illusions raised her eyebrows, but Kalanin nodded imperceptibly, and the Sorceress withdrew.

As they rode through the milling ranks, Kalanin told Baroda of the Sorcerers and their war against the League, how Julian and Galad sought the Truce Terms only to be countered by Houma at every step. As he spoke, Kalanin watched the Men of the Dragon's Teeth: "not-men," both furred and gaunt as wraiths, seemed to be assigned only routine tasks, and even with their modest efforts, many were becoming distracted, staring into the gloomy forest as though distant voices were calling to them.

And there were many, many wagons, carrying huge supplies of stores and weapons, as though they had long prepared for the struggle in Erivan. Kalanin trailed off.

"Yes, we were ready," Baroda said, following Kalanin's eyes, and his thoughts. "My actions were not altogether heroic, and for this reason, I wished to speak with you alone. After, you may tell others in our strange alliance whatever portion of the tale you wish. But first, hear what befell those of us fashioned from fragments of Dragon's Teeth, born into conflict on a blood drenched battlefield.

"Part of me wished to remain with you and share in the courage and defiance of your League, but the Mid-World also called to me, a never-ending world of wonders, where all things seemed possible. And *I* was changing — was it possible that a seedling Gift within me might sprout and grow? Now it has blossomed, but only bearing the Sight. I will never be able to manipulate the sorcerous matter of the Mid-World to fashion my own domain." Baroda paused, staring thoughtfully into the distance.

"Loran, known long ago as an Apprentice to your Wizards," Baroda continued. "Did you know of him?"

"By sight only, and that was many years ago. In the time of Orlan's strength, Loran was apprenticed first to Merlin, then Thorian. Later, he slipped away into the service of some Power. His defection was no source of pleasure to his Wizard Masters."

"He never did name his patron, but under the guidance of that Power, he passed first into full Adept's rank, then grew toward the level of a Sorcerer. He seems to have parted on good terms with his patron, and he sought me, proposing that we would together be lords of our own dominion, that our joined strength might be equal to that of a lesser Power. The thoughts in his mind were for the most part benign, though there were hints that Loran aspired to greater power while assigning a lesser role for me as captain general.

"We began the creation of our own world, Loran guided somewhat by my thoughts on the building of fortresses, and the needs of my people. Many others also flocked to us from Alantéa, wives for my people, orphans seeking shelter; while, with my insight I was able to turn aside all the spies of the Mid-World.

"Only a brief time passed before we noticed that many of my people were beginning to drift from their human shapes, becoming 'not-men,' as you call them, growing the fur of beasts or becoming gaunt. Perhaps four in ten changed. At first, they still followed my directions, but later they began drifting away.

"Loran was not greatly concerned about this matter, as most of his attention was focused on Houma and Cronar who were raising a powerful force under the banner of the Three Hands. News filtered toward us that the League was threatened, and Loran would glance at me from the corners of his eyes, as though uncertain of my allegiance, and there were Divinations that were not shared with me. As Loran grew less secure, I made some effort to ready my people and gather provisions. In truth, these were only halfhearted gestures — I was too comfortable in our kingdom, dazzled by the growth of our Mid-World domain.

"So, we continued, a little uneasily, but holding firm, until Cronar came to Loran, warning him from interfering in your League's destiny. I was included in their discussions, where Cronar, grim and humorless, put a deathly fear into Loran's mind: I could see the tiny beads of sweat merge and drip down my ally's face as he sought to reassure Cronar.

"The old, grim Sorcerer was well pleased when he left, for he had thought little of me, considering that Loran had power enough to restrain me. But I had stared more deeply into Cronar's mind and saw that our destruction was certain — that after the League's fall, we, and all others who had aided the League would be brought down without mercy.

"Later, when I shared this vision with my ally, he grew even more fearful, but in a short time later, he steadied, seeing that he might preserve himself if he abandoned his dreams of power. Loran is gone now, deeply hidden within the Mid-World, and I am here, no longer reluctant, as my fate seems intertwined with yours."

"And you are not our only reluctant ally," Kalanin said, face puzzled. "Have the Sorcerers a death wish that they desire to draw all possible enemies into this struggle? The Mistress of Illusions, like you, might have held back, had they not struck at her. Is there a reason for this rashness?"

"I was able to read only a portion of Cronar's thought," Baroda said, "but it seemed clear that he was acting on instructions, from some well-laid plans."

Kalanin nodded, then said quietly, "We should consider that one of the Great Powers is also at work; Zôs, or Wotan, Ra, or some other great Power, is seeking discreetly to forge an alliance against the Demon Princes. Striking first, the Sorcerers have smoked out portions of such an alliance, bringing them early into battle, before they might combine with many others and truly threaten those serving the Three Hands. The Sorcerers have been far, far ahead of us, and may yet surprise us here in Erivan Forest."

· X ·

Moving south and east, they marched with speed through the long afternoon and early evening. The Grey Captain seemed to anticipate Kalanin's wishes, and Géla, also foreseeing their needs, formed a rearguard, leaving parties of archers to screen for their opponent's rangers and outriders. The three Magicians rode apart, in silence, watching as messengers and tier leaders surged about, seeking Baroda and Géla. Only a small portion of Kalanin's mind followed their shifting tier-groups, for on the next day or the day after, they would be forced to turn and face the Sorcerer Houma, with his many men, his reawakened Creature of the Darkness, and his own unchallenged force of sorcery.

In forces of men, those led by Houma were out mastered both in numbers and in training, yet many of those following Houma were horsed, weighted with heavy metal on bulky chargers. In matters of sorcery, the balance might seem more even, with Julian, Héna and the Mistress of Illusions ranged against Houma. The three Magicians had grown quiet, reserved, after their initial failure, and yet their confidence seemed intact: they were grim rather than fearful. With The One, a Creature of the Darkness, they would encounter an unknown adversary, and perhaps the real reason for Houma's heedless, almost reckless advance.

During their last struggle, another Creature, the Dark Emissary, had been forced from the field, first by a mass of hundreds of men armed with pike and bow. Then Galad and Julian had joined forces to strike that being down. Galad would help again, with a thousand spears or more behind him. They would need spell guards, and more stratagems, more deceptions for Houma. Kalanin rode off, seeking Julian.

At nightfall, they made a hasty camp, still under the boughs of the Great Forest, but only a few leagues to the south the forest ended, leading to the rolling meadows and farms and wooded rangelands of Alantéa. Kalanin fell asleep sheltered by a slip of tarpaulin, dreaming of sunlight pouring over open country.

And he woke with a shudder, to find Baroda standing above him in the darkness, calling out his name. An ugly smell hung in the air, as though a cool but foul wind was passing through their camp.

"We've encountered some device of Houma's," Baroda murmured. "I, and the Wielders of Magic woke only moments ago. It was not directed at us, rather to another part of Erivan. Come, arise. Let us see what Houma has brought into this conflict."

Kalanin stood quickly, seeking boots and weapons. Sentries were trying to control scores of stumbling, only partially awake men, and women. "Not-men" were drifting to the north, faces all turned in the same direction. Baroda called out an order, and the second watch was called early, and rose grumbling, while others tried to quiet the turbulent camp. Kalanin and Baroda drew flaming torches from the watch and moved swiftly north, with a tainted wind tugging at their cloaks.

They found Julian at the edge of their camp's northernmost post, and with him stood the Mistress of Illusions, each of them bathed in pale mage light, a glow that seemed to retreat as the rays cast by flickering torches came closer. Héna was shuffling slowly toward Julian, just as Kalanin and Baroda arrived, and the old Sorceress was coughing: the north wind was blowing bits of dried moss and spores and fragments of shaggy bark at them as it stirred both the upper branches and the forest floor.

Kalanin and Baroda said nothing but stood facing north. Above them, the eagle sounded a warning, and in a moment, their eyes picked up a muffled light in the distance, a silver glow that drifted above the forest floor, winding its way toward them. Kalanin stood beside the others, with his eyes darting to the right and left. Both those born with the Gift, or the Sight were tense, waiting, though they were not expecting a battle.

A beating of wings came out of the darkness, and a weight settled on Kalanin's shoulder — the Eye of Merlin. As the eagle waited with him, watching the silver glow, the Eye hissed when the figure drifted into view: it was Haldor, or the ghost of the Elf-Lord, legs striding toward them, but its feet swept several paces above the ground as though held aloft by the North Wind.

When the figure reached them, it settled to the ground until it stood before Julian, but its eyes searched each face as though reaching for their minds. Mouth open, it began to speak, with harsh, choked sounds, as though a lifetime's phlegm lay trapped in its throat.

"Hold, and begin again," said the Mistress of Illusions gently. As the North Wind gusted, the figure glowed more brightly, like a lump of silver coal, then it spoke clearly.

"Do not fear me, mortals; there is no need to. Haldor lives and I am no Shade."

"No," Julian murmured, "a messenger, or emissary."

"Both more and less. I am a simulacrum of the mind of Haldor, a construct that mirrors his thoughts." A brief, sad smile flickered over the apparition's face. "My knowledge will last only a brief time before the decay begins, and then I will wander, growing ever more witless, until daybreak. Now, speak. Ask."

"We felt warfare in the darkness, and it woke us," Julian said quickly. "If your master lives, then Houma's sorcerous attack has failed. Is this so?"

"Yes, my master lives but wounded, seeking shelter far from here. The Kindreds will pass from Erivan, and monsters and the allies of Dark Lords will rule the Great Forest unless you defeat them. Even now, The Many in nightmare spectral shapes attack my people, and the Kindreds have strength barely enough to flee.

"I reached you only by rising above the grasp of phantoms," the construct continued, "though they groped for me with fingers sharpened like the blades of scythes. We fear for you, human warriors, and Mortal Magic Wielders. For Houma has mastered a Power's strength, and The One/The Many is the most fell of the Creatures of the Darkness. I, Haldor, have summoned aid: one called Armagh will come, with an Elf-Seer. Do not fear Armagh, he is powerful, seeming like a great beast but closer to mortal men in his wisdom and understanding. Soon Armagh's understanding will be greater than my own, for wisdom will slip from me after the briefest of times. Ask!"

Julian reached out a hand and would have touched the construct, but it backed away, saying, "No, you will only speed the decay."

"There should be some way for us to help you, to thank you and your master," Julian said softly. "In the beginning, Haldor seemed such an unwilling ally, yet you have done much, much more than we thought possible."

"I, Haldor, am the most cautious of Elf-Lords, yet I understand that the destiny of the Kindreds is linked with that of the Maker Servants. Our doom may be upon us, with Demon Princes, Marids, Sorcerers and Dark Lords seeking to destroy us, but the Kindreds will not pass without a struggle. Ask!"

"What does Haldor know of the Marids?" asked Kalanin. "Has he a way of countering them?"

"Their time is not yet come," murmured the simulacrum, it voice seeming to fade a little. "Yet when they come, we of the Endless Springtimes will stand helpless before them. Only the Powers...." The voice trailed off.

"Yes, the Powers! Why do I waste my short life with mere mortal conjurors? I will call upon the Mid-World of the Truce and summon the Powers!" The simulacrum began to drift back, silver glow rising and falling like an ember stirred by gusts of wind.

"No, wait," said the Mistress of Illusions softly. "See within yourself, how you are lessening. You will pass, soon, drifting alone amid the tree trunks. I will stay with you until the end if you wish." She stepped forward, chanting in a low voice, and as the Elven simulacrum hesitated, her chanting voice passed into song. Then, the two drifted away, the Mistress of Illusions beginning to glow with a silver light like her companion.

Julian turned to his allies. "So, Houma and his Creature Indomitable have swept the Elf-Kindreds from Erivan. Haldor sends aid of some sort, though he considers our survival unlikely. This sunrise brings battle, with only a few hours of sleep remaining for this night."

"Sleep is farthest from my thoughts," said Baroda, watching Sorceress and apparition drifting through the gloom. "Even now, I can feel the mind of Houma pulse and throb with dark designs; while The Many hunt and feast on the dark forest floor." They sat, facing north, talking in low tones, until dawn came sliding over them, with a heavy cloud cover that was both grey and distant white, like a tide of glacial ice.

·)(·

With the dawn, Kalanin paced the marshaling of their tier-groups so that they passed through food stations in shifts. There was still no sign of their foes, but from the upper branches came the first scurrying and fluttering sounds as the most fearful and wary of the forest's small creatures began fleeing south.

Sebastian turned first to the movements in the upper branches, then to the north where Houma wove spells that spread fear like a dark wind. Lastly, Sebastian watched Julian's face as the Apprentice readied himself for battle against the Dark Sorcerer. Sadly, and without saying farewell, the little Familiar led Rafir far to the rear, where they took refuge in a large tree trunk, watching above the battlefield from a crevice where owls had once perched and readied themselves for their hunt in the night's darkness.

On the forest floor, Magic Wielders and those sensitive to the presence of magic, waited. They watched their own forces marshal, while from the north a heavy weight of menace formed, a probing turmoil of fear. At the topmost branches, the Eye of Merlin saw that the migration of the upper forest was building to a floodtide, and steadily waves of dread grew heavier, beating without mercy against the eagle's Farsight.

Galad watched those sensitive to magic as their discomfort grew, and as it built, it reached beyond them, even into his own mind; while at his side, the Tarnished Sword was shifting and moaning as though preparing its hymn of battle.

Movement flashed from the edge — Galad reached for the Tarnished Sword, but it was only the first small herd of deer, bounding to the edges of their camp, then racing around them. Among the men of the Dragon's Teeth, a few began to murmur and hiss, baring their teeth, as the unhuman fur bristled on their backs and arms — yet their sounds were muffled, restrained, even when a wolf pack loped into the edge of their camp's perimeter, then sped away, howling.

Pressure built, though, as waves of fear reached beyond those with the Gift or the Sight, and into human ranks. Héna began to call out counterspells, while the Mistress of Illusions wove spells shielding the minds for those born of the Dragon's Teeth. But her own women warriors stood tall and fearless, facing north, their long dark hair unruffled in the stillness of the dimly lit forest.

Fear within the camp lessened — then surged, as by chance a Muon sauntered into their camp, half careless, half forced by waves of fear. With a bear's bulk, but lithe as a cat, the Muon stared scornfully at the wall of spears facing it, preparing to spring. From the west, a league distant, came a shriek of pure terror, of a man's throat, almost bursting with fear. The Muon shifted its bulging monster eyes from the rank of spearmen before it — to see that scores of grim arrows were ready to strike at it. Snarling, it scurried north, then east, vanishing into the gloom of the Great Forest.

More sounds came from the west: a heavy tread, a ground shuddering passage over the forest floor. More shrieks of terror rang out as the footsteps drew closer.

"No arrows, no spears," Julian murmured to those around him. Kalanin sent messengers to sub-tier leaders, and as the order rippled through their ranks, weapons were lowered, but all eyes were turned to the west.

A huge figure began to emerge from the shadows of the Great Forest, moving swiftly toward them with a hunched, shuffling gait. Beside the huge figure, an Elf-Seer rode on horseback, tall and proud, but dwarfed by the enormous brown furred creature behind it. Again, a shriek rang out, less strong, but much closer: the creature held something in its hand — a human, who thrashed, crying out in terror.

An image filled Galad's mind, and he realized with a start that a portion of his memory had searched through old images learned at Sea's Edge — and had identified the gigantic brown furred figure that strode toward them: a giant ground sloth, a stubby faced massive figure. But this creature was so much greater in scale than the image in his mind; this creature was a giant among giants.

Straight into camp, the Elf-Seer rode, his huge companion trailing just behind him. They came to a halt, standing before Kalanin and the Mistress of Illusions, the Elf features staring at them with the remote, grim look of a person sent on some distant, hopeless task.

"Armagh is my companion and ally," said the Seer. "I am Alfilas, sent by the Kindreds to your aid. One travels with us unwillingly, one who stalked us and now greatly regrets his recklessness." At a sign from the Seer, Armagh lowered his hand, letting his captive slip to the forest floor: a young ranger of little more than twenty years, wearing the emblem of the Three Hands, and weeping with fear.

"Armagh and I have had little dealings with mortals, so you must do with him as your customs dictate." The youth struggled to his feet, trying to run, but his legs buckled beneath him, and he lay twitching on the ground like a broken insect. Julian stirred as though waking from a long, dark nightmare. Only moments remained before battle. Less than half a league from them the mind of Houma seethed as though infested by dark, inhuman wraiths. Around the Sorcerer his human allies marched, growing steadily grimmer as conflict neared.

Julian stepped forward, weaving the healer's sleep over the captive, then casting a healing spell over his injured legs.

"Take him a little distance from this place," Julian said quietly. "Bind him lightly so that if his brethren find him, they will see that he was made captive and was never a traitor to his cause." He turned to the Elf-Seer, Alfilas. "We will try not to become akin to our enemies, to mirror their corruption. Yet it will not always be this easy."

Alfilas glanced north, sensing that Houma and his monster neared, but were not yet upon them, and he signaled to the giant beast beside him. Armagh sank to the ground with a *thumping* sound, the forest floor quivering from his huge mass.

The Elf-Seer looked at each of them coolly, clearly, studying Magicians, Captains, sorcerous beings and one sorcerous weapon. Then he sighed and spoke softly, almost to himself.

"It is surprising that you resist such corruption, for this violence ruins both mortals and immortals — yet now we are here. Your Sorcerers and Wizards mean little to us, but The One/The Many is an ancient foe, and among the greatest of the Creatures Indomitable — it seems only a few of the endless springtimes since I sought the Binder, and together we brought down this monster."

"Nablus, an age ago," said Julian. "But now the Binder is far from us, seated at peace in the Hall of the Dreamers, beneath the Cup of the Maker. Here, at this intersection, we can no longer seek to bind Houma and his monster. It is corrupting, ruinous, yet we must bring about their destruction. Mortal tier-groups serving the Three Hands may be dispersed, but the Sorcerer and his Creature of the Darkness must perish. Will you aid us?" Alfilas nodded, while Armagh simply watched their faces with his enormous, moist eyes. The Elf-Seer reached out, patting Armagh's shaggy fur.

"We will aid you, though both the task and the price to be paid seem likely to be great. For the One has been taught by Houma to choose a form we cannot master: the Seer's Sight within me brings visions of the Temple of Waiting for myself, and for Armagh, the Long Sleep. May the Maker be generous at the time of the Awakening."

"Thoughts have stirred in my mind that the Maker will take our best and most generous thoughts and move far beyond them," Julian said softly, and he, too, reached out and smoothed Armagh's beast fur.

Then his voice was raised. "Now, we are ready! One last testing, then if the Maker permits this will be my last battle! Houma, we await you! Houma, on this day we shall send your shrunken soul shrieking into the shadows!"

From the north came a piercing cry, then a clash of metal, as Houma's tier-groups smashed spears and shields together.

And then the eagle, the Eye of Merlin surged out of the shadowy forest, to light on Kalanin's shoulder.

"Not just yet," the eagle croaked. "This battle has a forerunner." As the eagle spoke, the Blue Amulet on Julian's chest began to flicker and flash with blue light.

"Just what *is* that thing?" Héna asked. "Sometimes it gleams with a blue light, but what does that mean?"

"Normally it means that Houma is coming," Julian murmured, "but for the moment he's too far away to —"

A booming sound echoed through the forest, and only a hundred paces distant from them an oval formed in the air, like a Portal leading to a far distant part of the forest. Gleaming within this Portal a huge projection of Houma's face emerged, sneering down on them; and on Houma's chest his Red Amulet flared with power.

"No need for all this intricate untidy warfare," Houma's sneering voice echoed down at them. "Red Amulet masters Blue Amulet again, and the Apprentice falls, with all the rabble around him fleeing to certain death. Farewell, Apprentice!"

"Not this time," Julian said softly, then to Héna and the Mistress of Illusions, he murmured, "Reach to me and link."

As they did so, Julian's Blue Amulet gleamed with power, as did the Red Amulet on Houma's chest. For the first time, Julian felt a burning sensation race over his chest, and both Amulets began to whine and moan as power gathered to their cores.

Slowly, the gloating, sneering expression slipped from Houma's face. Seconds later the projection in the sky of Houma's giant features began to radiate alarm, and finally, his Red Amulet burst, casting the Sorcerer's projection down, away from his Vision Portal.

On Julian's chest, his Amulet gleamed one last time, then faded into blue smoke and vanished. Only the empty, vacant midair Portal continued to radiate images from the sky of a different part of the forest.

Galad shook his head grimly; this *Projection* was something Houma had learned from Tel-Alantir, and so the Sorcerers were learning from the Gods, in addition to gaining all the tools passed to them by Demon Princes.

"What did all of that mean?" Kalanin muttered to Galad.

A voice, Houma's voice, came from the Portal overhead. "What it means is that one of the Great Gods supported the feeble Apprentice, and now, having accomplished that Power's purpose, the Apprentice is left to his natural end, which, of course, is death." Then the mid-air Portal closed and vanished.

"I think it means that we now have a chance, Galad said. "If Houma were completely certain about victory, he would not have bothered with a clash of Amulets. And yet our chances seem very, very slim."

"Better slim than none," Kalanin said, and he sent out messengers to again reorganize all the scattered sub-tiers and their supporting archers. "Anyway, all the pieces for this battle have now moved into place."

Chapter Ten

The Battle of Erivan Forest

NOW THE GREAT, COMPLEX Battle of Erivan Forest began at last. Tier lines began shifting slowly north. Woman warriors began to hum, then slipped into their war chant, their strong clear voices echoing beneath the upper reaches of the Great Forest.

Kalanin called out marching orders to their left flank but halted in mid-sentence. A vast feeling of unease was slipping over him, like an invisible, silent plague. Horses began to whinny, while tier ranks came to a halt. With a cry of warning the Eye of Merlin leaped from Kalanin's shoulder. The forest seemed to darken as great cloud banks grew swollen beneath a distant, unseen sun.

"Nothing stops Houma for long!" the Mistress of Illusions cried out, voice rising in anger. "Houma is using his Demon Tools and so matter blended with magic is shifting beneath the forest floor!"

"And from above," Héna muttered. The old Sorceress stood, stooped, staring into the upper branches. Tremors began rippling through the forest floor, shaking a hail of debris down from above. Thunder rolled in from overhead, as weighted lightning massed.

Then the ground bucked and heaved. Gigantic trees, some more than a thousand years old, began to split and topple. Horses began to run wild; tiers broke ranks, scrambling for shelter. No hiding places could be found.

"Now, lad, help us!" cried Héna. "There were only two of us before!" Julian picked up the chant; the three Magic Wielders spoke almost as one as tremors raced over the ground. A weighted lightning bolt crashed over the horizon, deflected, while soft rain pattered through the leafy upper branches as the ground subsided. Milling and resorting, tier ranks closed, and began moving forward again, the voices of woman warriors chanting their hymns of battle.

"Now, while he readies his next strike," Héna muttered between clenched teeth. The chant of the three shifted, no longer uniform, as three voices wove complex spell elements together.

Above them, an oily, black smoke began to form, swirling thick and dark. Grey hands emerged from black clouds, grim and menacing. At a word from the Mistress of Illusions, the black smoke shifted, scurrying toward their foes, grey hands groping for human flesh.

"That's a good, nasty piece of work," Héna murmured. Her hands trembled a little, but her voice was steady. "Let's see how those of the Three Hands enjoy our own fear touch."

Kalanin glanced to his left then to his right: clashes and the dim sounds of battle had begun as outriders on each flank met and began to skirmish. Overhead a patch of sky gleamed blue, where Houma's demonic tools had torn apart a section of the forest canopy, parting the clouds above them. Though as he watched, dark, rain-swollen clouds again swept over a ragged sky and all hints of blue vanished.

Down on the forest floor, a groping cloud hand made by mortals had reached their foe's center rank, with cries of fear and dismay greeting its arrival. Those the hand touched, fell stricken, but the Eye could feel the anger of Houma, and in moments, his counterthrust swept all the black vapor from the Great Forest. Then, the eagle felt a muffled concussion roll in from the north.

"Well crafted, a spell within a spell," the Eye called out, "but if you wish to teach fear to that Creature Indomitable, you will need more brutal lessons!"

"We have more than Amulets, more than complex spells," the Mistress of Illusions said grimly. "Linked together we three may nearly match Houma's great power."

Kalanin glanced at his old lover, then stood in his saddle peering over the battlefield: their right flank was smashing into the left flank of their foes, while in the center tier-groups were surging toward them, rank upon rank, only breaking file as they encountered massive tree trunks.

On Kalanin's shoulder the Eye of Merlin croaked, wings flaring in alarm, and moments later, Kalanin's eyes understood the eagle's reaction: deep within the ranks of their foes a Creature of the Darkness lurched forward, perhaps five hundred paces behind the front ranks of its human allies, a huge and menacing monstrosity, wobbling toward them as those serving the Three Hands scurried away from its path.

As the first ranks of the center tier-groups clashed, Armagh too, caught sight of his adversary and called out a wild cry, something between fear and hatred. Kalanin watched on as the Monster lurched toward them, and his own face became grim and set as his lips tightened over clenched teeth, forming a death mask. For this Creature of the Darkness was huge, bizarre, and terrifying beyond description. Men who followed fearfully behind it failed even to reach its knee's height, but its massive size held only the least portion of its terror: The One had chosen a form for battle, a twisted figure of might and terror.

Parts of the monster were shaped like a gigantic lizard, as it strode forward on massive stumpy legs — but other parts belonged to insects: overlapping black plates of chitin layered it, while each arm ended with a beetle's pincer claw that opened and closed as it wobbled toward them; and its lurching, swaying motions were caused by a scorpion's tale sting, a thing with the thickness of a tall man, that thrashed back and forth, leaking with a venom that smoked as it touched the forest floor.

On its shoulders was a head shaped in the manner of a third class of being — vague monstrosity, covered by hints of black fur while trailing wisps of smoke, regarding all before it with eyes that shone palely, like distant starlight.

Maker's Touch, but it's five times the bulk of the Dark Emissary, thought Kalanin, *and it's been shaped by poisoned dreams — from the demented visions of Houma.*

With an effort, Kalanin turned his eyes from the monster. He was trapped in some child's nightmare, facing a lurching, poisonous Creature of the Darkness, an immense being that dwarfed the humans scurrying from its path. And yet this nightmare and others were real — the fairy tales told by humans were the real falsehoods, for mortals had been born onto a battlefield, alongside the Creatures of the Darkness, and monsters would forever haunt the dreams of mortal men and women.

Without warning, light burst from the north, like a sunburst, intense, blinding.

All along the lines, men and women cried out, stripped of sight, while their enemies hacked and stabbed at blinded opponents.

"Houma!" cried the Mistress of Illusions, and she began to counter the Sorcerer's Sunburst Spell: waves of darkness flowed from her hands, rolling outwards, clouds of night fog billowing over the battlefield.

Kalanin's charger reared, wheeling in panic, while Kalanin held reins with one hand and shielded his own sightless eyes with the other.

"Baroda!" he called out. "Call your men to move back ten paces. Maintain their wall of spears. Tell them to call out their paces. Now!" The Grey Captain signaled with his mind and men began backing away, calling out their paces as they retreated. Woman warriors stumbled, sightless, beside them.

"Julian, can you see?" Kalanin called out into the darkness. The Apprentice was at Kalanin's side in seconds, the healing spell leaping from his lips. Kalanin's vision returned, to view a milling battlefield, with men, women, and horses stumbling through a boiling mist of black smoke.

"This can't go on!" said Kalanin, struggling to control his charger. Julian nodded, sighing, for from the north Houma's force of wind was lashing at their shield of fog.

"Sight will return in moments," the Apprentice murmured quietly. "We will try to counter Houma. Beware of their Monster, the Creature Indomitable." Julian turned, his mind again linking with Héna and the Mistress of Illusions. A thousand paces from his Master, Sebastian recoiled, gasping, as he felt Julian's mind twisting, changing — merging into something far more powerful and less good.

"Back ten paces more, then feint, then another ten," Kalanin called to Baroda. Tier-groups backed away, fog still swirling about them.

Sight began to return, as blinding light from the sunburst was lifted from their eyes. On the left, their lines settled slowly, and Baroda saw that those of the Three Hands were fewer than his own ranks and that their foes were wary and only partly trained. Slowly, Baroda stretched his sub-tiers farther outwards, gradually enveloping his foes in a vise of bristling spears.

As the mists cleared on the right, men serving the Three Hands massed their heavy horse, charging into a hailstorm of arrows, while men of the Dragon's Teeth struggled to hold their spear wall.

But in the center, tier-groups woke from blindness into a nightmare.

For now, The One was upon them. Towering above friend and foe, the creature advanced, huge pincers flexing at the end of each arm. Behind its massive legs, Kalanin could see its tail sting thrashing back and forth. In sum: this was monster enough for ten thousand men.

"Give way!" he called out. "Form a pike wall that's three deep!" But bands of Grey Men, becoming more like beasts than humans, heedless, leaped at the monster, stabbing at the joints of its armored shell. The One grasped several in each pincerclaw, slicing through shrieking armor and flesh. From behind, its tail sting swept forward, slaying those that it grasped or stabbed. As men sped from sting and claw, the Creature halted, raising its black, monster head, that was wreathed in smoke, roaring its challenge: no being, no power in Alantéa could match it, might against might.

Galad let out his breath, in a long, slow sigh. They had entertained horror stories of Marids, but this creature was monster enough for any foe. And it was bizarre that such a creature existed, madness to contend with it on a battlefield.

"Armagh!" called out the Elf-Seer. "Armagh, the mortals are no match for it. Come!" The huge beast eased forward into the press, humans seeming only small creatures beside it.

"You are no match for it either!" Kalanin cried. "First the pike wall!" At his signal, hundreds began to advance slowly, three layers of pikes lifted into the air like some deadly, steel-tipped forest. At Kalanin's side, Galad drew the Tarnished Sword.

"No, halt. Wait for the counterthrust," murmured Kalanin, then he raised his voice. "Pin its tail-sting to the ground, then ax it!" The wall of pikes advanced, the sweat of fear streaming down pale, grim, bearded faces. From their foe's ranks came a press of swordsmen, circling well beyond the Monster's reach, then stabbing and hacking at their foes and their walls of pikes. But Galad was on those swordsmen in a flash, and a dreadful reaping began, the air filled with shrieks of pain, as the Tarnished Sword slashed through armor and flesh.

Then the wall of pikes was raised against the Creature Indomitable, with scores of metal spear tips probing at the joints of its dense shell plating. And the monster laughed, a rasp of mockery, a rumble of malice. Rising higher, it leaned its bulk forward, snapping spear shafts before it — and massive legs flattened broken bodies as it waded forward. To the right and left, its tail-sting thrashed back and forth in a killing frenzy. The wall of pikes broke, its members all dead, dying, or in flight.

From his perch in the owls' nest, Rafir watched on in horror as the Monster trampled over dead humans. And then, as gigantic beast edged toward nightmare creature, inside him rose a terrible feeling that he, Rafir, was to blame: a collision of monsters was coming, something out of his most immature young fantasies. *If only, if only he could blink and blink, and blink again to have those daydreams disappear!*

"Armagh!" cried the Elf-Seer. "It is time!" From the Seer's hand, illusions of blazing fire leaped at The One, but it waded through, heedlessly. Bolts of force smashed against its shell armor — without any impact.

Alfilas, Elf-Seer and doomed immortal, pulled away, watching as the monster lurched forward.

"It has grown," murmured the Elf-Seer, heading back. Then he raised his voice. "Armagh! It has grown mighty!" Rasping words of magic sped through the monster's moist lips: nets emerged from midair, tangles of grey webs cast outward toward the Elf-Seer.

"Armagh, we cannot counter this form — do not close with it!" cried the Seer. Flames surged through one spell net; a second was evaded. "Armagh, choose wood or stone, but —" A third mass of webs caught the Elf-Seer, casting him to the ground. The One strode forward, as humans facing the One fled in fear.

"Galad!" Kalanin called out. Galad, unhearing, smote again, crushing metal and flesh, but the arms of comrades pulled him from the press, just as pincers tore life and Farsight from the doomed Seer. Galad pulled back, racing toward the confrontation between beast and monster.

For now, Armagh, sobbing, closed with the Creature, grasping its arms above its pincer claws. Men raced to either side struggling to pin the tail-sting, but The One thrashed like a mad thing, sweeping them away. Once, then again, its sting whipped at Armagh, piercing through its shaggy beast fur into soft flesh. The great beast began to stiffen, eyes glazed, mouth slobbering. Pincers tore at Armagh's arm tendons then its neck. Blood spurted, then Armagh toppled, dead, his fall shaking the forest floor.

Now Galad leaped forward, sword moaning, leading a great press of men wielding pikes and axes. The One hissed words of magic, and spinning nets formed in midair. The Sword swept through those nets effortlessly, but as it passed, a pincer claw caught the flat of the Tarnished Sword, sweeping it from Galad's hand. Galad leaped away, stumbling as the tail-sting swept toward him.

Then the Eye of Merlin cried out, diving downward, shrieking, and hurtling at the creature's eyes, then swerving to one side. Galad recovered the Sword, then backed farther away, slowly, watching the Creature Indomitable with a mixture of fear, loathing — and awe.

For now, the victorious Creature of the Darkness stood over Armagh's massive body, and smote its claws together, crying out its rasp of triumph and malice, eyes of bleak starshine searching for Julian and Kalanin. Yet as the Creature stood surveying the battlefield, its cry trailed off, tapering to a long venomous hiss.

The Sorcerer, Houma, was still locked in a spell test with three lesser Magicians. On the left, men serving the Three Hands were enveloped, crushed slowly in a vise of bristling spears, while on the right, those serving the League were mounting a fierce counterattack against a wavering foe.

Only in the center had the Sorcerer's puny rabble held, and that because of the One's unmatched power. But if the Sorcerer's might became unchained, then the humans would once again be reduced to insignificant, mindless prey.... The One stepped away from his fallen foe and began lurching toward the Magicians.

Kalanin slipped from his saddle, moving swiftly for a large ax, one requiring both hands, but then Géla was at his side, ripping at her armor lashings.

"Wait, this is our round," she murmured, then her voice raised to its fullest. "To me, O my sisters! Bring javelins and arrows and sling casts! To me, the light-footed dancers!" Kalanin grasped her arm, but she shook free.

"Go back to your battle!" she snarled, then lowered her voice. "Look again at The One/The Many, locked into a form it must hold until nightfall — did you not listen? If this form was chosen for its might, still it is less than agile."

Kalanin backed away, finally understanding her intent. "You may be right, but be *very, very* careful," he spoke softly, struggling with his own concern for her. "And you will need ax-men for a true distraction, with a screen of mounted spears for a shield."

Géla sped forward, gathering a score of lithe women warriors. Long haired, with grey eyes, they raced toward the hulking monster, hurling rocks, and javelins and arrow points at the creature, battering and scratching at its shellhide.

As The One lurched on, more joined Géla, casting weapons, then darting away. Bleak eyes seemed to flare and The One hissed, seething in frustration, poison bubbling from its tail. Twisting, it groped for its tormentors, but none were close enough. Again, it lurched toward the puny, soft humans, unaware of a lone ax-man slipping behind.... Ax hewed tailshell; The One whirled, bellowing, pincers grasping the ax-man, slicing armor and body in half. The casting of stones and weapons faltered, then resumed.

Kalanin stared, watching as the gap between monster and Magicians chanting spells was narrowed. With great reluctance, he turned from the battlefield and rode swiftly toward the Magicians.

As though sensing danger, Julian, Héna, and the Mistress of Illusions had fallen back from the struggle, drifting slowly south, yet when Kalanin reached them, they seemed locked to the ground. He paused before speaking: the three had changed, they were no longer the humans he had once known. They stood, linked but not touching, and their three sets of eyes had grown opaque, as though the whites of their eyes had absorbed greyish green irises. Tendrils of power, like sparks, leaped from form to form.

Warily, Kalanin turned from the three, and yet the monster, though harassed to a frenzy, was slowly stumbling toward them. Carefully, gently, he tugged at the arm of Julian the Apprentice, his friend, and ally.

Julian staggered, eyes casting about wildly as though waking from a deep trance.

"Houma, Houma is free!" he cried.

"The battle is ours," Kalanin said quickly, "except for a few tiny things like a powerful Sorcerer and the greatest monster known to humankind. And yet you are too close to the Creature. Come."

The three were led from the battlefield, scrambling, partly dazed, but no more than a hundred paces to the south, Héna stopped suddenly, then all three Magicians turned as one, staring once more toward Houma, and his Creature Indomitable, and his slowly shattering tier forces.

"Houma launches a great force of magic," murmured Julian, staring about, "but where?"

"Above!" snarled the Mistress of Illusions. "Baroda is peering into his mind...."

"And it's not sorcerous matter this time, it's a Maker cursed great sky stone, deflected earthward!" Héna cried, shivering.

"Again, link," murmured Julian. He stood between them, each hand reaching out to touch a Sorceress. As before, their eyes grew white, opaque.

A column of air and sorcerous energy leaped from them, slashing at the forest roof above....Kalanin saw that the sky that had become again ragged, torn, patched blue and white...and now a ball of incandescent flame was hurtling overhead.

A convulsion blew them from their feet. All around them the trees' upper reaches were shattering; a few of the gnarled ancient trunks were sliding slowly downward with concussions that brought showers of broken branches down upon battling tier masses. Men were shrieking and screaming everywhere, with horses bolting, racing into the unknown deep forest. In the distance, the One lay toppled, on its back, like some gigantic beetle — though now it scrambled up and was again lurching forward.

Kalanin stood and stared downward. Héna lay on her back, dead or unconscious. Julian lay next to her, while beyond the Apprentice the Mistress of Illusions lay stricken. For the second time on this day, Kalanin tasted a death fear.

Héna's eyes popped open.

"Help me..." she whispered, "...can't breathe...." At her side, Julian stirred, rolling like a drunkard toward the old Sorceress, mumbling spell words. Within moments, the three lay gasping, coughing on the ground.

From many paces away came the sounds of battle renewed, as left, right and center responded to Géla and Baroda's commands; and the baiting of the monster began again as its bellow of frustration echoed beneath the forest cover.

Yet there was something else, something beyond, or outside of hearing. Kalanin turned, anger mixed with wonder stirring in his mind. Why had the

Maker permitted so much dark power to be left, unchecked, in Alantéa the Forerunner?

"He's done it again," murmured the old Sorceress. "Maker, a forever curse upon this day." She coughed as Julian pulled her upright. Again, the three stood, hunched, fearful, facing a storm of power that rose from the north.

"But see, he cannot do this," Julian whispered. He touched the others, and his voice grew in strength as power surged again through his body. "A Portal Spell reaching beyond Alantéa, beyond the Mid-World! Not if we stand strong!"

·)(·

In the middle of the Great Forest, beside the litter of ruined weapons and broken bodies, a huge Portal began to form. Masses of dark water were surging on the other side, with huge malevolent figures lurching toward the Portal's gates. Beyond the Portal, luminescent decaying vegetation gave off only a dull glow, but even in the middle of dark waters, it seemed that the huge figures were mottled, diseased, with chunks of flesh drifting from their frames....

"Marids!" cried Julian. "Not this time!"

Power surged from the three, with many hues like a rainbow, arcing over Houma's counterspells — and the Portal Gates burst apart.

Marids vanished, but a torrent of ocean water swept through the Great Forest, an instant salt river, casting down friend and foe alike — but as it neared Kalanin it was only knee high and he held strongly against the water's tide as it spilled ever outwards, becoming only a thin stream, then vanishing into the forest floor, leaving only sodden ground and a few stray puddles.

Kalanin watched as men and women picked themselves from the ground, astonished to be alive. The Monster, too, stood bewildered, staring first to the hole in space where the Marids — masters of all monsters — had vanished, then to the tidal pools of water that seeped slowly into the forest floor.

Kalanin rode forward; the three Magicians followed, half stumbling, half shuffling like the newly blind. Orders were called, messengers gathered and dispatched. Bugle calls, at first halfhearted, wavering, grew in strength until echoes rolled beneath the forest canopy.

Tier-lines reformed and moved forward, at first tentatively, then with greater determination as they encountered faint hearted, stunned opponents. Many scores circled the monster, and the battering of its shellhide shook the creature from its trance.

As their lines knit and strengthened, and as those of their foes wavered and stumbled backward, the rage of Houma grew, looming over the battlefield like a storm cloud. With the battle shifting, Kalanin saw the Sorcerer's figure for an instant through a gap: Houma stood well back from his tier-groups, hunched over, mouth grimacing in rage, brows tight with concentration as words raced from his lips.

"Shatter..." whispered Kalanin, watching the Sorcerer's men give way. But then behind him came a single groan of agony — in three voices. He turned to behold the three Magicians as they gasped with strain, faltering under Houma's spell pressure.

"Bring Galad!" Kalanin called to the Eye of Merlin. "If they —" he faltered, and the eagle, aloft, let out a wild cry.

In the distance, at the side of the Sorcerer's slight figure, the outlines of a second Portal with a huge arch, were forming, and beyond it were wavering images of tier ranks shifting over a dark, gloomy plain.

"Bring Galad anyway!" Kalanin cried to the eagle, and as he turned to the Magicians, rays of power shot from the three, shaking the Portal's Gates.

But even as the Portal shuddered, its outlines grew deeper, stronger, and then firmed. Again, the Three groaned in agony.

"Un-Maurag..." whispered Julian, and the Apprentice seemed a being on the wrong side of Death, hunched, mouth gaping, eyes grown completely white, seeing only matters of sorcery.

"Un-Maurag," he whispered again. "We are doomed, but we do not need to be taken alive." Kalanin turned again toward Houma, the old rage building once more in him. Galad was racing toward them, battered armor mottled with blackened gore and red blood.

Where is the Maker? Kalinin's mind called out. *Where are the Maker Servants of old? And yes, where are those beings who dared to call themselves Gods?*

The first rank of their foes reached the Portal's Mouth: a grim subtier of massive Uraks, the advance guard of Un-Maurag, with their Master himself a few score paces behind. Galad reached Kalanin's side then turned and watched as the first ranks of Uraks passed through the Portal Gates. Kalanin's rage burst into speech.

"MAKER WHO MADE US OR LET US BE MADE!"

As if in answer to Kalanin's invocation, the air throughout the forest shuddered and twisted. Portals shimmered, flashing into view: many scores of enchanted gateways shimmered, firming into passageways. Rays of light and power lashed at Un-Maurag and his legions. His Portal vanished; the Dark Lord was swept from the Great Forest, with only the first rank of Uraks remaining as evidence of Houma's powerful sorcery: but these lay blasted to death by the Powers of the Mid-World.

"The Gods," Julian whispered. "The Mid-World of the Truce, at last." Across the battlefield, Houma picked himself from the ground, staring in rage at his faltering legions and his lurching, bewildered Monster. Julian raised his voice, freeing himself from his mental link and taking on his Voice of Command.

"Houma! Houma! You have defied the Gods! Houma, you have broken the Truce!" All through the Great Forest, men and women picked up the chant.

"The Truce! The Truce! You have broken the Truce!" Those pledged to Houma were falling back, the fears of their childhood concerning the Nine Billion Gods surging through their minds. Raging, Houma turned and blasted a score of those seeking to flee from the battlefield. Then the Sorcerer turned a face glistening with sweat, again toward Julian, Héna, and the Mistress of Illusions.

"Link again, lad," murmured Héna, and once more the three Magicians faced Houma. Desperately, the Sorcerer called out his blinding spell a second time — but this time it was blocked. And having blocked it for the first time, the three gained their respite, an advantage, and the initiative,

"Perhaps now, our counter," Kalanin said softly.

A Portal formed beside Héna. The Eye of Merlin leaped through, emerging on the battlefield just above the Creature Indomitable, and the eagle raked at its pale, glowing eyes, then vanished through a second Portal. Again, a Portal formed beside Héna, and Galad raised the Tarnished Sword, tensing. Houma called out a warning to his nightmare ally, just as Galad leaped through.

But the Portal did not open beside the Creature Indomitable.

It opened beside Houma.

And the Tarnished Sword whined as it met flesh that was knit by magic — but then it bit, slashing the left arm from the stunned Sorcerer.

Almost in the same motion, Galad dove through a second Portal and vanished. Houma was left alone, staring at his own arm, a thing that lay groping and twitching on the ground. All around the Sorcerer, warriors, and Magicians were advancing, while his own tier-groups were racing away, melting into the gloom of the Great Forest.

Houma backed from them, snarling, but suddenly filled with fear. A Portal flashed beside him, and he slipped through, passing from the battlefield. His stricken arm scrabbled about like some wounded, spider, one that had been struck by deadly poison, but then it too leaped through the Portal, hand first, groping for its master.

·)(·

The One lurched over the battlefield, half blinded by sling casts, with scores of its own wounds seeping fluid over the forest floor so that it trailed slime like some gigantic slug. Across its back the armored shell still smoldered where gobs of pitch had been cast on it, then ignited by flame arrows.

Why had he permitted the Sorcerer to choose this form? None of its endless battles had been like this before — it had always been so simple: power and terror by day, and dark, merciless hunting of warm flesh by night. Why had the Sorcerer failed to explain that these soft and succulent humans had become mad things — even dangerous?

Again, axes hewed at his tail, and again the monster howled and groped. But this time he was able to grasp only one; two others escaped. Raging, still puzzled, The One held the human to his damaged eyes. Of course, they were different, this one was covered with the fur of beasts! Why had the Sorcerer kept this knowledge from him? In anger, he slashed the shrieking human in half, and turned back to a battlefield that was filled with corpses, groping for more prey.

Though now, both lean warriors with long, dark hair and men holding axes were pulling away. Had they grown fearful? No — there were tugs of power, energies forming. Fear and rage and hatred surged through its mighty, tortured frame: the Mortal Magic Wielders had come.

All other humans were falling back, so that The One stood alone, in the center of a triangle of power. Rage overcame fear and it launched its own force of sorcery, calling for aid from lesser Creatures that served it. His spell was blocked and came to nothing. With a convulsion, The One sought to change, to become again The Many, but night remained only a hint of shadows over the horizon. Men and women were backing away, but the Magicians advanced, tightening their triangle. The Creature, no longer Indomitable, turned and lurched toward the youth — surely the easiest, the least dangerous — and why was this task no longer easy?

A dense wall of blue flame burst into life in front of Julian, drifting toward the stunned Creature. The One shifted away in mounting fear. It had been so easy before, what had gone wrong? A shaking and pounding wracked The One's shape: its present form shimmered then stiffened.

Gather Darkness!!

In front of Héna, a column of flashing steel formed, glittering even on the shadowed forest floor. The Creature turned again, beginning to moan in fear, pale wounded eyes filled with panic.

From the Mistress of Illusions emerged a column of glistening gemdust, an all consuming devourer of flesh.

Under the gloomy shadows cast by immense branches, a vortex of fire and steel, and devouring diamond dust converged about the Monster's gigantic frame, and as the vortex spun in violence, the Creature's shriek passed beyond human hearing. Within moments, every particle of its being had been consumed, so that not even its shadow was left to contaminate the floor of the Great Forest.

Chapter Eleven

The Sorcerers...

SLOWLY AFTER THE BITTER fighting, men and women drifted toward their camp gear and weapon racks. Julian remained on the battlefield with the other Magicians, working with the wounded. The Mistress of Illusions would not treat those pledged to Houma and the Three Hands, while Héna did so reluctantly; and Julian's healing strength was greatest among the three, so he lingered long after others had departed, laboring deep into the evening.

Sebastian alone stayed with Julian, watching his master's movements with a troubled face: Julian had paid a price for the day's violence and the sorcerous mental link with Héna and the Mistress of Illusions, and as a result, his spirits seemed weighted down.

At nightfall, Captains and Magicians spoke briefly then turned quickly to their resting places, as the long day's struggle had left them with a great fatigue, and a need for deep sleep. Yet their sleep was interrupted by the sounds of many men, milling about their camp's edge, speaking with the night watch. Men pledged to the Three Hands had come again — but as beggars rather than foes. At day's end, they were leaderless, lost in the Great Forest without provisions. Now they looked only for tasks as mercenaries or laborers. Baroda put them to work burying the dead, promising no more than food and safe passage from Erivan.

Morning in the Great Forest was signaled more by sound than by sight with the gloom lifting only a little; but the upper branches came alive with many flocks of birds calling out their morning songs. Shortly after daybreak Rafir sought Kalanin and returned with him to the battlefield. Captains and those with the Gift stood beside the fallen Armagh, while all about them lay many shallow graves. A deep pit had been started, but just a little way down masses of forest roots had grown so intertwined that the burial effort had been abandoned.

"The dead are buried, and their farewells spoken," Baroda said, "though many lie in shallow graves and may soon be food for carrion seekers. We cannot bury this one," he pointed to Armagh, "while a bonfire of sufficient heat would only bring more harm to the Erivan. Héna believes that she may have the answer."

"I have the knowledge, but not the power," the old Sorceress said wearily, hunched over, leaning on her cane. "If others will aid me, perhaps we can make something of this one's broken body, something to remember. Julian, to be linked with us in bitter battle magic was a challenging thing for you, but this is creation, work that the Maker would approve. Will you join with me?" Julian nodded and stood with the Mistress of Illusions, each with a hand touching the shoulder of the Old Sorceress.

Spell words came haltingly from Héna, as though she had difficulty in remembering her old magic or was feeling her way toward some new enchantment.

Before them on the ground, the stiff and broken body of the gigantic Armagh began to change: first, the crusted blood slipped from its body into the ground, then its fur grew less ragged, changing in color, becoming white. Slowly, the huge body shifted, bit by bit, until it sat upright, arms on knees, hunched forward. The figure of Alfilas, the Elf-Seer, also drew upright, to stand beside Armagh, his hand resting against the great beast's side. And then their forms began to harden into stone, frozen forever, but lifelike, as though they had just emerged from the depths of the Great Forest.

Spell words halted, and Julian stepped forward, touching the stone.

"Maker, if it is within Your Vision, may you consider this one, on the day of the Awakening." Kalanin stared all around the battlefield, where many of the huge trees stood upright, but doomed — their trunks were split, or root systems shattered or poisoned by a tide of ocean salt.

"Let their forms guard the Erivan from all evil beings," Kalanin added softly, drawing the Apprentice away. "And may the Kindreds shield these statue shapes from deadfall, for this portion of the Great Forest seems doomed."

· ☓ ·

By midday, the wagons were ready for the journey south toward Gravengate, while Julian, Galad, Rafir, and Sebastian were turning again northeast, toward the Ruins of Dahlak and their destination, the City of the Truce. Farewells were spoken, with wagons beginning a slow shift southward, but Kalanin and Héna and the Eye of Merlin lingered, speaking their last words to those on the quest for the Truce Terms.

"Houma is wounded, Apprentice, but most likely he will have access to forces that will provide great healing. Watch for him," the eagle counseled. "Also, do not fear that you have been soiled, damaged, by all these events. The Sight within me shows that the Gift within you remains clean and strong."

Julian smiled a faint smile. "Strong and clean, or stained and feeble, the thought of Houma will always fill me full of anger, though I will never stop fearing him. Now that pure force has failed, we will probably encounter more of his 'traps.'"

"Farewell, Captain Hangnail," said Galad to Kalanin. "Please destroy these Sorcerers. A stench of buzzards lies over everything they do, and the League will be much cleaner without them."

"The Sorcerers perhaps," said Kalanin, eyes passing back and forth between Galad and Julian, as though drinking in their images one last time, "yet the three of us know that there are Marids and Demon Princes still lurking in the shadows. Let us hope that Merlin finds some way to counter them. Farewell! May you bring the Gods down upon our foes!"

Lastly, the old Sorceress knelt beside Rafir, ruffling his soft fox fur. "Goodbye, Rafir. What a story we've gotten into! Do you remember those evenings in the cottage and all the images I showed you while telling tall tales?" The fox nodded, tongue panting, wide eyes staring up at Héna's face, though he said nothing. "You were young then, Rafir, and you liked all your stories to have happy endings. Now you are older, and understand that not all outcomes are happy, at least not for everyone. Think about me with kind thoughts, Rafir, if fate or chance separates us."

"Goodbye, Granny," was all that Rafir could say, but his face held a rare, distant, quiet look, as he watched his old patroness ride slowly away.

· ✻ ·

It was hard to imagine the ocean, after so many days under the leaves of the Great Forest, but he let his mind drift to the rolling foam lines that had once pounded peacefully against the shore at Sea's Edge. It seemed many lifetimes ago, in a different world, where the League had never been challenged. Kalanin's moment of peace ended, and he sighed, as out of the corner of his eye he saw Géla riding closer, ready to explore, once again, all their intertwined relationships. A few seconds later she was beside him.

"I liked Galad's name for you — 'Captain Hangnail,' was it not?" she asked in a voice tinged with a touch of malice. "It suggests someone grim and awkward, rather suiting; don't you think?"

"The Mistress of Illusions said something of the sort earlier," Kalanin said, "but in an hour or so, we'll be out from under Erivan's shadows, and that should leave us all a little less grim."

"And then where will Captain Hangnail lead us? To the Bariloch? Or do we become bold and take the road to Piranus?"

Kalanin nodded. "Yes, are we the griffin or the weasel? I've played both roles in the last year. Yet now it depends on matters outside of our control."

"Those serving the Three Hands?"

"Partly. The Elf-Kindreds will advise the Gods, and Tel-Alantir may well persuade many Powers that the Sorcerers have deceived them. Then those supporting the Three Hands will become less free to wage war against the League. Yet how long will that process take? Do the Powers mark time as we do? Will they act now or a year later? Perhaps your mistress can tell us." Géla nodded; as usual Kalanin had deflected her sharp comments, leaving so much unsaid, yet he was right in wishing to be free from the shadows of this stricken forest. She spurred her horse forward, riding toward their vanguard.

In late afternoon they passed the edges of Erivan. Even the wounded who were carried in carts were gazing skyward, glad for sunlight. They began moving more swiftly, though their passage over meadow trails grew more winding and less even. At nightfall, many slept out in the open under clear skies and welcomed the starlight overhead.

With their tier-groups settled, the Mistress of Illusions led their leaders — Kalanin, Géla, and Baroda — a few hundred paces from their camp, where

Héna and the Eye of Merlin stood in a small, treeless clearing. In the glade's center, runes had been scratched into the ground, left by the Elf-Kindreds, but the Mistress of Illusions scoffed at the inscriptions at their feet.

"Poof! I have no need for these things. Sit back and watch." They joined her, seated in a circle, watching her face as the lines of worry cleared and a distant dreaming look slipped over her enchanted features. Under the starlight, images of many colors flowed from her hands, taking shape in the middle of their small circle.

And the images flashed through a series of cities and villages, showing the many temples of the Gods of Alantéa the Forerunner. Each image showed men pledged to the Three Hands standing outside the temple gates, haranguing those entering or leaving — men were being stirred to anger against the Wizards and their League; gold was flashed, and power was promised in dark, hushed voices.

"This is as it was some months ago," the Mistress of Illusions explained. Images began moving forward at great speed, forming flickers of light that only the Eye could follow. "And now we see the last few days," she continued, peering forward intently.

Now the images showed fighting in the streets, as armed priests took up weapons against those pledged to the Three Hands, casting them from the temple gates. In other cities and villages, bonfires raged, with banners and devices of the Sorcerers' alliance hurled to the flames, with even painted shields melting into slag. Many men fled on horse or foot, casting insignia of the Three Hands from themselves as they raced away.

Illusion images faded slowly then vanished. Kalanin stood, stretched, and yawned. The Mistress of Illusions glanced at him briefly, then left, seeking her own quarters.

"So, the Gods have spoken for the second time," Kalanin said. "Yet if they are not happy with the Sorcerers, then why do they not declare against the Marids and Demon Princes?" He extended a hand to Héna, and gently pulled the Sorceress from the ground.

"That question will be asked many times," Héna said, "and we have no sure answers, only more confusion. We have learned this day that it was not the Gods themselves who barred Un-Maurag. Rather, all actions were taken by their greatest Emissaries, and there were scores of them, acting in concert on behalf of their masters." Héna shook her head as though to clear her thoughts. "Some mechanism was brought into play, but its nature and other devices of the Gods will not be understood until the Truce Terms become known."

·))(·

At nightfall, the Sorcerer slips from the siege of Gravengate, away from the accursed Wizard, away from the prying Sorcerer, Eudox, away from the always watchful Eyes of the Mid-World. Many leagues from the siege, moving beyond illusion into transformation, Cronar becomes as three: man, woman, and child. Even farther from the League, he reforms into a cloud of vapor, one drifting swiftly north, moving against the tides of wind.

Finally, in his hidden place of power, Cronar reforms his particles, while the powerful Gift within him confirms that he is alone. Cunning, daring, and mighty, Cronar is still fearful as he places his Demon Tools within his Divination pattern. Warfare against the League is turning against the Sorcerers, as they had known it might; but where are those Marids, the great ravagers?

Cronar whispers over his Divination, probing again for Marid and Demon Prince within the dark waters that swirl and surge through the underwater Isle of the Demons. He hisses as he finds his probe blocked — Demon Princes hold his life's blood and whatever is left of his shredded soul, or otherwise, he would vanish utterly. And yet there must be some answer, some counter, some power that will free him from the folly of his Demon Pact.

An image begins to form — immense, with an aura of power radiating through the waters that swirl and sway about it: it has only one great orb-eye, half closed, yet its open portion radiates blue, and its iris seems marred by traces of black lightning bolts! What is the other portion of its huge eye doing? Is it dreaming or dead?!? This thing radiates a strength of sorcery but what can it be? It is neither Demon nor Marid. A Guardian, overcome by the Demon Princes? An entirely different race of beings?

In mounting anger and frustration, Cronar breaks off his spell. To have dared so much and accomplished so little! What, by all the Maker's Cursed and Damned Nine Billion Gods, was that powerful, strange looking creature? And where are the Marids?

· ☿ ·

They moved south with more confidence the next day, traveling over rough but straight roads toward Piranus. Other travelers stepped aside, watching them warily, staring at the spectrally gaunt and beastfurred men of the Dragon's Teeth. Kalanin remained wary, but the Eye of Merlin soared overhead, a large, winged speck framed against blue skies, and it seemed unlikely that any force of men or magic could escape the eagle's Sight.

On the morning of their journey's third day, a quarrel broke out within their camp, a disturbance with several voices shouting and both men and women gathering. Kalanin drew the Mistress of Illusions from the scene, leaving Baroda and Géla to deal with the matter. Later, the Grey Captain sought him out.

"It was bound to happen," said Baroda. "I recall how Dargas argued against women warriors — and yet now it seems even more complicated."

"How so?" asked Kalanin.

"Liaisons will develop if unchecked. Géla and I knew that, but some of her people seem entranced by those growing away from human form — 'not-men' — as the Mistress of Illusions calls them. Who might have forecast such a thing?" Kalanin was silent; Baroda cleared his throat before continuing. "Also, the Mistress of Illusions seeks me out at every turn. We cannot afford rivalry among ourselves; and so, I will seek to discourage her if you wish. What are your thoughts?"

Kalanin laughed softly. "I almost wish Dargas were here — but there are two thoughts in my mind: first, that within a fortnight we will have another great test, and the fate of the League may be settled in a month's time. Thus, it seems wise to hold back, not to become entangled until fate shows us more. My second thought is otherwise. Death may come to us all in a few weeks, so we should take what pleasure we might have now." He looked directly into Baroda's grey eyes. "The second thought is the greater, but you must be discrete; we are at the cusp, without room for quarrel or error."

· X ·

That evening Kalanin sat at dinner with Géla, Baroda, and the two Gift Born. All seemed tense except for Héna, who sat, somewhat amused, making small talk to fill the silence. Toward the meal's end, the Eye of Merlin joined them, waiting impatiently for them to finish eating.

"So, a visitor," said Héna, looking to the eagle. "I sensed him before evening."

"And I, before afternoon," said the eagle. "There was no effort made to disguise its presence, only its nature, for it is carefully cloaked." The Mistress of Illusions rose and stretched.

"Another messenger, more advice," she said, yawning. "Best to see to it now, while the evening's still fresh." She walked out, waving her guards away. The others followed, moving through the dusk to a stand of trees that lay just a little to the east. Sounds of laughter and crackling watchfires receded as they reached their camp's boundary. The Mistress of Illusions strode fearlessly into the gloom that lingered at the wood's edge. A voice brought the others to a halt, for it was filled with hissing tones.

"Let those with the Gift approach, and the rest stay back." Héna shuffled forward, while the others stood at the wood's edge, though the eagle tensed on Kalanin's shoulder, wings flaring, ready to leap into overcast, darkening skies.

After a few moments, Héna and the Mistress of Illusions reemerged, with the still strange voice hissing at their backs, "Farewell, we will not meet again." Then, there came brief rustling sounds, as something moved stealthily away from them. Héna traced a shape over the ground so that they were enclosed within her inscription.

"That was a strange one," murmured the old Sorceress. She plumped herself on the ground, and sat, hunched. "It was neither mortal, nor Elf, nor Tanu, nor Sidhe, nor Shadow Mage, nor kin to Taurog, the leader of Trolls — nor any being I've been told of. I wonder what price Haldor paid for that being's help?

"Anyway, here's the gist of it: The Powers have barred the Elf-Kindreds from further interference in our affairs. Those of the Three Hands are to be strongly discouraged, except that the warfare within League lines remains an affair of the Mortal Magic Wielders, and no concern of the Powers. This much we knew or may have guessed. But there's more: the Kindreds believe that Mordred, Dark Lord of the Mid-World, will make one cast against us, some secret act of destruction."

"When?" asked Kalanin.

"Haldor believes that we will pass Piranus safely, that Mordred will strike when the Eyes of the Mid-World no longer view us from afar."

"Just let us reach Piranus safely, then we shall see what might be done," Kalanin said softly, staring south.

·)(·

The Sorcerer curses under his breath as he watches images of the Creature being harassed by fleet footed dancers, then hewed by masses of men: if the Marids are also bulky and slow moving, then lean and swift humans might likewise find ways to counter them. He signals and the image shifts once again, searching for Cronar and finding nothing — back to the battle — Eudox watches with amusement as the stricken arm of Houma flops and gropes for its master. Houma's discomfort is only just, for he has treated his ally with considerable disdain, even scorn, forgetting how valuable his own knowledge of the Wizards' behavior and lore has proved.

Again, Eudox signals and his Divination shows the many tiers of their enemies moving south. If only the dung-flecked Demons had brought forth the Marids! Then this struggle would be over, and he would rule, and grow stronger each day. But Marids and Demons have proven to be unreliable allies, and his "brother" Sorcerers barely trustworthy. If this struggle is to be won, he alone must turn the tide. When Cronar returns, he will leave the old Sorcerer, for a brief time, and strike down the feeble Captains and Magicians who approach from the north — except for the Mistress of Illusions, who might be of interest as a captive, enslaved by sorcerous potions.

·)(·

Taking their strange, mixed force of men, women, and not-men, Kalanin led them over rough roads toward Piranus, stepping up the pace each day, so that footsore and weary, few had the strength for the nighttime adventures offered by their mixed force. On the fourth day of their journey from Erivan, near sunset, they approached the walls of Piranus.

As they marched closer, a jumble of carts and wagons milled desperately about the gates, with drivers shouting and cursing, struggling to get within. Bonfires were being lit on the broad avenues inside, and men were moving swiftly to man the walls. As Kalanin neared, the gates crashed shut, and those few left outside scurried away in panic.

They moved closer, more curious than concerned, but then Kalanin saw rows of gallows outside the city walls, with many bodies sagging and drifting casually in light breezes. The sun was setting, blood red, to their right as they neared Piranus. The old Sorceress gasped as she watched dead bodies drifting with soft breezes in the last light of day.

Flocks of carrion crows lifted leisurely from the dead, calling out in what sounded like laughter. But then the Eye of Merlin hurtled through their ranks, *surging* through the air, talons raging, leaving broken black carcasses in his wake.

Arrows from city walls sped toward the eagle, but then there were commands and counters to those commands called frantically from within. Kalanin brought their tiers to a halt, and he stood with the vanguard, face grim with anger.

"They have warred upon the helpless," he murmured to Géla and Baroda, "refugees from the League. Curse them!" The eagle lit upon Kalanin's shoulder, talons still red with the blood of carrion crows.

"The fools!" croaked the eagle. "They have only a few tiers, poorly armed — most have gone south to aid the Sorcerers. And the walls to the east are flimsy wooden barriers."

"So, a shield wall, a fire beside the Eastern wall, then the city is open," said Baroda. Kalanin turned to the Mistress of Illusions.

"How to reach these?" he asked, face grim. "Either they come out for a parlay, or we go in and bring them out — and then judge them beside their gallows." The Mistress of Illusions touched his hand, watching his face for a moment, then she stood, eyes closed, face turned to the city walls. Images shifted, changed — and now there were flames licking along the walls of the city, with cries of fear from those within.

Then the flames vanished, and the walls were restored. Ghostly partial images followed, showing the gates opening and a shadowy party emerging from the city, meeting another group in parlay. Only the image of the Mistress of Illusions remained substantial, and her face was fixed in mockery as though she alone were real, and the others nothing but shadows.

Finally, the illusion vanished.

"They will come," she said softly. "At least the Priests will, for I have shown them a true vision of their twin fates. Either they come out to talk, or they are destroyed." Kalanin, Baroda, and Géla rode part way to the gates, followed by Héna and the Mistress of Illusions.

"Best to stay some distance from bow shot," Kalanin murmured. "Those who are most guilty may be anxious for an incident."

"Beloved, when I am with you, there's no need to fear bow shots," the Mistress of Illusions said sweetly, then with malice, "Unless I wish it." They rode further on until they stood no more than a hundred paces from the walls.

After a moment's hesitation, the gates opened slowly, only a little, with men at arms squeezing through, twenty of them, standing fearfully outside the gates, followed by their masters, the Priests, and Elders of Piranus. In the gloom of dusk, the two parties moved cautiously toward one another. The faces of the Priests were wary, but Elders and men at arms showed open fear. An Elder cleared his throat as though to speak.

"No, be silent," interrupted Kalanin. "It is obvious what has happened here. My brothers and sisters and their children lie outside your gates, dead, twisting in the wind, when they should have been inside, sheltered, and comforted. I know that the Sorcerers have sown the seeds of this hatred, but in Piranus, those seeds fell on fertile ground.

"Now, listen to me. We have the right and the power to lay waste to Piranus, but we have other business for the moment. If you wish peace, you will burn the instruments of your crimes, together with the bodies of my people, and vow that you will never again take up arms against those serving the League. Also, there are images to be conveyed to your Gods, future crimes that should be prevented."

Kalanin turned to the Mistress of Illusions. "Show them how Mordred, Dark Lord of the Mid-World, has been called against us. Let the Gods deal with the Gods; we have too many of our own worries." Then, turning back to the Priests and Elders, "And listen closely to me: if you fail to heed me, then Piranus will be forsaken, so that should we fall victim to Sorcerers and Marids, we will bring down Piranus even in our death spasms, with its ruins accursed down to its very last, broken stones."

Kalanin turned and left, leaving the Mistress of Illusions to give further instructions to the Priests. Others led their tier force a little distance from the city, where they made a makeshift camp. There, Kalanin paced long into the night, watching the lights fade as the watchfires within the city died down.

In the morning they again moved south, but behind them, they saw a thin stream of smoke build to a great column: ash and vapor rising then leaning into blue skies, as the slain were burned, together with the instruments of their deaths.

·)(·

With a grim face, Kalanin drove them harder, increasing their pace as they neared the League's borders. Those of the Dragon's Teeth who had grown spectral or more like beasts were now almost herded by their human brethren; but some drifted away each night, vanishing into the darkness.

As they neared the line of low hills that marked the League's borders, the Mistress of Illusions grew less mocking, more intense — now, she was beginning to feel the Gift reaching from Cronar and Eudox as they searched for her mind. The Eye of Merlin, too, could feel the probes of the Sorcerers, as he soared far above, watching the flow of men and women beneath him, moving like an insect horde toward the range of hilly forts that marked the League's borders.

But the eagle also saw that there was a countertide, a sparse stream of people moving from within the League out into the wide domains loosely ruled by the Powers of Alantéa; and among the refugees were the weak, the young, the old, the beaten — and strong, determined parties, with some who were Gift or Sight born. Troubled, the eagle waved off the mental probes of the Sorcerers. Later, in the afternoon, within sight of a heavily manned earthwork barrier, the Eye sought Kalanin.

"Almost, I would interrupt the mind of Merlin, as he sits in contemplation at Sea's Edge, but you might know, you understand the affairs of mortals — there are strong minds among the refugees, those born with the Gift or the Sight. Why should they now flee? They must understand that we are at a turning point. So why leave now?"

"Revenge against the Sorcerers?" Kalanin mused. "Delegations to the Powers?"

"There was a Priestly sense to them," the Eye replied, "like those at Piranus, but it was cleaner, harder."

Kalanin was silent for a while. "We will say nothing of this to the others, but *if* the League were greatly endangered, or *if* it were doomed, then those strongly turned to the Maker's service might depart to become prophets, seers, secret Servants of the Maker hidden in the Mid-World."

"Like a doomed tree, casting its final seeds," murmured the eagle. "Let us hope not. So, what is our next test of arms? Those pledged to the Three Hands have strengthened the hilly forts with earthwork barriers. How do we gain entry?"

In the end, a series of feints and brief skirmishes, together with promises of provisions and safe passage, were enough to breach the barriers. As they poured through several gaps, there were halfhearted counterattacks, then most of their opponents retreated, with large numbers of their men-at-arms abandoning their Masters, the Sorcerers, by fleeing north.

At last, far from the Great Forest, Kalanin stood once again on League soil, leading many well-armed tiers, and supported by cunning Magic Wielders.

· ◊ ·

Anger surges through the firstborn and greatest of Marids as he strides over the underwater Isle, seeking his Masters. Flesh trails from his body and he must slow every now and again to regenerate his body — but the healing barely keeps pace with the parasites' ravaging destruction.

How had his masters failed to shield their children, their most powerful creation? It was rending time, time to go forth to fulfill his destiny, yet he and his brethren were spending their powers rebuilding their own bodies, surrounded by scavenger fish that fed on rotted Marid flesh.

And where were his Masters, the Demon Princes? Why had they, so incredibly powerful, once again slipped into their enchanted resting place? Though it was not truly a resting place: it smelled of Guardian.

An enormous, evil-eyed shark drifts a fraction too close, and the Marid vents its rage, ripping the great predator apart. But after, the Marid is forced to halt, reknitting its flesh, while hooting and booming in frustration.

·)(·

Wearied by the border passage, forces under Kalanin's direction came to a halt less than a day's journey from Amalric. As always, a heavy night watch was set, but now guards encountered only League men, skirmish parties that had been cut off from the twin sieges, men who had fought in field or forest, struggling to intercept the flow of provisions southward. Skirmish parties, wearied by the long, slow defeat, now felt the shifting tide, and there were murmurs of joy as they met with the night watch.

Kalanin moved his sleeping pallet a little distance from the watchfires and lay alone, listening to the murmur of voices at the camp's edge, as the night watch greeted new allies. Every now and again, voices would rise above the murmurs: laughter and sounds of triumph, almost like ripples of music, and a suitable background for sleep.

·)(·

The old man makes slow, weary progress, shuffling along the beach to the water's edge. Cloud masses tower above him, casting a gloom over Alantéa's western coast, but the Wizard barely notices, for all about him are Spell Searches, Vision Portals, Divination Links. The Gods are studying the Wizard and his spells closely. Their probes are too many and too powerful to be turned aside, and so they must be ignored.

At the water's edge, Merlin draws a mass of black pellets from his pouch and whispers the final spell words over them: pellets come alive now, turning and twisting in his hand. White foam surges over the Wizard's boots as he casts the writhing creatures into the shallows. They seethe into the depths on a hunt for Marids, an epic journey that will take them far from sunlight.

The Wizard turns, shuffling back to the ruins of Sea's Edge. This ocean seeding is the last of many, and it is not a final solution; it will delay, not halt, the coming of the Marids, but more time is needed to seek a counter to the Marids, if there is a counter....

·)(·

Noise! Shrieks in the night! Kalanin lifted his head, ready to spring up, but then a tide of men surged over him like a herd. Men moving like beasts and gaunt spectral not-men were pounding over him. He shouted and one reached down, lifting him to his feet. Like a wild current, they swept him up, carrying him forward, strange faces tight with anger. More sounds of struggle could be heard in the distance, then the voice of the Mistress of Illusions boomed out: "Eudox! Come back and die, Eudox!"

Lights flashed as Demon tools struck down the night watch. But now there were thousands of Grey Men racing toward the unseen Sorcerer.

Kalanin halted by a wagon cart, letting the tide of men and not-men sweep past him to either side. Out of the darkness, the old Sorceress Héna emerged, shuffling, and panting, moving toward the Mistress of Illusions. Kalanin moved to her side, weaponless, bruised and shaken.

"One lone Sorcerer?" he asked.

"We were waiting, the eagle and I," Héna panted, struggling to regain her breath.

Watchfires were being stoked, and lights began flickering over their forms. They reached the Mistress of Illusions; she stood outside her tent, watching as the tide of Grey Men swept toward their unseen enemy. Baroda was at her side, willing the destruction of Eudox.

"We almost had him!" panted the old Sorceress. "We might have captured a Sorcerer and stripped him of his Demon tools!"

"And which of us was Eudox seeking?" asked Kalanin.

The old Sorceress touched Baroda's arm. "This one," she said, then sat, still trying to catch her breath. "With his death, the greater part of our force might have lost its will to fight. But Eudox failed because Baroda was not alone."

"I was with him to protect him!" said the Mistress of Illusions, defiantly. Baroda would not meet Kalanin's eyes, and Géla bit her cheek to keep from laughing.

"It's good that you were able to shield him," Kalanin said wryly, "and it's good that Eudox failed, for now. I think they must either meet us in an unequal battle or break off the siege of Gravengate."

· 🜨 ·

It was late afternoon when they rode through the streets of Amalric. Men serving the Three Hands had fled, and the gaunt, harshly ruled people of Amalric were on the streets, cheering, but watching Kalanin with awe, as though they were watching some long-lost Demigod.

As they marched further southward, their forces grew in number each day and their purpose strengthened, with all the petty bickering became subordinated to feelings of hatred for the Sorcerers and those serving the Three Hands. Not more than a day's march from Gravengate, word came that Cronar and Eudox had abandoned the siege and were shifting back toward Stone Mountain.

Gravengate, long besieged, but never broken was free once more.

Little more than a fortnight after the battle of Erivan Forest, Kalanin stood on a hillock overlooking the Plain of Gravengate, watching as Géla, and Héna, and the Mistress of Illusions with Baroda at her side rode toward the fortress. Coming out to meet them were old allies and comrades: Balardi, haggard but unbroken, and Dargas, Harlond and Rostov, captains who had grown strong in their service to the League.

A fanfare of trumpets drifted over the Plain, and to Kalanin, the echoes were the music of a slow and surprising triumph.

· ⵣ ·

Beneath the great heavy beating reptile wings, moonlight ripples over the sea's foam caps, and gives hints of the valleys and peaks that form and vanish in the ocean's night turmoil. Some struggle is taking place in its depths; perhaps the Demon Princes have lied when they vowed that the Powers of the Mid-World would not dare to oppose the Alliance of the Sorcerers and the Marids.

Alcman sends a thought to his winged steed and the creature turns back toward Stone Mountain, where the fortress lights of his adversary, Thorian, shine like beacons. It is unfortunate that the fortress will fall to Marids, rather than Sorcerers, but it is also amusing to feel the emotions of his brother Sorcerers: the dark rage of Houma, hidden, healing in the Mid-World; the frustration of Eudox, always slower, a step behind his Sorcerer allies; and the grim anger of Cronar, an emotion that caused the Sorcerer to take incredible risks.

And yet the others have more to lose, for their oaths bind them forever to the Demon Princes, while his own commitment has been subtly crafted, a carefully wrought net that might easily be brushed aside. Alcman laughs: the others are fools, and one day they will be victorious fools, dazed by power and easily controlled. He would rule the Sorcerers and the Marids, while manipulating the mighty Demon Princes, and become in all but name: Master of Alantéa and the Mid-World of the Truce.

Chapter Twelve

And the Marids

"AND THE MARIDS," MURMURED Eudox in deep tones, almost an invocation, but the rolling echoes of his voice were stopped by foggy clouds that were rolling in over the shoreline, and the soft sounds of wavelets slapping feebly against their ship's waterline.

"Where are the Marids?" he intoned again, slumping over the ship's railing. "And where are the Demon Princes? Where has Houma hidden? What of the Gods, and what will become of the four of us, the Sorcerers?"

"The Marids are hidden away," Cronar sneered, "in the same temple of lies where they conceal Ancient Guardians, Maker Servants, underwater Isles, and secret pacts. These, they bring out at bedtime to entertain certain feebleminded Sorcerers. Alcman, if you cannot shut this one's mouth, I am likely to do the Wizards' work for them and feed his whining carcass, piece by piece, to the carrion birds."

Images of death filled Cronar's mind, for, throughout the ocean surrounding Stone Mountain, the dead were bobbing in salt waters, having been thrown to the merciless crabs and tides. Wild mutinies had followed the Sorcerers' retreat from Gravengate, and now the rebellion's leaders and their followers were rough, bloated fare for the seagulls and black cormorants that flocked to the shoreline.

Eudox turned his moist, bulging fishy eyes away from the carrion birds, toward his brother Sorcerer, and said, again softly, "You might find yourself surprised."

"You! A surprise?" snarled Cronar. "You will die, whining —" Then the tremors again struck their vessel, and the three Sorcerers once more stared out to sea. Banks of vapor drifted toward them, interlaced with the debris of broken sorcerous emanations; and beneath the waterline, small shocks from distant underwater turmoil could be felt even in their huge headquarters ship, a vessel that lay heavy and sprawling on the water, like a floating palace.

"Merlin is powerful," Alcman murmured. "Yet a dozen Merlins could not hope to check both Marids and Demon Princes. Some other power stirs."

Cronar pulled back from the railing, the tension building again in his lean, spare frame. "Forget the other beings. Bring Houma forward; four Sorcerers will be enough. Tomorrow or the next day, we four will crush the Wizards and have done."

"Houma will not be joining us on this day," Alcman said, shaking his head. "This time he is beyond even my reach."

Cronar began to back away from the two remaining Sorcerers, with the stench of salty death seeming to stick in his nose and throat.

"No Marids, no Demon Princes, no Houma — and next there will be no Cronar. Farewell, my brethren —" He halted, having backed into a barrier: Alcman's unseen, invisible shield wall.

"Be not so rash," Alcman said gently. A silence ensued, with even the lapping sounds of the surrounding sea seeming to recede. Cronar's eyes narrowed, and his breath grew short as he readied to destroy or perish.

Alcman spoke the Words, and the walls fully enclosed them, taking the three far from the shoreline, far from Stone Mountain. The fishy eyes of Eudox bulged further from their sockets: without even a Portal Passage, they had been transported Elsewhere, even Otherwhen, to a place outside of time.

Alcman's Gift reached out toward the other two, and in the stillness, they felt the shaping touch of some immeasurably cold and hard power.

"The Gods have delivered fear unto to you," Alcman murmured. "Your dreams and those of others have been invaded. I will teach you the weaving of mind shields. But you should know that Hell and Damnation are lies fashioned by the Gods. There is no Hell. If we prevail, we will inherit the power of the Gods, with a lifespan so long it may as well be everlasting." As his brother Sorcerers bent to his will, Alcman lifted his barriers, until they stood, once again, on the deck of their floating fortress, surrounded by enchanted banks of vapor, and bobbing corpses that had been transformed by saltwater, with the cries of so many carrion birds echoing over the shoreline.

"You were always the most powerful of us," murmured Eudox, voice filled with submission together with a predictable undertone of low cunning. "Yet it still seems that the tide has turned against us. The hosts of Gravengate will reach Stone Mountain perhaps even tomorrow. Defeat lies before us. Have you a counter?"

"Defeat — not yet," Alcman replied. "We are evenly matched, and even if we were beaten on the battlefields surrounding Stone Mountain, we would not be destroyed. Since the beginning of our struggle, I have not wavered or felt fear. But now with this turmoil in the depths, even I feel the need to seek answers to the confusion that surrounds our war." His eyes locked with Cronar's.

"The Portal Passages are blocked," said Cronar watching Alcman intently, "and all my Divinations collapse into nothingness, as though weighted by slime and the smoke of burning corpses."

"There is a third way," Alcman replied. "Did you not mark how our foes countered Houma in the Erivan?"

"Mental linkage," hissed Eudox. "But there is too much power, and so we might easily be destroyed."

"Too much power for battle magic," Alcman said. "Let us seek instead a Seer's Sight, strength to peer into the distance, and into the future. Join with me. Come."

Cronar held his ground, but he looked at the two Sorcerers with growing revulsion. "We are entering a nightmare equal to the Gods' vision of Hell. I have my own darkness; I need not share others."

"Like copulating with serpents on a bed of maggots," Eudox added, inching away. "I prefer the Gods' nightmares."

"Come," said Alcman steadily, yet his own gorge was rising as he extended his hand. "There is no Hell — but there will be no darkness like our own darkness — come." With infinite distaste, the other Sorcerers touched Alcman's hand.

Then they linked.

For a moment, their thoughts swirled like some huge cesspool spinning in a vortex, then they steadied, becoming one intellect, a mighty, penetrating power that surged over Alantéa, over the Western Sea, and through the Mid-World of the Truce. Eyes distant with Farsight, standing stiffly like a stone oracle with three heads, the Sorcerers spoke in turns:

Eudox: "The Demon Princes have healed Houma, but he now lies locked in conflict with the Shadow People, and also with the Apprentice, Julian, and so is not free to aid us."

Alcman: "I must add that these Shadow People are a most ambivalent force, neither good nor evil, and so they may be used by the Gods as a powerful tool against *both* Houma and Julian."

Cronar: "The Apprentice is also caught up in this conflict; therefore, the Truce cannot be called down upon us, and the Wizard's gambit has failed."

Alcman: "Yet some unknown Powers contend with Demon Princes beneath the ocean's surface.... There is no feeling of Godlike power.... Even so, the Demon Princes are prevailing...."

Eudox: "And the Marids have healed, and their surface skins are now harder than steel; and so, Merlin's counterthrust is blunted and broken."

Cronar: "Twelve of the Great Marids now stride along the ocean floor toward Stone Mountain, ready to bring destruction upon our foes."

Silence followed, a pause, as flesh corrupted by salt water slapped feebly at their bark, and the Sorcerers peered more deeply into their *Web of Fate*.

Alcman: "Within the Isles of the Sorcerers and the Mid-World Kingdoms of the Dark Lords, the Demon Princes are weaving an alliance, a counterweight to the many Gods and all their servants."

Eudox: "Our war against the League has been only a skirmish in a much larger battle. We grow steadily stronger, yet victory will only come when our Demon Masters allow it to happen."

Cronar: "We have been only crude, blunt weapons, sharpened gradually throughout this struggle, being honed for a war against the Gods and the whole Mid-World of the Truce."

"And the Marids," Kalanin murmured, keeping his voice low. He rode beside Géla and the two watched as Dargas regaled Héna and those around her with another of his earthy soldier's stories. The old Sorceress slapped her thigh in glee and countered with her own scandalous version.

"Balardi rides toward his conflict with Marids at Stone Mountain," Kalanin continued. "He could speed his pace, but he hopes that Julian will reach the Vale of Whispers and call upon the Gods, or, failing that, he hopes that Merlin himself will come."

As Dargas heard the last of Héna's story, his mouth dropped open, his ears reddened, then laughter nearly swept him from the saddle.

"I and the others have heard tales of Marids before," Géla said. "Why is it that you and our Wizard alone have long faces?"

"The Wizard and I, alone, seem to be afraid," Kalanin said in a small, distant voice.

· 〤 ·

From far overhead, the Eye of Merlin looked down, watching the tier masses surge toward Stone Mountain like some unruly insect horde. A festive mood was sweeping through their tier ranks — a celebration begun far too early, the eagle concluded. Behind them, the setting sun was passing from gold to red; but before them, layers of ocean mists surged over the lands around Stone Mountain, and his view was blocked.

He reached with his mind, tentatively, then drew back — Merlin was preoccupied, withdrawn, hidden. And the other two Wizards were also shielded from his thoughts, caught up in unhappy visions.

With an effort, he lifted the burden of worry from his wings, and let them soar always more swiftly into the wind currents of sunset.

· 〤 ·

Géla lay, hands behind her head, watching the night sky as meteorites slipped from the cup of the Heavens and swept down toward a dark, foam crested ocean. Those flares of light seemed as large and as bright as stars. It was hard to consider them, as the wise men who chart the passage of stars, had taught her — that these lights were being made by nearby boulders flaring to earth against a backdrop of faraway suns, and even more distant clusters of suns.

With profoundly mixed feelings, she saw that a tall, blanket laden figure was moving slowly toward her. As Kalanin neared, she sat up, staring at him in an unfriendly fashion; but she left her sword sheathed.

"I suppose I should call the guard," she said. Wordlessly, he dropped his blankets a few feet from her and lay back on them, face turned to the heavens.

"And why should you expect to find me here, alone?" she demanded. "Each one of my tier leaders is out there with their counterparts, locked in feverish embraces, gasping under their breaths, hoping the sounds will not carry to other warrior maidens. Should I not be out there, teaching and learning from one of your young captains?" She turned on her side and looked at him — his eyes, unfocused, remained skyward.

"Is this courtship then, some crude, halfhearted effort?" She reached for him, tugging, though not roughly. "Come, an answer from you, even a grunt."

"I was alone, I thought I would join you in your star watch." His voice sounded a little distant, tense, as though he had not spoken for some time. "Even had I other wishes — love, or desire, I would hold back for a while. The Mistress of Illusions would be filled with resentment — I know it is inconsistent, that she is now close to Baroda — but she would still be jealous, and we cannot afford that."

"Ha!" she laughed. "Of all the Alantéan heroes to have adventured with, I've met the most dour, sober minded intellectual one. All the heroes of legend had as much trouble keeping their pants on as keeping their swords sheathed…. But still…." She pulled again at him; he embraced her gently, like touching a being made of glass petals. And he was chilled. *This is what I wished for,* thought Géla, *a beginning, but he feels as though Death already has slipped a cold hook into his body.*

·)(·

As they continued their measured, deliberate passage toward Stone Mountain, messengers came from all corners of the League, telling of the occupation's collapse, how those pledged to the Three Hands were casting weapons aside, or fighting their way to the League's borders and departing, never to return.

In the west, North Haven was abandoned by both sides. Amalric was freed, while at Tuvan the seemingly beaten town folk had arisen and destroyed the garrison. At Narsis, a truce prevailed, permitting those of the Three Hands to flee north. And at Khiva, sailors and fisherfolk had set fire to their foes' fleet, and there was slaughter along the long quays as those serving The Three Hands fought to the death, with nothing but salt water or burning ships to fall back upon.

Wagon loads of good were sent south from Piranus and Rigal, atoning somewhat for the earlier aid given to the League's foes. Barges filled with grain floated down the Asaram, the Saugus, and the Bariloch, sent, it was said, by the Elf-Kindreds.

None dreamed of easy triumph, with the Sorcerers fielding a force of arms at least equal to the League's and perhaps a greater strength of sorcery. Yet, to their astonishment, the Sorcerers did not meet them in battle, but broke the siege of Stone Mountain, and fell back toward the Asaram River.

There, at the mouth of the Asaram, Dargas, Baroda, and Harmadast led a test of arms against those serving the Three Hands — and were hurled back. The Sorcerers had caused great earthworks to be constructed not half a league from the river, while their fleet held the shore and the river's mouth in great force. At the same time, huge pontoon bridges were constructed over the river, so that if retreat was forced upon them, the Sorcerers and their armed hosts might escape nearly unscathed.

Less than four months after hurling down their avalanche of sorcery, fire, and steel, the Sorcerers held only a small, almost tiny fragment of the League, but they held it in such force, that the Powers of the Mid-World would have to come in force to dislodge them — and they had before them a concentration of the League's power, that now might be crushed in one swift, hard blow.

· ✶ ·

"Softly, now softly," whispered Dargas. Under the heavy overcast night skies, and shielded by the Mistress of Illusions, Dargas' words carried only a few inches. Even so, Baroda heard, or sensed, and signaling with his mind, brought their raiding party to a halt. In the distance were water sounds, as the Asaram, running broad and slow, lapped sluggishly at its riverbanks.

Now, the Archers? Baroda questioned, touching Dargas with his mind. The old soldier grunted, not caring for the mental intrusion, but his eyes remained on the earthen wall fortifications, watching the sentries of the Sorcerers as they stood only partially awake in the darkness, outlined dimly by watchfires.

Soundlessly, the archers slipped forward. The Mistress of Illusions followed their progress with a mixture of pride and concern: pride because her warrior women were lithe and deadly; concern because they were clad only in light leather, easy prey for bow shot or sling cast. There were twenty of them, and when they reached the river's edge, they waded forward without hesitation, bows held overhead. Here, at the northern edge of the Sorcerers' earthwork barrier, they hoped to emerge waist deep from the sluggish river and harass the defenders from behind.

Pacing himself carefully, Baroda counted to seven score, then touched the Mistress of Illusions. *Lights, madam...*allowing an afterthought to follow, *...my mistress, the incredibly beautiful lady, how you have changed my life.*

Spheres of light swept radiance over their adversaries' camp. Cries of surprise were followed by shouts of pain: the archers had loosed their first round.

Dargas watched as sentries began to topple. Others leaped from the walls, seeking hiding places in patches of darkness. Grey Men with rough hewn ladders were edging toward the walls, but Dargas held them back, listening to shouts of pain, and the singing of bowstrings. Then came a series of splashing sounds as the archers serving their foes cast bows away and dove into dark river currents.

Dargas leaped forward, but Grey Men passed him easily, sprinting toward the walls. Two score rough hewn ladders were placed against the sides of the earthwork barrier, and men sprang up, unopposed. Somewhere, far from sight, sentries were calling out the alarm, but at this point of attack, League forces were unchecked.

Heart pounding, Dargas reached the top of the walls' fortifications. All through the camp, their foes were fleeing or milling about in confusion. Grey men hurled javelins at knots of resistance or slashed at them with short swords. Something sprang at Dargas out of the darkness, a bowshot passing over his head by less than a foot. He scrambled to the ground.

"Find pikes and shields if you can!" he called out. The top of the earthen barrier would need to be held against men coming from the south.

Pacing himself, Dargas jogged toward the northernmost pontoon bridge that lay across the Asaram. A cluster of men formed around him, then sped ahead, sweeping all before them.

Panting, Dargas reached the bridgehead. Already men were hacking at thick ropes and metal restraints. Others were out in mid-river, pouring pitch on wooden supports of their foes' bridges.

"Maker curse them!" Dargas panted. Out of the night, reinforcements were coming on horseback. Dargas hurled his javelin, a long arcing cast, and it bounced off strong plate armor. But others leaped out of the darkness, slashing at horses and riders. Pikemen shifted forward, shielding the bridgework, and the prolonged thrust and counterthrust of battle began in earnest.

Now they were nearly done. The bridge creaked and groaned as those in the middle of the river raced back to shore. Soon the broken bridge sections would surge downriver, sweeping flames over a second crossing — perhaps even a third.

Out of the darkness, a force of magic groped for them. Like smoldering blue smoke, a floating cloud giant reached down and crushed two of the Grey Men.

But then light leaped out from the Mistress of Illusions, like radiant spear points, and the floating spell drifted away, howling as it died.

"Eudox! You dung licker!" cried the Mistress of Illusions. "Come yourself and taste death!"

Torches were cast on the bridgeworks as the last of the restraints was broken. Burning pontoons, still linked, began to drift down the river and out to the sea.

"That's it, lads!" Dargas called. "Let's be gone!" Sentries and outriders sent by the Sorcerers were battering at the shield and pike wall that had formed at the fortifications northern edge. At any moment, massive tier ranks would emerge from the darkness and their foray would end in disaster.

They ran back toward the earthwork barrier. As Dargas panted and slowed, strong hands grasped him from either side. With grunts of effort, they hauled the old soldier to the fortification's top, and he stumbled down the ladder and back out into the darkness.

Calling on all her strength, the Mistress of Illusions burst apart a section of the wall fortifications, so that the Sorcerers' sentries and guards became separated from League forces.

Men of the League hurled the last of their weapons at their attackers and were back over the wall, dragging their dead and wounded into the darkness.

They sped away, and in the overcast night skies, they could see flames glow and shift as the stricken bridge broke apart and drifted downriver. Still struggling for breath, Dargas reached Baroda and the Mistress of Illusions: the two were embracing with such a combination of triumph and lust that the old soldier laughed.

"Come now," he panted, "time for those things later. One of the chickenhearted Sorcerers may yet get a fire in his gizzard or his groin and come after us. Let's go."

"Yes, the Sorcerers," murmured the Mistress of Illusions, disengaging herself. "The Wizards predicted weather magic, but we shall see." She turned and strode west, with Baroda walking easily at her side. Dargas followed, listening as thunder and storm sounds began to gather over the river.

As the first warm raindrops pelted down at them, a cool, strong, chilly wind sprang from the west, and it swept the Sorcerers' rain weather from over their head and away from the river conflagration.

The Mistress of Illusions laughed, face still wet with rain. "See, the Wizards are too humble. I knew —" She broke off, and turned east again, for a great weight of sorcerous power was building in the skies above the Asaram.

Then the skies burst open, and a torrent of water swept over the burning bridge works, reducing all their night's effort to little or nothing: Alcman, the Weather Master, had countered the Wizards, and over the Asaram and the southern shoreline of the League, his power prevailed.

The Mistress of Illusions turned west again, her face set in a grim portrait of cold, wet fury. She walked in silence to the halfway point where men of Stone Mountain met their war party, bringing teams of fresh horses, and wagon carts for the wounded.

The three mounted, waving off questioners, Dargas, and Baroda each on one side of the Mistress of Illusions. Her horse sprang forward as beacons of sorcerous light kindled by anger shone over their path. Weaving through the fields and meadows, they raced over the rain dampened countryside, until the smoldering campfires of the night watch came into view.

The Mistress of Illusions slowed — a little — letting the night watch identify her. Then she was within League lines, surging toward the Wizards' great campaigning tent that thrust upward, puffed by winds, and billowing in the camp's middle, like some huge, ungainly mushroom. It was little consolation to her that tent creases were catching puddles of rain, and a weight of water threatened the inner scaffolding and outer guy ropes.

Guardsmen gave way before her anger, and she swept inside, with Baroda and Dargas trailing behind her, shaking moisture from their cloaks. In the far corner, Thorian and Balardi were seated on chairs with high backs, watching the three advance toward them through the smoky, sparsely lit interior. Kalanin was leaning over a charcoal brazier a little to the right, speaking in hushed tones to the Eye of Merlin. Both Captain and Familiar looked up, eyes watching as the rain soaked Sorceress confronted the Wizards.

"An alliance, mutual aid, assistance was promised," the Mistress of Illusions hissed, "yet all I received was feeble, halfhearted help! If I did not hate the Sorcerers with an everlasting passion, I would depart from here, and leave you to your melancholy gloom!"

She stared at them then snarled, "What...is...the...matter...with...the... two...of...you?"

"Alcman was Weather Master once again," Balardi said after a pause, glancing at his fellow Wizard. "He has overcome our weather spells before; in this one area, at least, he is our superior."

"Yet your first effort was so feeble! And a second counterstroke was not even attempted! Have the Sorcerers turned your guts into squirming eels? Has the courage within your hearts been eaten away by worms?"

Thorian spoke neutral, even-tempered words designed only to blunt her assault; the Mistress of Illusions raged on.

Kalanin led Dargas from the tent, but the Eye of Merlin remained within, watching on impassively. Outside, the air remained filled with drizzle and dampness, although the heavy rains had passed.

"A good plan nicely worked out," Kalanin commented. They stood beneath an overhang, shielded for the moment from the rainy aftermath of Alcman's weather magic. "The Eye says that all three bridges might have been destroyed by fire, and even the fleet at the river's mouth threatened. Pity about the Sorcerer's weather work." In the background, the Mistress of Illusions' voice rose, nearly to a shriek, and even the Wizards' neutral tones deepened with tension.

"Failure or not, it was a good night's piece of work," Dargas said, scanning the campground, seeking shelter. Then he paused. Voices inside the tent rose and fell, and the eagle's croak mixed with human tones.

"You know, they almost had me," Dargas continued softly. "A few inches lower and a bit of metal and wood might have been buried in my forehead. Do you recall how I drank a farewell goblet of wine for Envar? Do the same for me, then, if my end comes."

With one arm Kalanin clasped the old soldier, noting again how lean and spare Dargas' wounds had left him. "I would drink that cup for you, and celebrate your life," Kalanin said. "You came drifting down the roadway, almost stumbling in defeat, and then together we helped transform the League's fate." The mouth of Dargas was forming words, but then he stopped, listening as Baroda's deep voice rose in support of the Mistress of Illusions.

"Speaking of wine, and since daybreak's still far away," Dargas murmured, his eyes resuming their quest for shelter, "I think that this old soldier will search out a cask. Are any of the lads still up?"

"Not a good idea. Not on this night," Kalanin said softly.

"Eh?"

"Thorian has brought every last fighting man out of Stone Mountain. All others once shielded within his fortress have been sent to Tuvan, Amalric, or Khiva, far from this struggle."

Dargas stood straight, alert once again, eyes suddenly shrewd. "So, it's all or nothing, with Stone Mountain lost forever if we lose. When?"

"The Mistress of Illusions may well push the cautious Wizards over the edge. Tomorrow would be my guess."

Dargas sighed. "Then it's sleep for me — but I'll need to go far from this noise. Listen to them!" Within the tent, the Mistress of Illusions' voice rose again, shrill and demanding.

"Your Wizards are certainly a hangdog, down at the mouth pair," Dargas grunted. "What's the matter? Has the Apprentice failed?"

Kalanin shook his head. "He's been checked again. He and Galad and the small ones have been beaten back, but not defeated — it's unwise to count them out. Also, I believe, sometimes, that there is a Maker's touch on Julian the Apprentice."

"On Julian, on Galad, and their two small allies — and on yourself."

Kalanin smiled. "You've spent too much time with the old Sorceress."

"There's a wise one for you, probably warm and asleep at this moment," Dargas sighed, "as I should be. So, night's ease to you, Captain, and thanks for the warning: wine fumes mix poorly with the harsh choices of battle." Dargas waved and moved out into the drizzle, stepping carefully over the rain puddles and fresh horse droppings that littered their campground.

Kalanin listened for a few moments to the voices within the tent: they were lower, less tense, not as harsh. Likely a consensus was forming, with the next day bringing one final strike against the Sorcerers. He slipped away from the Wizards' huge command tent that sagged from water, and out into the night.

· X ·

Even in the darkness and drizzle, it was a simple matter to find Géla: no matter how her work crew struggled to mask their sounds, still the muffled thumping of metal striking metal echoed through their camp like a dull background noise. Workers were assembled in a series of tents that lay at the camp's edge, and as Kalanin neared, he could see stray light beams slipping from rips in the canvas.

Within, Géla was working alongside a score of men and women, linking thin plates of metal together. In the far corner, Héna, the old Sorceress, was chanting over the light armor, but in a tired, halfhearted fashion, almost mumbling. Only four hours remained before daybreak.

He picked up a corselet of mail, testing its weight: it seemed light enough, and with good fortune, it would stop the bowshots of archers.

"So?" Géla had stopped and was staring at him across a row of workbenches.

"Tomorrow, most likely. The Mistress of Illusions is forcing a decision from reluctant Wizards."

"Then, I'll raise the next shift," Géla said, wiping her hands, "though the preparation of armor is nearly finished. Do you need help on the longboats?"

Kalanin shook his head, and Géla left the tent, moving through the darkness on the thankless errand of waking fighters from deep sleeps. Within, the Old Sorceress finished her spell mumbling and came to Kalanin's side.

"So, tomorrow you'll be tigers doing a deathly dance among the mourning doves, eh?" she murmured, smiling up at him.

"Or kittens among hawks, depending on our fortune and our skill."

She touched his hand, the bleary smile still frozen on her face. "Don't seek refuge in Stone Mountain," she whispered, voice hoarse with weariness and tension, "and don't throw your lives away. We might prevail — on some other day — but Stone Mountain is doomed."

Kalanin held her hand, looking deeply into her eyes as though seeking the Farsight of the Gift Born, then he nodded.

· ⋈ ·

They labored through the night, sometimes catnapping in tent corners while others filled their bench spaces. Armor and reinforced bows, and longboats were finished, and the last of the wicker shielding was completed just an hour before daybreak. Most of the workers slept then, as total silence fell over the camp and all lights except their watchfires were extinguished.

A few remained outside, murmuring together in low voices until the sun crept up from its hiding place beyond the Eastern Ocean. No cocks crowed, having long ago been consumed by the land's despoilers, but a few birds woke in the surrounding fields and meadows and began tentative morning songs. The sun shone briefly, then dimmed, sliding beyond a massive cloud cover. Bird songs faltered then stopped, as bugle calls reached through the morning stillness, rousing the camp. To the freshly awakened foot soldiers, it seemed that the Wizards had at last put aside their uncertainty and were now prepared to drive the Sorcerers and their servants from the League.

A short time later, as their preparations gathered speed, more bugle calls came from the west. Harlond and Rostov were riding toward them with a great mass of the men of Stone Mountain, more than eight tiers of its defenders, adding four thousand men-at-arms. Shielded from the Sorcerers, they had marched from Stone Mountain a day earlier, camping less than a league from their allies.

Their camp was struck, with thousands of hands packing and loading, so that it seemed a full day's work was compressed into little more than an hour. Only the Wizard's huge command tent was left, a bloated, distended, poorly conceived palace that was already showing signs of water damage, as it listed and sagged in the early winds of morning.

The wounded and the poorly armed were sent west toward Gravengate, and more than two hundred men of the Dragon's Teeth were released, for they had grown so spectral or beastlike that they could no longer heed their master's commands. The rest began a slow, ponderous movement toward the Asaram, a measured pace, but the excitement and tension was building in each of them.

Watching from above, the Eye of Merlin could not restrain the cry of exultation that burst from his throat: the force below him was the greatest in numbers, most powerfully weaponed, most fell and dangerous that had ever moved under the League's banner.

Below, Kalanin raised his sword in salute to the eagle's war cry.

"Harmadast has passed to me the tier-group on the far left," Harlond said, "and to Rostov, that on the right...." He paused for a moment, seeing that Kalanin's attention was turned skyward.

"On such a broad front, four groups are best," Kalanin said judiciously, after a moment, "with the greatest weight in the two center groups under Dargas and Baroda — so it's well thought out."

"Then let me ask you one clear, simple question, my old Captain," Harlond continued. "Does it not bother you — even a little — that you are not in command of this, the greatest weight of power ever assembled under the League's banner?"

"Give our current leader some credit," Rostov interjected. "If he wished, or if great generalship would carry the day, then he would play commander once again. Instead...." Above Rostov's wispy beard, his shrewd eyes were touched by a wry humor. "Instead, we have Captain Hangnail, the leaper of ladders." He motioned to the longboats that were shielded by tarpaulins, with a scattering of ladders and siege rams lying on the canvas surfaces. Kalanin nodded, then raised his hand as though to forestall further comment.

"Yes, I know," Rostov said, smiling, "'Beware, lest the Sorcerers read your minds.' Somehow, I suspect that they have other concerns, that they will not bother with our thoughts or opinions."

Kalanin nodded. "Right on all counts, both of you, and all your observations, both spoken and unspoken are true — except that, I prefer my small role to that of Harmadast, our commander.

"Yet I do have some advice. *If* we fail, and even *if* it seems hopeless, save what you can. Then, we will make a stand, even a last stand, on the Plain of Gravengate." Géla repressed her scornful comments, but Harlond and Rostov let their eyes flash together, as though confirming something they had long suspected.

Kalanin turned their conversation again to the coming battle, yet much of his Giftless, though powerful mind, was far from the battlefield, building an invocation, almost a series of prayers:

Julian, reach your goal, bring down the full weight of the Mid-World of the Truce on the heads of our adversaries.

Merlin, greatest of the Mortal Magic Wielders, put forth your power now so that both Gods and Demons will be amazed,

Maker, I am greatly flawed, but Géla and Galad and Julian must gleam brightly among all your graceful children. If it is Your desire, I am willing to pass into the Long Sleep, but spare all these many other mortals.

No answers came, and clouded skies above them seemed to darken and drift lower.

· ☿ ·

As they neared the river mouth, shipborne catapults hurled stone and molten fire at them, and it was only with great difficulty that the ox teams were kept under control. Kalanin and Géla pulled their tier-group back a few hundred paces from the front lines, and they watched from a little distance as the first assaults began.

Four tier masses approached the earthen wall fortifications of the Sorcerers, feeling the bitter, war weary hatred of those serving the Three Hands beat down upon them. A silence, a pause followed, as Harmadast measured his foes and their fortifications. Bows were notched but not drawn. Drums quieted to low, rumbling, tapping sounds. In the distant upper air, many scores of those riding the Sorcerers' Reptile Birds wheeled and banked, far from bow shot.

Then there came crashing sounds, a roll of drums, an epiphany of trumpets, and many thousands of voices calling out as the tier-groups hurled themselves against the Sorcerers' fortifications. Flights of arrows arced and intersected in the upper skies, while at the river mouth, men sweated and pulled as catapults and huge ballistae were launched and reloaded.

Géla watched as several scores of ladders were thrown up against the wall fortifications, with men climbing them, while others smashed at the fortifications with massive battering rams.

"This is not the easiest time," murmured Géla. Her hands clenched and unclenched as liquid fire was hurled down on the ladders, with men bursting into flame, then falling, shrieking, from the fortifications. In the distance, their cries sounded like the hoarse calls of dying birds.

"Just let those in the air become committed," Kalanin replied, grim faced, "while all the ships' weapons stay focused on our land forces." Massive stones and balls of fire were falling among the tiers; men and women died where they stood, for they were too densely packed to fall back or flee.

Now there were shouts as one of the rams breached an earthwork barrier. Like the point of a spear, a half tier sped through the gap, meeting the thick ranks of pikes manned by their foes. Scaled wings of soaring lizard creatures that served the Sorcerers began to descend, as those manning the upper reaches drifted toward the breach, hurling javelins, and short spears downward.

"So," said Géla, drawing a deep breath and turning to Kalanin, "the Sorcerers have been our masters on air, and land, and sea."

Kalanin smiled. "Today we will test their mastery, perhaps even shake the hold on their watery domains — but recall my words: there may be a time to strike and a time to swim for shore."

"Yes, my sober minded, always thoughtful captain," she said as she signaled, and the ox teams were led forward, moving to the farthest right flank, where the Sorcerers' earthwork barrier met harbor and river mouth.

Arrows fell among them, piercing the tarpaulin and wounding ox teams. They neared the water. Galleys, harbor craft powered by oars, lay just a few hundred feet from shore — insolently, as though unchallengeable. Sweating men cursed and loaded, their boats rocking and surging with every cast. In the deeper waters, huge crafts with many sails were anchored, immobile, so that only the currents moved, sweet river water surging to either side of fixed craft.

"Now!" cried Géla. "Now the Wild Time comes for the Sorcerers!" Men and women sped toward the ox-drawn carts. Coverings were swept aside, and longboats were dragged swiftly to the water's edge. Oars flashed, and boats surged beyond the lines of foamy waves. Cries of surprise rang from nearby galleys, then a clatter, as men scrambled for their oar banks.

Kalanin smiled grimly: their longboats were swift and easily maneuvered, while the galleys of their foes were cumbersome when not at sea.

Wicker shielding caught the first halfhearted volley of arrows. But then it was too late for arrow and catapult casts: men and women were swarming up the boat sides. Lightly armed marine sentries were swept aside, their bodies seeping pink hues into clear harbor waters. Sailors dove from bow and stern, swimming away from the savage onslaught.

Géla stood on a galley's deck, and she cried out in exultation. Two boats had been taken, while on a third, the issue remained in doubt. At Géla's command, banks of oars were manned, and they sped seaward, white foaming water streaming to either side of their longboat. Kalanin pulled a second group together, passing heavy bows among them: carefully crafted bows of wood, reinforced with bone. On the shore, the Sorcerers' rearguard watched them with sullen surprise, while on the water, distant splashes seemed to be coming closer as catapults were realigned. They closed with the third boat, and the men serving the Three Hands faltered when they saw their foe's strength. A few dropped sword and shield, diving far from the fighters that surged toward them.

"Hold back just for a moment," Kalanin called out. He pulled his bowstring tight. Above them, masses of scaled lizard wings were hovering closer. "Loose!" he cried. Then there were cries of pain and surprise as winged steeds and riders faltered, then hurtled seaward.

"It's steel or salt water for you!" Géla cried, and she leaped from one boat to another. Kalanin and others followed. They swept sailors and sentries aside like ripe wheat slashed at harvest time.

Now they held three ships, with longboats surging toward them with reinforcements. Oar powered harbor craft were speeding away from them, while out on the deeper waters, craft manned by sailors serving those of the Three Hands, sails with many assorted colors were unfurled — to little effect on this windless, overcast day.

"So, water masters!" Géla cried out as they sped toward a larger sailing craft. "You have much to learn —" She broke off, and she turned, her eyes becoming riveted on the shoreline.

A Great Spell was slipping over the Sorcerers and their allies.

Under overcast, windless skies, the shoreline along the Asaram was undergoing an incredible transformation: slowly, unbelievably, sea growths and barnacles were creeping over those serving the Three Hands. Even now, many of the Sorcerers' allies were locked to the ground, not even able to cry out. A few dove into the water — and sank like stones.

"Wizard work," Kalanin hissed. "They warned me — where the Sorcerers hold sway will be transformed back into seabed." Men serving the Three Hands, grown heavy with stony growths, began to topple.

Then there came a great rending sound, as though the earth had cracked — and all the power of the Wizards' Great Spell was swept away.

"The Wizards feared Alcman with good reason," Kalanin murmured, turning to the banks of oars. Their three boats had faltered as all eyes focused shoreward on the Wizards' transformation work.

"Let the Wizards deal with the Sorcerers!" Géla called to them. "Pull! And pull again!" Then she cursed: their next target was being abandoned, with sailors manning small boats or swimming to the shore. And flames were licking the ship's deck so that it was made completely useless for them.

She called out a new command and their three ships changed direction, surging toward a second deepwater boat that had hauled anchor, sprouted sails — and stood becalmed, listless, under overcast, windless skies.

But now their foes' landing craft were returning from the shoreline, ferrying tier-groups back to the Sorcerers' fleet: reinforcements. Géla took a deep breath and steadied herself, forcing calm over the adrenaline that surged through her body. Her forces were only a few among many, with three harbor craft contending with scores of boats. However brilliantly they had planned and trained, they remained outnumbered.

She let out her breath and called out a different command, shifting direction again. Kalanin sighed in relief as they veered toward the shoreline and their foe's small landing craft. Moving to the middle of their ship, he readied the archers.

Their reinforced prow caught the first of the Sorcerers' landing craft and crushed it, while rowers leaped into foaming water. But others among the many craft hurled grappling hooks over the railings, and the wild fighting with men leaping back and forth between ships resumed. Whenever archers dropped bows and drew swords, winged reptile creatures hovered always closer.

"Not yet time for our swim, is it?" Géla muttered to Kalanin. Clusters of their foes had gained footholds on their galleys, forming shield walls, while others followed behind them. Kalanin and Géla drew swords, racing toward their opponents; once again a grim reaping time began.

The last of the boarders was repelled, and they turned to their sister ships: a second was nearly free, but the third was smoldering with flames below its deck. As they pulled alongside, men and women hurled buckets of water — then they gave way as the fire beat them back. They had come too late. Men and women leaped from the doomed galley onto their two remaining captured ships.

But now they were trapped in the river's mouth. To the west, the Sorcerers held the riverbank, while on the other side of the river, scores of ships were clustering, with catapults and flame arrows ranged against them.

They floated, drifting for a moment. To one side, the din of battle could be heard; while on the other came the wash of many boats, with seagulls crying in the background. There was no way out.

Oars tentative, splashing, they began to retreat south, back toward their starting point. But nearly a dozen galleys stood before them, now reinforced by sub-tiers of pike from the shore.

As they looked for an opening, the second of the Great Spells slipped over them, drifting shoreward over open water. Chilly air currents swept around them: an odorless, stale, vaporless mass, beyond the decay of death, utterly stagnant. Kalanin's mind leaped in recognition — and astonishment.

"Marids?" Géla asked, almost in a whisper. They were drifting, all eyes turned to the battle on the shore as greyish black apparitions began to form along the shoreline. Kalanin stood frozen, waiting.

Then the Shades of the Ancient Adversaries stood upon the shoreline: the Demons, the Dragons, the Creatures of the Darkness. Demons and Demon Princes, Dragon Lords with immense wingspans, dreadful misshapen Creatures of the Darkness — all of mankind's ancient nightmares stood silently on the overcast battlefield. Half solid, half aware, some of the dreaming dullness slipped from the Ancient Adversaries as they began drifting toward the Maker Servants holding the lines of the League.

Apparitions of the Ancient Servants slipped among the Adversaries, as the Mistress of Illusions countered — but they were misty apparitions matched against powerful sorcery and they vanished in seconds.

"What are these?" Géla demanded. "You know them — I can see it in your eyes."

"Row, then be ready to dive." Kalanin unbuckled his sword. "The Sorcerers have summoned the Ancient Adversaries from the Temple of Waiting. Immortals that have been dead for ages walk among us. If Alcman, Cronar and Eudox are that powerful, we are doomed. Row." Blasting sounds rolled over the waters as the Wizards sought to counter. Men of the League were falling back in fear, but those touched by the dead immortals became still and lifeless.

"Row," Kalanin said quietly. At Géla's side, he was forced into a role of Grey Councilor, but even now the old, impotent rage flared within him as matters of sorcery again mastered the Armed Host.

Oars tugged at water that was partly river and partly ocean. Arrows and javelins swept at ghost beings and cut nothing. Wizards' spell work sought the Ancient long dead Servants — and found not even echoes.

"I wish..." Kalanin murmured, "if you and I had only...."

But then a great darkness surged over them, and all sounds grew dim, muffled by nothingness, and the water's surface grew still as glass. The Ancient Adversaries halted, slumping, as the will and purpose of ancient hatreds slipped once more away from them.

All those on the shore and on the water found themselves in a vast Cathedral of Sorrows: the Temple of Waiting, where all the dead immortals waited for the Maker and His Will. A deathly chill ran through them, and the oar banks faltered.

The moment hung like forever, then it passed, and the Temple of Waiting was gone, with all the ancient, dead immortals drawn back to their gloomy, deathly sleep.

"Maker's work!" Kalanin called out over the stillness. "Alcman, neither you nor Demon Princes nor self proclaimed Gods can undo the Maker's Will!" Their oar banks came alive once more — and in the confused aftermath, a gap opened between the galleys facing them. They surged through, with hundreds of their own voices calling out in defiance as they sped through the opening.

Then they were safe for the moment, with nothing but open water between their two ships and their own tier-groups. Drifting shoreward, Géla and Kalanin turned to the river's mouth surveying the confusions in the harbor: splintered wrecks drifted into deep waters, interspersed with burning ships, and most of the shipborne catapults had lost their ranges when they had escaped into deep water.

"And yet, the Sorcerers remain masters of the surrounding waters" Géla murmured. Their two ships were ranged against many scores of fighting ships, both deep water and harbor craft. And now their foes were far more wary and alert.

"It may even have been the difference," Kalanin said, staring at the shoreland battle. "We will never know...but look...." Beside the shoreline, at the southernmost edge of the Sorcerers' earthwork barriers, a tide of League-tiers was swarming over the earthen walls of their foes. Bugle calls mixed with cries of triumph; sounds of rage and fear answered. The air seemed to shudder, as though some great dam trembled at the edge of destruction.

"Rostov!" Kalanin called out. "Rostov, the wily! Break them!" Figures moved along the bridgeworks: the first retreat, as litters carried the wounded to safety. Ships serving the Sorcerers began to pull away from the shoreline, ready to fall back into deep water.

"We may yet be masters of land *and* water!" Géla called out in triumph. On her orders, their oared galleys began a slow arced turn. "Now, we'll sweep fire over them!" Flame arrows were kindled; others stood with helmets filled with water, ready for a counterthrust of fire.

Again, they sprang forward, more fierce and swift than their uncertain opponents. Pitch-bearing arrows leapt with fire at their foes, like a thousand tiny smoldering sparks. Halfhearted flights of arrows flickered toward them, and most fell in shallow water.

"Again!" Géla cried out, and powerfully reinforced bows were drawn back. A cry of exultation slipped from her mouth as scores of flaming missiles arced high over their foes.

But Kalanin gripped the galley's side, peering forward: something had gone wrong with the arrows flight, as though they suddenly carried too far...or their targets were sinking.... And here, as the Sorcerers readied for flight, here the stage was set, and the final curtain was being tugged from center stage.

"Now, masters of land and sea!" Géla cried. "Perish in flames or saltwater —" she broke off. "By all the Nine Billion Gods, what is happening?" Their galley seemed to be settling, dropping, though they were still afloat.

Kalanin took a deep breath, then responded in a low voice that was both remote and filled with sorrow: "Here, unless I am very much mistaken, are the true water masters — the Marids. Turn back." She stared at him, face filled with defiance, but he continued, "Please — as we promised ourselves." All down the shoreline, the ocean was retreating as though a full day's tidal shift was sweeping seaward in moments; and now the sea passed beyond its lowest tidal mark, exposing large beds of shellfish to overcast skies.

"Please," he said again, and this time Géla called out the order, shaking her head in disagreement.

"Why do we not stand our ground and test these beings?" she asked, dark hair cast behind her, eyes alight with rebellion. "Are we not ourselves mighty and fell and dangerous?" Kalanin's face was turned to the harbor: swirls of water were moving closer as though a teeming undertow surged toward them.

"In our own way we are dangerous," he said, in a voice that was quiet, almost thoughtful, "but these have been fashioned as a death bane for Wizards, most likely creatures able to destroy our Nine Billion Gods... Ah...." They had struck a sandbar. Kalanin tugged at her light armor, pulling it off then casting it to the deck. The ship listed. "And the stage has been long prepared for these creatures; I cannot believe that they will be easily countered." Men and women were leaping into shallow water, splashing toward the shore. Kalanin cast his own mail aside and pulled Géla to the deck's edge. Then they both leapt into the sea.

Scrambling over newly exposed seabed shellfish and barnacles, they raced toward the sandy highwater mark; then they turned, panting.

From out of an uttermost low tide, the Marids emerged, striding through shallow waters that continued to withdraw into the ocean. Under an overcast, haunted sky, nightmare beings came out of the depths, rippling with power, five times man's height, but with the bulk of scores, so that as they strode toward their mortal opponents, rocks and barnacles lay crushed beneath ponderous, broad feet.

And their jaws were enormous, with huge, bright boar's tusks gleaming white from their mouths. Their skins were dark, mottled, brown and black, streaked with copper and red, scarred by angry, raw wounds. Greyish and green lamprey parasites with grim mouths were attached to those red wounds; but now the last few scores of lampreys were falling off, dying as the Marids waded into battle, while tens of thousands of parasites like tiny crabs, pink with the red flesh of Marids, spilled from the flesh of Marid necks and shoulders, falling dead onto the sands.

"What are those snake and crab things?" Géla breathed out. "Or what *were* they?"

"Merlin's unlovely magic," Kalanin said softly. "He tried to counter the Marids with sorcerous parasites, but the Wizard's efforts have only delayed them. Get ready to run for your life."

Now the Marids strode forward fearlessly, flesh rippling with healing strength, as though no creatures would ever again dare assault them, and they could take whatever they wished, ruin whatever they were sent to destroy, while all their foes fled in terror.

As they moved into battle, Marids raised their enormous heads and broke the silence:

— *Hoot!* —   — *Boom!* —

Echoes rolled over the battlefield like the deep sounds of huge horns emerging from dark caverns, filled with menace.

Ignoring both the noise and the menace of Marids, archers crawled over the deck of their beached galley, loosing arrows from powerfully reinforced bows. Metal and wood shattered against mottled, streaked reddish dark skin.

"You fools!" Kalanin called out. "Get away! Flee for your lives!" Behind the archers, another Marid emerged from the depths and strode toward the galley as archers dropped down to dark mussel shoals and ran. Clasping both hands together, the Marid smashed down on the beached ship: with a great rending sound, it shattered, spars of wood flying in all directions, impaling, or crushing those around it.

Kalanin pulled Géla to the ground, as wreckage hurtled overhead; then they scrambled to their feet.

— *Hoot!* —   — *Boom!* —

"Horses," Géla muttered, voice suddenly deflated. "We'll need them for either fight or flight." Demon spawned Marids reached the shoreline, striding fearlessly over sandy beaches. The tier ranks of their allies, the Sorcerers, pulled away from them, cowering. Marids strode toward League lines. Battle hardened tiers pushed toward the Marids, bristling with pike — but they were smashed like insects wielding weapons of straw; and yet the screams from the broken and dying sounded more like the death cries of crows, not insects.

— *Hoot!* —   — *Boom!* —

"Maker, who made us or let us be made!" Kalanin cried out. "How have You let these beings come to pass?" Scores of grim grey men wielding axes surged toward the tallest of the Marids. Those few who survived hewed at mottled Marid flesh and their axes fell, notched or broken, from their hands.

"Wizards!" cried Kalanin. "Where are your powerful spells? What of your own great powers?" As if in answer, a Portal flashed before the greatest of the Marids: an enormous being, with flurry of fangs and talons and scaled spikes leaped out — and in seconds that monstrosity lay in jumbled pieces, twitching in its death throes, still trying to shriek in a voice that could no longer even whimper.

Then Thorian countered: a fountain of molten rock sprang at the foremost Marids, engulfing them in blazing lava.

The first rank of Marids strode through unscathed, smashing, tearing apart both the living and the unliving in their paths while they stared out over the battlefield, seeking the Mortal Magic Wielders. Weapons were being dropped, with tier-groups turning into rabble — though some held, backing away with long pikes extended. Marids crushed those in flight and those in defense, indifferently, impartially.

— *Hoot!* —   — *Boom!* —

"Hold now, O my people!" Thorian's voice lifted over the battlefield. "At this, the last moment of battle, we invoke our pact with Taurog! Father of Trolls, aid us now! Taurog, see that we do not contend with the Gods, nor do we struggle in our own civil war as once we did!"

Then Balardi's voice too was raised, echoing over the battlefield, as Marids surged toward the Wizards. "Taurog, these Marids remain outside of the Truce! Taurog, in the Maker's Name, and for our commitment at the Awakening, aid us now!"

Portals flashed, with scores of Trolls leaping from them: stone giants, and ice golems, and Gograe bearing clubs, and many yellow-eyed, grey-skinned beings of the Troll Kindreds. Human ranks parted, backing away, as Trolls advanced toward Demon-spawned Marids.

The Marids, masters of all monsters, moved toward them relentlessly, fearlessly.

Trolls were shorter, squatter than the Marids — and yet only twelve great Marids now faced scores of the Troll Kindreds, with more emerging each second from Portal passages.

"We will never reach our horses," Kalanin murmured, eyeing the long boats.

— Hoot! —   *— Boom! —*

"There's no need." Géla drew her shoulders back and took a deep breath. "See, your Wizards are powerful, or have powerful allies —" She broke off as the tallest of the Marids stepped toward a Portal. Trolls smashed and battered — without losing a single step.

The Marid extended its hands into the Portal's mouth: it exploded with a muffled concussion.

"Shatterers of spells" Kalanin murmured, then he turned to those around him. "Now, listen to me: there will be a stand at Gravengate; we can be a part of that battle if we survive. We'll need boats and oars, with whatever food you can gather quickly. Take what weapons you can but leave any armor that will weight us down." Portals were detonating throughout the battlefield, shattered by Marids. Tattered bits of the bodies of Trolls were beginning to spatter over the battlefield. Tier-groups pulled back, beginning to race from the unequal struggle.

"Gravengate!" cried Balardi. "Merlin awaits us at Gravengate!" Portals flared, and tier-groups milled through. Those on horse raced for their lives. Others cast weapons aside, dying singly or in packs, beneath heavy, monstrous, Marid feet.

— Hoot! —   *— Boom! —*

Running like fire, those with Kalanin and Géla sped toward their longboats, scores of hands pulling wooden vessels over crushed mussel shoals, broken barnacles, and strands of seaweed. With nightmare sounds in the background, they rowed a great race, hugging the shoreline, arms aching, into the sunless dusk, and into a starless twilight. Hooting and booming sounds grew more remote.

Then, in the darkness, louder sounds of destruction rolled over them, echoing over the waters like distant thunder.

"A storm?" Géla asked. Her dark hair lay damp and matted on her forehead, plastered by sweat.

"The Marids are breaking down Stone Mountain," Kalanin spoke in low, distant tones. "As the Wizards foresaw, they will reduce both that fortress and Stone Mountain to rubble. Sea's Edge was never intended to be a physical bastion of the League. So, if none can check them, Gravengate, our last fortress, will be next. Then our League of Maker Servants and Mortal Magic Wielders will be utterly destroyed, gone forever."

Chapter Thirteen

The Marids Before Gravengate

"I HAVE ABSOLUTELY NO wish to leave this place," the Mistress of Illusions muttered. "Our final efforts to craft weapons ends at daybreak, with so little time remaining, and much left to be done."

"Yet you and I alone have felt the pain of losing our kingdoms," Héna replied. "I have one argument for Thorian, but I may need your support for any further discussions. Come. Recall how the Apprentice aided you in the aftermath of your loss."

The Mistress of Illusions softened. "Then we must go now, and only the two of us."

"They should go alone," Kalanin said, turning to Balardi. "The ruin of Stone Mountain is only the latest of many shocks for Thorian: the death of his mistress, the capture of his daughter, the complex traps laid for him by Demon Princes. But we should stay clear because we are part of those previous disasters — at least in a portion of his mind. Let the two of them go, alone."

Balardi nodded, wearily. Face bleak, gold hair turning whiter each day with stress, the Wizard faced the destruction of Gravengate by Marids in less than two days' time, as Sorcerers and Marids moved slowly toward Gravengate, destroying everything that lay before them. But Merlin was coming, Merlin was coming, he reminded himself, and there was still hope. His eyes drifted into the distance.

The Mistress of Illusions drew Héna aside and walked with the old Sorceress down the gloomy corridors that linked the many chambers within the fortress of Gravengate. Thorian was in one of them, and their Gifts led them toward the sorcerous emanation radiated by the Wizard's Divination Spells.

Lights flickered from Thorian's chamber, with low sounds rumbling down the corridor. The doors were unbarred, opened; Héna entered cautiously, the Mistress of Illusions just a step behind her.

Within, Thorian sat, engrossed by his own, grim, personal nightmare: Divination Images showing the destruction of Stone Mountain. Marids ranged over the fortress, rending bulwarks, crushing stone columns. Other Marids battered at its foundations, heedless of the huge fragments of the broken fortress that cascaded down upon them.

The three watched on in silence as light within the visions created by Thorian's magic shifted from darkening hues of dusk into overcast nighttime so that all that could be seen was the dim outline of a mountain slowly settling into rubble. Yet the sounds of destruction, muffled by darkness, still rumbled faintly from Thorian's Divination Spell.

"It always ends in the same fashion, does it not?" the Mistress of Illusions asked in soft, gentle tones. Thorian said nothing. "Wizard, I —" She trailed off, for Héna was waving her to silence.

The old Sorceress stood, weighing her words, stooped, leaning on her cane, looking down at the seated Wizard who sat very still, watching the destruction of his fortress.

"Thorian, your daughter still lives — did you know this? That means that not everything is lost."

"I know that Eléna is alive." The Wizard spoke in a small voice, as though contemplating something infinitely distant.

"Yet, you fear that she exists trapped in the underwater Isle of the Demons, held forever while she drowned, or tortured endlessly. It is not so." Thorian looked up from his nightmare, face grim, taut — and hostile.

"How did you come by this knowledge? Is Alcman speaking through you? Or that master of disguise, the Demon Prince, Zikar? Either way, do not seek to divert me." The old Sorceress sighed and sat on a chair across from Thorian, with the Divination Image, a rumbling sound of blackness, obscuring the Wizard's form. Yet, in a moment, the Wizard motioned the darkness away, and his nightmare vision vanished, together with its rumbling echoes of destruction.

"Thorian, I am by far your inferior in matters of sorcery," Héna continued, speaking softly. "Perhaps only Merlin and Alcman are your equals. Yet the Sight has grown within me. When I perceived — and accepted — my own death, it was as though layers of illusion were stripped from my eyes.

"In my night visions, your daughter Eléna has appeared many times. Her form is changed somewhat, and often she takes shape as an armed prince or young captain. Always, she contends with greater forces, and is beaten back, yet some hidden power or being shields her from complete defeat.

"Why the Demon Princes have allowed her this existence leaves us with still another mystery, but here is the truth: she lives a life that seems as real to her as yours or mine, with less sorrow than you or I now feel."

Thorian was silent for a moment, eyes peering into the distance.

"I always expected that the Sorcerers would seek to barter her," he said slowly, "and yet they have never even mentioned her existence."

"They may not even know of her fate," the Mistress of Illusions murmured. "It is no open alliance that we face, but rather a league of the treacherous, with separate bands of deceivers."

Thorian nodded and took a deep breath. "In my Divination Casts, I looked for the Sorcerers' faces as they first watched the Marids wade into battle: Cronar's teeth are clenched like those of a trapped wolf that must attack or flee; while Eudox stands with bulging, fishy eyes nearly slipping from their sockets; and even Alcman's face is filled with a strange disquiet."

The Wizard drew a second, deeper breath and stood. "There will be time, time for despair later. At least most of my people survived — so, for now, I will leave off from mourning the wreckage of Stone Mountain and prepare for the defense of Gravengate. Go back to your weapons' crafting; it seems so unlikely, but perhaps one of those devices might still make a difference."

"You have enormous will power," said the Mistress of Illusions.

"There is still strength within me," Thorian replied. "I am — or was — mighty among the Mortal Magic Wielders, yet I have no counter to Marids created by Demon Princes. Another will need to deal with the Marids; I can only seek to oppose the Sorcerers."

"There is still hope," said Héna, rising and clutching her cane. "Merlin is coming. I can feel him drawing closer."

· ☽ ·

Kalanin stood at the topmost peak of Gravengate, watching the tide of refugees moving west and north, fleeing both the disaster at Stone Mountain and the oncoming onslaught of Marids. Overhead, banks of clouds rolled in from the southern coast of Alantéa: an endless flow of overcast, rainless gloom, moving north, a suitable background for the League's last stand.

More than two thirds of their forces had survived the disaster at Stone Mountain. Many had been killed, but many more dispersed, and every few moments a string of soldiers would pull away from the tide of refugees, and moving in a halfhearted, faltering manner, would drift back toward the fortress and their tier-groups. A few even stopped and began working at the eastern side of the Plain, where many teams were digging huge pits — Marid traps, they believed. Kalanin shook his head; pits would never trap the Marids.

Why had the Marids not pursued immediately and broken the Wizards and their tiers? Perhaps Sorcerers and Marids could not yet communicate — or perhaps they wished to crush all their opponents in one tidy, well organized battle, with all three Wizards in their grasp.

In the distance, far to the east, the eagle seemed no more than a speck, but one that began to descend, in spirals, circling lower. Kalanin turned from the parapet and sped down the long, stark tower stairs. Taking care to avoid Géla or Dargas, or the Mistress of Illusions, he raced to the guardroom, and carrying a messenger's saddle pouch, he rode out from Gravengate, over the dusty, ruined plain. Patches of scrub grass were struggling for footholds on the withered plain, but even now they seemed dry, brittle, and lifeless.

He avoided the Greenway so that only at the Saugus' crossing did he encounter any of the refugees. A large mass of them packed the great stone bridge, but enough of them squeezed to one side that he was able to cross. Many refugees watched his passage with grim, haunted eyes.

A few leagues out, not far from the place where he had marked the eagle's descent, he encountered one lone, ancient traveler: an utterly nondescript, weather beaten old man on horseback; and the nag he rode was shuffling and stumbling as though she were on her last legs. This wayfaring stranger seemed so pitiful, that it was an effort for Kalanin to keep his eyes focused on his journey.

Kalanin turned and rode at the side of his master, who remained disguised as only another refugee. They picked their way through dying meadowlands, while a little distance from them, the tide of humans continued to choke the Greenway.

"Not many could have followed your progress," Kalanin said softly, "but all the Mortal Magic Wielders and the Powers of the Mid-World could certainly have marked your passage. And if you were to have come partly hidden, why not ride disguised as Great Wotan, with one eye, and ravens swirling in your wake? And why should you, a Portal Master, be traveling on horseback in any form?"

"The Portal Passages have been barred to me," murmured the Wizard, "and if I must take the Straight Path, then it is enough to be hidden from the storm tossed, the refugees.

"Yes, the Sorcerers have marked my progress; let them be most wary of me. The Gods have watched on; now let them abandon their unbenign, unneutral indifference." Kalanin peered out from the corner of his eyes, under the shadows of his eyelids, and the Wizard's form was still unclear, though now his eyes could see that the eagle's form was perched on his master's shoulder.

"The Gods are not as neutral as they once were," Kalanin said, lowering his voice. "Gifts have been sent of sorcerous origin, things that might be tested against the Marids. During the last few days, the Mistress of Illusions and Baroda and Dargas have sought to fashion weapons, huge spears, and projectile casting devices, with the Gods' gifts as spear points — from my understanding of these matters, such weapons seemed most unlikely to prove decisive."

The old Wizard shook his head, murmuring, "As well might flower petals seek to contend with a firestorm, as it is for us to contest the Marids' power using poorly considered devices at the very last moments of the League."

"Yet you have brought something or will introduce some new force."

"A chance, that is all, nothing but a chance."

"Should we wait for Julian and Galad? Are they free then? Free to call down the Truce upon Sorcerers and Marids?"

"I have done what I might, from a distance, to free them, but I fear that they have been halted, for the moment." The Wizard spoke in tones of distant, remote sorrow, so that Kalanin fell silent, keeping his many questions to himself.

The stone bridge spanning the Saugus still swarmed with the peoples of Stone Mountain and Gravengate, but the Captain of the Guard had now sent out a force of rangers to open a lane for Merlin and Kalanin. They passed over quickly, two messengers seemingly, one tall and powerful, the other dwarfed in comparison, but somehow quite difficult to look at.

Riding at an even, measured pace, they passed over the lip that curled at the edge of the great, ruined Plain of Gravengate. Above them clouds still surged northward, rolling over the heavens like huge masses of spun cloth. Riding over the Plain, Merlin veered from the fortress, a little to the north and west. Kalanin said nothing, only following the Wizard, then halting as Merlin paused: but here, he realized with a start, here he had fought the Ruined Seraph, and blood, golden blood, rich as sap, had surged from the ancient being's wound.

The Eye of Merlin dropped to the ground and paced over it, wings flared, as though seeking some serpent hidden in the dust.

"Gone," croaked the Eagle. "All traces have vanished."

"In my dreams some months ago, the Seraph stared back at me, face filled with mockery, sure of its own malice and power," the Wizard murmured. "Yet now I believe the Seraph drifts, mostly witless, with the other immortals awaiting the Maker's judgment. I am glad that he is not my servant to judge."

They turned once again to the fortress, increasing their pace as they moved under dreary, quickly moving skies. No trumpets greeted them, but two teams of honor guards stood, each to one side of the massive, carved gates. Within, Thorian and Balardi bowed, as Merlin, once the greatest of Mortal Magic Wielders, entered the last of the League's military strongholds.

"Come," said Merlin, alighting, "there is much to discuss." The old Wizard was hunched, almost shrunken, and he stood more than half a head shorter than Thorian and Balardi. Yet, now all three seemed to focus and become more purposeful.

As the three walked from the outer gates, Balardi turned and spoke to Kalanin, and the Wizard's eyes were clearer, his speech less weary: "For the first time since the beginning of this struggle, there is hope, and the ruin of Gravengate is no longer a certainty. The Sorcerers, I believe, will now speed their passage toward Gravengate. I have told Harmadast to prepare for tomorrow. Do not rejoice too early, but now there is reason for hope, at least."

"So, what are we supposed to do now," murmured a low voice at his side — Géla's voice, "kneel outside of their chamber and pray in hushed tones?" She had emerged from her weapon's work and stood now at Kalanin's right, leather gloves off for the moment, face streaked from the forge. Her eyes followed the Wizards as they approached the keep — the three figures were already locked in somber, intense conversation.

"Dig pits, forge weapons," Kalanin replied. "Either is better than despair or waiting for grim, uncertain Wizards."

"So?" She stood back, staring at his clean unsullied hands and face. He smiled at her: their eyes were almost level, and she smelled of charcoal wood smoke.

"No, I'm giving you my routine, neutral response. Don't go back to the forge, don't join the pit crews. Neither of those will make a difference tomorrow. Let the two of us, alone, make the rounds once before nightfall, to see that all is ready for morning. Then, if you are willing, stay with me tonight. What the Mistress of Illusions feels or does no longer really matters." She looked at him uncertainly.

"So, our hero does have desires," she murmured, "and he can make somewhat long if dry, speeches — but what's he doing, singing the old sailor's sea chantey, 'love is for forever, we are for tonight'?"

"You and I are for forever, or at least as far into the future as I can see. I say this not because our lives may end tomorrow, but because it is what I would wish for: to be wed with you, to have children, to have our own dwelling within the League, but far from the Wizard's gloomy fortresses. And there —"

"Yes," she interrupted, and the leather gauntlets slipped from her hands as she embraced him. "It's my wish also. But don't go on about our children and our farms or our baronial manors — if we survive, there will be more than enough time to disagree about those matters. Let's begin with tonight."

During the long afternoon, they rode out to the pit works, then walked through camp kitchens, and after, the wide chambers of Gravengate, where weapons were being forged: huge metal javelins were being honed, then fitted with weapon points made of strange jewels and metals and *Talismans* sent by the Gods. Everywhere the gloom seemed to lighten, as word of Merlin's coming had spread like a firestorm through the fortress.

At nightfall, she came to him, eyes soft with wine, her long dark hair still filled with wood smoke.

"This is the first time I have lain," she murmured softly, "with someone that I loved."

Daybreak brought strong cold winds, with lumbering, dark clouds towed behind them, so that most woke hearing the muffled thunder of the oncoming storm. By mid morning, a slow mustering had begun, with tier-groups forming outside of the fortress, passing rank upon rank through camp kitchens. As the tiers fed, the Eye of Merlin brought word to the Wizards that the Sorcerers had broken camp at dawn and were only a few hours march from Gravengate.

"A strange procession," the eagle reported. "Marids stride before all, hooting and booming to one another, while the Sorcerers follow on horseback, and behind them is an armed host, but a fearful, cringing one, fearful of Sorcerers, terrified of Marids. Thunder follows the Marids, as though their bodies were magnets for lightning."

The Wizards stood before the open gates of the fortress, with captains and Magic Wielders drifting one by one toward them. Muffled thunder rattled over their heads as a misty rain began sweeping over the parched, ruined Plain of Gravengate.

"Is this your doing, Wizards?" asked the Mistress of Illusions, pointing skyward. "Or has Alcman, the Weather Master, called this down upon us?"

"Neither," Merlin replied. His eyes ran over the faces before him, watching as Dargas and Harmadast drew closer. Only Kalanin and Géla had not yet arrived, but they were moving quickly toward the Wizards and their last Council. "The Powers of the Mid-World have at last learned to fear the

Sorcerers and the Marids, but the Gods are bound by laws that we do not yet understand, and so their storm magic will not even slow our enemies." Gusts of wind brought more water; cloaks were tightened, hoods drawn over bare heads.

"Wizard, something has changed," said Héna. "If the Powers of the Mid-World are not yet ready to set aside their Truce, then you have brought something, a spell, or some tool of power. Last night, for the first time in many moons, my night visions brought images of my own survival: I stood with Rafir and Sebastian in a meadow, with golden sunlight shining all around us — and we were well contented."

"There is a chance," said Merlin, then he turned to the others. "There is a chance — that is why we are gathered here. It will work or it will not work, and it may be over quickly. Beyond our sorcerous conflict, there will be escape hatches. The League may break, but it is not necessary for all the people of the League to die."

Kalanin's eyes flashed to the faces around him: Dargas and Baroda were grim, prepared for battle, while open rebellion flared within the Mistress of Illusions. Rostov and Harlond were staring away from Merlin, as though eye contact would reveal their thoughts.

"There will be a stand, Merlin my Master," Kalanin said gently. "You and your Wizard brethren have created a thing that is greater than the life of any man. If it ends, our League will be broken in bloody, red ruin, and not just melt away like an icicle in strong sunlight."

Merlin sighed. "The Marids are too powerful, and so I beg you not to throw your lives away...." He trailed off, staring away from them.

"Alcman," Thorian muttered, his face grim with anger.

"Yes, the Sorcerer is reaching toward us," Merlin said, looking into the distance. "Nothing is gained by speaking with him. Best to pull free...." No words were spoken, but there came a sense of invisible barriers shifting.

"Do not throw your lives away rashly," Merlin continued, "even should the League fail, there are other forces that —"

In front of them, shimmering in damp, misty, storm charged air, flashed an image of Alcman, and it showed the Sorcerer standing tall, fearless, filled with power, with a necklace of Griffin's teeth spilling over his broad chest.

"Old Wizard, so soon to pass into the everlasting darkness," the image said with surprising gentleness. "It was destined that Wizard and Sorcerer would speak, sometime before the end. It is passing strange that you and I, the Greatest of Mortal Magic Wielders, will never meet in a conflict of magic, almost sad that you are destined for death beneath the massive feet of Marids."

"We are Servants of the Maker," Merlin said softly, "transformers of Destiny."

Alcman laughed, and malice radiated from his seemingly gentle image. "Why do you continue to worship this ancient, departed Deity? Earth means nothing to Him, forgotten, no doubt, as He drifts through His strange passage among the star clusters. Invoke other Gods if you must — although our current deities seem astonishingly feeble."

Alcman pointed skyward to the storm clouds that gathered above the oncoming Marids, and the Sorcerer laughed once again. "Perhaps there will be New Gods soon, and I will be among them." Merlin waved the taunting image away, and it vanished.

"In victory or defeat Alcman, too, will sleep the Long Sleep, one day," Merlin murmured. "Now, is there anything else that needs to be said?"

"We are ready," said Harmadast. "If you can hold back both the Sorcerers and the Marids, we will deal with their legions."

"And we may ourselves even surprise the Marids," Baroda added, watching as one of their huge casting devices was wheeled to the gates.

"There are but twelve of them. With twelve good casts, the fortunes of the day will be completely changed." Merlin shook his head but said nothing.

"So, while you humans ready your tiers, and machines, and Sorceries," said the eagle, "I will find out what the Gods have woven for the Sorcerers and the Marids." The eagle's broad wings beat heavily, flapping through misty, rainy air; then the Eye of Merlin was in flight, sweeping upward into darkened, rainy skies.

Fierce, strong, and capable of flight in any weather, the eagle surged through a lower bank of storm clouds, into a clear zone between cloud layers, so that a rumbling grey darkness formed below him, with sheets of white clouds overhead, and no hint that sunlight or dry land had ever existed. Then, the eagle *surged* through the air, flying east, guided by the storm sounds and his own Farsight.

A few leagues to the east, storm clouds were massed, bulging upward, like mushrooms with greyish black caps. Thunder and lightning rippled through the upper reaches of the clouds, pulsing, then crashing downward. Carefully, the eagle selected a break in the clouds below, and descended, moving from serene upper reaches into a thunderstorm.

Torrents of water surged over the Marids, cascading over mottled brown, black and greyish red skin, yet they strode forward heedlessly, hooting and booming to one another. Rain gusts shoved the eagle downward, and as he struggled for height, a great mass of weighted lightning surged from black clouds, striking the tallest of the Marids. The great Child of Demon Princes paused — for half a heartbeat only — then moved on, unchecked and undamaged.

As though angered, the skies burst with light, as columns of lightning swept down over Sorcerers and Marids — who moved on, unharmed, heedless, with rain soaked, bedraggled tier ranks following behind them.

Watching the relentless Marids stride through blasts of lightning, followed by cunning, powerful Sorcerers, the eagle felt, for the first time, an emotion that was close to fear.

·)(·

Kalanin rode through the swirling rain, moving from the right tier-groups toward the fortress walls. Here, at the center, all their casting devices had been carefully aligned and ranged for distance; some were armed like counterweighted ballistae, while others were strung like huge crossbows, able to hurl massive steel bolts that were tipped with enchanted gemstones.

He passed beyond the center groups toward the left flank, where Dargas stood, head bare, speaking with Harlond and Rostov. Alighting from horseback, he embraced each of them.

"No farewells," said Rostov, raising his voice above the oncoming storm sounds, "if fortune favors us, Merlin with prevail, and our greatest concern will be preparing for the celebration that would follow."

"That would be a great moment." Kalanin touched the shoulder of Dargas. "I could never keep up with this master of wines, but I would join you for a glass or two — and perhaps more."

"Come what may," Dargas added somberly, "it was good to have you surging south, breaking the twin sieges. That tale will be told wherever men gather when they are left un-haunted by Gods and Demons."

"We have all been part of a legend," said Kalanin, and he remounted. "Let's hope that the story ends with us growing old, peacefully, in sunlit gardens and meadows. Farewell." He turned away, resolutely, but already a portion of his mind was flaring in wild rebellion: *You fool! You mushy-mouthed, senile fool! You will never see them again — had you nothing better to say?*

Storm sounds were growing louder with every moment. The last of their tier ranks spilled out from Gravengate, and behind them came wagons loaded with gifts given by the Gods — weapons, charms, and unknown, strangely crafted devices. As he passed the wagons, weapons seemed to shift, to lurch toward him and hope seemed to stir inside his mind — only to be crushed like tissue smashed by a forge-hammer: *Fool! Fool! Fool! These trinkets are nothing! There's no balance: Demons and the Spawn of Demons must be countered by the Gods, not by the Wizards!* Other portions of his mind rose in conflict:

— But sorcery is a wild force, the rule breaker that defies all balances —

— *Fool! Sorcery has its own laws, its own balances. And you will never understand them. Fool! Save Géla at least; be remembered by one, for a few more years* —

— But still, Kalanin's mind struggled with his thoughts: Enough! Here at least I will find a clean death, a warrior's death —

— *More like an insect's death. Save Géla* —

As he reached the right-hand cluster of their tier-groups, the Wizards were emerging from League ranks, riding out a little distance from their tiers, with rainfall sliding away from their sorcerous, weather-shielded bodies. As they rode forward into the shifting storm, the eagle was returning, settling to the shoulder of his Wizard Master.

Kalanin reached Géla's side, to find the Mistress of Illusions beside her, passing final instructions to her granddaughter. The Sorceress had time for only one, sharp, penetrating glance into Kalanin's eyes, then she was riding away, back to Baroda and the central tier-groups. Carelessly, she and Baroda had left one sub-tier of beast and spectral men on the right, and these stood not fifty paces from Kalanin and Géla. Some had become so much inhuman, that they stared at their weapons, puzzled, as though wondering what tasks these tools might accomplish.

"We might think a little on the Wizard's words," he began, "that it is not needed to die...."

But now, even though obscured by the great wash of water that swept over the ruined plain, the outlines of Marids were emerging, huge and menacing, as they neared the curved rim that surrounded the Plain of Gravengate like the edge of some vast goblet.

— *Hoot!* —   — *Boom!* —

Géla reached over and clenched his hand. "No blame to either of us if we never had a long life together. Perhaps the Maker will raise us side by side, at the Awakening." Conflicting words and thoughts fought for control of Kalanin, thus he said nothing, only watching the huge forms of Marids as they stepped on the plain.

Fool! Fool! His mind raged. *Now Géla will die too!*

Then the last roll of thunder spilled over the plain, followed by silence. The sky streamed in turmoil as black clouds boiled away into nothing. Within moments, only thin and distant upper cloud layers were left, and with this change of weather, the air over the plain began to shimmer as Vision Portals shifted into view.

"The Gods have cast aside their failed weather magic," Géla murmured, almost in a whisper. "Now they have arranged for clear, unblemished sight into our arena. Maker, at the Awakening, do not heed the clever, self-serving arguments of those Powers who now call themselves Gods."

Marids were still for a moment, standing in silence like twelve gigantic statues; their hideous, mottled skin still shone damply with rainwater. Then, the Sorcerers rode up beside them, tiny figures on horseback beside giant Marids. Behind the Magic Wielders, a fearful, cringing armed host began spilling over the edge and onto the Plain of Gravengate.

"I wish that we, you and I, had been given more time...." Kalanin trailed off. Nothing more could be said, as all those around him had fallen silent. Still, his mind raged on: *Whimpering fool! Be ready for death when the Wizard fails!*

No horns blew, no trumpets challenged. All drums had been put aside, and thunderclouds had been swept so far away, that it was as though they had never been. Silence ruled, heavy with menace.

The firstborn and greatest of the Marids stepped forward, his brethren following a half stride behind. Fearlessly, unchallenged, the Demon-spawned, ocean-bred Marids approached, ready to bring an end to the alliance of Wizards and Maker Worshippers.

But suddenly, without warning, the earth groaned, and four of the great beings vanished, with dust-swirls filling the air where their huge forms had stood.

"Pit-works!" cried the Mistress of Illusions, her powercharged voice lifting over the battlefield. "Impale yourselves and die, Marids!" Even as she spoke, the earth began to shake, tremors rattling through the stone fortress... and the dust-caked Marids blasted to the surface — unharmed, unfazed, undaunted. Tentative, filled with fear, catapult crews began to draw back winches, beginning to cock their huge weapons.

Wizards! Kalanin's mind raged. *The time has come for your final spells, the last, hazardous enchanted roll of the dice before the end of your League!*

· �X ·

Slowly, reluctantly, Merlin stepped forward a few paces. Ancient, hunched, and frail seeming, with a stunted, grey beard, almost insignificant, the Wizard shuffled onward — and he touched the muddy surface of the plain with his ash wood staff, murmuring spellwords in soft gentle tones.

Then the battlefield was suddenly transformed.

All the countless, enormous sorcerous energies of Alantéa began surging toward the Wizard's slight figure. Power hummed, nearly in song, a harmony of Makerwork; while rays of radiant power, barely touched by sunlight, arced toward the Wizard, coming to rest where Merlin stood.

Marids created by Demon Princes, Mortal Magic Wielders, countless legions, all stood frozen to the plain in the last, hushed moment before complete transformation. Merlin's form seemed to grow, while those of the Sorcerers and the Marids became diminished, as though Merlin had become the giant, and all the others reduced to lesser beings.

The bodies of Marids began to flicker, to tremble like faltering illusions; while the Sorcerers hunched in their saddles, leaning forward, nearly toppling.

But as the Wizard's spellwork reached its culmination, all the sorcerous elements drawn to Merlin began to whine and groan, stretching in turmoil as they reached for miracle work that exceeded the Wizard's grasp.

A vast tension hung over the battlefield for a moment — and then Alcman's voice, like an echo reaching out from a distant chamber, reached into their ranks, seeking Merlin.

"Old Wizard," the voice whispered, "how wisely you have plotted, how powerful you have become! You wished to send Sorcerers and Marids back in time to meet your God, to a time before the Maker roused the sleeping Demon Princes — It would have been the greatest of jests had we, the Sorcerers and the Marids, proved greater than this Maker of yours! Yet we shall never know!

"For we are your nemeses, O Wizards!" Alcman's voice rose, ringing over the stilled Plain of Gravengate that was frozen by magic. "See how your Great Spell whimpers and groans, straining at the very fabric of reality. Yet we, by a smallest of magics, can bring forward the last elements of your doom: behold the second birthing of Marids, a second generation untouched by the magic of Wizards! Behold! If you could not contain a lone brood of twelve Marids, now you face an additional five Marid broods, and you are utterly undone!"

A vast Portal, like some huge cavern mouth, formed beside Alcman's outstretched hand. There, within swirling, darkened sea water, skins unblemished, unscarred, were scores of Marids, groping for entry.

Merlin's spell work shrieked and groaned, at the edge of shattering. Power now flowed from both Thorian and Balardi, and yet water, thick with seaweed, first seeped then surged from the Portal's mouth.

His face turned ashen; shaking, the old Wizard turned from his spell testing, sorcerous energies slipping from his grasp.

"I can no longer hold them," he whispered. "Maker, oh my great God, I have failed...."

·)(·

And then the Portal burst open, with Marids surging from its mouth.

Merlin straightened, gasping, then he drew a deep breath and turned to the sky overhead. "Hear me, O Gods!" he cried out in a great voice. "The Wizards' League is at an end!" He shattered his staff over his knee, then cast it aside. "Now, save those of us that you will!"

As Marids surged over the battlefield, first scores, then hundreds of Portals sprang up over the ruined plain: the Gods, proud, but wary and fearful, were, at last, moving to save those mortals still serving the Maker.

Kalanin moved his charger a step forward and reached toward Géla.

"Listen," he said in a low, intense voice. "Here are the Wizards' escape hatches. Take one and join me. Everything else is nothing but slaughter."

Her face turned grim, she shook free from Kalanin, raising her voice, calling to Merlin, "A stand! Make a stand, Wizards!"

The Mistress of Illusions picked up the call, her enchanted voice lifting over the battlefield: "Make a stand, Wizards! There is no place left to hide!"

Time to die, Kalanin's mind raged. *Time to die!*

Tier-groups were speeding to safety, Portal Mouths reaching for them. But others pulled away from Mid-World havens, surging toward the Marids with sharp weapons.

"Loose!" Baroda called out; weighted projectiles arced outwards — and shattered against the chests of the oncoming Marids. Rage burned through League ranks, the anger of the powerless. More fled though Portal Mouths. Marids crushed their foremost ranks, and as the nightmare gripped them, men of the Dragon's Teeth grown bestial slipped from their master's control, cast their weapons aside — and sprang at Marids with tooth and claw raging against impenetrable hides.

Men circled Marids, hewing at knee joints and tendons. Their axes fell, blunted, broken. Marids crushed all those in front of them, rank upon rank.

Their final nightmare was upon them. "Make a stand, Wizards!" Kalanin cried, the old rage surging again within him. "There's a time to live, and a time to die! Make a stand!" As if stirred to life by his defiance, Mid-World weapons began lifting from carts, or slipping from Portal mouths, speeding toward Kalanin, hero and weapon's master. The first of the Gods' weapons, a colored silver, jewel studded spear, settled into his right hand as he spurred his charger forward.

He raced toward Dargas, toward the center, where the old warrior was leading a party of men who held corded wire, seeking to snare the Marids and drag them to the ground.

But metal was no more than straw to Marids, strands broken in one lurching step — and a huge mottle-skinned Marid leaned down, grasping Dargas. Huge fingertips flicked the old soldier's head from his body, as a child might pluck a daisy. Raging, Kalanin caught the Marid in its side with a white spear that shone with Mid-World magic; the weapon shattered, exploding, smashing Kalanin backward to the ground.

"A stand, Wizards!" he shouted, rising once again. As before, weapons were pressing toward him. One sword, curved, light as a feather, gleaming with power, forced itself into his hand.

"Time to die, Wizards!" He stood on foot, watching Portals swirling around the battlefield, as they drew humans away from death by Marids. He leaped from one, turning back toward Géla; but she stood in a vortex of coiling, twisting Portal Mouths. With a cry of great anger, she vanished from the battlefield.

"A stand, Wizards!" he cried again. And they were making a stand: Baroda and the Mistress of Illusions had fought free of all Portal Mouths and struggled toward the centermost casting devices. Dodging past fear-stricken horses, twisting beyond gaping Portal Mouths, leaping over broken bodies, Kalanin fought toward Baroda.

— *Hoot!* —   — *Boom!* —

Spell sounds rumbled as the Wizards tried once again to master Marids. But now the Marids were striding through the center, smashing catapults and casting devices. Baroda was crushed underfoot. The Mistress of Illusions was held for a moment, then, as the grip upon her tightened, life and illusions slipped from her, and she was nothing but a frail, aging, broken corpse.

"A stand, Wizards!" Kalanin cried, swarming toward the dead Sorceress. "Time to stand and die!" He lashed at a Marid, his "enchanted" sword shattering as it struck mottled skin.

"Time to die!" he shouted at Merlin. Marids were at the fortress walls, crushing and smashing its fortress walls. A stone hammer circled around Kalanin, pulsing with energy. He grasped it and cast it in one motion, barely noticing that it, too, shattered against the hide of one Marid.

At the last, Kalanin drew his own metal sword, one completely lacking any magic. "This is the end of nightmares, Wizards! Time to die!" The last tier ranks were fleeing now, with the Sorcerers slaughtering stragglers with blasts of power. A few hundred paces from him, Héna stood in shock as though waking into a nightmare. Suddenly alert, she began shuffling toward a Portal — but then a Marid's hand clutched her body, squeezing it then casting her broken corpse through the Portal's Mouth.

"Time to die, Wizards!" Kalanin stood, his unenchanted, useless broad sword clenched in both hands. Portal Mouths and the hands of Marids were groping for him. "A stand, Wizards! Time to die!"

Chapter Fourteen

The Quest for the Truce Terms

"TO DISAPPEAR, TO VANISH," Julian said softly. "We need to break free from all of the eyes and ears of the many watchers." Sebastian sat, hunched, shivering, and even in the starlit dusk, he could see the steam of vapor rising from Julian's mouth.

"I understand that the watchers keep following us, but does it really matter?" asked Galad, and he stood, folding a blanket over the shoulders of the chilled Familiar. "Let them follow our progress as we ride openly through the Vale of Whispers."

"It matters," Julian murmured. "Firstly, some of the Powers may intervene openly against us, led to us by their servants. Secondly, Houma can track us by following the Watchers, like fishermen searching for schools of fish by tracking the movements of sea lions."

"Houma — again?" questioned Rafir, interrupting the grooming of his red fur. "I thought we'd be finished with him, at least for a while."

"Houma is healing," Julian murmured. "He took a great wound. His own body was reinforced by powerful sorcery, then chopped brutally by a Mid-World Weapon, but yes, tragically, he heals. In my night visions, Houma's arm has reconnected, yet now it has become a dark, withered thing, malignant, filled with sorcerous power."

Galad shook his head. "Back to the Watchers. "What's to be done?"

Julian was silent for a moment, watching as fireflies swirled in patterns just a little distance from them — and it was too cold for real fireflies. Then, he spoke softly into the minds of his companions and allies: *Fog and vaporous mists will block those who follow us by sight. Running water will shake Divination patterns. Then we must pass underground to completely vanish, and after, emerge masked by illusions that block the sight of all onlookers.*

"At some point," he continued aloud, "they will lose interest in us — more serious matters will draw their attention far to the south."

"Kalanin will test the Sorcerers and their sieges," Galad said grimly, then he patted the Tarnished Sword. "Next time, weapon of the Mid-World, strike Houma's head from his shoulders. Houma would have a much harder time healing after that wound."

Only the whisper of a ring, a sigh, came from the sheathed, enchanted weapon.

· 𝕏 ·

Late at night a sleepless Sebastian arose, blanket clutched about his shoulders, and he sat watching the incredibly slow twist and turn of the great Wheel of the Heavens. For a moment, he rested his hand gently on Julian's side, while his eyes searched his master's face: even in sleep, Julian's features seemed clenched in tension. Sebastian turned skyward again, watching for signs that the Maker was preparing to save them.

The Wizards had given Julian a task far beyond his power, yet if the Maker truly existed, and watched down on them, great deeds were possible. Through much of the long night, Sebastian, the Familiar and conscience of

Julian the Apprentice, prayed silently, his monkey's eyes blinking upward, out into the starry universe.

·)(·

The next morning as they rode out, the day shone bright, carefree, oblivious to their difficult, grim quest. After they had emerged from the Great Forest, traveling eastward, they had encountered ranges of hilly meadows alternating with stony outcrops and stands of trees. Now, with the sun's heat, both hillock and meadow shook free from their cold night's lethargy, so that thousands of small creatures resumed their perpetual searches for food and occasional mating dances.

By late morning, their journey eastward had taken them lower, as hill country sloped gradually downward, leveling out onto a broad, partly cleared plain. Herds spilled out over rangelands: cattle and eland, bison and terazill, all cropping at rangeland grasses or drinking at shallow pools of water. Rotting tree stumps lay toppled, surrounded by lush grasses, while nearby, recently felled trees lay strewn about, showing that the seasonal clearing work continued every year.

Rafir watched as flies swirled over cowpies, then darted into the hides of shaggy bison. Sunlight and slender grasses were calling to him, and the fox took a deep breath then dropped lightly to the ground.

"Time for exercise!" he called up to Julian and Galad. "I'll be back to protect you in a few moments. Stay clear of the bulls!" The fox vanished, speeding away over cool, green grasses.

"You watch for sharp hooves, Rafir," Sebastian murmured, almost to himself, then the little Familiar smiled and relaxed in the sunlit warmth of the long afternoon. He drowsed on Julian's shoulder, wings folded, head bobbing as their horses paced, jostling through the pasturelands, long necks turning, watching warily for sudden shifts in the herds. Then something, a ripple of tension in Julian, a cloud moving swiftly over the sun, or a warning given to those with the Sight, something brought Sebastian instantly awake.

Galad was leaning over, helping Rafir up.

"To the east," the fox panted. "Large predators, with men and horses chasing them." The fox drew in his breath. "Though maybe they won't bother with us." In the distance, Sebastian saw small shapes moving swiftly toward them, and then there were horn calls echoing faintly.

"It's not some simple hunt," said Julian. "There are those with the Gift or the Sight among them — two, I think."

"Now, why did I think we'd be left alone for a few days at least?" Galad said, shaking his head. "I'm bone-weary of slaughter. Can we avoid them, ride to the north or south? Our horses are fresh."

"These men do not serve Houma," Julian replied, after a pause. "Perhaps a raiding party, but more likely, the masters of this land. We should wait for them." They stood their ground, watching the hunt, while their horses nibbled warily at slender grasses. Rafir vanished, and Sebastian hid carefully in a saddle pouch.

A pride of lions raced past them, passing less than a hundred paces to the north. Heads down, hard dark, yellowish eyes eyes seeking shelter, they swept west toward the Erivan, their lean, muscled forms outlined low against distant northern hills and stony landscapes. Arrow shafts extended from several, yet the pride surged on together, as though made up of one, defiant, gasping, creature with many legs.

A few hundred paces behind them, the hunting pack followed: three score riders armed with lances, and crossbows, and long, slender swords.

Horns and hunting cries swept over the plains, but their sound patterns changed as the riders became aware of Galad and Julian.

More than a score pulled from the hunt and turned toward the intruders, lances extended. Galad looked out over the rangelands: the herds, so casual and complacent moments ago, had scattered in all four directions. He touched the Tarnished Sword: it seemed to groan as though only lightly roused from its killing dreams.

"What are you doing in this place?" one man called to Galad. "Why are you on my lands?" The man signaled, and lance points lowered a few degrees, pointing to the ground. The man was in middle years, balding, with a grey beard, but in bulk and bearing, he nearly matched Galad.

"Lord, we are refugees from the south," Galad answered. "We wish only safe passage, free from harm." Another tugged at the cloak of the first speaker, and the second man was hunched, wily seeming, with soft eyes and a nose that was gently curved.

"Cendro says that the youth is your true spokesman," said the grey haired lord, "a Mage or Warlock with the Gift. Cendro says I am likely to receive sharper lies from this slender youngling — and Cendro knows a great deal about lies." He glanced a sideways sneer at his advisor.

"Lord, I am Rann," said Julian, "and my companion is Kelvin. Truly, neither of us is a servant to the other, and we are indeed refugees. Have not others sought to pass northward from the war down south? Surely we are not the first."

A second advisor caught at his warlord's arm, and this one was a strong, powerfully built youth, hooded, with dark fierce cauldron eyes looming beneath a mass of jetblack hair.

"Haakon urges your destruction," said the grey haired lord, "while Cendro cautions that the two of you alone might master us — but Cendro is always fearful, and Haakon always calls for destruction. I am Khond, lord of this land, and I will offer you what I have offered the other refugees: a weapon's test, one of you to match one whom I choose — not to the death, though that might come inadvertently." Haakon was gripping his arm, but Lord Khond twisted free. "Which of you is it to be?"

"Lord, I will offer myself," said Galad, "though my blade is unsuitable — perhaps an archer's skill test would do." A chorus of jeers rose from the riders, but Lord Khond unstrapped his blade and flipped the sheathed weapon to Galad. Jeers became grumblings and mutterings until Khond turned on his horse riders.

"Quiet down! When one of you rules, then you can choose — though none of you snot-nosed whelps is fit to be ruler even of a rabbit warren. Here...." Khond signaled to one, the tallest and fairest. Both the chosen warrior and Galad stepped down from their saddles and stood facing each another.

"This one is my fourth son, Barak-Kor," Khond called down to Galad. "Son or not, you have my permission to nick him, if he is less than swift or becomes stupid." Barak-Kor circled Galad easily, and Khond's son was taller than Galad, roughly Kalanin's height, though his shoulders were sloped, less broad, and his eyes glittered with amused scorn rather than understanding.

The two circled, Galad warily, testing the slender, unfamiliar blade, while his opponent watched with detached amusement. Both wore light armor, ringlets of metal backed by leather.

Then Barak-Kor was upon Galad like a whirlwind, sword flashing in glittering arcs and thrusts. Sounds of ringing steel pealed over the grasslands. Galad gave way, fending desperately. A crease of red showed along his left shoulder as he backed from the furious onslaught.

Slowly, Galad steadied. Their swords blurred, flashing sunlight; then it was Barak-Kor's turn to back, inch by inch, grudgingly — though not quickly enough. Like lightning, Galad's blade flicked out and a similar streak of red showed on his opponent's shoulder.

Barak-Kor steadied, detachment gone, eyes growing hard. Galad began to parry, backing, and circling, watching as a cool, determined anger grew in his opponent.

"Enough!" Khond called down. Galad took two quick steps backward, then lowered his blade.

"So, you are indeed Julian," Khond said softly, turning to the Apprentice, "and this weapons master is Galad, wielder of a deadly sword. While a second weapons master, Kalanin, marches south at the head of a strangely potent, many-tiered alliance."

"We are only simple refugees, Lord," Julian said reasonably, "yet others from the south have mistaken us for the ones you mention. And it is strange that you are even aware of those distant people."

Khond studied him for a moment. "So, it's Rann and Kelvin, as you wish. If you can remember those names, I suppose I can also. Yet, with a Seer and a young Warlock as my allies, it's possible to see and know of many things, though Cendro has the nerves of a titmouse, and Haakon is rash to the point of madness. Now that you have won passage, what is your wish? Where are you going?"

"We have distant kin to the east, Lord, a few hundred leagues short of the Gangean range," Julian said, as he dismounted. Galad came up quietly, and Julian began the careful binding of his lightly wounded shoulder.

"Although you remain intruders," Khond murmured, "as unnamed weapons master and Magic Wielder, I grant you free passage through my realm. However, I regret that our domain extends less than a score of leagues to the east. Beyond that, other chieftains, and range barons rule, ones with far less wisdom than I have."

"And to the north?" Julian asked, eyeing the hills that rose at the plain's edge. A troubled look came over Khond's face.

"To the north are the Shadow People, the shapeshifting underground dwellers. We are at peace with them, for we of the plains have no use for their caverns, just as they have no interest in our rangelands. You can, if you wish, bypass the plains by traveling through the hills — but travel warily, for the Shadow People are powerful, greatly feared by many. Here...."

Khond drew an armband from his upper arm and passed it to Julian. Angry murmurs came from those around him, and Barak-Kor pulled away from the washing of his wound, storming to his father's side.

But Khond raised his hand, slashing the air, and as if by some prearranged signal, they all fell silent, standing quiet, united at their Lord's side.

"This armband is a token of friendship given me by their leader, the Shadow Emperor. It may — it should, bring good will. Do not abuse it."

Julian bowed low. "You are strong and gracious, Lord, and I thank you." He looked up, watching Khond seated on horseback in front of his sons and allies: the facade of quarreling brigands had been cast aside, and the leaders of a powerful, subtle clan stood openly before him.

Julian nodded thoughtfully. "With your mighty sons and your own power, it is a wonder that you were not drawn south, by the Sorcerers, to serve under the banner of the Three Hands."

Khond smiled wanly. "Eudox did seek me out. When he arrived, Cendro vanished in fear, and Haakon fell into a near foaming rage at the Maker worshippers. My sons quarreled and argued among themselves, while I alternately blustered, dithered, and made impossible demands. In the end, the not altogether brilliant Sorcerer found other fools to do his bidding."

"It was a good outcome for the League," Julian said. "Had you gone south, you might well have triumphed."

Khond laughed a short, bitter laugh. "Had we gone south, we would all be dead, me, my sons, my friends and allies, all of us only partially buried in shallow graves, or fleshless corpses settling deep into the waters beside Stone Mountain. The Sorcerers can only deal with slaves and puppets, which we shall never be." He took a deep breath. "So, now we will follow the hunt once more. Go in peace to the north, or east as you wish, but —" Lord Khond looked at them meaningfully, "all your pathways may be perilous, and so we should pass to you some final words of warning. Cendro?'

Khond nodded to Cendro, his Spell Weaver and Sensitive, and began backing his horse away.

Cendro let his horse graze on surrounding rangeland grasses, then spoke directly into the minds of Julian and Galad: *Our comments regarding the Shadow People were incomplete. We have no natural conflicts with them and so our 'pact' is merely a convenience. They remain a mystery to all those outside their cavernous domains. We know that deep within their hidden empire, there are three species: shadowy beings, gnomes, and huge beetle-creatures that serve as tunnel makers. How these three very different creatures relate to each other is a mystery, but none have escaped and sought our assistance. We hope that you are not forced to learn more about them.*

Cendro backed away, following Khond and his allies. Other riders were more distant, moving westward once again, and their herds had long since resumed their slow grazing movements.

Within moments of the riders' departure, Rafir popped back into view, and Sebastian emerged from hiding.

"I could only sense traces," said Sebastian, "but Cendro was warning you and Galad, wasn't he?"

Julian nodded, watching the riders grow smaller in the distance. "Cendro warned us about the Shadow People, and we are hoping to avoid them. Also, Lord Khond knows a fair amount regarding both our errand

and the danger surrounding it, otherwise he would not have set aside his carefully crafted role as a cattle baron. It may even be true that he rode this way to warn us."

Julian spoke softly, then he whispered into their minds: *We'll move to the east and north, hoping that bad weather will shield us. Then briefly, to the hills, bypassing the Shadow People, then moving underground, to shake the last of the Watchers, and emerging shielded by a magic greater than illusions. With good fortune, we will never be forced to test the Baron's goodwill charm on the Shadow People.*

Chapter Fifteen

The Shadow People

ALTHOUGH THEY HOPED FOR cloudy skies, the weather held bright and clear for the next few days, even as they passed from Khond's domain eastward. Galad felt as though they were four insects trapped against a transparent pane of glass, struggling to get free, while visible to all in their fruitless struggle to escape.

If their weather luck was poor, at least the dwellers to the east of Khond's domain were inclined to let them ride free, perhaps believing that safe passage through their western neighbor's lands was an indication of the travelers' strength. But farther east, now under cloudy skies, swift outriders began appearing at the edges of their passage, shaking spears, and calling out. Also, the grassland herds seemed more skittish, as though humans acted more as predators than protectors.

"Next, the bow shots," Galad called to Julian, "and when those fail, then they will mass spears followed by sudden, surprised death grimaces." He drew a longbow from his side. "Shall I keep them at bay with this?"

"Only let them loose the first arrow," Julian called back.

They veered to the south, hoping to shake free of range guards and sentinels. Instead, they met a larger cluster of riders, more aggressive than their northern brethren, and arrows began to arc toward them.

"Back to the north, then!" Julian called out. Arrows tended to veer away or fall short of their party, but there were limits to Julian's control. Galad shot back from his saddle, cursing at the jostling motions. It was still dry and overcast, but to the north and west, low, dark clouds were gathering.

They rode swiftly, several hundred paces in front of their pursuers. Yet even now another cluster of riders was moving toward them from the northeast and would soon intercept them.

"Find rocks or a belt of trees!" Galad called to Julian. "Something that will force them from their horses!" Julian nodded, rising in his saddle. Northern hills were tiny, distant, but just to their left, huge tree trunks, nearly fifty paces long, lay rotting on the ground, felled many years ago, but never cleared or burned. Julian and Galad sped toward the tree fall, pack horses scrambling to keep up. Behind them, the two bands of horse riders merged, crying out hunting cries, as though they were tracking game instead of other humans.

They reached the tree fall, then slipped from their horses. Arrows were springing at them, and a few struck fallen tree trunks, sinking deeply into rotten wood. Galad shot back: only one fell, but two other horses reared, stricken, and toppled.

Their pursuers pulled back, then approached them on foot, shields extended.

"Stop for a moment, before the dying begins!" Julian called out. Men advanced, saying nothing. Julian sent force bolts crashing among them, but many wore charms under the insignia of Moloch.

"Servants of Moloch!" Julian called to them. "What does your God say about travelers, about the helpless?"

"The Fire God cares nothing for wayfarers," one shouted. More riders were alighting from horses and advancing with swords drawn, as though wishing a portion of the spoils. Julian began to whisper spell words, but Galad waved him to silence.

"Sorcery will draw the Powers, maybe even alert Houma. Best that I deal with them, even if it gives me little joy." He drew the Tarnished Sword and stepped forward. There were cries of malice and delight as their attackers saw how lightly armed Galad was, and that the youth seemed weaponless. Men broke into an eager shuffling run, each ready to claim a lion's share of the spoils.

Then the Tarnished Sword smote flesh and metal, hurling both backward in shrieking ruin. Bodies toppled, lifeless onto long grasses. With a flash, Galad struck again — men were now crying in fear, and beneath their high-pitched shrieks, the sword was moaning, crying out its death song.

Their opponents broke ranks, casting weapons aside, racing for their horses. Julian sent force bolts leaping among their unshielded steeds, and these fled with their masters while other riders followed in pursuit.

Julian looked down on the vacant, lifeless men, and there was pity in his eyes — but only a little.

"These have preyed on the unwary, the travelers," Julian murmured. "Who knows how many mortals they may have killed before death came for them." Galad was silent, only wiping the Tarnished Sword on a dead man's cloak. Then he put out a hand and looked skyward.

"Rain," said Rafir. "That's what you looked for isn't it, Julian?"

"Wet Vision Portals are almost as tedious as dampened travel," Julian said, staring to the north. With the oncoming harsh weather, the outline of ridges had vanished. He mounted, turning back to Galad. The young weapons master was staring glumly at the faces of the fallen.

"What were Kalanin's words in this matter?" Julian said, quoting, "'It's one less enemy to fell.' Galad, I don't believe you've struck down one decent man here. Let's go." Galad looked up, searching the face of the Apprentice, and Sebastian, too, watched on, filled with concern.

"Yes, I'm getting hard and mean," Julian said, smiling. "And that's not really the truth — the fear and hatred I felt for Houma are slipping from me, little by little. Let's ride now, then we'll have fewer conflicts, less reason for regret." Galad shook free from his deathwatch and mounted once again. They rode north, with rain and harsh weather beginning to challenge their passage.

Several hours later, in the long afternoon, they slowed, walking their horses, nibbling on provisions, that, once unpacked, were growing rapidly soggy with rainwater.

"Is this really what you've been looking for?" Rafir asked, wet and miserable. "A fog would have done —" He broke off, for Julian and Sebastian were both staring south, with long, unhappy faces.

"What's this?" asked Galad.

"A half tier, more than two hundred, at least," Julian said, mounting. They rode swiftly northward again, Julian chanting spell words as the rain slid down his face. A rearguard of apparitions formed behind them, an illusion of pikemen shifting south through rainy weather.

But shortly thereafter the Apprentice shook his head in disgust. "There's Seer Sight among a few, at least," he murmured to Sebastian, then he called to Galad, "They have some power at least. My spell work held them for only moments."

"No lack of talent on these plains," Galad called back, "though Khond seems to have captured all the mental power."

Northward they rode, with the hills still distant, and their pursuers gaining ground. Again, Julian chanted but longer now, and with greater concentration. With the last words, his hand extended into the mist before him, and it vanished. Grimacing, the Apprentice struggled, as though groping in the void for some elusive creature.

Finally, he pulled out a dark, twisted thing that seemed to writhe, slowly in his hands. Pulling his reins up, Julian turned and hurled the object into the air: it vanished into the dampness, but a few moments later, explosion sounds burst over them, and the ground rattled.

"That's the last bit of battle magic I have in me," Julian called out. "Now let's finish our errand so I can return to my old gentle occupation as a healer."

They rode north, swiftly, yet still, the faint rumbling sounds of many horse hooves were becoming gradually more distinct.

A gentle incline, followed by boulders, gave the first hint that they had reached the plain's edge. Then grey hills loomed suddenly in the distance: high, dark, and rainy, with scrub brush nestling in crevices. Behind them, the riders were calling out, spurring one another on as though sensing their last chance to close with their prey.

Julian and Galad raced over the last league, horses near exhaustion; then they were climbing a steep slope, slipping from their saddles, leading their horses upward over a stony hillside. Flights of arrows followed them, but the riders did not.

"Now, just to pass underground," Julian whispered. Rain and mist were heavy about them, and the eyes of remote watchers seemed dull and distant.

They moved up the hillside, looking for stony paths that twisted and turned upward over a damp rock face. Rafir slipped to the ground and raced ahead of Julian, darting around, sniffing furiously.

"There are smells I can't identify!" he called out. "At least two different kinds of beings — and there's cavern air seeping out from every crack."

"Hush, less noise," Julian murmured. "Try to find a passage unused by those beings — the hidden, unknown creatures, whatever they might be." They continued their upward climb, glancing back at the rangelands every now and again: only a few sentinels could be seen, and these were gradually fading from view as a harder rain washed over them.

A few hundred feet from grass level they passed into a lower cloudbank and chilled white vapor crowded around them so that nothing could be seen except damp rock surfaces and their own dimly perceived forms.

"Do we still need to go underground?" Galad asked, keeping his voice low. "Who can follow us through this mess?"

"A mass of stone will shield so many spells," Julian whispered, then he stopped. The fox, a few paces ahead, was sniffing at a cavern mouth. "What is it, Rafir?"

"There's room for us and the horses," murmured the fox, "though there's still a smell lingering —of Shadow People, I guess."

"Fresh smells?" Julian peered into the cave's mouth: beyond the opening, it was dark and gloomy, though the air seemed fresh.

"Not recent smells," the fox answered. They groped toward the opening, pulling reluctant horses through its entrance.

Within, it was lightless, but mists beyond the cave mouth seemed to glow with white phosphorescence. They stood quietly for a moment, letting the water droplets slip from their cloaks and drip onto the stony cavern floor. Far, far from them was a *ping-ping-ping* sound, of picks or hammers performing some distant underground tasks.

"This should be enough shielding," Julian whispered. "In moments we'll emerge transformed, and not just layered by illusions created to block our sight."

"A Transformation?" Sebastian asked in surprise. "You're doing this yourself?"

"Merlin's doing." Julian smiled down at his friend and Familiar. "Hidden among my healing potions is a charm passed to us by Merlin when we stood outside of the Dungeons of Un-Maurag. I was afraid of the Watchers as we passed through forests and fields, but now we can emerge completely changed —"

It was then that the cavern mouth vanished, as the surrounding rock face rolled outward, meeting like the closing of a wound.

"The Shadow People!" Julian cried, and his staff flared with light. He hurled himself against the wall, but not even a seam could be found.

In the farthest reaches of his mind came a whisper of dark malevolent laughter.

"Houma," the Apprentice murmured.

"Stand aside," Galad called. The Tarnished Sword whimpered as it arced high. In a whining flash, the blade carved rock as an ax might slash rotted wood.

But the rock face closed over his blade, healing almost as quickly as it had been cut.

Galad wrenched the sword free, cursing.

"That way has been barred," Julian said, casting about, fear and anger building inside of him. "Curse them, curse them. Were we steered to this place?" Again, his staff flared light over the cavern. "Was this but one of many stone traps? And is there a way out?"

Toward the back, a tunnel opened out of the cavern wall: one low, forbidding entryway.

"We're still being driven," Julian said, turning back toward their original entrance. Spell words leaped from his lips and where the cavern mouth had been, the wall began to fracture seeping dust.

"Stand back," the Apprentice murmured — but then the wall rippled, and its stone healed once more. Again, spell words leaped from Julian's lips, but this time the wall remained intact, and instead, their horses began to sag, drowsing with a healer's sleep.

They were left with only one entrance, one controlled by another power, and it was too small for their horses, who were now slumping to the ground.

"Is it fair to leave them alive?" asked Galad as he rummaged through their possessions.

Julian strode toward the tunnel opening, healer's pouch thrown over his shoulder, staff blazing with light.

"I don't know, and there's no time. We're trapped — again. But there's still a chance that this entry might lead to safety — somehow, someway." He stepped through the opening, radiant light beaming before his staff, and broke into a run.

The others followed, racing behind the Apprentice, with a trail of twisting, slanted shadows following them as they raced through dark corridors of a roughly carved rock face.

The tunnel curved left, rising a little, then dropping downward, taking them deeper into the hillside; but not five hundred paces from the tunnel mouth, their pathway forked, right and left.

"Rafir!" Julian called out. The fox ran, panting, toward the tunnel mouths, sniffing at each. The lefthand passage was low and wide, not even Julian's height, while that to the right was higher than Galad's height but narrower.

"Two smells," panted the fox. "The left is unlike any I've known, something acid and bitter, but to the right, there's something closer to human."

"Something that might recognize Khond's *Talisman*," added Galad. After a pause, a second's hesitation, they plunged to the right, with its "close to human" smells. Again, their pathway was humped, rising then arcing downward, deeper into the hillside.

Outside, Julian knew, moisture and mist were still passing over rain-soaked grasses, but here the air was dry and stale, not easily breathed.

Gasping, they spilled out of the tunnel, emerging into a large gallery with a high ceiling. Julian's staff spilled light over the walls: there was nothing, no hint as to the chamber's purpose. But at each of the four corners, tunnels had been carved, offering three new pathways. Rafir raced to each, breathing then listing, while within Julian, the Gift searched for a pathway toward freedom.

"All three tunnels seemed blocked," the fox said, struggling for breath. "Creatures, things, are moving toward us, many of them."

Julian's staff flashed, once more spilling light throughout the stone chamber. "Then this may be one of their marshaling halls," he muttered. "Bad fortune, curse it. Choose the one with the most surface air. Perhaps we can talk or cut our way through." Uncertainly, the fox led them to the far passage that hugged the righthand wall. Once again, they plunged through, running for their lives.

At first, the passage seemed well chosen: it broadened, leading upward into better air. Galad now ran beside Julian, loping easily at the side of the Apprentice. Sebastian alternately flew, then scrambled over hard polished stone. But now, as he soared in Julian's wake, shadows closed around him, clutching at his wings like a weight of black cloth. He dropped to the ground.

"Julian!" Sebastian cried out.

The Apprentice stopped, turned, and light flashed over retreating shadowy shapes.

"Shadow People!" cried Julian, struggling to catch his breath. "Let us go free. Let us out. See, we bear the...." He stopped, panting, as the flickering shapes retreated from view. Julian and Galad pushed forward once more, racing upward, their minds half dreaming of rain-soaked pastureland.

Once again, they spilled out into another broad gallery. But this marshaling yard was held in strength: gnome figures faced them, rank upon rank, with glowing luminescent eyes and dark, twisted bodies. They stood little more than half Galad's height, but they were weaponed with long bright spears, and there were many scores of them.

"Shadow People!" Julian called out. "Let us go free. We are not your foes. See, we bear the emblem of your Lord." With a sound like dry rustling leaves, the ranks of gnomes closed, dark grim faces tightening, their sharp spear points growing closer.

"Houma, the Sorcerer, will bring destruction down upon you if you conspire with him!" Julian cried. "Set us free!" Breaking away, he called out the sleep spell; only a few sagged. The stun spell toppled only three or four: their spell shields were strong.

"For the Maker, for the League, and for the Truce!" Galad cried and then he leaped at them, slashing. Gnome creatures fell, writhing and screaming. But scores of spear points pressed at them, forcing them backward. Again, Galad slashed, reaping flesh, blasting metal, but the press of spear points thickened, forcing him back.

"Too many!" he called out to the Apprentice, then he halted as shadow shapes that blocked his sight slipped over his face. Julian sent bolts of force leaping among the shadows, then flames surging toward the gnome ranks.

Once more his spell was checked, and as they backed from the press, a hailstorm of darts swept over them. Galad plucked one from his shoulder, letting it slip to the stone floor. As they gave way, more gnome creatures surged into the cavern, joining the spear press, stepping over the fallen.

"Back," Julian murmured, teeth clenched. "Go back. This fork of the tunnel is blocked." Galad nodded, then slashed at another rank. Julian's voice rose, calling out spell words in a great voice. Power surged upward from his staff, shaking the cavern's roof. They turned and sped away as huge slabs of stone came crashing down upon the ranks of shrieking gnomes.

Racing like fire, they sped back along their previous route, shadow beings twisting in the air behind them. And, as Galad looked back, scores of luminescent eyes gleamed as gnome soldiers pursued them.

Once again, they spilled out into a broad gallery, but here the gnome ranks were thin, marshaling not even half complete. They passed through the gnome ranks in a flash, cutting and blasting.

Panting, they stood once more at the tunnel fork first encountered. Julian extended his staff, light blazing from its tip, back into the righthand fork; shadowy shapes skittered out of range. He called out spell words and again the tunnel roof burst over their pursuers.

They stood, struggling for breath, staring unhappily down the low, dark, left-hand passage. A faint but sharp smell, a touch of acid, of bitter burning, was drifting upward.

"There's no other choice, is there?" muttered Galad. The Gift within Julian reached out, half expecting Houma, but it found only strangeness. Ducking their heads down, they entered warily, slowly. But their pace picked up as the tunnel grew higher and broader, while behind them came the sounds of loose rock shifting, as their pursuers cleared the debris from the passage behind them.

Down they went, with the tunnel hooking left. As they came around the leftward bend, they skidded to a halt: before them, luminescent and huge, stood a monstrous stag beetle, nearly as high as Galad's chest, but many times his bulk. It reared, huge rock-crushing claw breaking stone, while its antennae danced in the shadowy, partial light.

"A burrower, a tunnel maker," Julian murmured, holding Galad's arm back, then his voice was raised. "Let us pass, weaver of passages. We mean you no harm. Let us pass." They stood, panting, staff and sword held warily before them. Finally, the great burrower settled back, and its antennae twitched as though receiving many messages. Then it began backing, luminescent light dimming as it gave way.

The giant burrower backed into a side alcove, and they passed it warily, hugging the tunnel passage farthest from the huge claw.

"Will it hold the tunnel?" Galad murmured. "Will it block the gnome creatures?"

Julian shrugged. "No other way for us to go." Flashing light before them, they moved downward, with their tunnel passage curling and twisting like a nest of snakes.

Acid fumes, always stronger, brought fluids seeping into their lungs, and as they slowed, moving far more cautiously, Julian passed a measure of Heart's Ease to each, so that their breathing gradually grew stronger. As they drew deeper, and as their tunnel grew wider, the Gift within Julian began to flash warning messages: they were coming to a junction of power. Behind them, the sounds of pursuit had grown steadily, and now in front of them, their tunnel path became lighter, with sounds of rock crushing reaching them, for the first time clearly — and the stench of acid was growing stronger.

Now slowly, warily, they emerged into a broad, flat, shadowy cavern, a hive center for the huge burrowers, lit by their own luminescence. Huge burrowing creatures were scattered all around them, hundreds of them, most seeming at rest, while a few crushed idly at the cavern's stone edges. The ceiling was low, but shafts from above brought down waves of fresh air and carried acid fumes upward.

Antennae whirled in the air as burrowers regarded the intruders with a distant, mystified curiosity, as though flesh and blood beings were of little interest, while rock crushing was of everlasting importance. The light from

Julian's staff dimmed, and he searched for words —while inside his mind the Gift flared in alarm.

Then the last portion of Houma's trap was sprung.

Shadow Mages leaped from floor and ceiling. Passing through stone, they lashed at Julian's Gift and smashed at Galad's sword arm. Shocked, reeling and blinded by shadowy shapes, they fell back, but here a burrower's claw darted out, catching Julian by his right arm. With a snap, the bone broke, and his staff fell from nerveless fingers.

"Julian!" Sebastian cried. Galad cut wildly, severing the pincer claw.

Then beetle jaws opened, sending a torrent of acid at Galad, catching him at his knees, and he fell backward, his legs dying as he bellowed in pain.

Sebastian leaped for Julian's staff, dragging it from underneath the feet of milling burrowers. And yet already, sorcerous shadowy ropes were sweeping around Apprentice and writhing weapons master.

Then Julian put forth his full Adept's strength and burst the shadowy bonds. Right arm dangling useless, he took his staff from Sebastian, and sent bolts of power darting into shadow mages. A second spume of acid was vomited at them, but flame from Julian ignited it, and a ruin of fire washed upstream over its originator.

In great pain, Julian leaned over to pull Galad to his feet — but Galad remained thrashing on the ground, barely able to speak.

"O my Maker...take the sword, Julian...fight free...but leave me for my legs have died....I wished for a clean death, a warrior's death, one clean stroke under clear skies...but go...now, go."

Spell words were whispered over Galad to help ease his pain, then Julian pulled the stricken warrior to his feet. Blasts from his staff checked the first rank of burrowers. Galad stumbled forward, and the Tarnished Sword slashed through bone-hard external skeletons.

Slowly they fought free, surrounded by a nightmare of swirling antennae, fluttering shadowy shapes, and burning squealing beetle-forms: for as the burrowers launched acid, Julian ignited it and flames sped backward up the acid streams and incinerated the flesh of giant beetles.

Wounded, bodies ruined, they stumbled into a distant passage where a maze of tunnels branched out in front of them. Here Julian turned, face grim with pain and horror, and he put forth his greatest strength, and hard, joyless spell words brought masses of rock down on his pursuers.

Weeping, Sebastian bound Julian's arm to his side, while Julian did what little he could for Galad's legs: in places the acid had eaten almost into the warrior's powerful bone structure. Rafir watched the three, eyes big with terror: death was coming for them, an end to all their adventures.

Then they were moving forward again, slowly, tentatively, almost without hope. Somewhere, Julian knew, the sun shone brightly over fresh green growing things, alternately yellow, golden, then red, but here their last lights would be flames, luminescent glowing eyes, and darkish lashes of power radiating from shadowy beings.

As they stumbled forward, an understanding of the pursuit began to form in Julian's mind. The Gift, wary and fearful, was reaching out, exploring: above them, gnome beings marched, while from below, huge burrowers were actually herding Julian, Galad, and their small allies. Shadowy shapes flitted through rock surface, above, below, and behind them, leaving only one direction for the pursued to travel. And the Gift now brought an image of the Sorcerer, waiting and gloating.

"Quest's end," Julian murmured. "They have trapped us. We're being delivered to Houma."

They slowed, readying themselves for the final confrontation. Whispered spell words slipped from Julian's lips, and Galad felt new strength surging through his body, though he could not bring himself to look at his legs after they had been ruined by acid. Sebastian walked beside Julian on his left, watching his master struggle with spell and counterspell, and at last, he was able to make out the words.

"Kath..." whispered Julian. "Kath...mighty Kath...." No Portals formed, and the whispered words from Julian's spell seemed to slip down and die on the ground. Before them, their tunnel was ending, giving way to another cavern opening — but the lights beyond were multifaceted, more intense, and the echo sounds suggested a great hall rather than another roughhewn gallery. Julian stopped.

"Kath's entry is blocked," he whispered. "All my magic has come to nothing. We have reached our quest's end."

"I am dying, Apprentice," murmured Galad, "let us go and face Houma while I can still walk. But take some thought for our small friends: they do not need to perish."

"Rafir," murmured Julian, sinking down and patting the fox with his one good, left hand. "Vanish as only you can vanish. Seek Merlin first, and mourn after, mourning leads to healing — but find Merlin." The fox nodded in misery, eyes closed.

"Sebastian," said Julian, and he embraced his small friend and familiar. "Sebastian, I want you to live on if you can." The Familiar shook his head, weeping. "No, Sebastian, I want you to live. Bide your time, then free yourself to seek and serve Merlin. You will never forget me; I will be with you always in your mind's eye. They can never take that from you."

He rose, and clasped Galad with his one good arm, murmuring, "As for us, we have one last battle with Houma."

"Houma must die," said Galad. "Farewell, my small comrades. May we four stand together at the Awakening." Rafir vanished. Then Galad stepped forward, Julian and Sebastian moving a step behind him as they approached the cavern's mouth.

At the tunnel mouth before them were incandescent lights and a waiting stillness. Pain mastered for the moment, they stepped from the darkened tunnel out into the light, and as they emerged, rustling sounds echoed everywhere around them, as though they were performers entering from a stage wing, while their audience stirred in anticipation.

They stood at the edge of a vast oval shaped chamber, and above them, the domed ceiling glistened with polished stone. Rays of light gleamed from the facets of huge jewels that hung suspended from the ceiling by links of gleaming metal. All three underground races were represented in the great chamber: giant burrowers, gnome beings, and shadowy shapes. In the center stood a dais, raised only half a man's height, and on it stood a column of shadows that radiated pale lights, a being that dwarfed all those around it: their ruler, the Shadow Emperor. Beside him, tiny in comparison, but far from insignificant, stood a fourth type of being, a human, the Sorcerer, Houma.

The Tarnished Sword, as though sensing Houma, and his withered arm, began to shift and lighten in Galad's hand. Julian reached for an opening, and there was none — not yet.

"Hard fought, Apprentice," said the Shadow Emperor. "Hard fought, weapons master. Yet now it is over, and though the Sorcerer wishes a thousand trials, I will not toy with you." As the Shadow Emperor spoke, all the gleaming jewels shifted, light beams focusing on Julian, Galad, and Sebastian.

Cones of light formed around each of them: three separate prisons.

Julian's staff radiated power, and then a far greater power surged over him. Galad lashed out, his Tarnished Sword slashing light beams that were charged with magic, but then all the healing charms were struck from him, and he fell writhing to the floor, crying out in pain. Light beams tugged the

Tarnished Sword from Galad's hands, and a fourth cone formed over the sword, and it too was stilled.

"Well done, Lord," murmured Houma, "O, how well done. Surely these were never a match for you and your own immense power. My masters will be greatly pleased when these are brought before them in the underwater Isle of the Demons."

Julian heard everything. His own dreams and desires, together with his quest and his pain were distant, only partially understood things; but he listened as though he heard the doomed tale of some long forgotten, legendary being.

"It is in my mind, Sorcerer, that these mortals will stay here, held by me, until the true victors in your contest are known." The Shadow Emperor's tone was deep, thoughtful, weighty, and reasonable. "What are your thoughts on this, Sorcerer?"

Houma seemed to gather himself, to coil in tension, and he could not keep the menace from his reply. "You have seen, Lord, how mighty the Marids will become when they emerge. And the Demon Princes, greatest of the Ancient Powers, have yet to make their presence felt. A new order will emerge, a restructuring of power both here in Alantéa, and the Far Lands. If you truly wish to be a part of that new structure, you will permit me to take these captives when I depart."

Laughter, deep and dark like the caverns, spilled out from the Shadow Emperor. "Sorcerer, how I am tempted to toy with you! To bring forth all your threats and promises, as though you still dealt with Un-Maurag. But behold! I am not Un-Maurag, and so much more is known to me than at the beginning of this struggle. I know of your own power and of the hidden strength of these captives. I know of the Marids' forthcoming might, but no word will ever pass to them of your fate.

"Did you hear that, Sorcerer? You will never leave here. I will bring an end to all of your repetitious schemes and devices."

Houma murmured something under his breath, and his dark, withered hand seemed to swell, pulsing with power, then he smiled. "A lesson is here to be taught, Shadow Emperor. We, the Sorcerers, have become so mighty that few even among the Mid-World Powers may contend with us."

"Truly spoken, and so well stated, Sorcerer!" Like the Sorcerer's withered hand, the Shadow Emperor's dark form began to pulse with power. "But behold! Not only was one trap set for the Wizards' servants: there was another, a second one for the Sorcerer Houma! And it is sprung — now!" Portals, long prepared, flashed inside the great underground chamber.

Seven beings emerged, each wildly different from the others, and they ringed Houma, like jackals surrounding a venomous serpent.

"The Emissaries of the Gods," hissed the Sorcerer. "Yet it was said that these would never act in concert, that this collaboration was barred by the Truce. Is the Truce now to be broken?"

Again, the Shadow Emperor laughed, as though some prized student performed far above his master's expectations. "Sorcerer, you do not know all of the Truce Terms, though you have skirted them guilefully, like a skate bug skipping over pond scum. Yet now you know: the Gods are not pleased with you, and they have means to make their displeasure felt."

Houma snarled, saying nothing, and he watched for a moment as lights shifted within the cavern, and a cone of light — larger, more intense than those holding Galad and Julian — began to form around him.

Then Houma's dark, withered hand surged with power: all the jewels that radiated light shattered.

Darkness and wild battle magic surged over the cavern. Galad leaped for his sword, but his legs collapsed beneath him, and he fell, bellowing out loud in pain. Shadowy creatures surged over Julian, and he no longer had strength enough to resist them.

An invisible Rafir alone remained free, but in the turmoil, he was likely to be crushed. Darting, scurrying, he finally found his way to a far wall, pressing close to it as he watched the struggle.

Beams of light flared and passed suddenly as the Shadow Emperor and the Servants of the Gods fought to subdue the Sorcerer. Portals flashed into being but collapsed before Houma could escape. The Sorcerer's voice rose and fell in spell cursing vengeance. One of the great God Servants, a massive being with a lizard's face, straightened to its full height, then toppled, dead, crashing to the stone floor.

More lights flared as once again a massive cone began forming about Houma. The Sorcerer's voice rose, then trailed off with one extended moaning sound, as the Shadow Emperor's sorcery finally mastered Houma.

Bit by bit, other lights flashed on as jewels radiating light returned to life: but their beams were now ragged, blurred. Rafir, warily, padded toward the dais of the Shadow Emperor.

One of the Emissaries of the Gods stood over Houma, murmuring to the Shadow Emperor, "After all of this damage and destruction, you will still permit this Sorcerer to live?"

"I will not fault any being for defending itself," said the Shadow Emperor judiciously, "and besides, we are dealing with matters of aesthetics: look at them, partially living art, fairer than many of the visions of great artists, or architects of fabulous palaces and cathedrals."

Sebastian stood frozen in a cone of light, head bent in sorrow, while Julian stood, overcome by failure at their quest's end, holding his ruined arm. Galad's face was turned upward, stretched in agony. Houma stood with his face frozen in a snarl, teeth bared in menace, and his dark, withered hand still throbbed with power. Only the sword seemed serene, as it stood suspended in midair, point turned to the cavern floor, lost in its perpetual dreams of slaughter.

The Shadow Emperor, his substance twisting shadows, regarded his captives for a moment, then continued, "They will remain in this fashion for as long as it pleases me, but elsewhere, in their own gallery." Cones of light began shifting, sliding over polished rock surfaces. A second Emissary of the Gods began a muted dispute with the Shadow Emperor, but Rafir pulled away, following the cones of light and their prisoners as they drifted from the throne room.

They passed downward, deeper into the empire of the three races, and for the first time, Rafir could hear running water. A sub-tier of gnome soldiers followed, carelessly, as though their prisoners had been transformed into completely powerless statues.

At last, deep underground, the cones came to rest, set casually against polished rockface in a long, dark cavern lit only by the cone's rays. Gnome troops passed through, their destination unknown, and Rafir was left alone with his friends, and their enemy, Houma, all of them frozen in grief and torment. Slowly, warily, Rafir pressed up against Julian's light barrier.

He couldn't penetrate it…. The fox let himself slip back into visibility… and he still couldn't break through. Nor could he break into the others…but something, something else seemed to be changing, moving.

He turned to see that Houma's face had shifted. The Sorcerer's snarl was gone, and Houma's eyes were watching the fox with both malice and great interest.

Rafir vanished and fled from the cavern.

· X ·

Days passed, then weeks, with Rafir investigating a thousand passages, always seeking some talisman, or sorcerous tool to free his friends. None could be found, but other secrets, other mysteries were slowly solved.

Once, as he passed a troop of gnomes, one of its members grew vacant eyed, sagging, then, it toppled against a wall. Moments later, its skin split, with a beetle form emerging. As the gnome soldiery watched on disdainfully, the beetle consumed its former gnome's skin, then sauntered off to join its brethren with their work clearing rocks from tunnels.

Still another time, Rafir watched on as a huge burrower, groping for rock with its pincerclaw, began to grow vague, almost transparent, and its claw passed through the rock without disturbing a solid particle. The beetle form looked all around, suddenly filled with awareness; its shape seemed to coil and twist — to become a weightless shadow.

Rafir never saw the third portion of the transformation, but it was not difficult to imagine: a shadowy form would grow heavy, sagging with new weight, then it would coalesce onto the cavern floor, becoming a gnome being with dark, twisted skin.

Often at nighttime, the fox would emerge from the hillside, staring mournfully at the stars, trying to think of some way to free his friends. And he knew that if no way could be found that soon he would be forced to follow Julian's instructions and leave his friends forever, to see if he could find Merlin.

· ⚕ ·

Delight was in the starlit heavens, in the sparkling wheel of the universe. As crown princess of the Shadow People, she was lighter than others, able to dance thousands of feet above the hillside, far over the low cloud cover that hung about the hills and pastureland beneath her.

And her Sight was extremely powerful: she could see beyond the circles of the sun. Lately, she had followed the progress of the Spirit Lord, as he passed from earth, speeding far from the sun on his quest for the Maker. Yet now the Spirit Lord had halted, pausing beside the outermost icy wasteland of a half planet.

Why had he paused? Had he lost power? Or strength of will? Go forward, her mind called to the Spirit Lord. How wonderful it would be to speak with the Maker, with the First Fashioner, the Lord of the Beginning.

And what would you say to the Maker, Princess? came a thought to her out of the night. Would you tell Him of the Maker Servants you hold half dead, broken and bleeding?

Alarm shot through her, and she dropped a thousand feet in one second's pulse.

"Who are you?" she whispered into the night.

The Master of those you now hold, came the thought.

"Merlin, then?" she murmured. "The Wizard once known as the greatest of the Mortal Magic Wielders? I thought you were destroyed!"

I escaped the ruin of Gravengate — but only by a whisper's breath. Perhaps I was once the greatest of the human powers; others now have much clearer title. But my Princess, secret Servant of the Maker, what will you do for those your father holds? Can you free them? Help them with their quest?

"My father, the Emperor of the Shadow People, would not permit this, Wizard...and yet.... Perhaps there is something I might do, some forces might be set in motion...I will do what I can...before the wreckage brought on by the Marids. The Sight within me sees a ruin of destruction by Marids for both your people and for mine. Can that fate be averted?"

I will try, Princess and secret ally. And whether defeat or victory awaits us, I will speak for you at the Awakening when we stand before the Maker.

"I may never sleep, Wizard," she murmured with a fading whisper.
We shall all sleep. One way or another, we shall all sleep. Farewell.

· ☽ ·

Sebastian felt himself waking, slowly, pulled from troubled dreams back into the old nightmare of captured Julian, ruined Galad, and quest's end. Gnome beings stood before him, arms folded, spears set aside for the moment. What was this, a torture testing? He had no secrets to pass to them. Their goal had been clear right from the beginning: to discover the Terms of the Truce in the Vale of Whispers, a goal they would never reach.

"Creature, we were told to release you, to let you practice your healer's art upon your comrades." The gnome spoke in a soft voice, but its tones were filled with malice and treachery. "Though truly, if you wished to escape instead, none here would bar —" the Gnome halted just as a great shadowy being approached them, and there were hints of silver in its coiled darkness. The gnomes bowed and withdrew.

"Little Servant of the Maker, I have sought your release so that you may practice your healing arts upon your comrades — it is not fitting that their bodies' suffering should be felt even in their dreams." Before Sebastian on the floor was Julian's saddle pouch where all his healing charms and potions were kept: silver vials of Bindweed and Serpine, and Dragon's Breath, and Heart's Ease — and, he remembered with a start — the disguised transformation spell passed to Julian by Merlin.

Very carefully, the little Familiar dragged the saddle pouch over to the cone of light that held his master. He passed through the light barrier without resistance, and gingerly, rolled up the cloak of the Apprentice. Julian's fair seeming face was frozen in sorrow, and his broken arm was cold and swollen, skin torn by pincer claws. Gently, Sebastian washed the arm, setting it, then wrapping it with folds of cloth, with Bindweed and Serpine placed closest to his master's skin. Through all of this, Julian seemed no more than a dead thing, a corpse, cold and lifeless.

When Sebastian turned to Galad, the little Familiar burst into tears: flesh seared, white bone eaten away beneath the muscle, Galad's wounds were far greater than Sebastian's healing arts.

"Do not weep, little Servant," murmured the Shadow Princess. "Only do what you are able to do. Then I will add my healing strength to your own devices. In this, our kingdom, only my father and the evil Sorcerer have greater power than that which I wield. But there are limits to my reach: I can heal your allies but not free them. I can and will free your horses — because their enchanted sleep fades, and otherwise they would all die. Yet, there can be, there will be, a chance for your allies and their mission."

Suddenly alert, Sebastian began a careful cleansing of Galad's wounds. Then he bound them as he had Julian's, but more loosely, less certainly, and he touched each of Julian's healing vials as though pondering its use. One was clearly *not* a healing device, and this charm he bound carefully, like a talisman, onto Galad's right leg, just above the wound.

When he had finished, he stood before the Shadow Princess and bowed.

"You must sleep once more, little Servant, but now it will be part of a good sleep, a healing sleep." A white cone of light began to form about Sebastian once again. But one last message, a whispered thought, passed from the Shadow Princess into his mind: *And it is not over little Servant; your quest may yet continue.*

·)(·

As he always did in the middle of the day, Rafir passed quickly through the gallery where Julian and Galad and Sebastian were held. But this time he stopped short in sudden shock: their frozen images had changed. Sebastian's head was up, with a grim, determined expression fixed on his slight features. Now, Julian was looking outward, wary, and thoughtful, while Galad's face stared out in anger rather than in great pain. Both had the bandages of healer's work on their wounds — and Houma, even Houma had changed, he was glowering at Julian and Galad with unconcealed rage. What had happened?

Suddenly, the sounds of water surging and splashing reached his ears. These were new sounds, not heard before, and he sped away from the cavern, seeking their source.

Several levels down, Rafir had found a huge underground lake, fed by warm springs, cavern ceiling dark with fungus growths. Now he raced toward it, darting downward, slipping easily past gnome guards and crushers of rocks.

At the cavern's edge, two of the Emissaries of the Gods who served as the Emperor's Mid-World advisors were backing away cautiously, fearfully. Within the lake, thrashing in warm underground waters, was a gigantic beetle, larger than many temples, long, sleek, and now enraged.

"We could never reason with the Emperor in this particular phase of his transformations," murmured the first Emissary, backing away. This Emissary was garbed as a warrior maiden riding a winged steed. The second Emissary, on foot, had wing-growths on his ankles, fluttering nervously as he also retreated.

"He should have slain them all, long ago," said the second Emissary. "I am not mighty enough to counter Marids, nor is this Emperor. Soon they will be upon his doorstep." The two paused as they reached the corridor's refuge. One last stream of churning, warm water reached them, surging over Rafir's feet.

"My master says that Marids..." the first Emissary spoke in a near trance, "that Marids have emerged this very moment, from the ocean beside Stone Mountain —" A bellow, a cry of triumph interrupted her.

"The Sorcerer Houma sleeps only lightly," said the winged Emissary. "Come, we need to join with the Shadow Mages in their efforts to control him." They raced upwards, racing toward the Sorcerer's prison. Rafir followed, panting, in their wake.

All around Houma, the imprisoning cone of light flickered on and off, near failing, and even those rays of light holding Julian and Galad seemed to dim.

"Marids!" Houma shrieked. "Now stand and die, Wizards! Stand and die! First Stone Mountain, then Gravengate!"

"Maker, help our people!" Galad cried out. "Maker, do not leave us alone here on earth, grieving and forgotten!"

"Merlin," Julian whispered, struggling with his enchantments. "Merlin, Stone Mountain is forfeit. Go to Gravengate and save our people."

The sword, too, stirred, but it held steady, aware of its future task, but knowing that it was not yet *TIME*.

Power surged, once again, into the enchanted cones of light and the cavern grew silent, with only the faintest of sounds rustling in the background. Rafir lay panting, wondering, lying on the stone floor, staring upward into the supplicating faces of his allies, who remained frozen by magic.

Over the next few days, Rafir grew increasingly desperate, seeking ways to free his comrades. He explored every hiding piece, every barred passage, each crevice. He found Julian's saddle pouch, but no charm or talisman from it seemed likely to gain their freedom. He spent hours studying the Shadow

Emperor in his new form as he splashed endlessly through warm waters, caring nothing for the Sorcerers and the Marids. Emissaries of the Gods came and went, bringing tales of the destruction brought about by Marids, with most urging the death of all the Emperor's prisoners. The Shadow Emperor splashed on, heedlessly, in gigantic beetle form.

Then one day Rafir awoke, his small body filled with tension. Something was happening, something powerful enough to reach *into* his mind, and he was not even a Sensitive. He sped toward the throne room, the light chamber, seeking information.

Clusters of beings were shuffling around: shadowy beings, gnome creatures, beetle shapes, and many of their Emperor's greatest servants. They stood, grim and muted before Vision Portals. Rafir, blocked by many huge forms, could see nothing of what was happening on those screens.

"The Gods have grown feeble," murmured one being, a Shadow Mage. "Lightning bolts against Marids, like spears of straw hurled against Griffins." Emissaries glared at the Mage but said nothing. A tension tugged at Rafir as though Dread had slipped an invisible net over his unseen form.

"Time for the Wizard's last cast," said one Servant. Rafir edged away, slowly, weaving a path between the many beings gathered in the jewel-lit chamber. Gradually, he quickened his pace, speeding toward the chamber where Houma and Julian lay imprisoned.

Then a wave of sorrow surged over him. Something had gone wrong, his people, his allies had taken a forever wound, the cries of so many dreamers, their vision completely broken, as they thrashed in their death agonies.

Sounds then came from Houma, cries of triumph. Rafir slowed, recoiling in fear.

And then a second wave surged over him, a tidal wave of grief, and the image flashed into his mind of his old mistress, the Sorceress Héna, trembling on the battlefield, then being crushed by the huge hand of one, lone Marid.

"Marids!" Houma cried in ecstasy. "Marids! Now the Mid-World of the Truce is dying, and all those Nine Billion feeble Gods will be destroyed! Behold, all you fancy masters of hypocrisy, how your own doom approaches!"

"Merlin, I failed you! I failed! I failed!" Julian called out.

"Dead, all dead!" Galad bellowed. "Why am I still alive? Sword, come to me! Let us make a blood-red ending!"

But then the light cones, powered by Shadow Mages, and by so many of the Gods' most powerful Emissaries, surged once again over both Servants and their lone Adversary, and they slipped back into restless, tormented sleeps.

Rafir turned away from the chamber and padded slowly through the passageway, heedless of guards and shadowy shapes who wielded powerful magic, out from the maze of tunnels, until he stood, at dusk, on the hillside, staring skyward as distant, uncaring star patterns revealed themselves, and began gleaming in the darkness.

Then, he wept.

Chapter Sixteen

The Vale of Whispers

TWO MARIDS STRODE FORWARD in the darkness, moonlight rippling over mottled, grey hides and reddish, scarred skin. The Portal Passages were blocked, barred by beings who now called themselves Gods, but to Marids, tireless, undaunted, gliding effortlessly over lush rangelands through a grassy tangle of moonbeams, all pathways were opened, and no secret place in Alantéa was barred to them.

Behind the Marids, beasts and mortals seemed to follow, but these were utterly insignificant, like mice trailing in the wake of a Griffin.

"Stay well clear of them, Lord." Cendro's hoarse whisper slipped through the darkness like an asp seeking warm mammal flesh. "A thousand leagues are not sufficient distance." Khond grunted, riding forward in the moonlight, following immense Marids as they strode effortlessly into the gleaming night.

"Scatter, disperse more," Khond murmured after a moment, and horse riders slipped back in the half darkness, moving among the twelve score riders that followed in small clusters many paces behind. In the forefront, with Khond and Cendro, rode Haakon, Khond's three older sons, and Barak-Kor, his youngest son, and weapons master.

"Are they aware of us, sir fox?" asked Haakon softly, his dark, searching eyes watching the Marids for hints of purpose or perception.

"I know so little about them," Rafir whispered. "I'm just a small part of this business. I know almost nothing...." Khond's strong hands soothed the ruffled fur of the fox as Rafir trailed off.

"You did well, sir fox," Khond grunted, voice low. "You sought for those nearby, people with power to counter Shadow Magic, people who might wish to preserve the Mid-World of the Truce. You did well."

"But they're buried so deeply, trapped so far down," the fox murmured, anxiety building inside him again. "I searched forever for some spell, a talisman, some key to Shadow Magic, and there wasn't anything, just the Shape Changers, and the Emissaries of the Gods. Then —"

Khond hushed Rafir, for the soft voice of the fox had grown steadily louder. "Yes," whispered Khond, "then you and even your sleeping companions found that the Wizards had been defeated and that they, with all the peoples of the League, were dead or scattered. So, you sought us. But be calm now, sir fox, and rehearse to me once again what your tasks are this night."

Rafir took a deep breath. "There's going to be a conflict, some sort of battle underground...."

"The Marids are mighty," Cendro's soft voice interrupted, "yet the Shadow Emperor — in his present form — is among the most physically powerful beings ever to dwell in Alantéa or the Mid-World. As well, more Emissaries of the Gods have passed underground. There will be a struggle and a great confrontation."

"So, I'm to go underground, toward my friends," the fox continued doubtfully. "Some other force is supposed to wake Julian, then we're to fight our way toward you as best we can, though last time...." the fox trailed off.

"Yes, it sounds unlikely," Khond grunted. "Even so, I have learned to trust Seer and Warlock in their judgments. Your friends will wake to confusion, into a complex struggle. Then you must lead them toward me, while I and my people forge a passage. It seems unlikely, but on this complex, confusing junction of many circumstances, all of the slender hopes of your quest now depend."

Rafir said nothing, but his anxiety surged higher as he watched massive bodies of Marids reach the edge of the grasslands and begin their moonlit ascent toward the manycaverned fortress dwellings of the Shadow People.

· X ·

Suspended within a cone of light, and imprisoned by sorcerous rays, the Tarnished Sword drifted through its slaughter-filled dreams. Grey phantom hosts marched across desolate, insubstantial battlefields, under diffused, undefined light sources. Always these armies lashed at Sword and Master and always there came a rending of metal and reaping of flesh and the destruction of sorcerous Entities. The Manticore, and the Dark Emissary, and the golden hued Seraph, and Houma, whose sorcerous flesh had whined and resisted before losing his arm, all of these were among his enemies, along with many other powerful beings, so that the slashing and rending work became an endless, though not unpleasant task.

And yet some being, or power outside of his dreams seemed to have interfered with his consciousness so that he stirred periodically into a partially awake trance, in which he was held by an unseen hand beneath a cone of light.

Beside him were his master and his master's allies — these he would never harm, never rend — but across from his party stood the Sorcerer Houma, an enemy that crouched, filled with violence, always straining against his barriers.

And within the cavern were other powerful entities, both Shadow Mages and Mid-World beings, and these were prepared to slay both his master and the hated Sorcerer at a second's notice.

Here, the sword would strain and twist, trying to break free, but always the same soft voice would come to him, an invisible whisper, a shadowy sound: "Mid-World Weapon, sentient blade, I have strengthened your conscious portions and passed other powers to you, but you must sleep now, for the TIME is not yet at hand." As the words faded, the Tarnished Sword would sigh and settle back into its long, dark-harvest dreams of slaughter.

· X ·

"It is a cruel and evil design that your masters have created," said the shadowy being, the Princess, hovering on the moonlit hilltop. In spite of her soft tones, bitterness radiated from her voice. "My father in his current condition is at the point of least wisdom; otherwise, he would release the Sorcerer. Houma would then destroy his adversaries, and depart, leaving the Marids no reason to even enter our shadowy empire."

"Your Shadow Emperor is at his level of least wisdom, but greatest strength," the Emissary noted calmly, eyes following the first trace of moonlit Marid bodies, tiny in the fields below him. Belying its soft tones, the Emissary's long, pinioned batwings seemed to quiver in anticipation. It stood, armed and dangerous, beside the Princess, with spell-powered gemstones forged onto both ring and wrist ornaments.

"Yes," continued the Emissary, after a pause and a deep breath. "Your father is mighty, and we also will stand beside him. The Gods have created this test: by barring the Portal Passages, they will bring two lone Marids against the most powerful of Earthborn beings, supported by many of the God's greatest servants. The first Marid deaths will come this night."

More likely our own deaths thought the Princess, *and she sent a whispered word of awakening to the Tarnished Sword. And lastly, she transmitted an invocation to Merlin, if he still lived:* **Wizard, speak for me at the Awakening.**

· ҉ ·

"We're never going to reach them in time," whispered the fox. Marid forms were more than halfway up the hillside and still, Khond's band of mounted warriors followed at a discrete distance, picking its way through dark, stone littered ravines.

"There's both Shadow Magic and the scent of burrowers in the air," Cendro murmured. "At any moment...even...now...."

Above them, the hillside seemed to burst with beetle-forms as scores of acid streams leaped at the flesh of Marids, and wild Shadow Magic swirled about the Demonspawned intruders.

"Now, fox," said Khond, aloud. "Now, find your master. We will try to hold an escape hatch open for your friends. Haakon will send word to you with his Warlock's powers. Go!"

Rafir dropped to the ground and began racing up the slope. The acid stench of dead and dying massive insect creatures was already beginning to sear his nostrils.

· ҉ ·

Huge as a small temple, the Emperor of Shadows stirred in anger, sending sheets of warm water sliding over the stone ledges beside his underground lake. Intruders stood at his gates, and it was almost time to tear them into ten thousand pieces.

· X ·

Beneath its imprisoning cone of light, the Tarnished Sword gradually began to change, to glimmer and glow, and even its dull metals that were touched by rusty stains slowly gathered luster. A song stirred in its increasingly alert consciousness, for one of its greatest moments was about to begin.

· X ·

Rafir sped down the long dark passageways, panting with exertion. Just above, and a little distance from him, rank after rank of gnomes wielding spears were marching toward a second line of defense. The fox turned a corner and saw his first glimmer of light. Just one more marshaling cavern, then the downward passage. But when or how would Julian and Galad break free?

· X ·

Brilliant and deadly, Barak-Kor's blade darted among gnomes wielding spears, while behind him, the glowering Haakon blasted at strands of Shadow Magic.

"They are thinning — one more push!" Khond called, and he drew his own sword and forced his way into the press, to stand beside his tall, brilliant son. A deadly duet of rapier and cleaver followed as they cleared a path toward the imprisoned Maker Servants.

· X ·

The Sword watched on with growing alarm. The Sorcerer, as well as his own party, had been used as bait for Marids, and now with the Marids bursting through each defense line, both Houma and the Sword's allies were going to be killed. Many of the Emissaries of the Gods and Shadow Mages were approaching the Sorcerer and the Apprentice, elaborate killing tools in their hands.

No other choice was left to it, and for the first time in its newly awakened state of consciousness, the Sword tasted the bittersweet flavor of irony.

With a wrench of motion, the Tarnished Sword slashed at its prison, shattering its cone of light into translucent fragments. Then it leaped through the air, over the heads of startled onlookers, sweeping through sorcerous chains of light, and it freed — Houma! With a snarl of anger, the immensely powerful Sorcerer confronted his would-be assassins.

· ☾ ·

Rafir raced on, panting with exhaustion. Crashing and blasting sounds echoed through the maze of tunnels around him — even from the prison's gallery in front of him. Was he too early? Or too late?

· ☾ ·

Surging from its dark lakeside haven, the Emperor of Shadows leaped at the oncoming Marids. Like lightning it swept over them, whirling each from its feet, then hurling their dense, mottled, or scarred bodies smashing into the cavern wall.

Dust hung in the air as the Shadow Emperor trumpeted in triumph.

· ☾ ·

Rafir reached the cavern only to hear Houma's first cry of exultation. Mages sent by the Gods lay stricken on the floor while other Emissaries hurled spells at the crouching Sorcerer. Shadow Mages writhed in agony, twisting in the air, but others were surging through the grey rockface and into the chamber. What had gone wrong? Why was Houma freed, while his friends stood frozen, defenseless?

As if sensing Rafir's presence, the Tarnished Sword swept down from above, shattering the cone prisons that held Julian, Sebastian and Galad.

The three stumbled forward, dazed, then recoiled from the Sorcerer and his wild battle magic, as Houma backed against the cavern wall. The Tarnished Sword, shimmering with glee, came to rest in Galad's hand. But now, shadowy shapes were taking note of them, hovering in midair, drifting closer.

"Free — even healed," Julian said slowly, his words slurred in confusion. "But to what purpose? We'll never get out."

"It was no dream, was it," murmured Galad, straightening. "Our League is broken, with all its leaders dead or dispersed. A stand here is as good as any."

"No! No! No!" cried Rafir, bursting into view. "We're going to finish our quest! That's why I brought help. Follow me. We're getting out of here." Julian hesitated, confusion and turmoil flashing over his young face, as he watched Houma blast the forms of Shadow Mages into smoky atoms.

"Rafir's right," Sebastian said quietly, taking his master's hand, "and anyway, there will be all the time in the world to die, if that's what we need to do. Now, Rafir, what is this 'help' you've brought?"

Cautiously, they began backing toward the cavern's mouth. The Tarnished Sword was beginning to sing in anticipation, but its sounds made far less noise than Houma's blasting spells.

·){ ·

Complex weapons enhanced by dark magic probed and slashed at the Marids, wielded by Emissaries of the Gods. Unharmed and undaunted, the Marids rose to their feet, casually shattering any sorcerous weapons that passed too close to them. Then they turned to the gigantic Shadow Emperor in his beetle-like form with a strange, tentative approach, almost suggesting respect.

·){ ·

Houma stood in a vortex of magic, surrounded by the dead, and dying, fighting for his own life. But there were Marids nearby!

"Marids!" A cry of exultation burst from his mouth as his enemies began to give way. "To me, O Marids!"

·){ ·

Sounds of battle echoed through the hillside, and every now and again the hillside's stone foundations themselves seemed to quiver. In front of Galad, gnomes wielding spears were faltering, eyes twitching to the death agonies of their stricken comrades, then darting back to the Tarnished Sword. How many more gnomes had to die before the warrior and his enchanted weapon were allowed to escape?

From down below came a bellow of such agony that Sebastian cringed, holding his ears in pain.

"There's no need to die!" Julian called out to the Shadow People. "But find some place to hide, for the Sorcerers and the Marids are upon you!" Shouts were coming from a distance, human voices.

"Haakon is reaching for us," Julian murmured. "They can hold a passage for only a brief time longer." Once more Galad leaped forward, slashing at the faltering gnomes. Explosions followed as the Tarnished Sword smashed though metal armor and weapons made from steel.

Again, the Shadow Emperor swept over the Marids, and again a Marid form was sent hurtling against a cavern wall. But this time the second Marid grasped hold of the Emperor's pincer claw, standing between the claw's teeth, as they closed over its mottled body like an incredible, gigantic vise.

"You say you must go back? Are you mad?" Khond asked Julian.

"There's something among my stores, a *Talisman*," Julian said, then he stopped because the hillside was shaking. "Rafir, perhaps, can help me find it. And maybe we can free our horses from their enchanted sleep — if they still live."

"No, wait, Julian," Sebastian said, clutching his master with both hands. "Our horses were freed some time ago, but as for that 'Talisman,' we have it, or rather, Galad has it wrapped within the bindings helping him to heal. It was hidden inside a vial of silverfoil, wasn't it?" Julian stood for a moment, staring at Sebastian in surprise, then he took a deep breath and patted Sebastian's slender shoulder. Now they had a chance, perhaps, to break free from the Shadow People.

Unaware that he was dying, the Shadow Emperor fought on. One of his great pincer claws lay twitching on the cavern floor. Torn free from his body, the claw still groped for Marids, but blindly, hopelessly. Others were aiding him, both Emissaries and Shadow People, and yet the Marids were tireless and unstoppable. Again, the Shadow Emperor sprang at them, but this time he crumpled to the ground: strangely, several of his front legs seemed to have vanished.

·){ ·

Out in the moonlight, they stood amid lush rangeland grasses, eyes focused on the hillside: muffled sounds came from within, and the ground quivered, sending slides of loose stones bounding down dark ravines and out onto the moonlit plain.

"So, Apprentice, will you go on?" Khond asked. "It was my intent to free you to pursue your quest. Thus, the Truce might be maintained, and we, the free peoples of Alantéa, might continue to flourish.

"And yet in fairness, I must add this: though your League is broken, and its Wizards vanquished, Cendro tells me that the greatest number of your peoples were saved, and now shelter among the benevolent Mid-World Powers. Some that you loved and shared danger with may have survived. You might spend your days peacefully among them, shielded in a Mid-World haven."

"We must go on," Julian said after a moment's pause. "No haven would remain safe for us, not with the Sorcerers and the Marids, especially with Houma leading them. And besides, we must pull down the Mid-World of the Truce on their heads — if we are able to — and if the Gods are ultimately strong enough to deal with the Sorcerers and the Marids. Listen!" A death wail swept out from the hillside, passing through many octaves, then beyond hearing. Cries of lamentation followed.

"Best to be gone," Khond murmured. "Never again will the Shadow Emperor trifle with Sorcerers or Marids. As for me and my people, we must find a bolt hole and emerge only when these matters have been resolved and peace settles back over the land. Farewell, and Maker's speed to the four of you."

"Thank you once again, Lord," Galad replied. "Your gift of transport steeds is most appreciated. You and your allies are mighty among the free peoples of Alantéa."

"Lord," murmured Cendro, "we could speak all night of our masterful deeds, but morning would leave us as dead heroes."

"Pull down Deep Heaven on their heads," Khond murmured, and he turned, leading his battle group to the south. Julian and Galad watched them for a moment, then they also turned, riding eastward through the moonlight toward the Ruins of Dahlak.

"So, our people are broken, either destroyed or swept into the Mid-World," Galad murmured. "Why do we continue? I am willing to go on, but give me a motive, a reason."

"I suppose it is as Merlin said at the beginning," Julian said slowly, as though searching himself for a reason, "that this struggle may determine whether mortals survive at all — not just in the League, but anywhere in Alantéa or the Far Lands."

"Enough," Galad said, fumbling with his bindings, searching for the vial holding the magic of Merlin. "There will be time to mourn later — anyway, at this moment, I suppose you'll need this." He handed the vial over to Julian.

"Will we still need to pass underground?" asked Sebastian, shivering slightly.

"Not again, except in my nightmares," Julian replied, shaking his head. "And we have fuel for the nightmares of many lifetimes. No, Merlin's Magic is very powerful, and it should hide us completely. I also think, or hope, that our great lord and master has arranged his magic to have our mounts returned to us, so we won't have to look for Khond's help again. We'll see. Anyway, now is as good a time as any. Are you ready? Sebastian? Rafir? I'm not certain what this spell will do, but we won't be the same for a while."

Riding toward the Vale of Whispers, Julian invoked the transformation spell and each of them was utterly changed.

·)X(·

The sun rose in the east, bringing light to Alantéa, the Forerunner, the Land of Enchantments. As its first rays struck the peak of Mount Evergrey, the Mirage of Rainbows ignited once again, erupting in fountains of colors and images. Moments later, light came to Rivermeet, to the swirling waters and to the raised dwellings of stone that stood on the edge of the flood plain.

Light, too, came to the mound of rubble that had once been Stone Mountain, where gulls were beginning to nest, and no humans dwelt. The sun's rays reached even to Gravengate, a place where broken stonework still seemed to quiver with the pounding of Marid's fists.

By noon, the sun was reaching its fullest power, radiating light over Alantéa the Forerunner, standing almost directly over the Vale of Whispers; but here the sun's rays seemed thwarted, changed, altered, as though a veil of time twisted and transformed all light.

·)X(·

"You missed! It was a filthy sort of nocturnal emission that begat you!" The old crone raged on while Gar, a squinty eyed, pimply gangling, reached for another stone, cursing the old hag, his mother.

"No, it was no honest futtering that brought you forth, only a sneaky dark of the moon bit of slippery creeping slime —" She broke off, for this time when Gar hurled his stone, it struck crow, and their dinner fell dead to the ground.

"Skinny and wormy, no doubt," the crone muttered, shuffling over to inspect the dead bird. Other crows called out and dove toward them but recoiled as fire sped toward them from her outstretched fingers.

We should be eating real meat, she thought, *kill one of the two oxen. One would be left to draw the cart. Nothing of great weight was truly sorcerous, anyway.* But then rage surged over her as she remembered — again — that killing the oxen was one of the things she wasn't supposed to do.

"Someone has a magic hex on me," she called out, turning skyward. "One day that someone will be sorry — or dead!"

"Weren't me, Mum," said Gar wiping his nose on his sleeve. "Good shot, hey?"

"Get firewood, you ugly lout," the old woman muttered, knowing that none could be found. They stood in the Ruins of Dahlak in the haunted, spell blasted Vale of Whispers, where little or nothing grew in the aftermath of the ancient wars.

"Mum, you know —" Gar broke off. "There's one of them creatures again. I'd best get my spear."

"You know you're not supposed to touch it, you fool!" The old crone's eyes were too poor to see the distant hulking shape of the Marid, but the Power within her was beginning to flutter with warning signs. And now she could hear the booming, hooting sounds: two or more of the creatures hunted nearby.

"We've got to get underground, or find shelter, for all of us," she muttered. With the stone ruins all about them, it was simple enough to find a hiding place, but far less easy was finding one that had no occupant.

"Mum, I don't like it down there! It's scary. And you won't even let me hold my spear! You've got your powers and I've got nothing!"

"Listen, you little snot-nosed brat. You can be scared and alive down below, or scared and dead up here. Let's go. I'll bring the bird."

Half whimpering, Gar ran toward the oxen, pulling them down a long slant into the ruins. The old woman followed, dead crow in hand, half sliding down a layer of pebbles that covered the incline. Daylight was fading above ground, but down below a shadowy darkness covered the entrance to the crypt. Deep underground, now in complete darkness, Gar huddled against the crone, listening for booming Marid voices, and for other sounds....

"I was great among the Demon Princes," the voice whispered.

"Not again!" whimpered Gar.

"Hush," said the old witch, gritting her teeth. The oxen snorted and shuffled but steadied with the old crone's spell curses.

"I was great among the Demon Princes," the whispering voice resumed, *"mighty and powerful. When the Maker departed, I warred with Seraphs and Spirit Lords. How strange and wonderful were our battles! How long we fought! At last, I closed with Raphael, one of the greatest Seraph, mighty with energies I could barely perceive. Yet, in the end, I was the victor, and I sent his shade shrieking in sorrow down to the Temple of Waiting.*

"How great was my triumph! But the taste of victory was transformed so quickly to ashes, for the Seraph Sting of Raphael came to stay with me with every turn and twist of Earth, moon, and sun, rising with me in the morning, settling down with me at nightfall.

"So, I joined with the Mid-World of the Truce, and somewhere, far from here, the greatest part of me lives free of Seraph Sting, while I, a ghostly creature, and the slightest fraction of old Demon Princes, before the Maker roused them, I bear the entire weight of the Seraph's Sting, and it rises with me at the light of day, and it sets down with me as the sun departs.

"Almost," the voice lowered its fading whisper, *"almost, I wish that I, and not Raphael, had been sent, shrieking in sorrow, down to the Temple of Waiting."*

Then the voice was gone, leaving them with nothing but their own nervous scraping sounds, and the dim faraway hooting and booming of distant Marids.

"Mum, Mum, it was creepy and horrible, one of them old divils. Won't you hold me, Mum?"

"Shut up."

"You used to hold me. I remember."

"Shut up and wipe the snot off your nose." Fire sprang from the old crone's fingertips, and oily crow's feathers began to singe. She held the bird gingerly with one hand, roasting flames darting from the other.

Gar wiped his nose and stopped cringing; his mouth was beginning to water. "I guess they don't have more than one divil to a ruin," he said, eyes glancing at shifting shadows.

"That's it, boy. You just heard from one of the biggest, baddest old devils, Lucifrage or Satanis. Thank the Maker when we die, we're gone, not made to hang around forever...." She trailed off. "That's part of the magic of the geas; I see it now, every time I say, Maker, it stirs within me, like maggots chewing through meat that's been dead for a long time."

"What's a geas, Mum?"

"A compulsion, you slow witted lout! Something's trying to bring me to the City of the Truce." She tore the singed bird in half, passing one portion to her dimwitted son. Surprisingly, he hesitated before eating.

"Something's wrong with me too, Mum. I've had these dreams, where I'm standing there in the middle of no place holding this beaten, rusty old sword, and hundreds, maybe thousands are trying to kill us! And I don't even have sense enough to run!" He bit into the crow, wondering how hungry he really was: the fright had added to his appetite.

"The only way to find out about a compulsion is to trace it to its source," she muttered, biting into the bitter, burned flesh. "We've been led here, the last few weeks, spell hunting amid the ruins, always drawn closer, somehow, toward the City. So, tomorrow we'll pass into the City of the Truce. Should be some good spell work there anyway."

"Don't make me come too, Mum!"

"You'll come too, you air-brained scum! Just keep your mouth shut, no matter how many ghosts and bogeys yammer at you — they haven't touched either of us, not the way some filthy offspring touched by Demons has been tampering with our minds. We'll all go — if those filthy dragon-gobbling monsters let us by...."

She muttered her magic words, crooning them like an ogre's lullaby, and her loutish son stopped twitching and slipped into his overly exciting nightmares.

The crone also dreamed, but of nightmare caverns, and dark dungeons with walls of flesh that closed over them like a predator's mouth.

· X ·

In the morning they peered out from their shelter, watching for signs of the huge, booming creatures that were passing, so fearlessly, through the haunted Vale of Whispers. No beings were moving through the Ruins of Dahlak except the crows, and what those birds fed upon was a mystery, as even the mosses struggled for a foothold on the brownish-grey, spell-cursed surface of the Vale. Mounds of rubble lay interspersed amid the Vale of Whispers, but whether these had once been palaces, laboratories, or cathedrals, none could say.

It was early morning as they inched their way carefully up to the ridge that led down to the Vale of Whispers. Oxen followed, fearful of any change.

As always, sunlight within the Vale was dimmed, less than full strength, except in one direction: to the south, a few leagues away, stood the City, and already it seemed to sparkle, as though in bright noon, while morning had just broken.

"Can we talk about this, Mum? I mean, sometimes you talk to me, almost like we was partners —" He broke off as she began to mutter her often used spell-curse.

"No, Mum, I'll go! Look, my feet are moving down! Only, Mum," Gar's voice dropped, "when we get there, can I hold my spear again? I can't remember the last time you let me hold it." She cut short her curse, staring down at him from the cart seat with a mixture of pity and disgust.

· ✕ ·

Through the late morning and into the afternoon, they crept forward, only quickening their pace when the hoots and booms of Marids forced them to find shelter within the ruined mounds. None of the whispering Ancient Powers bothered them, as there seemed to be a gathering of ghosts to the south, where Marids were beginning to gather and circle around the City of the Truce.

Danger and terror faced them at their southern destination, but as they shuffled slowly toward the gleaming city, the old crone's fierce hatred began to lift and to transform itself into something entirely different. Walking beside the oxen, only half understanding her feelings, she reached out and patted the ox beside her, gently, on its rump.

"Mum, what are you doing? You're patting next month's dinner. We'll have to kill it and cut it pretty soon. Something's wrong with you, Mum. Let's go back."

The old crone shook her head and plodded forward, pace picking up; before them, the sun's rays rippled over the gleaming City, a place where all time seemed to have stopped, a single moment in eternity held frozen forever.

"Mum, if anyone's going to stop, it's got to be you. I can't. The Spear's singing to me, and I feel almost...brave. You've got to...." Great hammering, booming sounds overwhelmed Gar's thin whimper: Marids were smashing at the invisible barrier that shielded the City of the Truce.

Gar covered his ears, cringing. Hammers! Like thunder!

"I'm not afraid, not even now," Gar whispered. The old crone patted his hand, watching as the boils receded from his face, a rich brown beard replacing them. Prompted, the oxen began to move more quickly — and now they were drawing so close to the city that veins of gold and silver could be seen in the gleaming city's clear white, almost translucent stone.

"Geas end, the end of enchantment," murmured the witch. "We are like ripe water nymphs, hanging on broad stalks of reeds, waiting to be reborn."

Distant sounds of cymbals and chimes and organs with an incredibly wide stretch of sounds began to reach them as they neared the border. But sounds of destruction rang always stronger and deeper: the noise of smashing stone was only partly offset by the music of creation.

The Tarnished Sword, long hidden and restless, cast aside its spear image and leaped into Gar's hand.

Marids ceased their smashing, backing, and crying out in rage as the enchanted barrier repulsed them again.

Witch, loutish son, and oxen met the barrier and recoiled.

"Quest's end," murmured Gar, feeling the Change, as each step, the atoms of his transformed body resorted, rearranging themselves. "We always thought that you, alone, Mother, had taken the Straight Path..." he faltered, the Change within him not yet complete.

Again, Marids hammered at the barrier, but the sounds of many instruments were building, and the air was dancing as ghost beings flocked into the gleaming City.

The old crone stepped forward, wild thoughts lashing her strained imagination. The barrier rebuffed a portion of her but began to give way as her particles sorted, rearranged themselves, releasing the hidden Mortal Magic Wielder.

Julian, the Apprentice, stepped through the barrier into the City of the Truce.

"Quest's end, Julian," Sebastian called out. Julian turned and saw that loutish son, oxcart and oxen had been transformed: Galad, Rafir, and Sebastian stood behind the barrier, with the horses and supplies provided for them by Khond.

"Quest's end, Julian. Time to bring forth the Mid-World of the Truce," Galad called out. "We will await you here. Julian, pull down Deep Heaven on their heads."

Chapter Seventeen

Ashes...

JULIAN TURNED AND RACED toward the City's center. As he ran, the ghostly shapes of the Ancient Powers swirled alongside him, seeming to speed his passage, and whispers surrounded him, racing just ahead or behind, calling out to him:

"*I was a Spirit Lord, gentle, a being with little power.*"

"*And I, a Lord of Dragons, drinking deep at the Wellsprings of Sorcery.*"

"*What will the Maker say to me?*" whispered a Seraph. "*I should have been at Adonai's side, learning greater wisdom as we leaped from star to star.*"

Music gathered around Julian as he ran, like the music of creation, greater than ghost whispers. All around him were massive buildings, made of white marble, with runes carved on each block of stone, forged by sorcerous energies. These runes had been inscribed so that no single Power could dwell in any of these buildings.

Marids hooted and boomed, bellowing in frustration, as they smashed again at the gates.

"Maker, my great God of Gods, guide me now," Julian called out as he raced forward. What were the Words, what would invoke the shadowy ghosts of the Ancient Powers?

But no words came, nor were they needed: in the Vale of Whispers, the Wraiths of the Ancient Powers greatly desired to release their many sorrows by re-enacting the formation of the Mid-World of the Truce.

Within the City's innermost circle, masses of Wraiths were gathering, calling out to each other.

Julian came to a halt, panting, as misty Wraiths began to coalesce about him. In the distance, Marids roared and bellowed as they struck again and again at the sorcerous gates of the enchanted City. Ghostly images settled and formed. Standing among broken pillars and marble slabs stood the replicas of the greatest of the Ancient Powers: Demons and Seraphs, Spirit Lords and Dragons, all of them preparing to relive an event that had occurred so many hundreds of thousands of years ago.

Maker, what will become of me now, Julian prayed, shrinking against the stone walls, listening as the spell shattering Marids raged on, while before him, images of the Ancient Powers formed, lifelike, more real than any waking vision:

The Lords of Dragons dwarfed those around them; scales and wings glittered red and green, yet their eyes were greyish black, wise, and cunning, filled with sorcery;

The greatest of the Seraphs, firstborn of the Maker, stood fearlessly among the Adversaries; beautiful beyond imagination Many of them stood still as statues, yet when they moved, golden light slipped from them, gleaming effortlessly;

Demon Princes stalked about, dark, smoldering red, and it seemed that their vast energies and powers could not be contained by any council, nor by any combination of Powers. And their eyes darted over the shapes of Seraphs and Spirit Lords as though their own deep malice could barely be restrained;

Spirit Lords watched all with unblinking eyes. They differed from the other Powers in that they showed the first division into male and female: some bore shimmering beards, while others had sweeping hair cascading over soft shoulders. But all gleamed with a silver light, clear and strong.

Julian drank in these images, every sense alert, but in the background, Marids bellowed and howled, crashing at the gates.

Hurry, hurry, Great God of Gods before the spell shattering Marids come....

"Begin with the Maker, if you will," Lucifer, Prince of Demons spoke, his voice filled with mockery. "Begin with soft, pious words at the start, threats in the middle of your message, and promises at the end. Begin."

"It is not as though we alone brought about this parlay," Adonai spoke softly. "In all these events, the Maker's Hand is felt — a distant, gentle, guiding hand. Do you of the Left side of Creation understand this?"

"There are energies; we are in a convergence of power," said a Lord of Dragons. "A time of peace may ensue. Yet this remote, distant Maker of yours seems a bizarre and capricious deity. If ever I became ruler of my own realm, I would order all things as they should be ordered."

"Do not seek to judge the Maker." A Spirit Lord spoke, soft silver hair glistening over her shoulders. "I spoke only a few times with the Maker, as He taught me the weaving of life forms. He measured and understood me then, as he has measured and understood each of us."

"Think how evenly matched our contest has been," added a Seraph. "The Maker might easily have provided ultimate power to one side or the other, yet He wished a balance, a stalemate. Neither Servant nor Adversary has prevailed so that now we are free to join with others and seek the Maker in the starry universe. Recall His last words: 'You will need to seek Me.'"

Hammering! Marids at the Gates!

Baal, Prince of Demons, snarled, "He spoke of your needs, not ours. Leave. Be gone. We will wish you a safe passage." A laugh slipped from his lips. "Yet one of my children's children, a Creature Indomitable, wishes to meet the Maker. In its slow, sly mind, it wishes to corrupt the Maker and rule the universe in His stead. Will you take this being with you?"

"We will," said Adonai. "It is not necessary to be perfect, only to wish to begin the greatest of quests. Yet it is not the Maker's will that we leave Earth's gardens to be ruined, nor to leave our mortal servants defenseless. We must all go, or failing that, a few from either side must stay to be Stewards until the Maker returns."

"My brothers are adrift beyond the circles of the world," said a Lord of Dragons. "I have no wish to join them. Become flotsam to the tidal drifts of the endless numbers of stars if you wish. Here, I will remain."

"But they will not leave us to our own devices," said a Prince of Demons. "They feel that their Maker wishes them to meddle in our affairs. Here are terms which we may offer to the Servants: depart those that will, the rest may take the Far Lands; we wish only Alantéa. Take the ocean depths as well, if you wish, though the shorelines of Alantéa must also be ours. Think: if the Maker breathed life into us, surely He would allow us a small place where we might flourish."

"Yes, and the Maker left us witless, senseless, prey to the simplest guile," said a bearded Spirit Lord. "Alantéa is the wellspring of all energy; the Lands Beyond have but few of the forces that power us. Your terms would leave only a few of the Servants, and these would become prey to even one of the Adversaries should that being no longer adhere to the Truce."

"And also, what of the Creatures of the Darkness?" asked a Seraph. "Can you truly make peace on their behalf? They seem wild, ungovernable."

"It is far easier to rule your pitiful, feeble humans," sneered a Prince of Demons. "Your Maker left you responsible for a sorry, breeding maggot heap. What sort of God is this?"

At the Gates, the New Gods, The Marids, were massing, almost ready to break through.

"Nay, brother, there are changes in this struggle." A Prince of Demons with a grim face murmured, one who had been silent before. "Some of the mortals have grown sly, and cunning, attuned to the First Energies. Their Masters, the Spirit Lords, have nurtured this 'Gift' within them. It must be lifted: whatever else, I will not accept a future when humans might come to power; it is too much to ask of me."

"Yet the Gift comes from the Maker." A Spirit Lord stepped forward, silver hair shimmering over her soft shoulders. "We cannot take it from them. Possessed by only a few, the Gift was given so that mortals might survive in spite of the Adversaries, in spite of the Servants."

Hurry, please hurry.... A shattering sound echoed; images blurred then reformed as the shaken City's barrier struggled to restore itself.

A Prince of Demons stepped forward, quickened to anger, eyes blazing. "That such a whimpering soft lot should seek to counter us! I am moved to begin this struggle once again, to complete your destruction."

"Yet, you will not," Adonai said gently, "for at this conjunction of energies those breaking the Truce would suffer an enormous backlash. You would not survive."

"Of course, you are right!" the Prince of Demons blazed back. "Every whimpering word you speak is the truth. But I tire of this. Almost, almost I wish that the Maker had come against us, openly, without deception. He may have put me down, enslaved or chained me, but there would have been a great struggle."

"A contest with the Maker is no contest," said a Seraph. "A Word, a thought, and He would have set you aside, painlessly. You will see, at the End of Time, when the Maker reveals Himself."

"This talk of the Maker accomplishes nothing," a Prince of Demons snarled. "Offer terms, or we will depart, and renew our struggle. But hear me: I now understand your needs — you wage war, not for mastery, or even for the Maker, but to preserve your creations, particularly the feeble mortals. If we are forced to renew this struggle, we will no longer overlook the humans; we will destroy each and every one of them."

"Yes, it was bound to come: rule or ruin," said a Lord of Dragons thoughtfully. "Yet, you, the Demon Princes must also make peace, and give up your secret hopes for uttermost dominion over Earth. We, the Lords of Dragons, have followed the Demon Princes through war and devastation and the ruin of our seed. From this time forward, however, we shall choose a new path, one favoring our own interests."

The Demon Princes stood still, full of silent menace. "You are not your own masters in this matter," one Demon Prince spoke in a low voice. Silence swept over the convocation of Powers.

But in the distance, Julian could hear the booming sounds of Marids gathering together, to probe at one of the softest links of the barrier.

"Once that was true," murmured a Lord of Dragons, "that you could rule us; but no longer: we have found ways to counter your mastery." The Lord of Dragons rose to his full height, dwarfing even the Demon Princes, then his eyes scanned the faces of the Servants. "Yet you of the Right Hand are not free to impose your will, for if you mean to rule all of Alantéa, we of the Left Hand will oppose you with always greater passion. We will not depart; you will not permit us to rule. What, then, are your Terms?"

The Servants looked to one another, faces troubled. A bearded Spirit Lord spoke, at last, his words slow, reluctant: "If we join our energies here, at this intersection of power, the Terms will come to us. I have understood this necessity from the beginning; others must also perceive it."

"Yet then I would be different," said a Prince of Demons musingly, dark red energies in turmoil. "What use is power if another transformed being wields it?"

A deep sound boomed, and the ground shook, spilling Julian to a crouch... Maker, hold them, hold them for a moment.

"Brother," spoke a third Demon Prince, "see that your powers will be wasted, broken, if we continue. Even in death, the shades of the whimpering Seraphs, pursue us, sapping our strength. Perhaps the Maker was more subtle than we thought. The Truce may be our only escape from His cunning designs. We need to join together, even to fuse with one another."

"Many of us must join with the Truce to keep the balance," added a Seraph, "though not for power, only to preserve the Maker's works."

Adonai shook his head. "What is being proposed is not the best of choices; it is also not the worst. But do not be deceived, you of the Right Hand: if you join in this conjunction of energies to merge with this kaleidoscope of varied powers, you will be changed — forever."

"For the sake of Earth and its Gardens, we shall undertake this," a Seraph replied.

"For the Earth, and for the preservation of mortals, we will join with those of the Left Hand," said a Spirit Lord, silver hair flowing behind her, "and then become a blended Power of those of the Left Hand and those of the Right Hand."

"Then, stand with me, those who will instead seek the Maker," said Adonai, his voice raised. "And the lesser Powers taking the Long Journey must be within my circle of protection. Open the Truce Gates!" Five of the greatest of Seraphs drifted toward Adonai, then three of the Spirit Lords, and at last, a Demon Prince broke ranks, and came to stand beside Adonai, face downcast.

"Seraph stung, and feeble!" snarled a Prince of Demons. "Take him!"

Then Portals flared, and scores of lesser Powers emerged to stand beside Adonai: many Seraphs and Spirit Lords, faces serene; a few of the Demons and Dragons, irresolute, uncertain; and at last, a Creature of the Darkness crept through a cloudy, dark Portal. Massive, with the body of a serpent, its two huge arms ended in webbed hands, and its ghoul's face was contorted with a malice that seemed filled with delight.

Adonai and the other great Servants raised their hands, and lines of power extended about the Travelers as they shielded themselves from the Truce.

Others, the greatest of the remaining Ancient Powers, drifted into a vast circle, with Demon and Dragon, Seraph and Spirit Lord interspersed, standing so that none might reach out and touch another.

Tides of power drifted toward the Truce Makers. Flashes of light hovered about them: blue flickers like dark fires; drifting white lights like a sudden frost. Sounds of low, murmuring voices came, as the dead Ancient Powers were wrenched from their enchanted sleeps and called to witness the Mid-World of the Truce. Beneath their murmurings, a deep music surged, vibrating through the ruins of Dahlak.

Slowly, hesitantly, the Ancient Powers extended their arms toward one another — their own energies mingling with those of the Truce:

Pure Golden light radiated from the Seraphs,
From the Demons came a deep red, pulsing with power,
Dragon Lords shone green like the greatest envy,
Spirit Lords glistened silver, serene and distant.

· 𝕏 ·

And at this intersection of power, the world was changed.

Ancient energies stormed about the Truce Makers: they became engulfed, submerged in a tide of light, and already their forms seemed to be in the middle of a metamorphic transformation.

Energies closed over the Ancient Powers, and they passed from view, forever. Harmonies emerged, harsh and delicate, powerful, and obscure.

From the center of this intersection of power emerged the Truce.

A chorus of voices spoke as one: "All Powers who stand outside of the Truce will depart from Earth; all other Powers alive in Alantéa on this day will be governed by the Truce. Our War is over."

A Prince of Demons, voice low, rumbling with power: "Each of the Powers shall build his own domain, a place where that Power will be Master. None shall occupy the soil of Alantéa, the wellspring of energy."

A Seraph: "Nor shall any of us within the Truce, Ancient Servant or Adversary, forge an alliance with other Powers. If conflict ensues, each Power will act alone, within the Truce Terms."

A Lord of Dragons: "The Creatures Indomitable are outside of the Truce, unchanged, yet they are free to forge their own domains or dwell in Alantéa, as they wish."

A Spirit Lord: "The Powers are free to protect mortals, by shielding them within their own domains, or by fashioning havens for them in Alantéa."

A Seraph: "The Truce of the Mid-World is greater than the Truce Makers, and if the Truce is broken its power will be called against the offender. And even before the Truce is challenged, our greatest Emissaries must be free to act in concert to avoid a Truce breaking, or to enforce our wills against those outside our pact."

As Julian listened, a great rending sound burst over the convocation, as the Marids burst down the gates, and all the harmonies of the Mid-World of the Truce were transformed into whining noises. **"Maker!,"** he called out, **"just one more moment!"**

But from within the circle of power, a Prince of Demons spoke: "Yet the Truce shall not be called down lightly; there are words that will invoke the Powers — these shall not be spoken here but are now known only to us within this circle of power."

What! Julian sprang up in shock. They had been watching something that had happened thousands of years ago, hoping that some portion of the Truce Terms would allow them to stop the Sorcerers and the Marids today!

But now his people were all dead, while the Wizards' League lay in ruins, and he stood in the last moments of a fool's errand! There had never been even the least of chances! Tears of rage and frustration seeped down his face, blurring his vision, but within the Divination, the image of Adonai raised his hands. The Great Seraph stood apart from the convocation of energies, buffeted by whirlwinds of power. But he spoke intently, a counterspell — words that could not be heard! Words that were barred, words that were nothing!

Broken, broken, all dead, all ruined...and the Truce forever unknown....

Within the Circle of Power, Seraphs and Spirit Lords raised their arms, speaking the last of their Terms: "For the Mid-World of the Truce, we yield the greatest of our Ancient Secrets: we have learned how to free the most powerful of the Adversaries from their imprisonment within the ocean depths. This knowledge is now one with the Truce."

Demons and Dragons spoke, voices harsh and deep: "For the Mid-World of the Truce, we yield our Ancient Secret: we have learned how to summon the departed Servants from their distant haven in the Hall of the Dreamers. This knowledge is now one with the Truce."

All who stood within the circle were now changing, undergoing an incredible metamorphosis: The Gods of Mankind were forming: diverse, huge, powerful. Their voices rose in unison, one last time: "For the Mid-World of the Truce we yield our ancient forms and natures; these will never be regained until the end of time."

Julian stood, recoiling in shock, quest's end in ruins. The birth of the Gods had just been reenacted before him, but it counted as nothing: the New Gods — the Marids were nearly upon him, and it was time to die. Death, at least, would bring an end to ruin, an end to defeat, an end to horror.

· X ·

Galad crouched down, horses kneeling beside him, presenting a low profile to the ravaging Marids who battered at the Truce Gates. Julian was inside the City, struggling to discover how the Gods might be brought against their enemies — even after the loss of the Wizards' League, it might still be possible to overcome the Sorcerers and the Marids.

Rafir probed gently at the barrier, alternately visible then invisible, while Sebastian stood gazing into the gleaming city, tense, waiting, trying to hear calls from his master, the Apprentice.

Suddenly, the little Familiar leaped against the barrier, smashing at it with his tiny fists.

"Julian's going to die!" he cried. "We have failed, and he's going to die!"

As if recoiling from Sebastian's blows, the air burst around them, with the earth shaking beneath their feet, and a vast shattering sound rang through the air.

"Marids!" hissed Galad, and he straightened, probing at the barrier: it was soft, quivering, spongy. One sweep of the Tarnished Swords slashed the barrier's fabric into dead magic. Then Galad was on horseback, racing into the gleaming city.

Marids strode down the broad avenues, fearless and unopposed. Face set hard and grim, Galad sped toward the massive shapes, while at his side, the Tarnished Sword began a low, moaning hymn, a rumbling tribute to the power of death.

Ghost shapes hovered above the towering Marids, but no tales were told, for these Demon spawned beings were the first and the only intruders to force their way into the Vale of Whispers since the birth of the Mid-World.

And now, as Galad rode in fury toward the massive and mottled Marids, the City began to defend itself. All its gleaming stonework lost its luster, turning grey and dark with anger. A chorus of murmuring sounds grew in strength, as Mid-World energies surged back into their besieged birthing place.

Energies swarmed over Marids, circling, probing, attacking them — to no effect.

One Marid turned to face Galad, massive head regarding Galad impassively, radiating energies from its whole body, boar tusks gleaming from the corners of its mouth.

Galad's charger shied away as a rage of sorcerous energy attacked the Marid's body but recoiled from its impenetrable armorlike hide.

He steadied the charger, drawing his moaning Tarnished Sword. But behind him, faint cries could be heard: Sebastian had followed, riding Julian's horse, struggling desperately to control it.

"Go *around*, Galad," cried the little Familiar. "Around it, and *hurry!*"

It was then that the Marid began to levitate, lifting easily from the ground.

"This thing is the greatest monster of all monsters — and now it can fly?!?" Galad cried.

But the Marid — and its brethren, also rising from the ground in a storm-tide of sorcery — the Marid showed anger for the first time, turning, twisting, seeking for some being or thing to rip apart, something to destroy. Though now it tumbled, twisting, in midair, coming to rest on a cushion of nothingness.

Galad edged past, and it groped for him, huge hand reaching for some being to crush. Galad hewed at it, and with a blinding flash, the sword recoiled, falling stricken from his hand.

"No time to fight them!" Sebastian called out, urging Julian's horse on. Shrieking in fury, the sword rose from the ground and settled back into Galad's hand. They edged past the writhing Marid, just as it began to hoot and boom to its brethren in a voice that sounded like the coming of a storm.

All through the City energies pulsed and glowed like seething volcanoes. Marids hung suspended in midair, hooting, and booming: an invocation to their allies, the Sorcerers. Yet other Marids had found stonework within their grasp and were crushing, destroying towers with one hand, using the other to anchor themselves. Foot by foot, they were smashing their way toward Julian and the City's core.

Horses near panic, they raced through the broad, pulsing avenues, riding underneath writhing, twisting, suspended bodies of Marids. Portals were booming, then collapsing as the Sorcerers fought to create entries.

They found Julian in the heart of the City, where the Apprentice stood stricken, cloak over his face, leaning against a shattered pillar, ignoring the many energies that flared around him.

Grasping slabs of stone and massive pillars, one Marid had fought his way forward, eyes radiating rage, as foot by foot he groped toward the Apprentice.

"Julian!" Sebastian cried out. Julian looked up but did not move, only watching with detachment as the massive Marid's hand reached for him.

Face set, shrieking sword in hand, Galad raced forward, slashing at the extended hand.

And this time the Tarnished Sword slashed the Marid's flesh.

Bellowing with pain, the great Marid recoiled, losing its grip, and it drifted skyward, with dark red blood streaming to the ground below.

"Julian, we have to break free from this place," Galad shouted over the bellowing cries of Marids, and the raging windstorms created by Sorcerers. Galad slipped from his horseback. Julian said nothing, only staring at Galad with eyes that had witnessed too much horror and were now retreating into madness.

"There's nothing to be gained here, is there?" Galad turned to Sebastian. "No talismans, no hidden recordings, no sorcerous weapons?" The little Familiar shook his head, staring at Julian with horror in his small eyes.

"Then, we're gone," said Galad, and he lifted Julian from the ground, setting him on horseback. They rode to the east, their progress halting. Julian slumped and sagged in his saddle, while Sebastian struggled to hold him upright, and Galad led his horse by its reins.

Rafir rode in a pouch beside Galad, his small fox body so filled with shock that he could not even weep. They had been beaten, completely defeated after so many months of struggle. Julian was alive but might never be the same. And Granny was dead with all their other friends and allies smashed or lost.

They passed through the City's outermost ring, riding east, and only the fox turned back to stare into the City that had once gleamed so brightly: it glowed now, but with a turmoil of dark, sorcerous energies. Marids hung, still suspended, and yet now Alcman had come with Houma, as Marids gained handholds on the City's massive stonework.

The Sorcerers and the Marids are the victors, thought the fox. *Nothing, not even the most powerful place in the Mid-World — the City of the Truce — was able to stand against them.*

·)(·

All through the long afternoon and evening Galad drove them on, making Julian walk at intervals, leading him with a leash, as though the Apprentice had become some rough beast of burden. Water was forced on Julian, but food choked him, and he stumbled along or swayed on horseback, eyes distant, filled with images of destruction.

They pushed eastward, with the City receding gradually from view, then vanishing, to remain only in their minds, along with many other vivid nightmares. At nightfall they still trudged on, moving in complete weariness and sorrow beneath overcast, night skies that were haunted by clouds. When the first sweep of rain washed over them, Galad found shelter for them in a stand of trees, and there they halted, many leagues from the City and the failure of their quest.

·)(·

It was late at night, far beyond midnight, when Julian slipped from madness into a sorrow that felt as though it would last forever. He stumbled from their rough shelter, moving from the stand of trees, and he sat alone on long grasses, face turned upward to the rain.

Elsewhere, over sunlit oceans, heat and light and wind were lifting moisture into the air, to be cast back down upon Alantéa and the Far Lands. And the Earth wobbled and spun in its great, oval, everlasting journey about the sun. And the sun itself surged through the wide universe, drawing its planets spinning, in oval movements around it: but they were all bereft, abandoned, whirling, surging from nothingness into no safe place.

Here, under weeping skies, at quest's end, after many nightmares, all his carefully constructed barriers crumbled, and Julian confronted again his own personal first and most ancient nightmare.

They had been journeying southward, a party formed by Servants of the Maker, he and his parents and his mother's mother, along with a score of others, seeking refuge within League lines. He was only four, and yet he could smell the scent of fear all around them. But why should they be afraid? Had his mother not been born with the Gift, and his father not a weapons master and Seer?

Then, in the dead of night, the League within a day's march, there had come the shouts and cries of terror, and the jostling and panic, with his parents taken, captured; only he and his grandmother and two others escaping south.

Merlin had sheltered him, healed him, almost adopted him after the death of his grandmother. For years, the Wizard had searched for his parents, seeking word of them from the Powers. Yet no word came except for whispered rumors that they lived and were not in torment.

Julian had struggled to put aside all his fear and anxiety, learning from his Wizard Masters, always striving to serve the League, to become stronger, so that one day....

One day he might free his mother, free his father.

But now, as the skies wept at quest's end, and with the League's death, and the Wizards' failure, now he understood that there had never been any hope, that he would live, then die and be nothing forever, that the life of mortal men and women was nothing, and at life's end there was nothing — nothing but ashes, ashes mixed with broken dust, stirred slowly by the moisture of Earth's water cycle.

Chapter Eighteen

Visions

"JULIAN," MURMURED SEBASTIAN. "JULIAN, you'll have to come out of it, away from the horror." An hour before daybreak, the little Familiar had woken, small body aching with fatigue, and found that his master had slipped away from their temporary camp.

"Julian, there must be some good we can do, even if we save only a few lives. We couldn't preserve the Mid-World of the Truce — that was always too great a task for us. We were meant for lesser matters. But there still must be some good we can do." Alarmed at his master's disappearance, Sebastian had taken wing, rising above the canopy of leaves, finding Julian in the open, with overcast skies still raining down on the defeated, broken Apprentice.

For now, Julian said nothing, but he closed his eyes, and he touched Sebastian's small, frail hand with his own, and even at quest's end the warmth and love of old companions flowed through their touch.

At daybreak Galad and Rafir emerged from the stand of trees that sheltered them and came to sit beside Apprentice and Familiar.

"Julian," Galad said gently, "I was not willing to die at the Marids' hands, but I'm ready to risk my life for any good purpose. Is there anything we might do to bring down the Truce on our foes?" Julian shook his head.

"Is there any good thing we might accomplish?" Galad continued. "A thing that might make a difference for the future? Save lives, or preserve knowledge of the Maker?" Julian was silent, face staring at the rainsoaked grasslands.

Galad sighed. "Then we have only our own lives to protect. Which way should we go?" Again, Julian said nothing, but Sebastian smiled a brief, sad smile, touching Julian's hand.

"I'll search for directions this one time," said the little Familiar. "I can, when the need is great, borrow a portion of Julian's own power — that helped me to heal you, along with the power of the Shadow Princess."

Sebastian scratched at the ground, clearing a patch of earth, then he marked patterns in the soft, damp soil, tracing them with his slender fingers. After a pause, the little Familiar frowned, erased his work, then repeated the process. Rafir stared at the patterns, perceiving nothing, then he turned his mournful fox eyes to Julian: the Apprentice was staring with an unfocussed vision into the distance.

"Strange," the little Familiar murmured. "It's almost too clear, as though someone left this pattern for us to find."

"One of Houma's traps, no doubt," Galad said, a touch of bitterness creeping into his voice. "Even with his own victory and our complete defeat, the Maker-cursed Sorcerer would continue his endless schemes."

Sebastian shook his head. "No, I think I could sense Houma's work, after all we've been through — but we're supposed to go east, toward the mountains, the Gangean Range. Enemies lie to the south, to the north, and to the west."

Galad sighed. "Let's hope our pathway hasn't been chosen by the Wizards, leading us once more under their power. It is time now to be free of both Sorcerers and Wizards, with all their traps and plots."

·)(·

Under cloudy skies they rode eastward, grim, beaten, with little speech between them; and Julian remained completely silent, staring into the distance as a sun that was completely blocked by clouds rose before them and set behind them. Days passed as they traveled eastward, avoiding all human settlements.

Five days into their journey from the ruins of Dahlak and the end of their quest, Julian sat up suddenly in his saddle and whispered in a dry, almost croaking voice, "Houma is seeking us."

"Do we hide?" Galad looked around: the land was turning drier, as though the distant peaks of the Gangean Range had swept much of the moisture from their cloud cover, and nearby trees held a parched, almost withered look.

"Probably not needed," Julian said after a pause, and again his voice was a whispered croaking sound. "There's no urgency in his search. To Houma, our destruction is only a minor, uncompleted task. Perhaps he will again seek to move some Power against us."

"Somehow I doubt that," Galad said, shaking his head. "All of the Powers used by Houma have found only grief or destruction. Think of Un-Maurag, or Tel-Alantir, or of the Shadow Emperor."

Julian said nothing, his eyes resuming their vacant, distant look, as though even the names of Powers could rekindle sorrow and madness.

·)(·

Rafir watched the foothills of the Gangean Range draw slowly closer with every step. Green and brown vegetation was interspersed with a dark rock face, rising a few hundred feet then vanishing into dry mists. Grim beings must dwell in the Gangean Range with its many mountains because his old mistress, Héna, had never mentioned those peaks, keeping all her stories limited to lands of beauty, where good people resisted evil, with brief struggles that made them stronger and wiser, and then their lives were much better afterward.

She told me only stories with happy endings, and then I helped to kill her — had I stayed with her, she never would have gotten so deeply involved. We'd be alive, together somewhere, and she would be telling me a story where the great heroes, armed and aided by Powers, defeated some far away not really frightening evil creature.

"Watch now, Julian," Sebastian's voice called out. "Galad, can you see them overhead?"

"The first Watchers," Julian murmured, gazing upward into a cloud cover that seemed stripped of moisture, "and look at them swirl in excitement — they must have been seeking us for many days." Rafir stared upward, watching winged creatures circle overhead. They seemed larger than hawks, floating like sleek carrion seekers, but they lacked the curled, bobbing buzzard's necks and hooked beaks.

"So?" asked Galad.

Julian shrugged. "They will seek Houma; at some point, the Sorcerer will forge a Portal Passage. Let us be sure that we are not taken, this time, alive."

Galad pulled up his reins, halting and staring grimly at the Apprentice. "Somehow, th —"

Harsh shrieking cries swept over them from above.

"The eagle!" Sebastian cried, pointing upward.

Galad stared skyward, watching the Eye of Merlin. "Caught again in the Wizards' plots," he muttered in a low, grim voice, "like being trapped in the webs of spiders that have been dead for centuries."

Above them, the Eye of Merlin surged and swept among Houma's winged spies, talons ripping apart their wings and spines. One of the three fluttered to Earth, hopping, scrambling over dry ground, with keening sounds slipping from its gargoyle mouth. Almost in a trance, Julian raised his staff and blasted the last strands of its life from the stricken creature.

A second fell to Earth like a sack of meal, but the last surged free of the eagle and raced westward. Julian sent phantom shapes of hawks in front of the creature's path, and as it swerved, the Eye of Merlin swept over it, the last of Houma's spies spun and plunged to its death.

Sebastian watched on, thinking how the eagle — so long ago, in such a different time — had destroyed a winged serpent, a predator that was seeking Sebastian.

All of them sat still, even the horses watching as Merlin's winged emissary circled down, coming to rest on a stony outcrop a few paces from them.

"I cannot say, 'well met'," croaked the eagle, "but it is good to see you alive in the middle of ruin and disaster."

Neither Julian nor Galad spoke.

"From the mind of Merlin, I know of your grief, and of the failure of your quest for the Truce," the eagle continued after a pause, "and from my own mind, I still have nightmare visions of Sorcerers and Marids, and the final ruin of the League. And yet, it is not over."

"If Merlin has somehow discovered the Truce Terms, where are the Gods that serve the Mid-World of the Truce?" Galad asked, his bitter irony spilling forth. "And if he has fashioned some new and powerful weapon, why does he not destroy the Sorcerers and the Marids with it, instead of tracking down his pitiful, useless pawns?"

"Merlin, and Balardi, and Thorian, all still flee Sorcerers and Marids by Portal Passages, but believe me now when I say that —"

"Which way are you going, eagle?" Julian interrupted, speaking for the first time in a clear voice. "I, for one, will travel in the opposite direction."

Fierceness flared in the eagle, then subsided. "I was to gather you, then return to Kalanin. And Géla."

"Alive? Kalanin, alive?" Galad asked in disbelief. "Is this some Wizard's ploy?"

"Wait," said Julian straightening. "No, Galad, it's unlikely the eagle would tell such a direct lie — Merlin gathers the remnant of his ruined pawns, the last of his pieces. We will go to Kalanin and Géla. But think about this, Galad. Is Kalanin any more likely to do the eagle's bidding than we are? Is he your willing servant, Eye of Merlin?"

The eagle said nothing, only regarding them with a skulking, wary look never before shown by the winged emissary.

· ҉ ·

When they reached the foothills of the Gangean Range, they began a slow ascent, riding up a gentle incline, only dismounting and leading their horses as their passage became steeper. Galad led them with some eagerness, but Julian followed more warily: even during his long interior retreat, images of Shadow Mages and sorcerous snares were still sliding in and out of his mind.

As they climbed, they passed through masses of low clouds, and as they emerged, the true extent of the Gangean Range became clearer to them: to the west, dry, hazy cloud cover erased all hints of land, but to the east, peak after peak rose, with white snow covering its upper reaches.

Even at low levels, it became cooler, so that they wrapped cloaks over chilled bodies, while Sebastian and Rafir conserved body heat by retreating into saddle pouches. The two small beings peered out, watching as every now and again, columns of sunlight would slash through the upper cloud reaches, sweeping over distant peaks like scepters conveying divinity to a race of demigods.

Galad's eyes were the first to mark the distant, tall figures of Kalanin and Géla in their grey cloaks, as the two stood together on a ridge, watching the slow progress of Galad and Julian. None waved or called out, but Galad's pace increased so that he was first to reach the ridge, and there he cast sword and pack aside and embraced Kalanin.

"'Dead, all dead,'" Galad murmured. "I remember waking from my charmed sleep and calling that out. I never dreamed that you still lived. It seemed that everything had been destroyed."

"Dargas sleeps the Long Sleep," Kalanin said, "and Baroda and the Mistress of Illusions were destroyed, as well as Rafir's old patroness, Héna. Yet in the end, the Wizards called upon the Gods to save them, dissolving their League. I and Géla ...." He halted, watching the bent and stumbling form of the Apprentice as Julian struggled upward. Kalanin and Géla descended and helped him to the ridge's crest.

On the ridge, Géla and Kalanin embraced the stricken Apprentice, with folds of grey cloth wrapping about Julian's hunched, limp body.

"We have all been defeated, beaten and ruined," Kalanin said softly. "I envy Dargas who sleeps the Long Sleep."

"You were summoned," croaked the Eye of Merlin, "because there is yet much —"

"You should fall silent, eagle!" Kalanin said, raising his voice. "You have been a trusted ally, but our League has been defeated, so we wish to hear no more about it." He took a deep breath then turned back to Julian and Galad.

"But here, on this ridge, at the struggle's end, each of us will have questions about the other's journey. So, my counsel is this: we should take shelter, and talk for a while, each of us recounting his portion of the tale; then, we will mourn for the League. After, we may talk about what is to be done with the rest of our lives."

Julian said nothing, only staring out over the cliff's edge: it would be simple to cast his staff over, with his own body following as easily — but Sebastian was at his side, clutching at his cloak as though restraining him.

"Whatever else," added Géla, "we will not wish to remain in the Gangean Range. It is said that at the middle level the Indomitable Creatures of the Darkness roam night and day, hunting the lesser Stone Giants."

"And higher," added Galad, "Vespoids feed on human worshippers, feasting on living bodies that have been raised on Pillars of Silence. It is a strange, unlovely place the eagle has brought us to. But yes, we will sit, and talk, and then mourn, though I fear that I must tell most of our sad tale, leaving only the Truce Terms for Julian."

Galad put his arm around the Apprentice. "Come, a brief time for mourning, as though attending the funeral of a loved one, then it will be done, over forever."

· X ·

They gathered at a hollow in the cliff's side, a place too shallow to be called a cave, though it gave shelter from cold updrafts that surged over the ridge's edge. They sat quietly for a moment, the eagle studying their faces warily, as though seeking a gap in the steel bars of some complex prison.

Géla spoke first, talking in low tones, telling how the Sorcerers had abandoned the twin sieges of Stone Mountain and Gravengate; how a tide of Marids had saved the Sorcerers from defeat at the mouth of the Asaram. Then, as she trailed off, Kalanin told of the last stand before Gravengate, where the Wizards had disbanded their League and fled.

"Many died, but by far the greatest number of us were swept up by Portal Magic; and this happened, not just on the battlefield, but escape hatches opened for every village and township of the League. In my last moments of our battle, both Portal Passages and Marids groped for me, one Portal seizing me a single second before a Marid's hand could touch me, and I was transported to Géla's side at the Courts of Auai Kuan Yin.

"The Goddess Auai Kuan Yin is akin to the Dark Lords in that she seems only lightly bound to the Truce, though if the Dark Lords are transformations of ancient, unrepentant Demons and Dragons, the Goddess is closer to a sister of the Spirit Lords, being now what Llara might have become had she entered the Truce.

"There, at the Courts of Auai Kuan Yin, I found the beginning of peace, with rest and silence bringing a quiet time of healing. But then the eagle somehow persuaded the Goddess to deposit us here on this barren shelf.

"Also, we learned at the Courts of the Goddess, about the Wizards' fate, how they lived on, fleeing by Portal Magic as the Sorcerers and the Marids pursued. I think that they should have had the courage to stand their ground and die."

"You know so little!" snarled the eagle. "The Wizards remain powerful — mighty beyond your imagination!"

"You repeat yourself, eagle," Galad said evenly, "like some mindless, mimicking parrot. At this point in our struggle, silence is more suitable. Now I will tell our portion of the tale, except for the Truce Terms." Galad spoke of their journey through the rangelands, then of the Shadow People, with their escape followed by the Wizard's transformation spell.

"As Merlin must have known, the unlovely sorcery worked upon us began crumbling as we approached the gates of the Truce: The City would not permit any sorcerous work but its own." He turned to Julian, hesitating. "As for the Truce Terms, and our quest's failure, we must ask Julian, though he has been able to say little of these matters."

In faltering tones, voice little more than a whisper, Julian spoke of the Truce Terms, how the last of them barred all but the greatest of Powers from invoking the Truce.

"So, all our long quest and pain and torment were fruitless, a wasted effort from the beginning. Yet even at the end, when the invocation was barred from me, Adonai, the Greatest of Seraphs, spoke a counterspell, and still, I could not hear it — either the words of that spell were shielded from me, or the spell's power was overwhelmed by the Mid-World of the Truce. How could the Maker, so wise, so powerful, so mighty, how could He leave this planet forlorn, with so few and such feeble defenses?"

"We should not seek to judge the Maker," said Kalanin, "even if Demons and Marids and Sorcerers come to rule everything...." He trailed off for a moment, turning the Truce Terms over in his mind. "And so, the Truce Terms were forged to prevent any resumption of the old wars. But why are the Powers so reluctant to call down the Truce upon the Sorcerers, the Marids, and the Demon Princes?"

Silence settled over them a short while, then they spoke for a long time in low tones, as they might at the funeral of a loved one, recounting their favorite aspects of a lost one: Kalanin of hunting in the frosty hills above North Haven; Géla of Amalric's broad avenues and teeming market place; Galad of Khiva and the coast; Julian of the foaming shoreline along Sea's Edge; Sebastian of the wide, seething Saugus, with floods of sweet water surging seaward; and Rafir of the Wizards' great stone fortresses, with their endless passageways and inner corridors. Then, they were silent once again, each lost in his own thoughts.

Finally, with daylight passing and dusk nearly upon them, they emerged from their shelter, where outside, the last filtered strands of sunset cast a red glow over the range's snowcapped upper reaches. Returning to the cliff's edge, they faced south, bidding a last farewell to their ruined lands.

Then, they wept, with even the indomitable eagle bowing his head in sorrow.

Darkness and defeat swept over them, and Sebastian began shivering as though touched by a plague. They returned to their shelter, huddling together against the chill. On the shelf, their horses cropped at small ferns and greyish green mosses.

"If ever there was a time for wine, it's now," said Galad. "Yet, I'm sure that our host the eagle has given little thought to these matters."

"Wine?" Julian asked in a soft voice, then louder as though his thoughts gave him new strength. "Wine? There's no need for wine. Dream visions can be created that are more potent than any narcotic."

"Are you mad, Apprentice?" the eagle croaked. "Do you not recall how the Mistress of Illusions became lost in her own tangled dreams?"

"No need to fear that," Géla said softly, "not if we all go. I have traveled on an enchanted pilgrimage with the Mistress of Illusions. When I forced her vision from my mind, the journey ended for both of us."

"But you are, all of you, the tools of destiny!" cried the eagle. "Do not imagine that you can embark upon such a journey without tempting fate!"

"Eagle, it is over," Galad said quietly.

"Not while you live!" raged the eagle. "Not while the mind of Merl —"

"It is over, eagle," Kalanin interrupted. "Please be silent — or leave us." The Eye of Merlin seethed, beak and talons raging, but all faces watched him with open or subdued hostility, and in a moment the eagle turned and studied the distant mountain tops as they lost the last rays of sunlight.

"I cannot even reach for counsel to the mind of Merlin," murmured the eagle, "for he flees even now from the Sorcerers and the Marids. What would he say? Likely, he would not bar you from your enchanted pilgrimage. Dream on, then. I will guard your backs. Dream on if you must."

"Come then, those wishing to travel with me," Julian said, staff in hand. "Sit beside me, for our minds will leave this place, then share one vision." All except the eagle came and sat beside the Apprentice. Outside of their partial shelter, it was now dark and gloomy, with an icy wind shearing up against the barren cliffside.

Julian began murmuring, and the powerful Gift within him strove to beat back its defeat and depression, seeking use of magic as a temporary escape.

Sebastian felt nothing for a few moments, only an easing of his unhappiness, then a lessening of cold. It was good to be beside Julian, good for all of them to be released from sorrow.

Julian rose, an expression of peace on his face. Wordlessly, he gestured to the others, and they, too, rose easily, as though drifting upward, free of the weight of earth. As they moved from their shelter, Sebastian turned briefly, and he saw that all their slumbering, peaceful forms lay slumped together against the face of the cliff, with only the eagle standing guard, a fearful and wary sentry.

Then their sleeping forms vanished. All the light around them shifted, and all the chill, dry, mountain atmosphere seemed swept away by currents of warm, moist air, as though a river had surged into being beside them.

They emerged from their shelter, drifting out into a sunlit alpine meadow, where wildflowers blossomed, and swallows swooped and darted. Shining green and lush, with flower tendrils reaching for sunlight, the vale extended for leagues, surrounded first by snow capped peaks, then gradually descending, and merging with rolling grasslands.

Again soundlessly, Julian, their host, and Vision Master, turned to his fellow journeyers and bowed. They returned the gesture, then applauded the Apprentice, though no sounds came from the clapping hands of ghosts.

Julian reached skyward, as though invoking some new mystery.

But then — the ground vanished.

And they fell like stones into a dark chasm, shrieking without a single sound, thrashing with arms that were able to grasp nothing.

Light fled, leaping into darkness, then the light reentered with subdued, far more real, and powerful tones. They were standing beside a riverbank, watching figures of — themselves. But their phantom shapes were straighter, stronger, robed in majesty, standing tall and fearless. As though impelled by an utterly powerful, distant force, their own forms stepped forward, each merging into his own magical image.

Music, a deep hymn of victory with many chords, surged out over the river, a powerful processional and celebration of triumph. Julian stood beside the riverbank watching as Kalanin and Géla advanced toward the water: they seemed like monarchs of middle years, tall, greying, but still mighty, immeasurably strong, and confident.

Before them stepped a tall young woman, of perhaps fourteen years, so like Kalanin and Géla that she could only have been their daughter. With grey eyes and born with the Gift, possibly a Seeress, she carried a second child, a brother, down to the river to bathe, moving in front of her parents in a stately procession, with the music, a deep hymn of triumph and peace, marking their pace.

Kalanin walked arm in arm with Géla, pride and love surging through him as he watched those on the riverbank: Julian, less youthful, but so fair of countenance, subtle and mighty among the Mortal Magic Wielders; beside him, holding his arm, was a young woman of great beauty and power, whom Kalanin had never before seen.

Galad stood beside Julian, tall, powerful, untouched by age, and about Galad images of fair young women flashed into being then vanished, as though his own vision of the future included many different possibilities. Sebastian and Rafir sat one on each of Galad's shoulders, with the little Familiar's wings flapping, slowly waving in exultation.

Harlond and Rostov stood a little distance from Julian, and yet their figures seemed to fade and flicker, then surge back into view, as though their future presence was less certain.

Watching Kalanin and Géla, the Gift within Julian felt the presence of another human with the Gift at his side, and he turned — to find himself arm in arm with Eléna, lovely as an Elven princess, the daughter of Thorian who had been born with the Gift.

Kalanin and Géla reached the river's edge. They took the child from their daughter's arms, and kneeling beside the smoothly flowing river, they bathed the laughing infant in clear, fresh waters.

In a luxury of sunlit joy and triumph, the scene held for a moment, engraving itself forever in their minds' eyes.

Then the music dimmed and faded. A haze of vapor began slipping over the sun, and from the river, a mist that was more than vapor began to rise from the surging torrents of water.

Huge figures — the forms of pitiless Marids — were approaching the river from the opposite shore.

All the images of maidens flickering around Galad now vanished and the figures of Harlond and Rostov faded, dissolving like smoke before a cool, strong wind.

Huge Marids, four of them, reached the river on the opposite side, and each of the mottled-skinned Demon spawn held a creature as small as a dwarf on its massive shoulder: the Sorcerers — but their bodies were shrunken, while their heads had grown huge and bloated. Only Alcman's figure was vague, as though he alone might avoid the ruinous transformation of the Sorcerers.

Sunlight was blotted out, and as the Marids extended the shrunken forms of the Sorcerers over the water, torrents of vomit spewed gargoyle-like from mouths that had once been human. Steam rose from fouling waters, and a stench of decay and death swept over the river.

Julian reached for his staff, and as he did so, he found Eléna's fading form staring at him, with a look of sorrow, fear, and everlasting loss. Then she was gone.

Géla stood, handing the infant back to her daughter, enabling her to draw her weapons. But as the child left her hands, it whimpered, grew insubstantial, then vanished.

And as clouds of vile steam swept over them, the daughter of Kalanin and Géla began to fade, casting a last beseeching look at her parents: *Why is this happening to me, I who lived so briefly, why am I now reduced to nothingness?*

Then she, too, with her baby brother vanished, leaving Kalanin, Géla, Julian, Galad, Sebastian and Rafir to stand alone on the riverbank. Now, their garments changed, and weapons were drawn; armored and grim, they stood prepared for battle.

On the opposite side of the river, only dimly perceived, three figures came to stare at them across the expanse of fouled water. They were less than half the Marid's height, yet the three still seemed to dwarf the Marids: radiating unchecked, unrivaled power, three Demon Princes regarded the humans with implacable malevolence.

But now there were sounds, first dim, then growing louder: the harsh desperate cry of the eagle, striving to wake them from a dreaming vision that had turned into a nightmare. And as the eagle's cries echoed over the ruined waters, all the images began to blur, became vague, more distant, and then they vanished — into nothingness.

Chapter Nineteen

Rivermeet

RAFIR WOKE IN THE darkness a little distance from the sleeping forms of Julian and Kalanin. On the other side of Julian, Sebastian, too, was awake, and the little Familiar seemed to be shivering from the deep chill of the Gangean range.

"Sebastian," whispered the fox.

"Shh...."

"Get a blanket and come talk to me," Rafir whispered, "then I'll make less noise." Sebastian paused, listening: Géla and Galad had woken earlier, gone out to wait for the eagle, and now in the last hours of darkness, they were beginning to gather their belongings for the next day's journey.

Stepping gingerly around the sleeping forms of Julian and Kalanin, Sebastian found a cloak and came to sit beside Rafir.

"All right," said the fox, "now tell me — slowly, carefully, what those dream visions were all about."

"Somehow the eagle was right, all along," Sebastian murmured in hushed tones, his voice shivering a little with the cold. "But now the Eye is too worried even to boast about it, and he's gone off seeking the mind of Merlin — he's afraid that we've called attention to ourselves, and we'll have to leave here, very, very quickly."

"But what were those dreams all about?" the fox whispered again. "Kalanin muttered something about triumph still being possible. Though if that's triumph — with Sorcerers, Marids, and Demon Princes ready to crush us, I'd hate to see what defeat looks like."

"Images of victory came first, but it seems we'll have to deal first with the Sorcerers and the Marids — then the Demon Princes."

Outside of their partial shelter, it seemed to be growing lighter, but it was only a false dawn, with daybreak still hours away. Through the last hours of darkness, as the great ocean of night grew thin and shallow, the two small beings whispered to each other, hunched together against the cold.

At daybreak, there was still no sign of the eagle. Julian, rose, bone weary and bleary eyed, but with all his withdrawn, ragged, defeated manner cast aside. Carefully, he scraped dry moss from a portion of the shelf, and carved a Divination pattern, erasing it, then fashioning a second and finally a third pattern.

"Down." He looked up at Kalanin. "Down, then southwest to the Zor." He erased his spell work from the ground, carefully replacing the brittle moss scrapings. Géla and Galad had already packed their belongings, and shortly after the first light of day they began their slow descent, moving cautiously through the upper gorges, then down the mountain's spine, gradually quickening their pace as they descended under overcast, dark skies.

·)(·

The eagle was gone for one entire day, then a second. On the third day, as they neared the headwaters of the Zor, the eagle with its broad wings was seen spiraling gently, peacefully downward to the riverbank. Yet when they reached the winged emissary, he was far from peaceful: haggard and wary, the Eye seemed to twitch with tension.

"Again, after a brief interval, the Wizards have been forced to flee," the eagle murmured, with the harsh croaking sounds slipping through even his muted tones. "And that brief respite was so dearly and bitterly earned. The Greater Goddess Auai Kuan Yin renounced the Truce, and cast aside her claims to Godhood, declaring for the Maker. She and all her mightiest servants and legions made war against the Sorcerers and the Marids amid the Ruins of Dahlak. Mourn, Maker Servants, for she is dead now, drifting with only partial awareness through the Temple of Waiting."

Kalanin bowed his head, while Géla stared at the eagle with open shock and disbelief.

"Did I not say that she was kin to the Spirit Lords?" Kalanin said softly. "Yet I wish greatly that she had held back from her last desperate Service — because now, we have hope, real hope, though of what nature we still do not know."

"Again," continued the eagle, "out in the Western Seas, some Power seems to be contending with the Demon Princes, so that storm and turmoil and the ruins of ocean beds are cast to the shorelines of Alantéa the Forerunner. Neither seers, nor priests with the Gift know what power dares to face three of the Demon Princes, and none of the Gods will claim responsibility. I know that it is not the work of Wizards, for they are struggling just to stay alive."

"Yet, at least briefly, you must have brushed against the mind of Merlin," Julian prompted. "What does he wish from us?"

The eagle gazed over the water, twitching in anxiety. "An intersection of power builds at Rivermeet, a place where good and evil will collide. I greatly fear that the Sorcerers know more of this than we do and will be there in force. Yet here is Merlin's bidding: speedy night passages to Rivermeet by watercraft, for you must conceal ourselves during the daylight. Boats have been hidden for us along the riverbank. We should not seek to discover the gift givers, for they greatly desire anonymity: Merlin has many partial, hidden allies among the benevolent Powers, and the Tanu, and the Elf-Lords, and the Sidhe, and the Sires of Trolls. One of these allies has dared much and may well be endangered if the minds of the Sorcerers discover our hidden benefactors. How I wish that I could peer into the Sorcerers' minds, just for a moment! Yet I fear we will learn of their intentions only at Rivermeet."

"Eagle, we are yours to command," Galad said, interrupting the Eye's musings. "We'll journey to Rivermeet, to Nemesis, to Grave's End — wherever we are needed. But first: what did Merlin say about our various visions of victory and defeat? Did he name the Power that brought forth those images?"

The eagle was silent for a moment, then he croaked a short, mirthless laugh. "Power? That was no earthly Power, nor do I need Merlin's mind to identify their author — it was the work of the Maker. Could you not sense that yourself?"

· X ·

Barges, two of them, had been hidden high on the riverbank, buried deeply in the brush. So massive were those flat-bottomed boats, and so far from the water had they been concealed, that it was the hard, sweaty work of a long afternoon before they were floated on the river's edge.

They began the river journey at sunset, poling themselves out into deep waters, then stepping down below to examine the holds. Trade goods had been stored there: tanned hides, ornaments of silver — slightly tarnished, nondescript pottery, and several vats of raw red wine that Galad pronounced barely drinkable.

"With these goods," Galad noted wryly, "there's no danger of our group abandoning the Wizards to become tradesmen." Nevertheless, Galad drained two goblets of red wine before pouring a third into the river's surging waters.

The Eye of Merlin rode at the forefront of the first bark, with Kalanin and Géla. In the second, Galad, Julian, Rafir, and Sebastian followed the lead raft, with Rafir's night vision marking the progress of the first vessel. Each barge held two of their horses, but their steeds were restless and so ill at ease that Galad promised himself that when they took shelter at daybreak, he would find some method of shielding them, a wood frame enclosure, perhaps.

On the first night of their river journey, Sebastian kept watch for stony hazards or movement on the river that might reveal intruders. Movement came only from the skies, but a soft call signaled that their ally, the Eye of Merlin, was floating down to their barge.

"I bring news from the mind of Merlin," the eagle croaked softly, "news for you to pass on to your human allies when they wake."

"Let me wake Rafir," Sebastian said, heading for their sleeping hold. "I trust our combined memories better than mine alone."

Once the sleepy fox was out into the overcast night, the eagle continued. "Here are the insights and fears of Merlin concerning the Marids; he refers to the birthing of Marids as broods. The first brood of monstrosities numbered twelve, their mottled skins scarred by the magic of Merlin. The second birthing of Marids consisted of five broods of twelve for a total of sixty, so we now face more than seventy monstrosities, and we have not managed to damage even one."

As the eagle flapped away into the night sky, Rafir muttered, "What did I say about those visions not being much more grim than hopeful?"

"A faint hope is better than no hope," Sebastian said, shaking his slight head. "Anyway, it's time for your shift. With the Eye's bit of nasty news, that alone should keep you wide awake."

So Rafir paced round and around the deck, under a night sky speckled with traces of stars, while the infrequent firelight of scattered human settlements slipped into view then passed behind, as they surged south on heavy water wheeled chariots.

·)(·

With the first light of dawn, they sought shelter along the riverbank, casting themselves down in surrounding woodlands, then slipping into fitful sleeps. Sebastian found himself awake, unable to sleep in the warm, moist air where insects thrived, and he busied himself batting gnats and horseflies from the sleeping forms around him.

Also restless, the Eye of Merlin stood amid tall reeds, staring southeast toward Rivermeet, as though seeking a message, a signal that had been missed, or lost, or never sent.

·)(·

Julian watched the shimmering lights of unnamed, unrecorded townships as they ebbed and flowed, and their watercraft surged through the pitch black waters of the river. His thoughts drifted, as they had with every breathing space, back to their visions and the Vision Master.

Even in uttermost victory and complete triumph, there had been no image of his parents, not even a flicker, or a hint of their proud, strong faces. Thus, the Maker, with implacable justice and everlasting mercy, had shown them images, not of what their hearts desired, but of what truly might still be accomplished. So, just as he had learned from his first years, some matters would have to be postponed until the Awakening.

But how, then, had the daughter of Thorian been cast so strongly into their dreaming visions? Would the Demon Princes yield her and make peace? Or, far more likely, and almost beyond his worst nightmares, would they be forced to journey to the underwater Isle of the Demons to rescue her from the Ancient Adversaries? It was a task that the greatest Powers of the Mid-World might fear to undertake. Why then would Julian and the others, the lesser pawns of the Wizards, be sent on such a task?

The river gave no answer, only continuing its southward surge, preoccupied with its epic quest toward the salty, chilled, watery arms of the great Atlantic.

· ⅄ ·

Kalanin's eyes searched overhead, hunting through the darkness for the shape of eagle wings. How strange it must be to have the eagle's piercing sight, to see so far, to follow and understand patterns of sorcery and enchantment. Had the eagle fully understood how completely he had loved his own children as seen in their dream vision, who had been so briefly alive, and how he had ached when his daughter's pleading face had dissolved into mist? And could the eagle name the princess who had stood so vibrantly at Julian's side? There was one possible answer, but its implications filled him with a great fear of drowning.

From out of the darkness with a *whoosh* of wings, the eagle broke into his reverie. Simultaneously, the snap of a bowstring could be heard, with cries of pain coming out of the darkness.

"Galad launches arrows at river pirates," the eagle croaked in muted tones, "are you armed as he is?"

"No." Kalanin could hear them now, the sounds of muffled paddles speeding sleek watercraft toward them. Géla was racing for their barge's hold. He followed as they pulled light chain mail and swords from their stores. Outside came cries of surprise and fear as the eagle raked at the first pirates trying to board their vessel.

Then they were back on the deck, swords slashing at a surprised boarding party. Armed with long daggers, faces blackened for night raids, their attackers backed toward their boats, crying out in shock, watching comrades fall like scythed grasses that spurted red blood.

In moments, the river pirates were repelled, numbers halved, their night's work in ruins. Kalanin and Géla heaved bodies into the water, where they floated poorly, if at all. Several of those heavily wounded by Galad's bowshots drifted, moaning, in the barges' wake, but after a brief time, these fell silent, leaving only the night sounds of surging water as the great river carried them toward Rivermeet.

·) (·

They pulled up short of Rivermeet, unable to reach it during the fourth night of their river journey. Daylight shelter that was free from human intrusion was becoming harder to find, but finally they discovered a marshy slip of an island that stood surrounded by decaying grey trees. They rested there, trying, with little success, to sleep in the overly warm holds of their barges.

Unwilling to wait for the gloom of dusk, they set out for Rivermeet just after sunset. Not knowing what to expect, they hoped to find allies or at least clear instructions left by the Wizards. Just outside of Rivermeet, the Zor merged first with a lesser river, then the two rivers encountered the powerful Saugaram. As the three rivers thrashed white foam against one another, a time of sweaty, heavy paddling took place before they were able to push far enough east to reach Rivermeet. In early evening they were still paddling and poling hard, hooking into a sheltered estuary, where scores of pilings and the long docks of Rivermeet reached out into sluggish waters.

For Kalanin and those who were Giftless, Rivermeet was a lush, dense, teeming city. Standing on the edges of a flood plain, most of its older buildings stood raised on pillars of poured stone: temples, counting houses, ancient inns, and the dwellings of the wealthy, all seemed raised on massive stilts, surrounded by much lower, more recent wooden houses of the poor and recently arrived. Still, many of the lower dwellings threatened by floods seemed long established, secure, and well lit. Around many of the stone pillars surrounding them, were ornaments, tapestries, or decorative carvings, as though the floods had been kept at bay for a generation.

For those without the Gift, Rivermeet seemed rich, teeming, expanding in many directions, filled with adventure and mystery.

But for those with the Gift, Rivermeet seemed like a sandcastle under the shadow of a great wave. Sorcerous energies were flocking toward the city like clouds surging into a powerful thunderstorm.

"Merlin, my Master," murmured the eagle, as they docked, "choose well, this time, at the last." Then the eagle went below, hiding with Rafir and Sebastian in a deep hold that had probably been built for smuggling goods.

As they lashed their barges to the torchlit quays, bored clerks with sleepy eyes straggled toward them with schedules of fees, and taxes and temple tithes. But the Harbor Master waved the clerks aside and approached the newcomers himself, searching their faces and examining their goods in a nervous, haphazard fashion. Shorter than Julian, the Harbor Master was balding, paunchy, beyond midyears, a man whose serious, busy life had recently been greatly shaken.

"Rumors gather at Rivermeet, as always," said the Harbor Master, his eyes darting from face to face like a pair of frightened shrews. "We hear that the creatures known as 'Hooters' are moving toward Rivermeet, while those pledged to the Three Hands have declared themselves openly, and the Priests no longer force them to leave the city. Do you know anything of these matters? Are there any who have been born with the Gift among you?"

"Hooters?" Julian questioned. "Do you speak of Marids, the huge creatures with boar's tusks curling from their jaws?"

The Harbor Master watched them narrowly, naked fear now showing openly in his eyes. "And so, you know of them...."

"Only as you do," Galad said easily, "by rumor and horror stories. As for being born with the Gift, we are lovers first, and fighters if need be. Of Magicians, we have little knowledge of them and avoid them always. Note the bloodstains on our barge decks if you have time, then join us for a cup of admittedly imperfect wine."

The Harbor Master, feet dancing in twitching uncertainty, stared out at the grey wood pilings and sluggish, swirling waters. "It is not that we bar those born with the Gift, it's just that the Priests and Adepts and Seers have all fled so that no one with any sense of magic remains in Rivermeet."

Torchlights hung extended from the quays, looming over dark waters, and now its light flickered over the master's forehead where drops of sweat beaded and slipped down into his cloak.

As the Harbor Master, wiped sweat from his forehead, he muttered, "Danger, misunderstood, unseen, is all about us, but what are we, the Giftless, to do? I am imperfect, bribable, haughty, sometimes even stupid — but do I need to die for these things? And what of my family? If I am guilty, they are many times more perfect than —" Julian put his hand over the sagging shoulders of their fearful host, then spoke into his mind.

We are neither the forerunning clouds nor the storm. The Stormbringers, the Sorcerers and the Marids, are almost upon you. Flee now with your family. In payment for your own perceived flaws, I ask you to also save your partial friends — and even those that you count as enemies. Do this in the Maker's Name.

"So, you are Servants of the Maker," murmured the Harbor Master, eyes glancing around to make certain no one could hear him. "May the Gods and their Priests forgive me, but your people were always clear of sight, and tellers of truth also. So, I will pack and depart at dawn, together with any that will listen to me."

"Leave now, even with your family's midnight wailings and lamentations," Julian said softly. "Wait at the farthest outskirts if you wish; it may be that the Sorcerers and the Marids will focus only briefly on Rivermeet."

The Harbor Master bowed once, then hesitated as though anxious to speak a defense of his long life that had been so filled with compromises, but he fell silent, then leaped to the docks, and began a shambling run up the quays.

Kalanin tapped on the hold, and Sebastian, Rafir, and the eagle emerged, staring warily down the long piers that led to the harbor front. Beyond the warehouses and open yards, the city sparkled with many lights, and night breezes carried faint sounds of scores of voices, their distant echoes hinting at laughter.

"Looks inviting, doesn't it," Galad muttered to Kalanin, "but fortunately — or unfortunately — we have those born with the Sight among us who will tell us about all the dangers lurking inside of Rivermeet."

"An intersection of many forces," the eagle rasped.

"With all participants heavily disguised by illusion," Julian added, "so that even I cannot tell whether Sorcerers or Wizards are nearby. We should also proceed in other than our true forms...." His voice trailed off then merged with spell tones as the Apprentice wove dense strands of illusions over them.

Kalanin watched as Galad and Géla shortened, becoming wider and bowlegged, with tangled unkempt dark hair; now they looked like nearby river pirates, who must be little welcome in this city of tradesmen.

"We may well be hung before midnight," Kalanin murmured, and Julian nodded, his chanting voice shifting their ages and sizes. The three thinned, with leaner legs, but they became even shorter, and older. Kalanin and Galad became bald, with sagging stomachs, while Julian kept for himself a lean, grizzled, sardonic look.

Géla stared down on her dowdy, grey haired form and cursed under her breath. "I'll find some way to repay you for this, Julian."

"You have not seen fit to include us, Apprentice," said the eagle.

"It's beyond my power to disguise you properly as humans, and the presence of non-humans, in any guise, might easily advertise our presence."

"But *I* can come," Rafir interjected.

"Not this time, Rafir," Julian said, with a brief, sad smile. "An image comes from the Gift, of many beings, thrashing and stumbling in panic. You would likely be trampled. This once, wait for us here."

"Do you truly believe," rasped the eagle, "that you will be free to return here after a brief expedition? Apprentice, if you survive, you will be fleeing for your lives, racing far from this city, and you will not be sliding away on a barge, riding a sluggish wash of water. No, we will await you, but my own Sight will anticipate your movements. Look for us when you flee for your lives."

· ✕ ·

Their horses shied from the unfamiliar, transformed riders that sought to mount them, but a few words from Julian calmed them. Then the four dowdy humans were astride wobbly horses, moving slowly from the partially lighted docks, into the dark, shadowy warehouse area. Lightly armed sentinels lurked near darkened doorways, moving quietly through the shadows, ready to call down the night watch should fire, or theft arise. Galad wondered what sort of alarm the sentinels would sound if and when the Marids emerged from torchlit shallows and stomped toward the teeming city.

· X ·

Cloaked in shadows, the eagle watched as the four humans turned into the winding streets and vanished; but with his powerful Sight, he followed the riders as they moved toward the city's heart. On either side of him, Rafir and Sebastian were growing restless, fidgety; to calm them, the eagle began recounting the images and sounds brought by his Sight — as an adult under stress might tell two children a tense, grim, bedtime story.

· X ·

It was early evening with starshine growing steadily brighter as they passed beyond the docks and warehouses and on into the city's winding, narrow streets. In reality, it was two cities, thought Galad. One was low, a youthful place with wood frame buildings jostling against one another, surrounded by scattered saplings and fruit trees that rustled gently in the evening breezes.

A second city loomed above them, of heavy beams and masonry resting on enormous pillars of poured stone. Another forest of trees also hovered overhead: huge, craggy, gnarled growths that creaked and groaned in the upper breezes; and some of their root systems had fought free of huge tubs, extending twisted, groping fingers down onto the flood plain.

For Julian, there was a third, almost invisible city, of masked, shifting sorcery, with heavily shielded Mid-World Spies and Emissaries moving from the city's outermost edges into the city's center. Above them, Divination Portals fashioned by the Gods were slipping into place, so that the stars overhead wavered and shimmered.

To Kalanin, watching every corner warily, only one thing warned of danger: the temples above them were dark and silent, and those entering or leaving did so with furtive scurrying movements, as though the Gods had abandoned Rivermeet.

For Galad, all the city sounds were welcome, inviting: mealtime festivities, the clinking of glasses, bursts of laughter, voices raised in loud celebration. But at his side, the Sword was beginning to hum, in an invocation of coming death and destruction.

"So, O wise and crafty leader," Géla murmured to Julian, "have you chosen a dining place or our night's lodging?" To her disgust, her own voice croaked, with tones that wavered and whined. Julian shook his head, and under his breath, he continued whispering his seeking spell. Turning left at the next intersection, they wove their way east toward the city's innermost heart.

·){ ·

"A great gathering place," the eagle croaked in hushed tones, *"an inn; an intersection.... I can almost see its name...."* The Eye's audience, Sebastian and Rafir, were listening to Merlin's Familiar, their faces tight with tension.

·){ ·

"Stormhaven," Julian murmured, staring across the avenue with his head tilted upward as he examined the huge building. "Though it's unlikely to be a haven for us."

"But there'll be wine, a half decent goblet," Galad said softly, though cheerfully, "before we breathe our last. Let's go."

Julian shook his head. "Let's take a moment, to make certain that our exit will be as quick as our entry."

Stormhaven was immense, larger than any of Rivermeet's temples, as the building's many wings were supported by massive beams resting on pillars of stone; and around each pillar, wooden stairs curled, with high banisters protecting the impaired or unwary from pitching helplessly out into the darkness. Beneath the upper building, storage rooms held masses of provisions. While on the eastern side, neighing sounds could be heard: stables for the travelers' horses.

They dismounted, crossing the street warily. One drunken party swirled down the circling staircase and spilled out into the street, laughing as they continued to turn around as though made dizzy by their descent; while above the revelers, unnoticed dark shadowy shapes were twisting around the building's upper peaks.

As they crossed the street, Julian whispered charm words under his breath, touching each of their horse's foreheads, then their reins. Within the stables, they lashed their horses to hitching posts, passing coins to the stable hands.

Then, as befitting their aged, dowdy forms, they mounted the circular stairs slowly, pausing at mid-level — and here Julian touched each of them, whispering soundlessly into their minds.

Our horses will come when called, and their bindings will unleash themselves. If we must depart in haste, only cling to me and we will fly down — after a fashion.

They resumed their slow climb, moving to one side as yet another group clattered noisily down the stairs, singing some off-key tune that only the revelers could recognize. Then the four were at the doors, tentative, hesitant, like grandparents at some unsettled gathering that threatened to deteriorate into wild courtship rite.

·) (·

"Houma is inside Stormhaven!" raged the eagle, wings flaring. *"He is shielded from Julian but not from me! O Merlin, my Master, why have you led us to this place?"*

·) (·

Noise and smoke and fumes from wine surrounded them as they entered the inn called Stormhaven. Their eyes adjusted quickly, for the interior was sparsely lit, with scattered vat candles casting pale shifting lights over scores of tables. Meek, hunched, and dowdy, the four picked their way to an empty table that was set against a far wall. Youths gave way to them, moving chairs aside with exaggerated courtesy, while others laughed openly at the meandering, slow passage of their elders.

"Old age is indeed a shipwreck," Géla murmured as they sat. Their table was pulled away from the wall, so that all four sat facing outward, backs against broad beams with seams of mortar.

·) (·

"Others have found their way within," rasped the eagle. *"The Emissaries of the Gods. Yet we know that these forces will be no match for Houma — Wizards, you can never rely on the Gods or their Servants!"*

· ❌ ·

After a short wait, wine was set before them, with coins passing from Kalanin's hands to those of a sour faced servant who frowned openly at the prospect of serving such an unpromising, dowdy group. Galad sat back, hoping for a moment's relaxation, but at his side, the Tarnished Sword was beginning to stir, humming softly with threats of violence.

Kalanin sipped wine, then drew on his pipe, while his eyes searched the sea of faces that surrounded them on three sides. Most spoke animatedly among themselves or argued between sips of foam. Others watched on warily, groups of them mostly silent, as though waiting for instructions from their masters; and still others, each of them alone, watched on with eyes darting from face to face. No sure way existed to identify those cloaked by illusion, or those serving the Three Hands. Kalanin turned to Julian the Apprentice, their leader in matters of magic.

Julian watched on silently, with the Gift searching everywhere around him. Many of those nearby were hidden, shielded by sorcery, waiting for a sign…. And as for a sign, there was none…except now in the distance, in another wing of the inn, music was beckoning, the soft tones of the lute, with a woman's voice, raised in song.

· ❌ ·

"Those serving the Three Hands have slipped into the inn, disguised and well-armed," the eagle murmured. *"As I feared, a trap has been set and —"*

The eagle broke off, for now, faraway echoes were sweeping across the swollen, merged rivers: the booming sounds of Marids striding toward Rivermeet.

· ⋊ ·

Julian rose, wine glass in one hand, his other hand signaling to his companions. As they meandered across the broad hall, other patrons, singly, or in twos or threes, began to drift toward the music. As Julian turned into a second, larger hall, the sounds of music grew louder, the woman's tones clearer — and now he recognized the singer's voice: it belonged to a friend, one first encountered in the early part of his journey, a time that seemed an age ago.

· ⋊ ·

The eagle panted hoarsely from the exertion of lifting Rafir. Sebastian flew beside them, able for the first time to keep pace with the eagle. The three settled on an upper roof then peered down from the building's edge, staring down at the harbor.

From out of the water a single Marid emerged, immense and fearless, towering over their barge, with red torchlight glistening over damp, mottled skin. Effortlessly, the Marid tore the decking from their river craft. Peering into the hold and finding nothing, the Marid then turned and looked up — staring directly at the panting Wizard's servant, the Eye of Merlin.

· ⋊ ·

Maeglan, the powerful Seeress, was singing in a language Julian could not understand. She had aided Julian at the beginning of his journey, then had grown mortally afraid that she would be destroyed: Houma and Un-Maurag had been seeking Julian and had become aware of Maeglan. Why had she not hidden herself away as she had promised? Now she played serenely, sitting on a small, upraised dais, staring into the distance as scores of onlookers who were masked by illusion crowded toward her. Why was she endangering herself?

Slowly, almost imperceptibly, Maeglan's song changed, the music growing stronger and her language merging into the common tongue of Alantéa.

Voice rising in pleasure and joy, she sang of the five great Lords of Dragons, how they grew in wisdom and might, sweeping through galaxies in their Quest for the Maker. Images grew in Julian's mind of beings grown complex beyond the dreams of Dragons, moving at many times light's speed, each of them now encompassing more energy and power than a single star system.

And she sang of the Maker, waiting at the center of all understanding, watching the approach of these brilliant Lords of Dragons with a joy that radiated throughout the universe.

As they, Servants of the Maker, listened with pleasure and delight, others around them began murmuring first in low tones, then louder:

"Scum licking slave of a long lost, feeble deity...."

"Break this off! The Gods do not permit such talk of the Departed."

While a third snarled at the second speaker, "Your Gods also have grown as feeble as demented ghosts. Soon there will be New Gods." The forms of both speakers shimmered as each struggled with the other's mask of illusion.

Maeglan played on, rising to her feet, voice lifting above the mockery and abuse.

· ℳ ·

"Now it will burst over us," croaked the eagle, "like a flood." As the huge Marid strode toward them, the Eye of Merlin grasped Rafir and flew toward the city's center, with Sebastian fluttering a little distance behind them.

· ℳ ·

Abuse and more than abuse was hurled at Maeglan: spittle streaked her face and shoulders, then the contents of wine glasses blinded her. The strong arms of Kalanin and Galad grasped Julian from either side, yet the Apprentice could feel the anger mounting in them, too.

Finally, a heavy ewer was hurled, striking the lute from Maeglan's hands. Blood spurted from one hand, spilling over her broken fingers.

Stepping back, she cried in a great voice: "Julian! Julian! Stay back but heed me! Your quest was not in vain! Another being knows the Truce Terms! A Sentinel rests upon —"

A dark hand twisted, and Maeglan was frozen in silence.

"So *that* was the lure for the Apprentice," Houma murmured, and again his black, malignant hand twisted, wresting illusion masks from those beings standing near the dais.

Emissaries of the Gods tried to flee but could only move a few paces before striking unseen barriers. Maeglan fell, twisting in pain, to the floor.

"Let her be, Houma!" Julian called out, staff clenched in both hands.

"Houma, the Sword calls out, singing for your blood!" Galad cried. Kalanin and Géla drew weapons, but more slowly: there would never be children, not even one, only a stand, here against the mighty Sorcerer.

On the floor, Maeglan ceased to stir, as life slipped from her frail, soft form.

"Houma! Is no torment enough for you?" Julian cried. "This time —"
He broke off, for behind him, a powerful but gentle hand was pulling him
back.

He turned and stared into the strained, weary face of Balardi. The
Wizard's eyes were bloodshot, his gold and grey beard in tatters — and yet
his grip was like stone.

Houma laughed in malice and contempt. "I wondered if we would also
trap the whale among the minnows! And the bait was pitiful in comparison
to the catch!" Houma's hand twisted again, and a second figure stepped to
Houma's side: Alcman, mightiest of the Sorcerers.

"Get away from this place," Balardi murmured to Julian. "Flee — now."

"You will *not* stand alone," Galad said, feeling the Sword's power, and
his own anger was icy, sharp, and grim.

"But I am not alone," Balardi replied softly, and there came a twisting
of shadows, like the swirling of fallen oak leaves in some faraway ghost
forest; Thorian emerged.

"Leave," Thorian said to Julian, "now, while there is still time."

Houma's withered hand surged with dark power and the inn's massive
roof hurtled out into the night.

And now, with the night air flooding into the roofless inn, they could
hear the hooting and booming of Marids.

"If you do not die at our hands," Houma snarled, "then the Marids are
certain to destroy you."

Julian felt the spells surging from Houma, and he pulled away. Galad
pushed in front of Julian, shattering the invisible barrier with one sweeping
slash of the Tarnished Sword.

Bands of men sought to oppose them, but they were shaken to the
ground as spell shocks vibrated through Stormhaven.

One being still blocked their passage: a servant of some dark God, it stood in front of them, all illusions cast aside. Now it stood as a vortex of spinning energies, cloaked by dark shadows, with tentacles probing outward from the edges of its shadowy essences. Neither face nor eyes were visible, yet somehow the creature was regarding them intently. They paused in front of it.

"Hear me," Julian called out. "Tell your dark Master that the Truce is at an end. Sorcerers and Marids —" He broke off, for tentacles leaped from the shadows, swirling around him, grasping his body and his staff. A second set of appendages coiled around Galad and his Tarnished Sword.

The Sword whined in frustration, while Julian's Gift reached out and grasped the Emissary with a clutching spell. Behind and around them, beings were dying at the Sorcerers' hands or fleeing from oncoming Marids. Their escape hatch was closing.

Kalanin grasped a massive plank bench and smashed the shadowy Emissary aside, while Géla chopped and stabbed at its tentacles until they were all severed. Then they sped around it, scrambling for an exit, slashing through any humans who struggled to stop them.

Out in the night, the inn was creaking as it swayed with the violence of battle magic, and the night air echoed with the booming sounds of oncoming Marids. Géla locked her arms around Julian's chest, while Kalanin and Galad each caught hold of Julian by the shoulder. Julian called out spell words, and they hurled themselves from the inn's upper balcony, fluttering to the ground like a cluster of wounded moths.

They landed heavily, rolling through the dust. Down one avenue a huge Marid could be seen, pushing, toppling, rending, as it raged toward Stormhaven. Red fires were beginning to burn against the night sky as Marids smashed through wood frame buildings. Alarms were pealing through the city, but the residents were climbing up into tall, stone sanctuaries that would no longer save them.

"Do not seek the heights!" Julian called out, then his voice grew louder, charged with powerful sorcerous energies. "Flee the Marids on foot! You will find no safety in tall buildings!"

Their horses came when called. Mounted, seeking an exit far from Marids, their eyes turned back to the inn called Stormhaven, watching as bodies pitched, shrieking, from its heights. And now, its foundations crumbling from the warfare of complex magics, the great inn was toppling, crashing into ruin. Hesitating, uncertain, they turned and began riding east.

"To me!" the eagle croaked, panting in the darkness. "Merlin calls upon you to escape once more from a ruin of Marids." The Eye of Merlin lumbered into view, clutching Rafir, with Sebastian fluttering behind him.

They followed Merlin's winged emissary as sounds of terror and ruin echoed all around them.

"Flee! Get away!" Julian cried to the city's people, his enchanted voice lifting over the sounds of destruction. "Go far from here! Forget all your gold and jewels!"

"One day, O Marids," Géla called out into the night. "One day we will no longer flee, and we shall turn on you with weapons that will do you harm!"

"Yes!" cried the eagle, panting, but his voice also was filled with defiance. "Yes, Sorcerers and Marids may rule in Rivermeet. But complete victory will evade them until they have dealt forever — with the Wizards!"

Chapter Twenty

On the Slopes of Mount Evergrey

RAFIR SLIPPED SILENTLY THROUGH the forest glade, passing through shadow and sunlight, watching insects as they buzzed through the shadows or burrowed into decaying plant matter. Above him, the sun shone brightly, peacefully over Alantéa the Forerunner, as though Sorcerers and Marids and Demon Princes were faraway, forgotten tales of horror.

Where were they? Another night of flight filled with terror had been interrupted — not by dawn and hidden shelter — but by passing into a different climate, a different season, and an early morning rather than daybreak. Rafir lifted his head, listening; he was close enough to hear Julian's voice, but not near enough to understand his words. All the answers to his questions lay back in the glade's heart, with his companions and not with the insects' sunlit dance. With a shrug and a small sigh, the fox followed his trail back toward his allies and their Master.

For a long time, the Wizard had sat motionless, listening closely to Julian's tale as the story rose and faltered, then picked up again. All the others had avoided interrupting or prompting Julian, sitting in silence as the Apprentice finished the story of the Truce Quest.

"And so, in the end, I broke, Merlin, my Master. In despair, I looked only for release into the Long Sleep. I am sorry that I was not greater, more equal to the task." Julian's grey eyes remained fixed on the form of the hunched, seated Wizard.

"You are not alone in this, Julian," Kalanin added softly, speaking for the first time. "Twice during our struggle, I've looked for an exit, an escape. And even now, with the imprint of a Vision from the Maker engraved on my mind, even now I cannot promise that some future event will not cause me to fail and falter and seek to free myself once again."

"Yet, neither of you *did* fail," said the Wizard, looking up. "To have fought through torrents of nightmare sorcery, and then to have reached the Vale of Whispers and forced the speaking of the Truce Terms was a triumph. To have hurled the Sorcerers and their legions from the League was a triumph, and we the Wizards shared in that triumph. If any have failed, it was the Ancient Servants who have permitted a state of affairs that would allow the Adversaries to triumph.

"What you felt was despair, a hopelessness, when forces beyond your comprehension ripped victory from your desperate, outstretched hands. Even I have felt despair; standing before Gravengate with our League in its death agony, it would have been easy for me to have perished, raging at Sorcerers and Marids. But that was not the Maker's will, nor did He promise that our tasks would be easy. Indeed, our tasks have been bitter, brutal, almost hopeless from the start."

"Yet, you must know now that we are not without hope," Géla said. She stood, looking down on Merlin's hunched form. "I confess myself to have been a faint follower, a vague believer, yet now I perceive that the Maker sees all with the clearest of visions and even if He has chosen not to interfere, He alone is a Power; the others, in the end, are all illusions."

"All other Powers may grow beyond illusion," said the Wizard, "if they seek or serve Him. That was the last message of Maeglan as she sang of the Lords of Dragons and their quest for the Maker through the starry universe."

"Maeglan sleeps the Long Sleep, Merlin, our Master," Galad added. "Yet we assume — or hope — that your fellow Wizards have escaped from the Sorcerers and the Marids."

"They remain in flight," Merlin replied, "though their danger lessens with each passing moment — it was hazardous, though vital, that Alcman be drawn away from me, even for a short while, for he alone has a grasp of temporal magic.

"We are all learning, Wizards and Sorcerers alike. Before the coming of the Sorcerers and the Marids, during our civil strife, I noted how the stresses and strains of powerful magics at war with one another hurled Sebastian and Rafir into a far future city. After, I struggled to learn a little about forces that might tamper with time. As a result of my learning, we are seated here in an eddy, a backwater of time. Alcman, too, understood the interplay of temporal magic; he alone might have been able to follow us to this place, yet I believe that our trail is now very, very cold."

Merlin took a deep breath before continuing. "Here, during this lull, we will seek to find a gap in the barrier that has kept us from those Truce Terms — a barrier fashioned by the Ancient Powers, but now maintained by a strange alliance of Gods and Demons, Sorcerers and Marids.

"Through Julian, we shall now relive, reenact the telling of the Truce Terms. Then all of us will consider these conditions with great care, to see if there is not some way to call upon the Gods to confront our foes. Julian, you need not yourself endure this reenactment: so much pain remains within you, that it might be better if you lay healing under an enchanted sleep."

"There will be time enough for healing later," Julian said, drawing a deep breath. "I will watch with you. Begin now if you wish."

"Hold for a moment, Julian," Kalanin said. "Merlin, if our minds and understanding are to be involved, there are two questions that many of us are likely to share. Firstly, why have the Gods not taken it upon themselves to invoke the Truce against our foes? Surely, they must realize that the Truce is at an end. Secondly, where are the authors of our ruin, the Demon Princes? Why have they called upon other beings of power to fight their battles? Why have they not themselves come forward openly to rule Alantéa and the Mid-World of the Truce?"

Merlin laughed to himself, a short, sad, fading sigh. "If I understood those mysteries, we might begin to dream of victory. I know them not, but in answer to your questions, I will conjecture:

"The Gods must fear the Sorcerers and the Marids for their alliance was forged as a weapon to destroy the Gods, so that even mighty Zôs or one-eyed Wotan, or Ra or dark souled Set might be sent drifting like a mindless Shade down to the Temple of Waiting if they fought openly with Marids supported by Sorcerers.

"As for the Demon Princes, they may fear the Gods, for a goodly number of their own kind live transformed within the Truce. Also, of the Great Gods and lesser Powers of the Mid-World, there are many scores, hundreds, perhaps more than a thousand. So, the Demon Princes must bide their time, perhaps fashioning an alliance of many different sorcerous beings.

"But aside from these likely reasons, the Demons and the Gods must fear matters that are now outside of our understanding. Why else is there an enormous struggle beneath the ocean's surface, with stormy ruins still cast upon our shores? What has held back the grim, brutal deities such as Marduk, or Quarezokziil, or Moloch of the Endless Fires? These things we may never know. Are you answered, Kalanin?"

"Partly answered, but well answered, Lord," Kalanin said, smiling. "If all else fails, I will seek you out at the Awakening. Then, I think, all of Earth's secrets will be open to you."

"Whatever we now learn or fail to learn, I am ready." Julian drew himself together. "I will yield the Truce Terms to you, Merlin, my Master. May they be of greater use to you than they have been to me."

Uncertainly, Sebastian went to stand beside Julian, touching his cloak, staring at Merlin with anxious eyes.

Merlin stood, but then his face turned skyward, watching as their sentry floated downward: serene, unhurried, the eagle came to rest beside his Master.

"Our once cold scent has now been completely washed away," said the eagle. "Alcman will never find us."

Merlin drew a deep breath and hesitated for a moment, watching breezes and golden light brushing over the glade's wildflowers, then he murmured, "We have stolen a moment of peace from never-was in a long-ago never-when. Remember this time when grief crowds in upon us, once again." Leaning forward, the Wizard reached out to Julian, with an almost inaudible murmur of a spell passing through his lips.

· X ·

Slowly, the glade began to darken, fade and blur. Then, as the light rays reassembled, the glade vanished, and they stood watching recreated images of the City of the Truce. From a distance came sounds of Marids hammering at the gates, disturbing the deep, welcoming harmonies that had greeted Julian as he passed through the Vale of Whispers.

All the watchers stood together, Sebastian on Julian's shoulder; the great eagle resting on Merlin, seeming to become one with his Wizard

Master; while Galad, Kalanin, and Géla peered into the Wizard's vision quest. Again, Marids hammered at the gates as the images of the ancient Demons and Seraphs, Dragons and Spirit Lords began to form.

Before them, to the right, was the wary, fearful image of Julian the Apprentice, a struggling, slender human who stared at the images of Ancient Powers with awe, his own frail body cringing as Marids pounded at the gates.

And before them, just to their left, now stood the recreated Ancient Powers, Servants and Adversaries, gleaming with hues of silver and gold, smoldering red and green with envy. Merlin and the watchers outside of time formed one side of a triangle, with Julian's cringing image a second point, and the Ancient Powers at the third.

We are watching a reenactment of a reenactment, thought Kalanin. *The greatest of the Ancient Secrets is being revealed to me, and I remain astonished. Yet what I feel most intensely is horror and pity for the Apprentice. Look at his face! Like Sebastian, I can hardly draw my own eyes away from him. How could I have indulged in so much self-pity while the Apprentice bore a much greater burden?*

Merlin shook his head in sorrow as the Ancient Servants and the Ancient Adversaries contended with words, dueling over the fate of Alantéa and the Far Lands. *Seek the Maker,* Merlin thought, *then all of you will gain power beyond the imagination of any Mid-World being. But now, let us watch, watch to see.*

For now, the Ancient Powers were moving beyond their long struggle, most of them prepared to enter into the Truce.... And at this point, Adonai, greatest of Seraphs, called on those bound for the Maker Quest to join him, to shield themselves from the transforming energies of the Mid-World of the Truce.

Then the others, linking energies of good and evil, blending powers both subtle and raw, began to speak the Truce Terms:

A chorus of voices spoke as one: "All Powers who stand outside of the Truce will depart from Earth; all others alive in Alantéa on this day are one with the Truce. Our War is over."

A Prince of Demons, voice low, rumbling with power: "Each of the Powers shall build his own domain, a place where that Power will be Master. None shall occupy the soil of Alantéa, the wellspring of energy."

A Seraph: "Nor shall any of us within the Truce, Ancient Servant or Adversary, forge an alliance with other Powers. If conflict ensues, each Power will act alone, within the Truce Terms."

A Lord of Dragons: "The Creatures Indomitable are outside of the Truce, unchanged, yet they are free to forge their own domains or dwell in Alantéa, as they wish."

A Spirit Lord: "The Powers are free to protect mortals, by shielding them within their own domains, or by fashioning havens for them in Alantéa."

A Seraph: "The Truce of the Mid-World is greater than the Truce Makers, and if the Truce is broken its power will be called against the offender. And even before the Truce is challenged, our greatest Emissaries must be free to act in concert to avoid a Truce breaking, or to enforce our wills against those outside our pact."

Interrupting this re-telling of the Truce Terms, with great rending sounds, the Marids burst down the gates, and all the harmonies of the Mid-World of the Truce were shattered into whining noises.

Maker! Just one more moment! cried the mind of Merlin.

But from within the circle of power, a Prince of Demons spoke: "Yet the Truce shall not be called down lightly; there are words that will invoke the Powers — these shall not be spoken here but are now known only to us within this circle of power."

Pity humanity; fear the Creatures Indomitable, Merlin thought. *But now they were close to the crux, barring knowledge of the Truce Terms, and the blocked counterspell of Adonai. Which of the Powers might check such a spell, and how had they gained the strength to do so?*

Merlin shook his head gravely. *Julian, my gentle servant, my foster son, it pains me to watch you twist in turmoil, but now let us see how, or why, Adonai was barred from countering this twisted Truce Term.*

The Great Seraph, image unshaken by a storm tide of transforming energies, turned to meet Merlin's eyes, and with a wave of his hand, the noise of the Mid-World of the Truce diminished, and the destructive sounds of the Marids became as faint as a distant whisper.

From across a void of many thousands of years, Adonai spoke directly, distinctly, to Merlin and those surrounding him. ***"Know, greatest of Mortal Magic Wielders, that the Maker's Sentinel, Alanthéa, the Tree of Heaven, abides near the topmost peak of Mount Evergrey. If the TIME is indeed upon you, Alanthéa will yield the Truce Terms to your Far Traveled Servants."***

·)X(·

Sunlight swept through the glade once again, with the silence of slow, rustling leaves settling over them.

"So, for many ages, the voice of Adonai was stilled," Julian murmured, "waiting until this time to speak to Merlin, our Master. And so, the Quest for the Truce was not in vain."

"At least there is hope," Kalanin said, "though it seems that our Quest will take us to the Slopes of Mount Evergrey. But, Merlin, my master, so much was happening that I almost missed the last portion of the Truce Terms, how the Adversaries and the Servants each yielded the greatest of their Ancient Secrets. To free the Demon Princes from their underwater imprisonment was one such, and the other, a haven for the Servants? What of that?"

The old Wizard's mind seemed to return, with great slowness, from an infinite distance.

"The Hall of the Dreamers," he murmured, "though I understand, as the Adversaries did not, that these are barred from conflict or warfare. The Dreamers might be called, but they would never take up weapons against the Sorcerers and the Marids, for the Gods must rise to do battle.

"But further I can now guess how the Truce became broken: one of the Ancient Adversaries, a Dark Lord, whose form was altered by the Truce, but who was never reconciled to it, found some device that freed the Demon Princes. Un-Maurag, perhaps, or Mordred, or Haeglin. These things we may never know until the Awakening, or unless our foes triumph and that hidden Adversary stands forth to claim his reward." Silence returned, for a moment as the mind of Merlin retreated into his remote contemplation.

"So, Wizard, what now?" Géla interrupted, with mock cheer. "A picnic on the slopes of Mount Evergrey? Perhaps in the afternoon a gentle stroll to its very top? Shall we pack a luncheon? Are the Gograe and other Troll-Creatures invited as well?"

"Yes, and plan for several score Marids," Galad said with a laugh, "leading the four Sorcerers by leashes — and yes, at sunset, when the Mirage of Rainbows is at its most colorful, we should expect all three Demon Princes to entertain us with spiced wine and cutlets of roast Phoenix. Delightful!"

Merlin smiled a half smile at them, then slowly, imperceptibly, the Wizard's form grew thin, fading until he vanished.

· ҉ ·

They stared for a moment at the vacant space, then Kalanin commented wryly, "It is one of the greatest privileges of being a Wizard, that he need not respond to sardonic observations."

Through the long afternoon, they strolled through the glade or napped in the shadows. Toward evening the air in the glade's center began to shimmer, then a flood of goods burst through, as though shoved hurriedly in their direction: boots of many shapes and sizes, and beneath them was a note in Balardi's hand.

Elven boots for walking on crusts of snow. I, too, wear them, ready for our next foray. Heed me. If the Sorcerers are sharks, the Wizards are akin to dolphins newly returned to water: we have learned to swim in the sorcerous Mid-World. Wait — my message is too long — they are coming for me — B.

"The Wizard's messages were always too wordy," the eagle noted dryly. Julian and Galad changed footwear, carefully lacing the soft ankle length boots: they seemed frail and thin in comparison with their weather beaten, travel stained footwear. Géla and Kalanin were elsewhere in the glade, and none of their company, not even the headstrong eagle, was willing to disturb them.

A short while later, long pikes appeared, each shaft stiffened by metal molding, and below their points were guards to prevent deep penetration. Galad hefted a pike, driving its base into the ground.

"So, the Gograe await us —" He halted as fur lined cloaks and gloves tumbled from nothingness into the glade; and seconds later, almost as an afterthought, powerfully reinforced bows followed. Galad stared down at the weapons thoughtfully: it seemed that their time of peace in this strange underworld was coming to an end.

At sunset they gathered around a small watchfire, looking dolefully at their meager food rations — shattered nuts and coarse oats were all that remained. But as they picked at it, torch lights flared at the outer edge of the woodlands. All stood, weapons drawn, listening to the approach of low, mumbling, huffing sounds.

Torch bearing imps came lurching into view; and behind them, other imps bore steaming platters or lugged beakers of wine. All the imps sagged with disease, groaning and breaking wind as they neared.

Platters were set before them — a feast, surrounded by torches set into the ground. As the imps finished their tasks, each of them toppled, collapsed, and melted into the ground.

The followers of the Wizards were silent for a moment, as the air cleared in the glade, leaving only the smells of rich food.

Kalanin leaned over, lifting the lid from a steaming dish. "I have seen many illusions crafted at Sea's Edge, but diseased, wind-breaking imps are a new creation, likely designed for insolent questioners. It is interesting, however, that Merlin now has time for such detail."

Galad sat, pouring wine into a silver goblet, and he murmured, "Hereafter I will reserve my biting wit for the eagle, alone, if he promises not to relay any of my observations to his master."

They ate, seated on the ground, breaking their tension with a long feast they had never expected to encounter. Before midnight they readied for sleep, spreading sleeping rolls on the ground. Above them, intermittent breezes brushed back a canopy of leaves, revealing a sky that had grown crowded with stars. As silence swept over them, and after their watchfire dwindled into dark red embers and pale grey smoke, they turned and slept.

· ⋊ ·

In Julian's dreaming vision, the underwater kingdom of the Demon Princes seemed strangely different from the dry land of Alantéa. Air surrounded him, eerie, moist, and heavy, though it was clearly not water, and above, the sky shimmered, glistening under a vague, diffused light source, far from sun or moon.

Before him stood a single, lean watchtower, with two figures at its base, battling back and forth in a strangely unequal contest: one was slight of build, a princeling or young knight, but swift and fierce; the other was mighty and massive, battering the slender form's shield with a huge mace, and the blows echoed dully through the moist, heavy air.

Yet now, leaping away from the battle, the slender figure turned to Julian, calling out for aid in a voice he knew he should recognize, but could not....

The eagle's talons were tugging at him, drawing him from his strange dreaming vision. Julian opened his eyes, seeing that it was still pitch dark.

"What's happening?" he whispered. "Has Alcman discovered us?"

"Morning comes to Alantéa, the Forerunner," rasped the eagle. "Our leaders, the Wizards, will forge for us a Portal Passage to Mount Evergrey, then attempt to hold back the Sorcerers and the Marids while you seek the Sentinel."

"No sign of daybreak here," Kalanin said softly, a little distance from them.

"The hours pass in a different fashion, within this time eddy," the eagle replied with surprising gentleness. "Come. Dress for cold. Arm yourselves against the Gograe. On this day, many hidden secrets may be revealed to us."

They rose, gathering light chain mail for themselves, then adding layers of heavy furs, so that despite the night chill that still lingered over their resting place, traces of perspiration began beading on their foreheads.

"Eagle, I should have spoken more about our plans last night," Galad murmured, "instead of sipping wine by our peaceful firelight. What of our horses? What weapons do we take? Mount Evergrey covers a huge area — and so, where do we begin our search?"

"Your horses will remain here, in this temporary shelter," the eagle said distantly, as though he listened simultaneously to some faraway voice. "Take the weapons provided for you. As for the mountain, I do not believe that the

Wizards can bring us to its highest peak, not with the Sorcerers contesting our Portal Passage. Are you now ready? O my friends and companions, another great test now begins! Merlin, my Master, may the Maker's Touch guide you on this day!"

Light shimmered over them as a Portal with a huge arch burst into view. Brilliant, varied light, bringing colors: a dull white from snowfields still shielded by night, and a blue sky overhead foretelling the brightest of sunlit days. Grasping long pikes, the four humans leaped through, with Sebastian on Julian's shoulder, and Rafir on Galad's. The eagle, croaking defiance, burst through just as the Portal collapsed under a weight of counterspells.

On the slopes of Mount Evergrey, they took deep breaths of thin, ice-cold air. But the air's thinness alone had little to do with their deep breathing: facing east from the upper slopes of Mount Evergrey, the view was staggering.

Below them, a sea of clouds pulsed white and red with the first rays of dawn. They stood on an island of granite and snow, surrounded in all directions by oceans of water vapor. And as they stared downward, the sun brought light, yellow and golden, over the sea of clouds, bathing Mount Evergrey in brilliant light. Memory jogged Julian's mind as hints of color tugged at his eyes.

He turned north toward the Mirage of Rainbows, where patterns of Alantéa's enchanted vapors were beginning to gather the sun's rays and focus those rays like an enormous prism. Others also turned to behold how sunlight renewed the Mirage of Rainbows, where color and form ran riot. Patterns of light, at first unrecognizable, were molded within the Rainbow's seething depths, then they were launched skyward, as though offering homage to a Sun God.

As they watched the churning Mirage, light patterns altered, shaping, forming: the image of a bull, gigantic and red, leaping skyward with bright lightning flashing from its nostrils. Then, from the depths, a dark rich blue figure surged upward: a unicorn in deepest blue, white horn reaching skyward to duel with red bull over the skies of morning.

A snarl, a deep rumbling bellow pulled them back to Mount Evergrey like a riptide dragging unwary swimmers back into deep water.

"The Gograe," murmured Kalanin, turning slowly, reluctantly.

"Fight or flight, warrior and captain," cried the eagle, "choose what you will. As for me, I will be seeking the Sentinel at the mountain's peak." The eagle, gasping in the cold, thin air, began to climb skyward.

Kalanin watched as three troll creatures thrashed toward them, wading through drifts that were nearly as high as their chests.

"Flight upward is my choice," Kalanin said in a low voice. "The Wizards gave us nothing to cope with thin air, though. Did they leave that for you, Julian?"

As Julian murmured spell words, touching each of them, Galad fired a warning shot over the swarming, onrushing Gograe. If anything, the troll-creatures' pace grew swifter.

"Let's be gone," said Galad, pointing up the slope. "It's coming back to me, how difficult these Gograe are even to wound." They turned, jogging upslope, enchanted boots skating over the snow's surface. Behind them, the huge troll shapes bellowed in anger as they fell further behind.

Above them, the multiple peaks of Mount Evergrey shone white with snow and dark with granite, impervious, serene in the new light of day. The eagle seemed to have vanished, swallowed whole by an expanse of incredibly blue sky.

"A second airborne seeker," Julian panted. "The Sentinel might be anywhere. Sebastian?" The little Familiar winced at the thought of flight through cold thin air.

"It's cold. I know," Julian panted. "I can help. Make a stand first though." Doubtfully, Galad slowed, then halted. Kalanin and Géla came to a halt a few paces beyond. Then they turned, drawing bowstrings back.

Arrows sped toward the Gograe, while Julian murmured spell words over Sebastian's wings and shoulders. Wading forward behind massive shields, the Gograe deflected arrows, but slowed, hunching down beneath their barriers of metal covered with hide.

Drawing his reinforced bow back to its fullest, Kalanin shattered the nearest Gogra's shield. As the creature bellowed in surprise, Kalanin and Géla grasped long pikes and sped over the snow's surface, jabbing at the necks and shoulders of their pursuers.

Sebastian was launched, warmth and strength surging through his shoulders and wings. But from a distance came sounds of battle, a deep rumbling as though the mountain had just cast an avalanche into a distant chasm. Galad launched another arrow, then drew the Tarnished Sword as it began to whine in anticipation.

"Defenders of Mount Evergrey!" Julian called out. "Did you not hear the sounds of distant destruction? The Sorcerers are upon you, with Marids in their wake. Leave us to our destinies! We may be intruders, but the real invaders are below us!" The Gograe ignored the warning and brushed aside the pikes as they waded closer through snow drifts.

Surges of electrical power darted from Julian's staff, flowing through the damp snow surrounding the Gograe. Stunned, the trolls fell back, as the Apprentice turned and sped once again toward the peak of Mount Evergrey. The others followed, panting, dragging pikes, with pike-shafts trailing in the snow.

But further ahead their way was barred. As the slope curled upward, arcing toward the peak, two massive Gograe watched them from above, impassively, clubs still sheathed. One, almost casually, kicked at a drift of snow, sending waves of white flakes and ice crystals shuddering down upon them.

"Hear me!" Julian cried, and he took on his Voice of Command. "Hear me! Defend yourselves or flee! The Marids are nearly upon you! We are not your enemies!" Behind them, other Gograe advanced so that the humans stood, soft as grapes trapped inside a nut crusher.

Then, alerted by an event almost unseen, a change of light barely observed, all eyes turned from weapons and confrontation toward the Mirage of Rainbows that lay in the northern skies.

There, a gigantic red bull and a blue unicorn contended endlessly over glistening, blue skies.

But now, an even larger figure was lumbering upward, slowly, heavily: the huge image of a Marid, skin mottled grey and red, hooting and booming as it groped skyward. Reaching up it clutched first the bull, then the unicorn — and broke their spines effortlessly, as though snapping slender reeds. Then, the Marid turned and glowered at the beings that met in a confrontation on the Slopes of Mount Evergrey.

Julian let silence descend over them, to be broken seconds later by the downslope sounds of hooting and booming; once again the Marids had come to battle, fearless, unchallengeable, implacable. Eyes narrowed, heads tilted upward as though listening to distant, barely audible instructions, the Gograe turned, moving downward, letting their massive bodies forge an almost effortless passage through snow drifts. The four humans backed warily to one side, letting the Gograe sentries pass.

"Now for speed," Kalanin said, and he cast his pike aside, together with his furlined cloak. The others did likewise, leaving trails of brown fur and dark metal as they raced upward, speeding over frozen drifts like water striders on a pond's surface.

Below them, battle cries of the Gograe lifted upward from the slopes, together with the clash of energies as Wizards and Sorcerers struggled for mastery.

They slowed as their way grew steeper, with jagged grey cliffs now jutting from snow drifts. Panting, they paused for a brief rest, eyes searching for signs of Sebastian or the Eye of Merlin. From downslope came avalanche sounds, as Gograe loosed the Mountain's stony power against the Marids. Gulping thin air, they resumed their climb, with Galad leading them.

Their lungs pounded with strain, and even their travel-hardened bodies faltered. As they slowed, struggling with leg cramps, Galad pointed upward, wordless, to a ledge where the eagle perched, staring vacantly out into space. Sensing that some evil lurked nearby, Galad felt the Tarnished Sword beginning to stir, moaning softly. Julian's hand drifted to his chest as though wishing for a Blue Amulet that no longer existed.

On the shelf above them, Houma stepped forward into view, his black withered hand idly stroking the eagle's head.

"Do you approve of my new pet?" the Sorcerer called down to them. "I have half a mind to make pets of all of you, though I doubt that any of you can warble as sweetly as this one." Obediently, the eagle croaked out a song, chirping like some mindless, songbird stuffed with hemp.

Teeth clenched, Julian grasped his staff with both hands, while the others drew weapons, edging upward. The Sorcerer laughed down on them, a mockery filled with hatred.

But from high above the Sorcerer, a Portal flared. Balardi dove through it, his tattered cloak rippling in thin air, he dropped like a stone, sweeping Houma from his perch, over into the gulf. The two spun in violence, hurtling toward the Cloudland Plateau. Halfway down, they burst apart, like a meteor exploding in Earth's atmosphere.

Kalanin drew a deep breath. "Is that Houma's end? Balardi's death?"

"They have become so powerful," Julian panted, staring into the cloud cover. "Both Wizards and Sorcerers have become exceedingly difficult to destroy." He took a deep breath. "Now it's upward for us once again. We'll help the eagle in shifts, if Galad...."

Julian's planning was interrupted as the eagle, stepped to the far end of the ledge, eyes fixed on the Mirage of Rainbows, and cast himself off the brink, wings flapping heavily.

"Wait!" Julian called. "Eye of Merlin, stay with us!" The eagle's great wings pulsed on. Partly visible coils sped from Julian's staff, entangling the great form, but the Eye, snarling, broke free and began dropping downward, as though it had sighted prey on the cloudy surface, thousands of feet below.

"Merlin must save him now," Julian said, almost in a whisper. "For us, we must climb, then crawl if we can."

Like wingless insects struggling up a cliff's face, they groped upward foot by foot, enchanted boots finding footholds where none seemed to exist. Bodies aching, lungs shuddering, their pace slowed to a near crawl. As they struggled skyward, they glanced to the north, where the huge images projected by the Mirage of Rainbows, were beginning to shift, and refocus: a lone Marid stood, glowering as before, but bull and unicorn had vanished, and instead, the Marid stood on a mound of many dead and dying Gograe.

For now, the battle cries of the Gograe were turning to lamentations as they fought Marids and died by the scores.

Julian halted, collapsing against the icy slope, gasping for breath. "Never make it," he panted. "Where's Sebastian — Sebastian!" No answer came. Julian, gasping, tried to steady his breathing. "Sentinel!" he cried. "Tree of Heaven and Maker Servant! Recall Adonai's words and aid us now!" Silence came as Julian gasped three times before calling out, "Sentinel, the *TIME* has come!"

Only the hooting and booming Marid voices and wailing Gograe cries reached the stillness of the upper crags.

Then, a still, soft mental communication came, like a distant whisper of a ghost who had been long dead:

*Yes, Maker Servants, I greatly fear that the **TIME** is upon me, after so many ages. For your small servant, Sebastian, now stands before me: the first of Earthborn to know and speak to Alanthéa, the Tree of Heaven.*

"Sebastian — good work!" Julian said. "Sentinel, where are you? We must reach you soon, before the Sorcerers and the Marids reach us."

I am at the topmost pinnacle of Mount Evergrey. Did you think to find me elsewhere? The Tree's voice tones were at a middle level, neither male nor female, but they rang with the gentle sounds of wind chimes.

Julian looked up to the topmost peak, many hundreds of feet above them, where few handholds existed, nor had they hammers, spikes or axes for the ice. The Apprentice searched the faces of Galad, Géla, and Kalanin, and they shook their heads: equipped as they were, the climb was impossible.

"Great one, Sentinel of the Maker, we will never reach you in time," Julian said quickly. "Yield the Terms, the Words to my ally Sebastian. Then the burden placed upon you by Adonai will be lifted."

A pause came, with the hooting and booming Marid sounds growing always louder, then the voice spoke:

It is...not...so...easily done. The end of my days is also upon me, for even now, hatred from the Sorcerers and the Marids lashes at me like a howling windstorm. Because it was foretold that the Far Travelers would open many of the hidden passages to me, I believe that I am entitled — even required — to draw you to my sanctuary that has been hidden for so many ages. O my Maker, Greatest of Fashioners, I stand at the end of my lifelong watch, for now, I shall bring your Far Traveled Servants to stand before me....

Caught by surprise, they began floating free from the ice and granite mountainside in a slow and heavy fashion, as though the pull of Earth threatened to drag them down to the clouds that lay so far beneath them. But then they gathered speed, surging with a rush through thin mountain air, as the sounds of turmoil and destruction beneath them grew distant and dim.

At last, they stood on the pinnacle of Mount Evergrey; an ice covered, wind blasted wasteland devoid of life. A single misstep seemed likely to send them sliding then crashing downward with many tons of ice crystals following to form a burial shroud. Julian looked around him warily: there was no sign either of Sebastian or the unseen Sentinel. Had they been ensnared in the last of Houma's traps? The greatest, most treacherous, and final trap?

Be at peace, little Servant; Houma of the Withered Hand is still some distance from us. Though now, at this moment I feel my first fear — something that shrivels my roots and rots my bark with inner decay — yet at the end, I will put aside my semblance as a crag. Now, let the Powers also know fear: for they believe that the Maker has departed, leaving only halfhearted, feeble Servants. I, too, was left: the Sentinel, Alanthéa, the Tree of Heaven.

Irresistible forces began pushing them back from the peak; they scrambled, seeking to hold their places, to avoid being cast down.

Above them, cloudless blue sky began to give way to greenleaf foliage, with scores of leaves forming, each of them as small as petals, but deep green and rich with life. And the force pushing them back was the tree's massive base so that each stood holding greyish brown bark around the base of a trunk that was so great in circumference that none could see another. At their feet, mosses sprouted, while in the torrents of green above them, warm breezes were blowing with rustling sounds, like thousands of tiny echoes in a chasm.

"Julian," Sebastian's voice murmured from the lower branches. "Julian, I saw Houma snare the eagle, but I couldn't do anything. Did Houma —?"

"The Eye is damaged, perhaps even ruined, but he lives," Julian said softly, then he raised his voice, "O Sentinel, you must hear the sounds of Sorcerers and Marids, Wizards and Gograe below. In the Maker's Name, will you not yield the Truce Terms and allow us to depart?"

The Gograe, my unwitting protectors, the Tree of Heaven spoke into their minds, *are nearly done, but the Wizards and Sorcerers, including Houma and Balardi, still fight on. Mortals, the TIME is here, with my ending nearly upon me. At this end, it was foretold that much that has been closed to my Sight would be revealed. After you have shared your innermost visions with me, then the Truce Terms will be yours.*

Julian glanced around the pinnacle, full of tension and fear of failure: the sounds of Sorcerers and Marids were screened off, and they were held in an oasis of green with both blue skies above, and white mountain slopes below hidden from their eyes. But within moments they might again stand in a final circle of destruction, with the Truce Terms lost forever.

"Julian, begin!" Kalanin called out.

Far Travelers, the Tree continued, *understand that I am a devourer of knowledge, while you hold in your minds my last great feast; so, do not consider me another weak-willed partial friend. Apprentice, you will not be cheated — even now, I will forge an escape hatch for you.* The ground beneath them seemed to hum, to murmur, and it shook beneath their feet; but the movements had the feel of building, of an opening forge for escape, and not for destruction.

Julian took a deep breath, and murmured, "Great One, we are in your hands." Kalanin and the others came to stand beside Julian, some sinking to one knee on soft, moss covered ground, struggling to shake the stiffness from their bone weary bodies.

First, began the Tree, *beyond the Mid-World, and the edge of its borders, a Spirit Lord once called Délea, forged her own domain, dwelling there in a land of diminishing energies. One day the Gods, too, will pass into the Waning of Energies. What will this be like, warrior, and sentient blade wielder?*

Galad rose and placed his hands upon the Tree, with the images of the Lady of the Hill, the Manticore, and the Dark Power at the Portal racing through his mind.

So, at the Waning, there will be desperate and foolish strife, touched with a bittersweet sense of loss — and at the end, small Servants of the Maker, beyond the Waning, when even Faerie has faded into nothingness, what then of Earth's gardens?

Sebastian and Rafir came forward, touching the Tree's bark, staring up into a forest of tiny, rustling leaves. Almost unbidden, the images of a vast city raced through their minds, with its buildings choked with life, and teeming streets, filled with mechanical contrivances, soot falling always from the air like light snow. But within the city, the Ancient Energies had long ago faded, dried up, and were now reduced to fairy tales that entertained children.

This does not seem like the Maker's Will, that Earth's gardens be overwhelmed by stone and lifeless dead matter. Alas, that I have not Dragon wings to fly skyward and seek Him! On this day I fear that I will take my forever rest in the Temple of Waiting, among the dead immortals. Show me this place, warrior, and captain. Is there pain within? Is there surcease? Show me!

Head bowed with sorrow, Kalanin placed both hands on the shaggy tree bark, as dark visions filled his mind, of that immense Cathedral of Sorrows, where the dead immortals drifted endlessly without purpose, in a gloomy partial light.

Alas! Though there is no pain, the Temple is without solace. And there is no place for me in the Hall of the Dreamers, is there, Apprentice? Nor is there even a place upon the hillside beneath the Cup of the Maker. Show me, Apprentice with an Adept's Strength, show me while there is yet time!

Warily, every sense testing for a hint of Marids or Sorcerers, Julian approached the Tree, his hands reaching for soft bark. And he straightened as a vision of the Cup of the Maker swept over him, of sparkling waters leaping skyward. Then, he seemed to stand once more within the Hall of the Dreamers: but now the Greatest of the Servants no longer stared skyward, uncaring and at peace; instead, they watched as one, staring directly into Julian's face, as the Sorcerers and the Marids extended their power over Alantéa the Forerunner.

Even the Dreamers now fear that the Adversaries will triumph. As well they might, for the Sorcerers and the Marids have been forged as a force with the capacity to destroy the Gods. And behind them, the Demon Princes have fashioned an alliance with Marids and Dark Lords and Sorcerers, with Creatures of the Darkness and corrupted Guardians swelling their ranks. Beyond.... A pulse of powerful magic shook the pinnacle.

Now, they come.... Swiftly, within.... And after, the Tree no longer spoke into their minds.

A crack opened in the Tree of Heaven's massive trunk. Julian stood still for a moment, reluctant to be confined again in a narrow, closed space. Anger was stirring inside his mind: where were the Truce Terms? In moments they would fail once again, this time forever.

Now came shouts below, with all four Sorcerers blasting three Wizards from the slopes, and Marids advancing unchecked, booming, and hooting. Surviving Gograe were fleeing downslope, filling the air with cries of woe. As Julian hesitated, strong arms pulled him through, although the Apprentice resisted, clenching his staff with both hands.

Within it was dark, shifting and groaning, as the Tree of Heaven slowly expanded its root system outward and downward, and now there came a soft, whispering voice, echoes growing louder as their shelter became larger: *"I will not fail in my last Service, small ones. Firstly, you should know of the Isle of the Demons, a place where you..."*

Rumbling sounds rolled through the pinnacle as the Tree of Heaven hurled snow and shattered rocks down on Sorcerers and Marids, before continuing its whisper, *"...have not yet traveled, and which even my senses can see only dimly."* Beneath their feet the ground was changing, shifting, and massive tree roots fashioned tunnel passages beneath the pinnacle.

"Within the Isle of the Demons, the Guardians are believed to have been overcome and subjugated by the Demon Princes. Indeed, this has been accomplished, and yet three times the greatest of the Guardians has cast off his sorcerous shackles, his lone, blue orb-eye blazing with power as he battled once again with the Demon Princes. Only the Great Guardian has saved Alantéa, preventing the Demon Princes from confronting the fearful Gods before the TIME. Now...."

A great rending sound tore through the Tree's whisper, and Alanthéa shrieked in agony, shuddering throughout its massive structure.

"...the pain...."

"Tell us now or fail utterly!" Julian cried.

And the Tree whispered into their minds: *syllables of power, in a language their minds failed to understand, words that meant nothing to them, and yet their intellects and bodies seemed to surge with newfound power and purpose.*

A muted silence followed, with only deep grating and thrusting sounds reaching them as the Sentinel's roots forged a passage for them. Dull light glowed from Julian's staff, as slowly they edged into the largest shaft.

"Now, you die, Sentinel," came a voice from far above, Houma's voice, "and your life and death will benefit no one, neither the tepid Gods nor the feeble Maker Servants." The sounds of snapping branches filtered down to them as they picked up speed, beginning to slide down the expanding, thrusting passageway.

"No, you should..." whispered the Sentinel. Ripping, splintering sounds swept over them, and the tunnel writhed.

"You should not do this!" The Sentinel shouted at Houma. Crackling sounds came as sheets of flame blackened green foliage. Smoke billowed behind them as they sped downward.

"Maker...the darkness...." The Sentinel cried out with an even louder voice. A vast shattering sound split the air.

"MAKER, WAKE ME AS WELL!!!"

Chapter Twenty-One
The Mid-World of the Truce

JULIAN SLID DOWN THE long shaft and halted, the Gift inside him still shuddering with shock. Alanthéa, the Sentinel, the storehouse of knowledge, lay dying above them, and as it died, images were fleeing from its fading consciousness: of the Ancient Wars; of the Birth of the Gods; and of the Mid-World of the Truce, seething with all its sorcerous empires. Sebastian clung to his master, hunched, eyes shut, his small, enchanted mind buffeted by the death throes of the Tree of Heaven.

And now, in its final death spasms, Alanthéa shook the mountain top, sweeping all of those beneath its collapse from their feet, casting their worn bodies against the rock walls of their underground passageway. Even the dim light from Julian's staff was extinguished, and they lay in the darkness, waiting for the tremors to subside.

"So, Houma is above us," Kalanin murmured into the darkness. "What of the other Sorcerers?"

"Alcman stands beside Houma," Julian said, staring into the dark ceiling. "Cronar is joining with them as the three use their powers to search for us. Eudox stares into the distance, wondering how all his many unwise choices have led him to the slopes of Mount Evergrey."

"Yet you yourself are well, are you not, Julian?" Galad asked. "You feared that the Sentinel would delay too long or deliver us to our foes."

"I feared those things," Julian murmured, "but the Sentinel's duty has been fulfilled. I cannot believe that the Maker will let Alanthéa sleep the Everlasting Sleep." Tremors were subsiding, but there were sounds from above as Sorcerers and Marids picked through the rubble, searching for them.

"Yet now the Apprentice, along with ourselves, has been delivered into another fear," Géla murmured, "a dark underground passage, with evil beings in pursuit."

"This time —" Julian broke off, for the vibrations were starting again, with dust falling from the tunnels' upper shafts, and there came crushing sounds: Marids battering at Mount Evergrey, seeking frail mortals to destroy.

"This time there are more of us," Kalanin finished, "and we are better armed." Rising, he pulled Julian to his feet. "Now, farther and deeper, into the Mountain's heart if we must." Again, they fled downward, Julian's staff radiating bright lights and leading them, sliding over sheets of rubble as their passage grew steeper. Around them, echoes of destruction rumbled through the Mountain's interior.

"One day, O Marids," Géla called out. "One day we will turn on you, with power to do you harm!" Responding to her threat, the battering intensified, and in front of them, the downward shaft collapsed in a tumble of stony matter, with dust swirling back at them. They were trapped — again.

Julian slowed then stopped, spell words leaping to his lips. But to their right, the air was beginning to glow: a Portal Passage was groping for them.

"Houma!" Julian cried. Bolts of force leaped from his staff into the coalescing Portal Mouth. Then the Tarnished Sword arced through the air, shattering the Sorcerer's spell work.

They stood, coughing, and breathing heavily as the air remained choked with dust. Once again, the air shimmered, but this time Julian approached the Portal Mouth cautiously.

"Thorian," he whispered, then he turned to the others. "Bid farewell to Mount Evergrey and another trail of destruction: Thorian has found us. Come." He stepped through the Portal Mouth and vanished, with the others following only seconds behind.

Above and outside, the Marids halted their stone crushing destruction, and the Sorcerers ceased their probing Portal magic. Sorcerers and Marids all turned to the Mirage of Rainbows: there to the northeast, the Mirage still radiated the huge image of a Marid, yet now that Marid was standing over the broken ruin of the gigantic Sentinel, Alanthéa, the fallen Tree of Heaven.

· Ӿ ·

Winds, lifeless and stale, brushed over the darkened plain; they sat, hunched down, cold, and hungry, wishing for the warmth of a fire and food to ease their hunger. But only lichen and dust lay around them, with nothing to burn and nothing to eat. In this eddy of time, a place that never was, in Otherwhen, the Maker had chosen *not* to arouse life forces to grace the planet. So, they sat in the stillness, waiting for the Wizards to end their Divinations, and let their furrowed, worry ridden faces relax.

Rafir sighed, then drew a deep breath of stale air. "Why can't this — at least once — be like the old fairy tales?" he asked, for the third time. "In the old stories, when the quest was over, and they've learned the magic words, or found the *Talisman*, then the evil ones are defeated, and the story comes to its usual, happy ending. What are we doing here? Why aren't we celebrating our victory?"

After a moment of silence, Kalanin laughed, a low quiet sound that traveled only a short distance through the still, almost lifeless air. "I admire your persistence, Rafir. You've asked the same question three times in three different ways." Kalanin waved at the bearded figures who stood together several hundred feet from them. "Since the Wizards are still mumbling at one another, and since Julian is keeping his own counsel, I will speculate for you.

"It is true, that we, or at least Julian, should be able to call the Gods to battle — if he can pass again into the Vale of Whispers. But the Sorcerers and the Marids must know of this threat, and they will have taken steps to keep us from entering the Vale.

"Secondly, Rafir, the Gods have shown great reluctance to come to battle; thus, they must fear the Marids greatly. So, were I a Wizard, I might consider that the Demon Princes, the Sorcerers, and the Marids, together with others of their alliance, that these might destroy the Mid-World Powers, and then the triumph of the Adversaries would be utterly complete. So, the Wizards mumble, seeking answers through Divination or Seer's Sight, while we, no longer of any real consequence, sit here in the frosty air of Otherwhen."

"To think that the Powers of the Mid-World, the Gods, might actually be defeated," Rafir said, shaking his head, "after all we've done...." The fox finally fell silent, his small, enchanted mind wrestling with a thought that was too complicated and confusing to understand.

Many paces away, the Wizards, too, were struggling in weariness and muted argument with concepts that exceeded their comprehension. In the distance, a dry thunder crackled, with lightning flickering feebly over an ocean that remained barren.

Julian lay back, his thoughts turning to their long journey, and to the trail of destruction that had followed them: the ram-shaped Adept of Tel-

Alantir, the Elf-Seer, Maeglan, and the Sentinel, the Tree of Heaven. It was only a noble sounding falsehood to call themselves the Far Travelers; instead, they were carriers of a deadly plague, ruining those — like the Elf-Lord, Haldor — that they avoided luring into destruction. Now, it seemed that rather than calling down the Truce upon their foes, that the death plague might be spread to the Gods, with the Adversaries ruling in the aftermath of the Gods' destruction. If so, perhaps the decay of evil would bring about an Earth like this one: lifeless, barren, dead.

But then Julian's eyes met Sebastian's, and the little Familiar was slowly, imperceptibly shaking his head. Julian smiled, reaching out to touch his small ally — Sebastian was right, they had come too far to let one last barrier discourage them. Julian closed his eyes and struggled to clear his mind.

When evening came, the partial warmth of daylight passed quickly, and they sat, shivering, waiting for an even cooler nightfall. With the last light of day, however, the Wizards broke off their long debate, walking back toward their servants across the lifeless plain, with slow, ponderous steps.

"This remains the safest of havens," Balardi murmured wearily, "but it is unsatisfactory in so many other respects. Come." In front of him, the air shimmered, and a Portal with a huge arch flared, leading to an Alantéa that seemed infinitely more inviting. Still shivering, they passed from a barren world into a land that was now shrouded in darkness, but its warmth and rich scents, and the night murmurs of many small creatures suggested a world teeming with life. As the chill passed, sleep came easily, with the rustle of leaves and the Wizards' hushed voices forming a low, background murmur.

· X ·

And the Wizards were still mumbling at daybreak, but their words seemed blurred and indistinct, as though speech and language themselves had slowly been transformed. In the middle of the morning the three finally lapsed into silence and stared for a time at cloud patterns with unblinking eyes. Then came a time of more complex contemplation, with three bearded faces studying shapeless inscriptions.

Géla stifled a yawn, then broke the long silence. "At least the Mistress of Illusions had the courtesy to perform her tedious rituals out of view and far from the sight of lesser mortals."

Balardi stirred as though waking from a dream, then came over and addressed them haltingly:

"We have decided to try it; it is not dangerous, though it seems most unlikely to work. Therefore, you may stay. Also, you have been catalysts before, and may serve as such again — though none of us really believe that our efforts will produce what is most needed." The Wizard turned back to his inscriptions, but Kalanin's voice rose in tones that demanded attention:

"Wizard, we have become baggage from this point on. We know that. But you owe us a better explanation than your mysterious words. What are you going to try? What is its purpose? Why is it likely to fail?"

With a sigh, Balardi returned and sat beside them on the ground. Setting his staff aside, he rubbed his face with both hands then sat with his eyes closed for a moment, as though meditating.

"The death of the immortal Powers, both Ancient and New, can be a long, complex process," he began, eyes still shut. Puzzled glances were exchanged, but the Wizard continued, ignoring their reaction. "So, it was in the struggles of Servants and Adversaries that some who seemed destroyed might actually recover over an age or be recalled to life before they reached the Temple of Waiting. The Ancient One, my Spirit Lord ally, and longtime friend was one such; yet he has departed from Earth, to seek the Maker, as was his destiny.

"Another, a Lord of Dragons, was recalled by Merlin, but the Demon Prince Zikar sent him again on Death's journey toward the Temple of Waiting — Julian knows of this one, for it was Julian who invoked the Lord of Dragons, sharing his form and consciousness for a few, brief moments. That Ancient Power now stands almost at the Temple Doors. We are going to attempt the retrieval of this being from a very great maze of death."

"And if he comes as called?" Kalanin asked.

"If he comes, we will seek his aid in dealing with the Marids, his recently created brethren. Neither the Gods nor the Wizards have solved the riddle of the Marids. Perhaps a Lord of Dragons might." Balardi looked up, turning toward his Wizard brethren: they stared down at him with grim, heavy faces.

"It is time," Thorian said.

"We have been avoiding many seekers," Merlin added quietly. "Not only do all four Sorcerers search for us, but many Gods fear that the Truce will be called, and that their own destruction will follow. So, Mid-World Powers are also trying to discover our hiding places."

Balardi said nothing, but he rose and bowed to the Far Travelers. Then all three Wizards turned, staring out in silence over green fields and meadows where sparrows arced through the sunlight and butterflies fluttered in gentle breezes. Thorian began first, murmuring a spell that was tentative, reaching, uncertain. Merlin's voice came next, chanting, strengthening the first theme, adding power and direction. Lastly, Balardi's voice rang out with bold, strong words, adding a framework for their tapestry of spells.

Here are the greatest of Magic Wielders, Julian thought, *weaving spell strands into a vast, complex tapestry of sorcerous energies. It was not surprising that no single Greater God had chosen to challenge the Wizards.*

And as they wove, enchanted energies surged from earth and air, from hidden fire and distant water. The ground beneath them seemed to tremble, while the air grew sharp and still — and fragile, as though it might be transformed into glass.

Gradually, all the arcing, and fluttering and swooping flights of winged creatures began to slow, until they stopped, held frozen in midair, with only the whining of sorcerous energies seeping through a stressful silence.

Before them, in the midst of meadow grounds that were filled with sorcerous energies, the image of a Lord of Dragons began to flicker and fade, seeping like a lump of dying coal stirred only by a whisper of winds. Wizard voices rose, chanting interwoven spells around the form: the Dragon's shape ceased to flicker and fade.

But it was still no more substantial than mist, less than the feeblest of phantoms.

The Wizards faltered and grew silent, staring again at failure.

"Too late," whispered the Lord of Dragons, and the sound came to them as though it was only an echo from a great distance. "Too late, even though I add my strength to yours." The figure stirred with effort and concentration: if anything, it became less substantial, more misty and frail. Stillness hung over the meadow.

"Wizards, I stand outside the Temple Gates." Even its distant whisper seemed to fade. "No power might draw me from such a distance, except for the Maker's.... Tell the Maker that I tried, that...." More words came, but they passed outside of hearing as the image dimmed.

Sorrow swept over Julian. He and this Lord of Dragons had fought against a Demon Prince in the battlefield of Stone Mountain. Before him was the fading image of a being with whom he had once merged, however briefly — a brilliant, powerful Servant of the Maker, and now it was passing into the shadows.

The Apprentice stepped forward, touching the fading image, feeling nothing but dry mist.

"Great One, I will tell the Maker —" Julian broke off, for power was beginning to flow through him, power, mighty forces, unlike anything he had felt before, rising, surging through his own body and into the Dragon-shaped mists. Julian stood linked, again, to a Lord of Dragons. Now, the Apprentice was a conduit: energy shrieked through him as the Wizards' voices rose in alarm, and Sebastian cried out in fear.

Energy, power that he had never before imagined might exist — his own voice passed from a groan into a cry of terror, and then he collapsed, senseless, to the ground.

The Lord of Dragons shook himself, flaring huge, scaled wings in triumph.

"Birth-Strength," murmured the Dragon. Reaching with one taloned claw, he raised Julian from the ground, breathing on him gently as though arousing fire from an ember.

"Birth-Strength, thanks to you, Mortal Magic Wielders, and to you, young Magician." Setting Julian on his feet, the Lord of Dragons turned from them, studying the sky-patterns of early afternoon, as though his powerful Sight could penetrate through the refracted light and peer into the star systems of deep heaven.

Then the Lord of Dragons turned to the Wizards, murmuring, "What are your wishes for me, Mortal Magic Wielders? Clearly, my rescue from the Temple of Waiting was not an unselfish, purely altruistic act. Have you a new task for me?" The Dragon's tones were soft, muted, yet energy and power seethed behind them.

The Wizards said nothing, letting thoughts, images, sequences of action speed from their sorcerous minds into that of the Ancient Power who regarded them in a coiled, partially swaying manner.

"Marids," murmured the Dragon. "Mighty dealers of death and ruin, God Banes and destroyers of Mighty Powers. You wish me to probe and peck, and test, to become ensnared once more in the traps of Earth?"

The Dragon's voice built slowly into a snarl, with anger and cunning seething behind its gleaming red eyes. A wall of cool, translucent stone shimmered in front of the Wizards.

"Wizards, I am Wild Magic!" cried the Dragon, and a torrent of flame leaped from its mouth, blackening the Wizards' stone barrier. All the meadow's small beings woke from the magic that held them and fled in panic; yet within a few moments both stone and flame vanished, as Dragon and Wizards confronted one another impassively.

Julian came to stand beside the Dragon, and he touched a scaled wing gently. "Great One, what are your desires? Will you still serve the Maker and his followers?"

"Do not be afraid, young brother. I will not enter a contest of power with your Wizard allies — though such a struggle might prove most interesting. No, we merely debate tactics while I am wild with power, after ages of sinking slowly through the shadows.

"Wizards, I will not lie in wait to ambush a lesser Marid. The Spirit Lord awaits me at the outermost circles of the Sun. Even now, I yearn for star flight. Bring forth the First Born, the greatest of the Marids. I will solve the riddle of the Marids for you or sink, for the third and last time, toward the Temple of Waiting."

"This might be done, yet then it is all or nothing," Merlin said softly, "with little hope if you fail. Lord of Dragons, we need your aid. Will you promise to survive, to avoid death, should the Marid prove mightier than you? You are brilliant and subtle, a mighty wielder of sorcerous energies and your second or third contest with a Marid might transform our struggle. Will you agree to avoid ruin if you can?"

"Compromise is not among the Dragon-paths, but yes, I will even beg for mercy, or swear fealty to the Powers of the Mid-World if I must." The Dragon's head shifted skyward, and once again a torrent of fire leaped from its jaws. "But the Birth-Strength is in me and wild power surges through my frame! Bring forth this second child of Demons, the greatest of Marids to me, Wizards! Bring it, now!"

"So much has happened, Lord of Dragons, so many defeats, so much destruction," Merlin said quietly, as he glanced into the faces of Thorian and Balardi. "Forgive us if we seem hesitant — even now our minds are probing the Vale of Whispers where the Sorcerers and the Marids stand guard. The one you seek stands within the Ruins of Dahlak. Only let him be separated, just for a few seconds...." Wizards turned from the Lord of Dragons, facing north, minds following from a vast gap of time and space, the progress of the many Marids as they paced tirelessly through the Ruins.

"Great one, or Dragon Lord," Galad said softly, "we, the 'baggage,' wish you good fortune in your contest with the greatest of Marids." He drew the Tarnished Sword and extended it, hilt first, toward the Ancient Power. "We have little to add, though this weapon, alone, has slashed the flesh of a Marid." Watching the Wizards warily, the Dragon drew the sword, tiny in its huge claw, closer to its red, far-seeing eyes.

In the Dragon's claw, the Sword stirred, moaning in trembling tones that became almost harmony. In a tune unrecognizable, and in a language unknown, the Tarnished Sword sang of battles and destruction, while the Wizards searched, and the Far Travelers attended the Lord of Dragons.

"A strange minstrel," said the Dragon, searching their faces, seeing Kalanin and Géla, Galad, Rafir, and Sebastian as though for the first time, "and you are all heroes, each of you, though that should not surprise me, as you are companions of my Young Brother. If I reach the Maker, I will —" Sensing a great force of sorcery, the Dragon turned north, toward the

Wizards, where a great arched Portal was beginning to form, partly obscured by clouds of grey mist.

"Yes, my thanks to you, half mocking, unsubservient mortal," the Dragon said quickly. "Your blade is mongrel magic, not easily understood, and yet it might help. Now, if you will stand far back, but remain within view...." Kalanin tugged at Julian and they sprinted from the meadow, racing toward a stand of trees. Géla and Galad paced them as they ran, with Sebastian fluttering above them and Rafir trotting easily behind them. Half-forgotten, the Tarnished Sword sprang through the air, settling hilt first into Galad's outstretched hand.

As the Lord of Dragons moved toward the Wizards, Portal Gates burst open. On the other side, there seemed to be nothing but ruins, yet dust surged upward, and the rubble was shaking. After a few seconds, the First Born and greatest of the Marids emerged from his destruction of ancient, underground ruins, and stood, regarding them fearlessly with clear eyes.

A jet of flame lashed through the Portal, blackening grey stone, but Dragonfire left the Marid unscathed.

"Marid, I am a first child of Demon Princes as aided by a Greater Seraph!" the Dragon called out. "Come now and let us see if you, the second offspring of Demons, are yet equal to me!" The Marid stared at the Dragon with eyes that had never known fear, then, without a second's hesitation, the Demon-spawned God-bane stepped through the Portal.

"We must guard the Portal Passages," Merlin called out. "Neither Sorcerers nor Marids nor Gods of Alantéa will be allowed to disturb your contest. Maker's strength to you, Lord of Dragons!" All three Wizards vanished, but the air about the meadow began to shimmer and glow as Portal bars slipped into place.

The great Lord of Dragons backed away from the advancing Marid, and the Dragon's eyes pulsed red with enchanted Farsight and cunning.

Both beings were huge, but the Marid bulked larger, taller in height and broader of chest than his scaled opponent.

"What are your innermost desires, Firstborn of the Marids?" asked the Dragon, red eyes pulsing as he backed away. "Is there anything in your mind besides the tearing of flesh, or the pounding of stone, and grim servitude to your Demon Masters?" Huge Marid hands reached for Dragon flesh, but the great Ancient Power sprang back, huge, scaled wings flaring as he settled back to the ground.

"Have you given thought to the Maker, First Born of Marids? Great is my desire to speak with Him. We might take you also, if you desire, for others of the left-hand, side sinister of creation have made that journey. The Spirit Lord and I might forge a passage for you if you wish. Have you no such desires?"

Again, the Marid groped, and again the Dragon leaped back.

"Maker, behold how I restrained myself!" cried the Dragon. "Even with wild magic surging through my frame!" A torrent of red flames surged over the Marid's body; heedless, the impenetrable creature advanced. The Dragonfire focused, growing thin and blue, probing at the Marid's eyes, its neck, then its shoulders and thighs.

"So," hissed the Dragon. "My old masters forged you well, God Bane. Yet there are other forces, other powers!" The Dragon's voice rose, filling the meadow. "Wizards, let this one through!" Spell words hissed through Dragon lips: a thin, high mist shimmered beside the Dragon Lord, then the mist grew black and deep, like some gigantic tunnelmouth.

An immense being stepped through, snakes rippling from its dark, moist body, and it stood far taller than either Marid or Dragon and was greater in bulk than both together.

"Behold the Lord of Snakes, O Marid," said the Dragon, eyes pulsing with malice. "Unlovely but loyal, he is my unlooked-for, first born child.

Let us see how you fare against his strength." The Marid turned, regarding the Creature of the Darkness impassively; from the Lord of Snake's body, a score of mouths opened, and forked tongues darted toward the Marid's flesh.

A half-silence hung for a moment, then shattered as the Creature of the Darkness bellowed: though not in defiance — the Lord of Snakes was crying out its own Portal Spell, its own summoning.

From a gap in the air, masses of huge serpents — both Kath-sized and far greater — hurled themselves at the Greatest of Marids. The Demon Spawned Marid vanished in the coils of serpents, and beneath those coils, streams of venom were sliding down its mottled Marid skin.

Marid arms groped beneath the coils; massive snakes writhed and died, with groaning and crackling sounds filling the glade — and the Marid stepped from the mass of dead and dying serpents, grasping the Lord of Snakes with both hands.

In turn, the Lord of Snakes grasped its opponent with hands as large as the Marid's shoulders. A score of serpent mouths extended from the Creature's body, probing at the Marid's skin.

The two swayed and struggled for a moment, but then snakeheads began to quiver in alarm, as the Marid's grip tightened.

Hissing in malice, eyes pulsing as though aflame, the Dragon seized one Marid shoulder in its jaws, talons ripping at its massive forearm. Swaying backward, using the Snake God as leverage, the Marid wrenched forward, hurling the Dragon across the clearing. Then, hands wrenching into the chest cavity of the Creature, the Marid began ripping at the oily, unnatural organs of the Lord of Snakes.

Bellowing in pain, its snake forms writhing in agony, the Creature of the Darkness struggled to free itself from the Marid's grasp. Half hidden from the contest, Galad drew the Tarnished Sword, and its war song rang out in defiance; but Julian and Kalanin held him back, for now it was too late. Arms extended into oily, pulsing organs, the Marid reached the Creature's vertebrae and burst its spine apart with a *crack* like the shattering of some huge tree.

Wild and free, pulsing with sorcery, the Lord of Dragons took flight, circling the glade once, then launching a torrent of smoking venom at the Marid — a being that stood unscathed, impenetrable, invincible.

Puzzled, the Dragon dropped to the far end of the clearing, again watching the advancing Marid with red, pulsing Dragon-eyes.

"A stillness of inner density, reinforced by sorcerous co-matter," murmured the Dragon, then, raising his voice, "O Marid, I fear that I must take on more Earth-weight to deal with you." Stepping forward, the Dragon seemed to grow in bulk — and weight, for its passage began to rip apart the meadow's green growths, leaving trails of torn brown earth.

Circling around the carcass of its fallen child, the Dragon rose on its hind legs and sprang. Crushing claws grasped the Marid's arms, while the Dragon's jaws closed on the Marid's shoulder. A deadly tension hung silently over the meadow. For the first time, the Marid's voice grated in its effort; but then one arm broke free, and it battered, crushing a Dragonwing. A second arm smashed at the Dragon's jaws, then both hands closed over a scaled throat.

"Great One!" Galad cried, springing from the tree line. "Great One, you do not fight alone!" Others followed, as bolts of force lashed out from Julian's staff.

With a last burst of strength, the Dragon broke free, springing back from destruction at the Marid's hands.

"Back," the Dragon mumbled through broken jaws. "Get back," it said again — more clearly as its bone and flesh re-knit. They halted, watching as the Dragon retreated, body healing with each step.

"O Marid, it is the beginning of the end," murmured the Dragon, regarding a line on the Marid's side where from the slightest of scratches, Marid-blood, at last, was beading. With a shrug of its shoulder, the Marid's own wound healed over, and it resumed its battle with the Dragon.

Now there came cries of torment and wild pain and fear from both beings, and when the Dragon once again saved itself by wrenching free, one Marid arm dangled uselessly at its side, with blood rippling down its massive chest.

"Your end is coming, O Marid," said the Dragon, backing, flesh, and bone re-knitting — but the Marid healed as quickly, and it advanced with only a hint of uncertainty.

"You are not invincible, God-Bane," murmured the Dragon. "And you have blind spots...."

Suddenly there were twelve Dragons in a circle about the Marid, and it halted, bewildered. Twelve jaws closed over Marid-flesh; only one of them broke its skin, yet that was sufficient.

"It is over, O Marid," said the Dragon, now alone, still backing, eyes pulsing. "Your flesh is most bitter to my taste, child of Demons, and I have tasted both mortal and immortal — yet now I am able to fashion a Marid-bane."

Again, there were twelve Dragon-shapes, and as they closed on the Marid's flesh, their jaws seethed with intricate, subtle venoms.

In the end, the Marid burst free, turning toward the sea, arms raised in supplication; and as it boomed its last wordless tale of fear and terror to three Demon Princes, it fell to earth, tearing apart the ground in its death agonies.

As the Marid stilled, the Great Lord of Dragons placed its head upon the ground, eyes closing in contemplation. Julian came to stand beside the Ancient Power, touching the Dragon's powerful claws with his own small, frail-seeming hand.

"Young brother, I have grown again heavy with the weight of Earth," murmured the Dragon. "It is not wise to begin a quest for the Maker in this fashion, to seek the Lord of Peace and Understanding through a gateway of violence. Now, I have cause to fear the Traps of Earth, and all the new snares woven by ancient Demon Princes."

"Great One, the strength to depart remains within you. I can feel it," Julian said softly. "And it is not necessary to be pure or perfect — we must either serve or seek the Maker." Into Julian's mind came the image and words of Voritar, Prince of Demons and great Servant as he spoke to Julian in the Hall of the Dreamers: *Here, in the Hall of the Dreamers I watch my children often, as they leap from sun to sun, and the dross burns away from them.* Then Julian shared Maeglan's song with the Ancient Power, how she sang of the great Dragon Lords nearing the Maker, themselves grown mighty beyond the comprehension of both mortals and immortals.

As Dragon and mortal dreamed together, the peace and stillness of sunlight returned to the meadow, and insects began, tentatively, to investigate the strange, enormous carcasses that lay broken upon the surface of ruined meadows. After a time, the Wizards flickered, one by one, into view, regarding them with only partial concentration, as though the greater portion of their minds were working to guard the Portals.

"It is finished," said the Dragon, raising itself slowly, "and the price has been — nothing!" Voice rising in exultation, the Dragon cried, "I am free! The Birth-Strength is still within me! May the Maker guide my path!"

Settling, the Dragon glanced one last time at the First Born and most powerful of the Marids, murmuring, "Mighty are the Marids, the second offspring of the Demon Princes, yet they are not the equals of the Lords of Dragons. For was not Adonai, Greatest of Seraphs, and co-fashioner of Dragons, not also a forebear to us?

"Now, Wizards, open your minds to me — here are talismanic patterns of ruby and onyx, sapphire, and emerald, that will break into the Demon-wrought Marid-hide; here are the shapes to these patterns....

"Know that there are subtle blends of Serpine and Silverfoil, Nightshade and Starstone, that together form a Marid-bane; here are the admixtures....

"Should deception be needed, there are complex illusion patterns that are utterly deceiving to the eyes of Marids; into your mind, I am placing the weaving of those patterns....

"Now, I am done! The Birth-Strength is in me! The Ancient One, mighty among the Spirit Lords, awaits me at the outermost circles of the sun! Together we will forge a passage to the Heart of the Universe, where the Maker sits at the Center of all Understanding!"

Its great wings trembled with power, then came a moment of hesitation, as the Lord of Dragons turned to Julian. "As for you, young brother, if the Maker permits, I myself will raise you from the Long Sleep, at the End of Time. Now, farewell!!"

· X ·

Hooting, booming Marids strode through the Ruins of Dahlak, through the Vale of Whispers, tireless sentinels guarding the City of the Truce. Two of them walked together; one was somewhat larger, and its skin was scarred, while the red-dark, thick hide of the other was without blemish, and it moved a half pace slower than the larger Marid, with a touch of reverence in its manner.

— *Hoot!* —   — *Boom!* —

Any stone that blocked their passage was smashed. And ghosts no longer whispered to them, for the Marids heard nothing, their own speech being ripples of thought at the edge of booming echoes.

Brother, we still do the bidding of the cunning-softs who call themselves "Sorcerers." Will this always be so?

— Hoot! —   — Boom! —

Patience, brother. Soon the Demons, our First Masters, will overcome the last Guardian, the mightiest of those beings. Then the great rending will come about.

And after, after the last rending, we will no longer serve the cunning-softs?

There will be a realignment, a time of changes.

Let us change much, my brother, for I tire of destruction. It comes to mind that twisting a thing so that it becomes what it would not be, that this is more satisfying than any devastation. I long to change all green growths so that they feast on night shadows and no longer the light of day.

— Hoot! —   — Boom! —

Patience. Over time, I have learned a little of the cunning-softs' weaving of energies and a little of their speech, so your desire for destruction through the use of magic may someday be possible.

— Hoot! —   — Boom! —

Yes, but first must come a time of changes, with shifting unknown forces that must be brought to dust. I have learned from the fear-filled minds of our cunning-softs that the First Born and mightiest of our kind has vanished into nether regions.

— Hoot! —   — Boom! —   ?!

Just so. I am not pleased with the support given us by the Demons, our fashioners, nor by the cunning-softs our allies. A realignment must take place. Whether we will seek an alliance with Dark Lords or corrupted Guardians lies in future chance. But first must come the complete destruction of the Old Gods and the cunning-softs of our foes.

Scarred brother, you are older than I, wiser, and...

Break off, brother. Both Demon Princes and cunning-softs send images to my mind, of soft un-cunnings.

A haze builds before me, brother, like a wall of dark water.

Destroy them!!!

Tiny sticks leap from the mist, from stringed soft-tools! Brother, my shield-skin is broken!!!

I, too, and — Inner Rending!!!

Great Brother, I come, but a darkness, like the last wave, closes over me! I Rage! I shall ruin! I....

· X ·

They burst through the Portal Gates on Wizard-crafted steeds. Dark smoke poured forth from the nostrils of their enchanted steeds and sparks flickered from the passage of steel-shod hooves. Kalanin led with Géla on his left, Galad on his right. Behind them Julian rode, calling out spell-words that blinded all the Marids that were racing toward them.

Two Marids faced them, one mottled, one clear-skinned, and they staggered in angry confusion. Charmed projectiles leaped from singing bowstrings, plunging deep into the Marids' flesh.

"I said that we would turn, upon you, O Marids!" Géla cried out, "with power to do you harm!" Again, they released their arrows, then rode hard, speeding past staggering, toppling Demon-spawn.

Before them, the City of the Truce stood gleaming in the new light of day, spires and towers radiating whiteness. Murmuring Shades began to gather around them, swirling and flocking, while in the distance, battering Marids again smashed through the City's enchanted barriers.

"Too late, O Marids!" Julian cried out. At Galad's side, the Tarnished Sword began to sing in exultation. Their steeds, tireless, enchanted, built to a pace unmatched by mortal creatures of flesh and bone.

And they sped into the City of the Truce on the crest of a storm-tide of ghosts.

In the howling storm-center, a once fearful Julian called out the binding invocation of the Truce in a clear, strong voice, in tones the Maker might use when summoning the Earth to Judgement Day.

· X ·

So many God-beings were completely unprepared. The Lord of the Dreamways rose from his couch; haggard and drawn, he was awake for the first time in ages. Around him, the old crones, his Dreamweavers, fluttered like dying moths.

"Sleep, Lord, sleep," they cried. "Who else will guard the Dreamways? Who else will harvest the Night Visions?"

"The Truce," he murmured in a dry voice that had not been used for centuries. "That ancient binding spell still has power over me. We must arise and go to defend Alantéa the Forerunner."

"Then, we shall all die!" they shrieked. "All die...all die...all die...."

· X ·

The Sorcerers struggled to rally their legions. Trumpets were echoing, bells were pealing, and throughout the marshaling yards, beaten men were stumbling to their ranks. Some were already half drunk, weaving and toppling, then helping one another to their formations, struggling to escape the Sorcerers' deadly wrath.

The Captain-General of Cronar's hosts listened to the marshaling sounds, transfixed by the music of his own death sounds: in moments, the Great Dying would begin, and all his people would perish like straw in a firestorm.

He stared for a moment at his long-prepared cup of poison — that was too slow; then he stared at his sword — and that was too sharp. At last, he emerged from his quarters, cup still in his hand.

Seeking his Sorcerer Master, he found Cronar at the edge of massive Portal Gates. Hurling both cup and poison at the Sorcerer, he cried: "Death to the Maker-cursed Sorcerers! Death to all these Demon-spawned Marids!"

He was dead before his mind could grasp that his stratagem had worked.

· ⋇ ·

A few of the Great Powers had long foreseen this moment. At the head of his legions stood one-eyed Wotan with ravens swirling about him, croaking aloud as they, too, heard the Summons. Wotan signaled, and with a vast rustle of metal, his people stepped toward the Portal Gates.

The TIME was upon them, long overdue: his fearful co-rulers of the Mid-World should have understood that there were conditions more terrible than destruction, matters more fearful than death.

· ⋇ ·

Even in the League's abandoned fortresses came shifts in power: sudden shadows swept over the sun and the bird flocks took flight, calling out in alarm, scattering seaward from the ruins of Stone Mountain. Gulls and terns, black cormorants and even darker crows were all mingled together, swirling like a clumsy cloud over an ocean that foamed white at the shoreline. They returned slowly, as an uneasiness, a disquiet built within them, a strange sense that their empire-nest amid the rubble might not last forever.

·)(·

Only half aware of its complex death-journey, the Tree of Heaven drifted slowly toward the Temple of Waiting, absorbed in its barely understood sense of loss. Then, as Julian spoke the Words, energies surged over it, like shafts of sunlight beaming into the deepest of caverns. A healing strength flooded back into its Shade, and it cried out in wonder. Casting deep roots downward, Alanthéa the Sentinel halted outside the Temple Gates.

Leaves sprouted. Thousands of millions of images and memories surged through its frame, and as they passed through its vast canopy of leaves, tiny rays of light began flickering from leaf to leaf, so that the Tree's outermost branches sparkled in the gloom.

·)(·

Julian felt all these changes, like enormous shifts in the tectonic plates of sorcery that supported Alantéa the Forerunner. And yet....

And yet, in the City of the Truce, no signs of battle came, only a long silence. Ghost beings had grown quiet, and at the outskirts of the City, Marids were hesitating in confusion. Overhead, the sky was clear, motionless, without even a trace of clouds.

A sense of wrongness slipped over the Far Travelers, like the first frost of fall coming with a sudden daybreak. Dismounting from their Wizard crafted steeds, they stood in the heart of the Vale of Whispers, and they waited. Julian drew a deep breath, and again the Apprentice called out the Words — to no effect. As he prepared to speak them a third time, an oily, menacing voice muttered, "Enough."

Their war party turned as one, facing east into the new light of day, to regard: Houma. The Sorcerer stepped from his Portal passage, confronting them once again with all his boundless malice and hatred.

Houma no longer wielded his fiery red amulet, though his darkened, gnarled arm still gleamed with power.

Behind Julian, he could hear the Tarnished Sword whining in Galad's hands, and he could sense that Géla and Kalanin had drawn bowstrings with arrows with the power to pierce Marids, ready to launch them against Houma and his dark, withered hand. Rafir had vanished and was circling behind the Sorcerer, while Sebastian gathered his small bit of magic for one last burst.

Harsh laughter burst from Houma's mouth. "So, we have abandoned another contest of Amulets. Still, you must realize that you are out mastered, and now you must die. So, die!"

Houma's dark, withered arm gleamed with dark sorcery, but as its power surged toward Julian and his allies, a vaguely greenish mist seemed to absorb it.

"Some sort of feeble magic of your failed Maker," Houma muttered, "though it will do nothing for you —"

"Where are the Gods?" Julian interrupted. "The Truce has been called, and so, where are the Gods?"

Houma's mouth twisted into a snarl. "You will have your war, Apprentice. In that war, the Gods will be crushed, and yet you will not live to weep, or even — "

Suddenly, Houma was smashed scores of feet from Julian, as though an invisible giant had *flicked* the Sorcerer away with one lone, gigantic fingernail.

As Houma struggled to get his breath back, the eyes of Julian and his allies were drawn to the east, staring into the rising sun. Marids were marshaling amid the Ruins, scores of them hooting and booming as they gathered together. Behind the Marids, Portals were flaring, and the Dark Lords of the Mid-World began to emerge, mustering countless legions behind them. A pounding began with thousands of the drumbeats of their foes.

Houma rose, gasping for breath, and they could hear his voice, made smaller by distance as he cried out, "Great Lord Satanis, let me have a few more moments to eradicate these human vermin, and then...."

Flick! And Houma was hurled off into the distance, shouting at the top of his voice as he rose high over the City of the Truce, through a greyish black Portal, and then he vanished.

"I don't want to sound like Rafir," Galad murmured, "But by all the Nine Billion Gods, I have to ask — what exactly is happening?" In Galad's hand, the Tarnished Sword was whining in confusion.

Julian lowered his staff. "I have no idea," Julian said softly, shaking his head.

"We did everything we were supposed to do," Sebastian said, fluttering up to Julian's shoulder, "and now we're left staring at each other like idiots."

"Look," Kalanin said. "Thus far, only one side is coming to battle." He nodded to the east, where the Adversaries were mustering, with drums pounding, and legion after legion forming ranks. "If we're supposed to face them alone, our lifespan can be measured in seconds. Géla, if that is what is to happen, I am so very, very sorry."

"Watch and wait," Géla murmured, "and say a prayer to this Maker of yours. Perhaps this one last time He will listen."

In the heart of the City, all its ghostly creatures had vanished, and the gleaming whiteness of the shimmering towers was slowly losing its luster. Watching in silence, they stood in the middle of a moment that was so strange that it had reached the level of the bizarre — after all their struggles, they had succeeded in summoning only the Adversaries, while from the Gods came only a curious silence.

And as they watched, the situation grew even more grim: now the Sorcerers were moving to the battlefield, joined by more of their brethren from the Isles of the Sorcerers, with rank upon rank of human warriors emerging. Mortals, once at least partly allied with Seraphs and Spirit Lords, were now swelling the ranks of the Adversaries.

"How can we possibly be reconciled with this outcome, Apprentice," Géla said, drawing a deep breath. "It is grim enough to have our human brethren marshaling at the Adversaries' side. I hoped, I dreamed that most of our peoples would serve the Gods — if the Powers of the Mid-World would ever come."

"A few will come at least," Kalanin said slowly, hesitantly, "those most like Auai Kuan Yin. Yet it's clear that the Ancient Servants are much less eager than the Adversaries...." He trailed off, watching as the formations of the Adversaries grew larger and louder. For now, the Creatures of the Darkness were emerging, wild, unruly, and savage. And then in a short time, the mightiest of the Adversaries would stand forth: the Demon Princes, and the unknown, untested, corrupted Guardians.

"The Gods must come," Julian murmured. "I...." He turned west, the Gift within him stirring in hope. The faintest sounds of many trumpets were beginning to reach out, as though calling to them from the edges of the world.

"We have stayed too long in this place, Apprentice," Kalanin said quietly. "We need to be gone."

"I am so slow, and you are so right," Julian muttered, taking a deep breath. "We are in the middle of what will be the greatest of pitched battles. We —" He halted, for powerful forces were lashing at their spell shields so that the air about them rattled and glowed. Their shields held, but their wizard-crafted steeds vanished into smoke.

"Thrust and counterthrust!" Julian cried. "Why do I always believe that we have completely won or absolutely lost? And yet we still have our own speed of foot. Come, let's be gone from this place." He took two quick steps in his elven crafted boots — but then they began sinking into the stone, drawing him downward, and his own body was becoming insubstantial, ghostlike. Julian called out in fear, turning to see that the others, too, were slipping downward, like wraiths sinking into stone crypts at the first light of day.

"Thrust and counterthrust," Kalanin called out. "This should be the Wizards' counterstroke. Julian?" The Gift within Julian stirred, and it sensed the powerful magic of Thorian.

"Intervention by Wizards," Julian murmured, then louder, "magic for our protection." He turned westward again, where vast Portals were forming tunnels into the depths, leading to the underwater Isle of the Demons.

Then the stonework closed over his eyes, and Julian cried out in frustration, for the Gift sensed the entrance of the last unknown, untested Powers in this struggle: the corrupted Guardians.

"Easy, Apprentice," Kalanin called out in a soft voice, muffled by surrounding stone. "It is enough to have called down the Mid-World of the Truce, and perhaps even to survive for a few moments after that act." Some distance from Julian, the Tarnished Sword was whining angrily as it struggled to slash magic that it couldn't touch. They sank slowly into the rock, drifting downward at a pace that might take them to the Earth's core in a few thousand years.

They sank in silence, struggling to hold back their own fears, and above them, the sounds were growing less grim, more heartening. Bugle and trumpet calls and the pounding of deep bass drums built to a crescendo as the mighty Gods assembled. Powers, who were aware of one another only by distant Farsight, were now standing together on the battlefield, facing a new alliance of Adversaries. The sounds peaked, then lessened, as the marshaling calls quieted and they, the Far Travelers, sank slowly through damp earth and cold stone.

We have come so far, thought Kalanin, *through so many victories and defeats, yet even now we have little idea which side will emerge as Masters of Earth. Maker, my great God. Maker, you wished neither Adversaries nor Servants to triumph; grant that the neutral Gods will preserve themselves against the Demon Princes and their new alliance of Adversaries.*

Now, above them the sounds of battle were beginning: a testing of lesser powers as mortal legions from each side fought one another, joined gradually by Creatures of the Darkness and the Emissaries of the Gods. Yet as they slipped deeper, even the sounds of chariot wheels, and battle calls, and the clanking sounds of metal gear were growing less and less distinct.

A long, slow time passed, with Earth's destiny being decided above them. At last, they slipped slowly through a cavern roof, floating feather-like to its stone floor, and here their journey came to an end. Pale light flashed from Julian's staff: Thorian stood in the cavern's darkness, his face drawn and haggard, eyes staring into the distance as though grim visions played over the veined, lime-eaten walls of the cavern.

"The Gods," murmured Thorian. "The mighty Gods; the poor, foolish, self-blinding Gods. So many would not heed our words concerning the Marids, while the Demon Princes have countered by fashioning armor for their second offspring. Beyond that, the corrupted Guardians are wielding a magic that the Gods do not understand." Above them came the shudder of a groaning Earth, then a wild cry that passed beyond the edge of hearing.

Thorian sighed softly, like the last pant of a dying man. Pale lights played over his haggard features as he murmured, "One of the Mightiest has fallen. Tor-El-Baldur, felled by Demon Prince, slips toward the Temple of Waiting…." Thorian trailed off, then his face jerked as though some distant, mental leash tugged at him. "Yes," he said, speaking to some faraway voice, then he turned back to the Far Travelers.

"Beyond our imagination, outside of belief, we, the Wizards must go to help save the Gods. As for your war party, you must vanish utterly." Again, they began to sink, this time more rapidly, passing into dark, slowly warming rock and seeping clay.

Above them, a shaking and pounding began, as though the First Fashioner had grown angry with the Earth and was determined to smash it into rubble.

Chapter Twenty-Two

A Spell-Cast at Sea's Edge

JULIAN LED THEM ALONG a ridge of rubble that curled jaggedly up the hillside. Moonlight, not magic, guided their path, and they moved with some stealth, Géla, and Galad following directly behind Julian, with Kalanin forming a rearguard. Rafir was scouting the hillside above them, while Sebastian sat on Julian's shoulder, humming softly to himself, staring with interest at the interplay of moonlight and green foliage. After more than a year's growth, seedlings and long grasses and brush teemed everywhere amid the husks of fallen trees and patches of volcanic ash.

They reached the hilltop, passing quietly over its rolling crest, halting partway down the far slope. In the valley below, lanterns swayed in front of rolling carts, with music raised in the darkness, as refugees returned in slow, winding processions toward Sea's Edge.

Hesitating, Julian came to a stop, the Gift testing for any sign of surveillance. In the pale moonlight, the cicadas droned on, with only a whisper of wind ruffling the soft new growth of the hillside. "We should be all right," Julian murmured after a moment, "though truly the Wizards could follow our passage to the Far Lands if they wished to."

"They seem preoccupied, withdrawn, and not very communicative," Kalanin said with a slight smile. "That's why we're creeping about in the moonlight. Let's begin."

"I agree that it's rash," Galad added, "but the close-mouthed Wizards have only themselves to blame."

"You judge, Apprentice," Géla said, smiling. "Pay no attention to these heedless, reckless wild men."

Julian took a deep breath, found a level area, and began clearing brush from it. The others bent over, pulling up grass and seedlings until the ground for a hundred square paces became brown soil, standing cleared and lifeless in the still moonlight. As they finished, Rafir emerged from the shadows, panting for a moment, then curling and licking his soft fox fur as he watched in silence.

Julian stood quietly for a moment, staring down into the valley below. Then he began tracing lines in the soil, carving runes within the square, until its outer edges began to flicker and glow. If they had been barred from the greatest of all contests, there was no reason not to view the battle in its aftermath, by Divination spellcraft.

· ✕ ·

Slowly, reluctantly, the images began to flicker and firm within their Divination pattern, showing the Vale of Whispers shining in the bright light of day. Portals were flaring in the east as the Adversaries assembled: Creatures of the Darkness, battle tiers of mortal men, Sorcerers and Marids and Dark Lords followed by many legions of Uraks and Vorrs.

Watching warily, Kalanin sat, and the others did likewise, except for Julian who stood to one side of the Pattern, staff touching the edge of his outline. The images seeped and faded, as though fitful forces interfered periodically, and three times Julian was forced to add greater power to his design.

The Far Travelers sat, bathed in moonbeams, but the images before them rebuffed all outside light sources, radiating their own light, as they showed the enchanted Vale of Whispers as the Adversaries gathered.

Now Portals to the ocean depths were forming, three of them, and from each emerged one of the mightiest Powers on Earth, a Demon Prince; so that Zikar, Satanis and Iblis stood together upon Alantéa the Forerunner for the first time in many ages. Radiating power and majesty, they stood far less in bulk and height than the Marids or the strange unlovely Creatures of the Darkness, yet the Demon Princes stood forth in might and grandeur, prepared to challenge the self proclaimed Gods for the lordship of Earth.

Behold the true rulers of Earth, thought Kalanin. *Even reduced by Divination to tiny images in the dust, they still radiate incredible, pitiless power. How can we hope to withstand them a third time?*

As the Demon Princes readied their challenge, their last summoning brought forth more Portals, dark, shifting underwater gateways to the corrupted, Demon-ruled Guardians. Indistinct in diffused daylight, the Guardians were unlike Demon or Seraph, Spirit Lord or Dragon; and they seemed to stand in a trancelike state, their orb-eyes glittering with red radiances as matter and light shifting all around them, as though their inner visions could transform reality.

Yet now, as the Demon Princes called forth the last portion of their alliance, the Divination blurred and shifted, showing Portals that flared in the west, with the Heralds and Emissaries of the Gods emerging, bearing the banners of mighty Zôs, of one-eyed Wotan, and Quarezokziil, and Marduk, and Tel-Alantir, and Arioch and darksouled Set, and Ptah, the Opener of the Ways, and scores upon scores of others. An epiphany of trumpets preceded the Gods, as the Powers of the Mid-World stepped forth into battle. The music of the Gods filled the Vale of Whispers, a harmony countered only by hoarse cries from the Creatures of the Darkness, and the hooting and booming of the Marids.

Scores of thousands of mortals stood on either side, the brave, the meek, the fearful, and the angry, multitudes of insignificant, tiny pawns, so small now, as the scope of the Divination widened to show all the many participants, that the mortals seemed no larger than grains of dust...and as the mortal legions began to clash, Sebastian looked away in sorrow, into the faces of the mortals around him, his friends.

But as he looked away, the little Familiar heard a sharp intake of breath from his master; when he turned back, Sebastian saw that the images within the Divination were growing hazy and indistinct. Mist, like a heavy cloud cover, was surging over Julian's spell, and in a brief time, they stood staring at a mound of whiteness, one that shook and vibrated with muffled concussions. Kalanin looked up at Julian.

"Very nice," he commented. "Is this the Gods' doing, or is it Merlin blocking your spell search?" Julian watched the clouded, indistinct Divination for a time, perceiving little more than the others, as within, miracle work confronted *The Great Spell*, with Gods and Demons struggling for control.

"It must be the Gods," Julian murmured after a moment. Down below in the valley, more voices were raised in song: hymns to the Maker, sung at quest's end, with the long journey to the coast nearly finished. "The Gods were challenged, fought to a standstill, some destroyed." Julian watched for a moment, striving to penetrate the haze. "In the end, it must have been the Wizards who saved them — likely calling on other allies. The Wizards are crafty, with many hidden alliances forged with Mid-World beings: the Tanu, the Elf-Lords, and the Sidhe. Those beings would fear the Mid-World's end should the Adversaries triumph."

"So, Apprentice, we tried, at least," Galad said, rising to his feet. "Perhaps one day the Wizards will cease to be hermit crabs and emerge from their shells. Though what they might say to us, mere —" He broke off, for Julian was waving him to silence, staring off into the distance, as though listening to sounds unheard by the others.

Suddenly the Apprentice burst into laughter, a sound of joy that none had heard from him during their long struggle. Tears flooded Sebastian's eyes as he sensed strength returning to Julian. They had been trying to view matters that the Wizards had wanted to keep hidden from their lesser allies, but the Wizards had caught their intrusion and stopped it.

"O Merlin, my Guide and Master!" Julian called out. "We are like small children caught in a foolish escapade. Do not treat us harshly, we beg you!"

Kalanin laughed softly, murmuring, "Tell the Wizard that it's his own fault."

"Yes," Julian said, listening to his master's distant voice. "Yes. Tomorrow then." He turned back to his Divination Spell, face now frowning in concentration. The others, too, turned to the white cloud before them, the obscure mound that rumbled and shook on a tiny patch of the Earth's surface.

Slowly, the shaking and quivering passed, and the white haze thinned, becoming a mist that rose from the Vale of Whispers to reveal the reddish sunset in the aftermath of the greatest of battles.

Merlin stood in the center of the Vale of Whispers, hunched, leaning on his staff. Before him stood a score of the Emissaries of the Great Gods: some were pale and worn, streaked with soot, while others struggled to heal bitter, deep, sorcerous wounds. Most of the banners they held were ragged and torn.

Emissaries and a lone Mortal Magic Wielder stood upon a battlefield that lay seeped in red blood and strange fluids. Many thousands of mortals lay broken and lifeless, scattered carelessly throughout the battlefield. But to either side of the Emissaries, dead things, both massive and mortal sized, lay carefully arranged, as though forming an offering to the Wizard.

Scores of the Creatures of the Darkness lay there, torn and broken, seeping strange fluids into lifeless soil. Marids, too, lay twisted in lonely death agonies, more than a score of them with mottled though unbroken skin, but three of the great Marids with reddish scarred skin had fallen face downward, hands extended into the Earth as though fulfilling one last moment of destruction.

Faces turned skyward, two of the Guardians lay, each of them with a single orb eye open, a look of wonder frozen on their strange, hairless heads, as though death were the final, most astonishing dream vision.

To one side were two, tiny, insignificant forms: the bodies of Cronar and Eudox. In death, all of Cronar's tense, grim energy had passed into a slumped nothingness, while Eudox was now beyond all surprise, deceit, or low cunning.

"You were wise, Wizard, not to use the full Summoning Spell," said one Emissary, breaking the silence. Sunset was turning the Vale into an even deeper shade of red. "Yet you now seek from the Gods that which they will not grant."

"We ask that your Masters consider that we have won only one battle," Merlin said softly, "while the War still hangs in the balance. Demon Princes and Dark Lords, Marids and corrupted Guardians, all these may have been expelled from Alantéa, yet they have not been destroyed."

"Have there not been enough deaths, Wizard, enough suffering? Even some of the Mightiest have fallen," said another Emissary, face clenched in pain as sorcerous flesh strove to knit over sorcerous wounds. "And the Gods are not unmindful of your own losses. They will release all your people who were sheltered in their domains, together with others once prevented from joining your League. Grow, prosper, be a shield to the south of Alantéa, the Forerunner."

"Our League will be what it will be," Merlin murmured, "but we will all perish if we do not confront and defeat the Ancient Adversaries. Yield to me the great jewel, the Cornerstone that Summons."

"Wizard," said a third Emissary, a dark Wraith that loomed above the others, dark hues blending with the red light of day's end. "Wizard do not presume too much. Should the Gods, even one of the Great Gods, grow angry at you, all your most powerful spells will come to nothing."

A pause came, a moment of hesitation; Merlin was silent. "But as a token," the Wraith continued, "we have taken and healed your servant, the eagle. Only his memories are gone, and yet his strength of mind and body have been restored."

Shadows shifted from within the Wraith's body, and the eagle, its mind wild with a thousand thoughts, but without knowledge of its past, emerged with wings flared, and savage, fearful cries echoed over the stilled battlefield. Merlin said nothing to the eagle, but his mind beckoned, and slowly, reluctantly, the eagle moved toward his ancient master.

"The eagle will be well, for I have shared in his thoughts and can replenish them," said the Wizard. "I am not ungrateful but behold! Much more must be done, for if we have upheld the Mid-World of the Truce here in Alantéa, we have scattered monsters and Dark Lords to the Far Lands. Men have woken there, Third Servants without a Maker, and they will find only the nightmares of Alantéa the Forerunner. What shall be done about them?"

More silence followed, a pause, as thoughts leaped among the minds of Emissaries and their Masters. Merlin watched on, eyes darting from face to face as though he followed much of the unspoken communication.

"Wizard," said one Emissary through clenched teeth, struggling for control of his own pain. "Wizard, the Gods will fashion outposts in the

Far Lands. Priests and Servants will dwell there — and moreover, the Gods Themselves will journey to the Far Lands."

"Pity mortals waking in Alantéa; pity mortals waking in the Far Lands," the Wizard murmured. "It is the fate of mortals that they should wake to confusion and the half truths of the Powers. I cannot avert this, but I must ensure that the Adversaries do not triumph. I must take the *Talisman*, the Jewel."

"Wizard, we cannot conceal from you that there is a debt to be paid." A new voice spoke from the Emissaries: shorter in stature, less mighty in appearance, this God Servant was more like a seer, a Grey Councilor perhaps. "We have endeavored to placate you by releasing the Maker Servants, healing your emissary the eagle, sending delegations to the Far Lands. We have even sought — without success — for the forebears of your servant, the Apprentice. Are these things not enough? Will you not now depart?"

"Your masters must yield the *Talisman*, the Jewel," the Wizard said softly, studying the faces before him.

Rage slipped over the smiling countenance of another Emissary, and its form shook at the edge of transformation. As it struggled to master both its own form and inner anger, the Emissary snarled, "Not much time has passed since wild battle magic surged through me as I confronted Monsters and Marids. I yearn to turn those powers on you, Wizard, and yet a curious forbearance lingers among us — Wizard, forget this 'Jewel.' Our Masters, in turn, will grant the Maker Servants the privilege of fashioning their own houses of worship. It is a great concession from the Gods...." Here the Emissary laughed in malice. "Yet any competition to our masters, the Great Gods, would not be a challenge, for the Maker never answers any pleas, He never responds to any prayers."

"For your own destinies it is wise to cease persecuting the Servants," Merlin said softly. "Yet I say to you and your Masters, the Great Gods, without challenge, without hostility: I must have the Jewel."

"Our Masters do not treat your request lightly," said the Emissary with the semblance of Grey Councilor. "Yet they have looked beyond your intentions and desires. The fate of Alantéa itself is tied to the Cornerstone, to the Demon Princes, and to the Guardians. For both enormous magic and doom were linked with the creation of the Guardians and the imprisonment of the Demon Princes. What would it profit should you win your struggle with the Demons and have Alantéa the Forerunner, the Wellspring of Power, slide seaward into nothingness?"

"Your Masters have looked deeply into this matter," sighed the Wizard, "as I have. Yet, they should look one level deeper, take one step further into their exploration of all the many, possible futures.

"At that deeper level, they will see that the Demon Princes have not lost their creative powers. Indeed, when they have overcome the greatest of the Guardians, they will be stronger than ever; then they will fashion a new race of beings, mightier even than the Marids. After, they and their Third Seed, and the Dark Lords and the Guardians, and the Sorcerers and the Marids — all of these will confront the Gods, and this time the Gods will fail. Ask your Overlords to explore that potential future, then yield to me the Cornerstone, the *Talisman* that Summons."

Silence slipped over the Emissaries as they and their Masters contemplated the Wizard's words. Night was slipping over the Vale of Whispers, and the night ravens, cloaked by darkness, now dared to investigate their vast harvest of death.

More time passed, then one by one the Emissaries vanished, leaving Merlin alone on the battlefield — except that where the Servants of the

Gods had stood there lay a Jewel, a huge, multifaceted *Talisman* that lay gleaming in the darkness.

· ℵ ·

On the hillside, the image of the *Talisman* faded, its last strands of light blown away by a whisper of wind. Moonbeams ruled once again amid a silence broken only by the cicadas and the music of travelers in the valley below, voices raised in song.

"So, in the end, victory," murmured Kalanin, "with still more to be experienced and explained."

"I can't believe there's more," said Rafir, "that we haven't gotten to the end of this story. What in all the names of the Nine Billion Gods was that stone?"

"It may be...but no, that's not right...and I won't speculate." Julian took a deep breath. "No need to try and guess, for much will be revealed tomorrow. That was the last part of Merlin's message, that we should rise early, and not lie abed in the morning."

"I thought we were more discreet," Géla said smiling, "but it seems that our secret is out: Old Captain Hangnail has the desires of one half his age."

"No end to surprises," Galad noted dryly, "but since we're to be up with the dawn, prepared for new wonders, perhaps we should sleep now. What do you say?"

"Sleep," Sebastian said, yawning. "No charm or potion for me tonight. Just find me a warm, soft spot, somewhere in the darkness." They descended back down the ridge of rubble, guided by moonlight and the chorus of voices below them. Cloaks and cowls were drawn tighter, and Julian's use of illusions subtly altered their features so that they would not be recognized.

Falling in behind a long caravan, they followed the winding procession back to Sea's Edge, their own voices swelling the chorus of hymns to the Maker that reached up into the starlit heavens.

·)X(·

Galad felt a dreaming vision slip over him and his sleeping mind stirred in curiosity. All their dreams had become more vivid, more real since the Gods had come forward to defend the Truce; it must truly be that the Lord of the Dreamways had perished, and that night visions would be more powerful until the Gods found another Power to guard the Dreamways.

In his dream he found himself in a strange land, far from Alantéa, a place where indistinct, quivering light shone from above, shimmering as it passed through moist, heavy air. He stood a little distance from a watchtower, where two beings fought in a grim, unequal contest: one was slender, a young captain or princeling, while the other bulked huge, in a form that barely seemed human. The young knight darted and leaped but was battered back by sledgehammer blows of a huge mace.

Galad stepped forward, reaching for the Tarnished Sword, but as he unsheathed it, the blade collapsed into bits of broken metal, as though its binding spell had broken. Before he could find another weapon — or even search for one — the great mace dealt the princeling a ruining blow, crushing the arm holding his shield, so that the young warrior fell back, defenseless, crying aloud in agony.

A second blow smashed the warrior's chest, bursting through plate mail and flesh. The princeling toppled slowly backward, face a death mask, a fountain of blood spurting from his wound; but as he fell, a dove sprang from his ruined chest, leaping forth white, untouched by all the bloody, red ruin surrounding him, and it flew from the battle, white wings pushing effortlessly at the dense, moisture filled air.

· ⋈ ·

Kalanin, too, dreamed a new dream, and like Galad, he stood in the underwater Isle of the Demons, but in his night vision, air and water were not blurred; here they were separate and distinct.

He stood in an oval pocket, in a chamber of air bathed in green and blue light. Above and around him, dark waters thrashed and swirled, as though threatening to engulf him in a single second. He stood on a tile floor, one that alternated black and white so that he felt again like a small piece on some great gaming board.

Before him stood one of the great unknown pieces: it was held motionless like some huge frozen statue, except that now and again its chest would rise and fall with intermittent breathing. Hairless, it seemed kin to the other Guardians, except that it was larger, a colossus, and its enormous head held one huge orb-eye, that was struggling to open, with shafts of blue radiances sliding out periodically as its massive eye slipped slowly open and then slammed shut.

Water rushed all around Kalanin, loud and threatening, ready to collapse down over him.

Warily, he circled the colossus, his feet passing over a light coat of sand that lay upon the tiles. And the huge statue was garlanded with seaweed that still dripped moisture so that it seemed as though the tide of water had just recently receded.

Kalanin looked up into its face: it must have been dreaming powerful, disturbing dreams because its eyelid spasmed and its head shook as though warding off danger. Yet now as Kalanin stared up at its quivering face, its lone orb-eye slipped partly open, while its mind struggled to communicate.

Help me, its mind whispered to Kalanin, help me....

· ꗏ ·

Julian's night visions took him far from the Isle of the Demons, far from their struggle with the Ancient Adversaries. He was climbing to the topmost peak of some tower, striding up a circular stone staircase two steps at a time. From above and below, windows opened to the outside with shafts of bright sunlight beaming through blue skies and white puffy clouds could be seen beyond the window's edges. He climbed tirelessly, speeding toward the pinnacle.

At its peak, he stood for a moment before a heavy door that was carved with many runes. Beyond, he knew, would be a sunlit chamber in an intersection of high breezes; and within he would find his heart's desire and his greatest sense of loss.

As the door swung open, two figures, a man, and a woman, rose from chairs, faces shining with joy. Unlike his other dreams, they were older than he remembered but still tall and powerful, still his parents.

Struggling not to wake, Julian felt hot tears surging from his eyes.

"My Mother, my Father, I am sorry I was not strong enough to free you," he said, voice shaking. They stepped forward, embracing their son with strong, tender arms.

"You have become great beyond our imaginations," said his Father. *"Because of you, we, the hidden Maker Servants can now share the Dragons' dreams of star flight. Our minds have Dragon wings and can reach out to follow the flight of Dragon Lords as they sweep through the Galaxies. Never again will we be completely chained."*

Julian clutched them again, murmuring, "*I love you, even though I know you are only images from my own mind, created by a great yearning.*"

"*We are much more than that, child,*" said his mother, brushing back the long dark hair from Julian's face. "*The Lord of the Dreamways has fallen, and the paths of night vision are open to those who have the willpower. Our minds are strong, as is yours, my son. And do you think that even our Master, who is jealous though not brutal, would deny you, the Maker Touched Summoner, a taste of triumph? Come, sit beside us. We will have this night and others before some other Power again masters the Dreamways.*"

Through their long, shared, dreaming visions, the three talked and wept, in a tide of tears and love that might have turned the heart of the grimmest, most pitiless of Gods.

· Ϫ ·

Kalanin woke slowly, gradually realizing that Géla was no longer at his side. His eyes slipped open and saw that she stood by an open window, watching as men labored with stone and mortar in the vale beneath their wood frame cottage. Outside, the day seemed overcast and damp, with the air stirred only by the thrust of nearby ocean currents.

Géla stood tense and waiting, fully dressed, but without armor or weapons. He swung his body to the bed's edge and began dressing quickly.

"You are the last abed, my beloved," she said in a soft voice. "Julian, Galad and the small ones have drifted from their dwellings and are walking slowly down to the sea. Galad wore no mail, so I judge we are still only onlookers to this day's events — though perhaps they will not even wait for us."

"Privileged onlookers, I hope, the so-called 'Far Travelers'," he said, dressing quickly and finishing by pulling his boots on. Brushing his hair back with both hands, he followed Géla outside, and they walked quickly down the gentle incline. As they passed, sentries and stonemasons, and haulers of goods came to a halt, bowing or staring openly at them.

"We will not have many close companions," Géla murmured, smiling to those around them, "even in our old age."

"It's hard to be a demigod," Kalanin replied also speaking quietly. "Hardest now on Galad, though I think we'll see Harlond and Rostov quite soon; and after it will be easier for us all."

She looked at him sharply. "So, you've talked with the Wizards then?"

"No, I've found a higher and more reliable source," Kalanin said laughing. "The fox, of course. Rafir is too friendly to be held forever in awe, and besides, no one can detect him when he doesn't wish to be seen, not even the Wizards." They walked on down into the vale and up another slope, moving toward the shoreline and Sea's Edge.

The air was touched by salt and dampness, and the ocean smell still held hints of death. Warfare had raged in the depths, a struggle between Demons and Guardians and the ruins of the ocean's seabed had been cast upon the Western and Southern coasts of Alantéa: thick wedges of dead shellfish and coral and barnacle-coated boulders littered the long beaches, together with the carcasses of huge sea creatures that had not been swift or strong enough to escape.

They found their four companions on a bluff overlooking the ocean. Julian and Galad stood looking down at the desolation of Sea's Edge, while Sebastian and Rafir were turned inland, as though watching for the last of their friends.

"It is good to stand again at Sea's Edge with all the other 'Far Travelers,'" Julian murmured, turning to Kalanin and Géla as they reached the ridge. The face of the Apprentice was still worn and haggard, as though wasted by a long fever, but his eyes were light and dancing, filled with joy as if a lifetime's weariness had been lifted from them.

"Behold the last act, Apprentice," Kalanin said quietly. "Some final mystery unfolds, likely dealing with the Jewel or the Truce Terms." *Or both, an echo in his mind whispered.* Géla stared down at the shoreline seeing images of defeat and desolation rather than victory: the ocean was dark and turbulent under overcast grey skies, while broken rocks and dead creatures littered the beaches. Plunderers of the depths lay dead and rotting on the shore, huge whales, and enormous sharks — Carcharodons that stretched threescore feet and more. Many were beyond the scavenging of seabirds and were now feasts for swarms of black flies and the salt wind's edge that picked at the whiteness of their bones.

They stood, cloaks fluttering in the wind, gazing first at the shoreline, then out to sea. Somewhere in the depths, scores, and hundreds of leagues from Alantéa, lay the underwater Isle of the Demons, a place of dread, a nightmare for drowning men — and a place where their own dooms or destinies seemed to lie.

From the corner of his eye, Sebastian saw motion along the southernmost curve of the long shoreline. He turned, as did the others, to see three tiny, faraway figures moving closer toward them. From a distance, the three cloaked Wizards seemed like squat, bearded gnomes, shuffling slowly over stony beaches that were still littered with strips of wood and broken weapons.

They looked to Julian to see if they should descend to meet the Wizards; instead, Julian sat on the bluff, staring downward at the Wizards' slow, meandering passage.

"Do we wait here," Géla asked, "until the Demon Princes again sweep the Wizards away with a wall of water?"

"Thrust and counterthrust," Julian said gently, his greyish eyes shining as he watched Merlin, his foster father, and Master. "The Demon Princes were seeking to overthrow the greatest alliance of power known to earth:

the Mid-World of the Truce. Now, if the Demons Princes are not wounded, at least they are worn down, with all their powers spent for the moment. Also, there may be other balances, other forces, of which we may learn more on this day." Géla did not respond, for there was joy in the Apprentice, expressions of contentment on the faces of the others — and inside herself, a sense of anticipation was becoming increasingly strong.

Halting below them, a little to the south and left of their bluff, the three Wizards stood motionless on the shoreline, staring toward the ocean in silence, drinking in the sea's greyness. After a time, the Wizards began to speak, but haltingly, intermittently, as though engaging in conversations that could not quite be sustained.

The air seemed to change, to become more wholesome even on the bluff where the Wizards' Servants watched on. Warm breezes swept over the shoreline, sweeping swarms of black flies out to sea, as though salt air could cure a plague of insects. Above them, the bleakness of the overcast sky began to change, with creases of blue opening gaps in a gloomy dark sky.

The Wizards' conversation seemed to change, to become more animated. Sunlight began to flash over the dark waters of Sea's Edge, and foamy waves filled with light began lifting from the ocean's stormy waters. These were ghostly waves forming, like the images of ancient waters that had once sparkled at the edges of Alantéa the Forerunner.

The onlookers rose and stood, watching the division of waters at the shoreline beside Sea's Edge: one was light and sparkling, the flickering images of what had been, or what might be, or what never was; the second was dark and battered by storms, holding all the misery of the uncontrolled conflict between Gods and Demons, Servants and Adversaries.

Now, the first curl of ghostly water reached out over the sand at the ocean's edge, slowly, tentatively, a force that was insecure and uncertain. Made of froth and radiant light and sorcerous matter, the wave struggled for a moment before its charmed particles grasped a mat of dried kelp and dead mussels; then these were dragged back in triumph out into the ocean depths.

Other ghostly waves reached out, curling over the long expanse of shoreline, touching, groping for debris. Gathering strength, sparkling light and foam swept over the shore, cleansing, transforming. Even broken boulders were being dragged away. But as waves filled with magic passed over the sands, not even a trace of moisture was left behind them.

The Wizards stood in the center of their transforming magic, ghostly surf passing to their chests as charmed particles wrenched carcasses and boulders from the ruin of Sea's Edge. Light broke through the gaps in the sky, with shafts of sunlight beginning to beam over the shoreline.

Behold the Wizards, Kalanin's mind murmured, *who have grown in power as they struggled with the Sorcerers and the Marids.*

From over the ocean and in the upper air, Vision Portals began shimmering into existence as the Gods became aware of the cleansing at Sea's Edge. And the Gods' power over the weather was clearing the upper reaches of all cloud barriers, so that shafts of sunlight were becoming broad banks of bright daylight, until, at last, the shoreline was bathed in broad sunlight, sparkling over white sandy beaches.

More Vision Portals slipped into view, and light rays shimmered, with brightness falling from the air like an enchanted, glistening dew.

Ghostly waves passed one last time over a newly cleansed shoreline, then they retreated into darkened waters, moving charmed particles through the turbulent shallows, filtering, settling. As the waters at Sea's Edge returned to an aquamarine that was pierced by sunlight, the Wizards turned from their purification work, and they moved to the right a few paces to begin their own Divination crafting, their own Vision Portal to some faraway, distant place.

The faintest music began whispering from afar, and suddenly Julian understood the purpose of the Wizards' Divination work: they were clearing the scene for their own battle group, the Wizards' Far Traveled Servants.

Beckoning to the others, Julian stepped from the overlook, striding down the long, sandy cliffs as the others followed. At Galad's side, the Tarnished Sword began to quiver and hum, adding its own song of vengeance and triumph to the music that was gathering around them. Galad shook his head once, then raised his face into the broad sunlight and laughed.

Sounds of music grew more distinct, and the last of the Vision Portals sprang into being as even the most preoccupied of Gods grew aware of the Spell-Cast at Sea's Edge. Caught up in events they were only beginning to understand, the Wizards' servants stepped over clear, sunlit sands, coming to stand beside the Wizards and their Divination Portal.

Standing under blue and brilliant sunlit skies, the Far Travelers saw that the Divination Image portrayed a scene of overcast turbulence in the middle of the ocean. Enormous whirlpools of water spun over the ocean's surface, while turmoil seethed in its depths. Far below, they understood, Demon Princes and Maker-Serving Guardians fought once again for control of the enchanted underwater Isle of the Demons, with sorcerous debris sent surging toward every shoreline of the Far Lands.

Julian stood a nearly a dozen paces from the Wizards' magic: their Vision Portal was twice his height, and the images beyond seemed so real, so vivid, that he imagined extending a hand through the image, where it would emerge, like that of a giant, over the turbulent sea's surface, bathed in the sheets of swirling salt water.

The Wizards turned back to the open sea; their features had become remote and distant, as though they no longer sought to make judgments over the struggle between good and evil. Sounds of music deepened. Sunlight shimmered as the Gods crowded closer to their Vision Portals.

Gone were Merlin's machineries of power whereby he had attempted to master the ocean more than a year earlier. Gone were the Wizards' staffs, their amulets, and their elaborate Great Spells. Gone were all tools except....

Merlin drew forth the *Talisman*, the Jewel yielded by the Gods. Huge in Merlin's outstretched two hands, with broad sunlight spilling over its many facets, the Jewel gave forth complex rays of emerald and green, sapphire mixed with blue, and ruby-red.

Julian's mind trembled at the edge of understanding: *All of this has to do with the Truce Terms, a part of the ancient balance struck between Servants and Adversaries. But which of those Terms, and how could these possibly affect the underwater Isle of the Demons?*

Kalanin's mind struggled to grasp another aspect of the Wizards' purpose: *The ruin of Sea's Edge has been cleansed, not for the Wizards or their Servants, but in honor of beings who were to be summoned. But what beings? The Gods? He turned back to the Vision Portal that portrayed a scene from perhaps a thousand leagues distant. In that place, at least one Guardian is struggling with Demons and Demon-spawned Marids, and their own corrupted brethren. In his nighttime vision, the Great Guardian had begged for aid, but what aid could be brought? And how could the Guardians be supported when they lay beneath a mountain of dark, storm struck waters?*

Pulsing light pulled the Far Travelers from their study of dark, stormy waters. Now, the Jewel, the *Talisman*, was lifting from Merlin's hand, moving slowly skyward so that it caught more of the sun's rays, refracting, reshaping them into thousands of different patterns.

Music deepened, and the air shimmered as the *Talisman* pulsed with light.

Suddenly, understanding flashed through Julian's mind like lightning flashing over a darkened field.

The Truce Terms! The last of them dealt with the Ancient Secrets: *For the Mid-World of the Truce we yield the greatest of our Ancient Secrets: we have learned how to free the most powerful of the Adversaries from their imprisonment within the ocean depths. This knowledge is now one with the Truce.*

Yes, yes. And the Demon Princes were free now. But there was another of the Terms juxtaposed to that dealing with the Adversaries: *For the Mid-World of the Truce, we yield our Ancient Secret: we have learned how to summon the departed Servants from their distant haven. This knowledge is now one with the Truce.*

The Hall of the Dreamers. They intended to summon —

Without a second's warning the Jewel shattered into a thousand fragments.

Julian cried out loud, half blinded by the last surge of light released by the *Talisman*. But he could hear — how could any Earthborn being fail to hear? And he could sense....

Music was swelling over the ocean at Sea's Edge, as though cliffs and sandy shorelines and ocean waters formed a huge amphitheater, with the deep chords of triumph ringing over sand and salt water.

Specks of light emerged over the waters as though stars were rising in the middle of the day. Radiating light, pulsing with power, the Dreamers passed over the ocean, floating effortlessly in their midair passage, Vision Portals shattering as the Dreamers passed through them.

Julian's mind radiated exultation. *Know fear, all of you self-proclaimed Gods! For truly the Maker has not forgotten or abandoned Earth!*

As the Gods pressed closer to their Vision Portals, and the music of triumph surged over Alantéa the Forerunner, the Dreamers, glistening in the full light of day, descended to stand beside the Wizards on the shoreline of Sea's Edge.

Six of them there were: Orissa, Seeress and High Priestess; Hestaur, Predecessor of the Wizards, and one of the fashioners of *The Game of the Masters*; Nablus, Binder of the Creatures Indomitable; Voll, Elf-Lord, mighty among those serving the Maker who were born with the Gift; Llara, Spirit Lord, patroness of those mortals who had been born with the Gift; and Voritar, Prince of Demons and great Servant of the Maker. But each of the Dreamers had grown and changed: like the Lords of Dragons seeking the Maker, the Dreamers had passed beyond their strength at birth into something that was fuller and more rich.

Wizards and Dreamers bowed to one another, then they turned and bowed to the Far Travelers.

Kalanin's mind raced. *Yes, there was a balance — against the Isle of the Demons stood the Hall of the Dreamers. But to what purpose were the Dreamers called? Merlin himself had said that they were barred from conflict, and so what now?*

Dreamers and Wizards now turned seaward with their arms raised in an invocation. A chant, partly sung, and partly spoken, surged from their mouths, as the harmonies in the air about Sea's Edge deepened and grew stronger.

A flurry of motion caught Julian's eye, and he turned from the Dreamers, back to the Wizards' Vision Portal. There, above the underwater Isle of the Demons, strife and disharmony ruled: the ocean was passing beyond turmoil into open warfare. Columns of water were shooting skyward, spewing masonry, debris, and the shattered husks of great predators into the air.

Julian's mind groped for understanding and retreated into prayer: *My Maker, we are at the edge of another wonder, yet what actions might you allow these your Servants to perform? We thought they were barred from strife, yet now....*

Now, before them in the Vision Portal, the image of the ocean shook and shuddered with strife, rocked by concussions, by the complex sorceries of Guardian and Demon, and Wizard and Dreamer. Tidal waves radiated from their warfare, sending ruin to the Far Lands.

Now, my Maker, Julian prayed, *something great is happening, a work of opening, of revealing....*

Now, in the middle of the ocean, tsunamis rippling from its shore, foliage unbroken and lush, untouched by turmoil and destruction....

Now, torn from the ocean depths, raised above sea level, beset by the contending powerful dreams of corrupt Guardians, and those striving to serve the Maker....

Incompletely ruled by Demon Princes who lusted for the overlordship of Alantéa and dominion over the Far Lands....

With booming Marids striding among newly formed hills and valleys, calling out their promise to completely corrupt and destroy every last God....

Wrested from its hidden ocean sanctuary by Maker Sentinels and Servants, their power extending a thousand leagues into the heart of their Adversaries' Citadel....

Now, shining green and red in the light of day, filled with malice and mystery....

Now, there stood: *The Isle of the Demons.*

The Sorcerers and the Marids is the fourth of five books.
The Isle of the Demons is the sequel.

Manufactured by Amazon.ca
Bolton, ON

24601475R00296